Eli Chronicles

By

R. David Dugger

Dedicated to my family: Renee, Adam, Aaron, Natalie, and Kelly. They lent both their names and their spirits to the telling of these tales, which had their beginnings with Adam's request to, "Tell me a story, Daddy."

Special Recognition: to my beautiful wife, Renee *(Fini),* my editor-in-chief, and our future voyagers: Daisy and Ike.

Part I:
Awakenings

Chapter 1 - The Men

He awakened to the sensation of falling and landed hard on his back.

Opening his eyes, he saw a blue and brilliant vastness. He traced the curve of the expanse to where it intersected green waters. Then his eyes continued their sweep to the point in his near vision where the waters joined the crystal sand upon which he lay.

The man rose and steadied himself as the world spun around him. After a few seconds, the spinning sensation passed, and he walked to a fallen palm tree where he slowly sat down.

He took inventory of what he knew and was disappointed in the limits of this knowledge. He knew, for example, that the blue dome was sky, the expanse of water was ocean, and the sandy bed was a beach, but additional details came to him only in a disjointed manner which left him disoriented and empty.

Grabbing a handful of sand, he allowed it to cascade from his palm. As he watched it flow to the ground, he was reminded that sand was used to make glass. Thinking of glass conjured the image of a glass bottle full of cool water, which in turn gave identity to the thirst he felt. This was the unsatisfying process through which he found memories returning.

Soon he knew the thousands of minor details that make up the daily course of life. He knew what it meant to hate, to love, to be lonely. His mind was full of general facts, figures, and emotions.

But this multitude of statistics and information would not coalesce into self-identity. Each fact recalled led to an additional memory, but he soon found his mind meeting an unyielding barrier. He knew that his being was so much more than this jumble of facts. Despite all he came to recall about the mechanics of life in general, he knew nothing of his own life and history.

Even as the man contemplated this last thought, he realized the way he framed the thought gave a clue regarding his own character. Apparently, he was the kind of man who when faced with a situation that was pregnant with unknown possibilities did not respond through anger or dread. He was curious.

Although the man continued in his attempts to appease his curiosity, he ultimately could recall no other enlightening information. He slowly came to accept that for the most part, everything he knew about himself was no more than would be available to any casual observer.

He had no idea by what name he was called or the country in which he was born. There was no knowledge of family, friends, or occupation. The man could not recall if he had a wife or children or a home.
He did know, somehow, that he was thinking in a language he knew to be English. Although it occurred to him that he could read and speak several languages, he could not be certain which of the languages he spoke when among friends and family. He knew he was well educated but could not recall the university he had attended or his field of study. He knew he was on a beach but had no understanding of how he got there or on which continent he found himself. He knew, by the position of the sun, that it was midday but did not know the date.

Looking at his bare arms he saw skin the color of cocoa. He was dressed in an open white shirt, brown trousers, and laced brown shoes. The only thing remotely noteworthy was the gold metal band around his right wrist. There was no design or markings of any kind on the surface of the band.

His interest in the band was short lived as his mind immediately returned to the task of reclaiming his identity. Perhaps he was a scholar or teacher, for there seemed to be countless facts and details on the fringe of memory waiting to flood his thoughts. Perhaps he was a diplomat, which would explain the large number of languages that seemed at his disposal. Or maybe he was a scientist as suggested by the analytical way his thoughts formed.

The man continued to ponder possibilities suggested by the limited information available to him. He had no sense of passing time as he sat on the beach regarding the things he knew and the things that seemed to be just beyond his reach. It was well after sunset when he again noticed the gold band around his wrist.

As he began to explore the surface of the wristlet, he soon found that if squeezed anywhere along its sides the diameter would expand. So, he earnestly compressed the band and removed it from his wrist. It was then the man saw for the first time the greatest clue to his identity.

~~~~~~~~

The soiled ship was boxy and lacking in elegance. As it neared the island the captain knew that the wind could easily carry the stench from the hold to anyone on shore. But the full Caribbean moon revealed that the beach was deserted.

Although he wore clean and tasteful clothes, in his soul the captain felt he was as unclean as his ship. In his tormented mind he and his ship suited the unholy cargo. Although his trade was no longer legal in Jamaica the captain readily endured the dangers of his business. After all, demand elsewhere remained high, and he found the Caribbean an excellent source of experienced and work hardened slaves. By proclamation of their government, the Jamaican blacks could no longer be forced into slavery. However, the captain did not allow such a small detail to impede his resolve to fill his hold with any local blacks unfortunate enough to cross his path. This was confirmed within the ship's vile hold which he had filled by force these last few months.
~~~~~~~~

Tonight, would be the captain's last raid before heading to South America and the customers who were willing to pay handsomely for as many slaves as he could supply. The captain had calculated his profits for this voyage and confirmed they would be more than sufficient for purchase of the plantation located for him in Virginia. In fact, the captain determined that his profits would be sufficient to allow him to keep five of the strongest slaves for use on his new property. Yes indeed, this was promising to finish as a very profitable voyage. All this helped to calm his increasingly active conscience.

The captain considered turning the ship immediately for the rendezvous with his customers. But in the end, the idea of having one or two additional slaves for his own use persuaded him to continue the night's activities.

The Captain's name was Arturis and his ship, the *Middle Passage*, was supposedly out of Boston. However, for the last twenty-three years Captain Arturis had plied his trade among the sugar plantations of the Caribbean. For most of those years Captain Arturis had purchased or traded for slaves and delivered them to those plantations. But as the islands began freeing their slaves, he confined his actions to raiding near those same plantations during the dark and moonless nights. He found he could fill his holds much quicker and at lower cost than that required by the more traditional passage to Africa. He even found this approach to be relatively risk-free since the plantation owners usually assumed their former slaves had merely decided to exercise their new freedom by leaving the plantation. It was unusual for anyone to attempt to locate the missing blacks, and those few who did invariably followed a trail that ended in disappointment. Captain Arturis and his crew had become very efficient at collecting their shameful cargo and he made it a policy never to visit the same island twice during a given voyage. The Captain had coolly managed everything except for the one item that birthed so many sleepless nights. He had yet to find the secret to managing his increasing guilt.

~~~~~~~~
~~~~~~~~

As he sat on the fallen tree near the location from which he awoke, the man looked closely at the engraving shown on the inside of the gold band he had removed from his wrist. In the fading light he could just make out the characters *Ben-Ja-Bar*. He pronounced the phrase slowly to himself and was surprised to hear his voice carry a mild Caribbean accent. An accent perhaps muted by the influence of advanced education. It indeed seemed strange that he would notice his own accent. This was particularly true since he was not sure what was meant by "Caribbean". But then again, everything about him was strange and new.

He repeated the phrase to himself twice more. There was a feeling of near familiarity in the phrase. Whispering to himself he said, "I think Benjabar is my name." This seemed correct, but he could not quite confirm the fact in his own mind. However, the more he repeated the name to himself the greater his certainty that he indeed was Benjabar.

Even as his certainty grew a flood of questions filled his mind. *What nationality is suggested by the name Benjabar? Is that my family name or my given name? Does it include both first and last names, such as Ben Jabar or Benja Bar? Is it hyphenated, as suggested by the engraving on the interior of the band, or is the hyphenation just to help in pronunciation?*

Another hour had passed without further insight or understanding regarding his identity. He had come to solidly think of himself as Benjabar, but an understanding of his past was no clearer than before.

The sun had now set, and a cool breeze was blowing in from the ocean. Benjabar became aware of a growing hunger and determined that his continued well-being would require he change his focus from his internal searching to addressing his physical needs. His first order of business was to find food and drink, and he began his search in the vicinity of where he awoke on the beach. Logic suggested that he may have brought supplies with him from wherever he came.

His search was soon rewarded as he found a duffle that, in his general confusion, he had earlier ignored. The words *Sea Queen* were printed boldly on the side, and within the duffle was a bag of dried beans, a canteen of water, flint for making a fire, dried beef, or pork, and what appeared to be a hunting knife with belt and sheath, as well as sundry additional items. He buckled the knife around his waist and pulled it free from the sheath, hefting it in his right hand with a definite feel of familiarity. As an afterthought, he once again removed the gold band and placed it in a hidden pouch that he somehow knew was inside his left shoe.

Benjabar struck the flint against the knife to build a fire with dried grass and wood found near the beach. He prepared the beans using some of the dried meat and the water in the canteen. As he ate, he muttered to himself "Good bee-uns mon", smiling at his use of what he instinctively knew as Jamaican vernacular. He recognized this phrase as one he would have used as a youth. Perhaps he had spent his youth in this Jamaica.

It was then that he heard the footsteps crunching on the sand behind him. He whirled and pulled the knife from the sheath and shifted it to his left hand with an ease that suggested this was an automatic response. Standing three meters away was a man carrying a heavy club. Immediately the intruder rushed forward and expertly swung the club at Benjabar's head. Benjabar easily side-stepped the swinging club and delivered a chopping blow to the side of the assailant's neck. The attacker groaned and collapsed on the sand.

Benjabar immediately sensed two new aggressors coming at him from either side. He dropped to the sand and kicked in a round house fashion that knocked the feet from under one of the men. The man fell heavily to earth and did not move.

The third man dove and grabbed Benjabar around the waist before he could recover. The two men tumbled in the sand with arms and legs flailing. Benjabar was able to stand as he momentarily grasped the front of the man's shirt. He then rolled on to his back and used his momentum to fling the other man in an arc to the ground. Before he could rise, Benjabar delivered a blow to the side of the man's head. The man became still and appeared unconscious.

Before he could rise completely to his feet two new opponents grabbed Benjabar and each pinned an arm to the ground. With a strength that surprised Benjabar, he easily broke free from the grips of the two men. In one fluid motion he jammed the knife into the sand and grabbed the two men by the sides of their necks as he brought their heads together with a crack. The bodies of the two men collapsed to the beach. He pulled the knife from the sand and started to stand.

Before he could rise Benjabar heard a metallic click followed by a coarsely spoken, "That will be enough my boy." Still gripping his knife, he looked in the direction of the voice. A man, wearing a long black cloak, was pointing a musket at his head. The man continued, "I must say that I am extremely impressed. You defeated five of my best men in short order. You will bring a high price at auction." Benjabar inherently knew he could throw the knife and kill the man but doubted the intruder would die before he could pull the trigger. And he also knew somehow that killing this man would be against a deeply ingrained principle. Benjabar sheathed his knife.

Three more men appeared from the shadows, and two grabbed Benjabar's arms and pinned them behind his back. The third removed Benjabar's knife, tied his hands behind his back, and placed a gag in his mouth. Only then did the man in the cloak continue. "My name is Captain Edward Arturis, and you are now my property."

~~~~~~~~~

The ship sailed sharply through the crystal Caribbean waters. This ship was clean in both the lines of her form and in the sense that obvious effort was concentrated on maintaining her hygiene.

The eyes of the captain were both determined and saddened as he peered in the direction of his heading. He was a tall man with muscles conditioned by frequent strenuous activity. He was clean shaven with dark hair and eyes of a blue, not unlike the color of the waters through which he sailed.
~~~~~~~~~

The captain was a man of great integrity whose manner suggested kindness, but with an intensity of purpose that would not allow him to be diverted from any goal about which he cared deeply.

The crew of the ship was small given her large size, but they were efficient and well trained. All were handpicked by the captain, with none selected from the coastal taverns and other traditional gathering places of seamen. Instead, the captain visited mines, mills, and factories and watched as the workers left their jobs for the day.

He would revisit the factories the next morning and watch as each returned to their jobs. He noted the way they carried themselves, how they interacted with their fellow workers and how much, if any, respect was shown for them by others.

Soon thereafter, he would select a few and initiate conversations with them while approaching them on the street or the marketplace. He noted how they responded to his questions, both in what they said and how they said it. Primarily he looked in their eyes.

From the dozens of potential candidates, a very few were selected by the captain for a special test. The captain would seek an invitation to their houses and observe them in their home environment. There was much poverty in the world, and invariably the captain would identify a need that he, with his significant resources, could address. It was how the recipient responded to the offer of assistance that told the captain the most about the candidate.

Most of the candidates responded to the help with expressions of appreciation. Some followed thanks with requests for additional support. Some grew hostile and harshly rejected the assistance. Still others tried to refuse his help from a sense of embarrassment.

But some few thanked the captain, and then looked him in the eye and assured the captain they would do whatever it took to repay him. If he felt they were sincere, these were the ones the captain sought to join his crew. The captain paid well and paid a year's wage in full before the ship left port. Most of the crew could see the honest goodwill in the captain's face, which was reinforced by his insistence on ensuring the crew's families would be well cared for during their absence. He confirmed to them that this absence would only be for the time it took to take on a permanent crew unless they requested longer service. The captain also secured assurances from their employers that, for up to a year, the crew's jobs would be waiting for them after they returned from the voyage. Few candidates turned him down.

Most of the crew had never sailed previously, but the captain's experience had long since proven that given a proper attitude most can be readily trained. And a proper attitude was a key criterion in the captain's selection of his crew.

The design of the great ship was forgiving and easy to crew. In part, this was because the designers knew his crew would likely be new to the sail. But its designers passionately believed in spending great effort in planning and design when executing any endeavor. The result of this early planning effort was an outcome that was a joy to behold and employ. And the reality was that the design of the ship was such that, in a pinch, the great ship could be sailed by a single experienced sailor.

Standing at the bow of the ship, the captain recalled how he, his new crew, and his magnificent vessel were first tested on this mission.

The ship was sailing the Mediterranean, and not yet fully manned, when the first mate came to the captain and reported that three sails had been spotted. All three were flying the colors of local pirates. With this news the captain felt his chest tighten as his thoughts raced. In an instant he recalled the many conversations with merchantman captains who plied their trade in the Mediterranean waters. Without exception, the conversations had turned to the ruthless pirates that harassed the trade occurring in those waters.

Also, without exception the advice had been the same; if confronted with unfavorable odds in which retreat was not possible, you must surrender your ship and your crew without resisting. For if you resist, it is certain that you and your crew will not live to sail a single day more. However, if you surrender immediately there is a reasonable chance that you and your crew will be marooned in a location in which survival may be possible.

 The great ship was making way for an offshore rendezvous with another merchantman when the three pirate ships had approached seaward from directions that would make retreat impossible. For this reason, the words of warning received from these captains seemed prophetic. Despite these doubts and concerns welling up within his mind the captain managed to maintain a calm exterior. Yet the very act of remaining calm seemed wrong and a betrayal to his crew as he considered their right to know the dangers that his actions would precipitate. For the captain knew for certain that regardless of the outcome, he would not, could not, surrender his ship. For without this ship his plans and future would be destroyed.

The captain reached the quarter deck, surveyed the situation, and immediately noted that they were still well out of range of the pirates' guns. "Hoist flags advising the vessels to withdraw or face action," the captain had ordered.

The signal flags were raised, but after five minutes the pirates continued to close on their position. "Very well," said the captain, "Bring the bow twenty degrees starboard and prepare all three bow guns for firing." The sleek ship turned easily until her bow was in line with the intruding ship furthest from their position.

"Place a shot fifty yards forward of her bow," the captain ordered as he pointed at the menacing vessel. "Fire when ready," he continued. Even though this was the first action most of the crew had ever seen, they worked quickly and effectively. One of the three bow guns belched fire and seconds later a plume of water erupted in front of the opposing vessel. But still the pirates' ship continued to close.

"All bow guns target her main mast and fire when ready," ordered the captain. In quick order the guns fired. The first shot missed the mast by two yards, but the second and third shots slammed into the main mast and the vessel lay crippled.

"Bring our bow another thirty degrees to starboard," ordered the captain. "When the bow is in line with the second vessel target her main mast and fire at will."

As the ship turned into the unfavorable wind with an ease that amazed her crew, the captain's orders were flawlessly executed, and the second ship was crippled as well. With that, the third ship signaled withdrawal.

The captain's crew raised a cheer as they stood amazed at a victory seemingly won without their opponents managing to fire a single shot.

"Signal the two vessels to push their cannon overboard and surrender immediately," said the captain to the first mate. While one of the wounded ships complied with the signal the other hesitated. In response to this refusal the captain immediately commanded his vessel be brought in line with the pirate's crippled ship, and that the forward and aft port guns be readied for firing.

As his ship cleanly turned as ordered the captain said, "Place one shot forward by five yards and one aft by five yards. You may fire when ready." The guns fired almost in unison with the intended results. The enemy vessel's guns were immediately pushed into the water and its flags hoisted signaling surrender.

The captain then ordered his ship be brought to within ten yards of the closest pirate vessel. With the guns primed, and ready to fire at point-blank range, it was an easy matter to persuade the entire crew to abandon ship using their long boats.

"Send all available dinghies to collect any treasure they hold," the captain ordered. The captain would return any loot to its proper owner, if known, and keep the remainder. The captured ship would be taken to the nearest port and sold with the proceeds given to the poor. This action sent a clear message to all pirates terrorizing these waters, and built good will between the captain, the local population, and the other merchant vessels operating in the area.

After the captured treasure and ships were secured, the crewman acting as first mate came to the captain with a quizzical look on his face. His name was Dick Bruan, and he was one of the few crewmen with any significant sailing experience. It was clear that he, more so than most, understood how unexplainable and unexpected the outcome of this action had been.

"Captain" he began, "I thought you insane when you refused to surrender. But I see now your actions grew out of your confidence in this wonderful ship." The captain's response was a simple nod of his head, but he did not voice the reality motivating his actions. He simply had no other choice but to fight.

The captain later walked to his quarters and sat at his desk. He took a key from his vest and opened the middle drawer. The captain removed a small gold band from the drawer and stared at it for several minutes as the sadness returned to his eyes.

He removed a logbook from the same drawer and began to write:

January 1, 1837. I do not wish to fight, but after today's action I know I am prepared to do so if anyone attempts to deflect me from my goal...

These last thoughts jolted the captain back to the present and the action at hand.

Benjabar lay chained to the putrid hold of the *Middle Passage*. In the moments following his unhappy introduction to Captain Arturis he had gasped as a flood of cultural memories invaded his mind. The gasp was not in response to any immediate concerns for his well-being, but rather at the horrible images associated with these new memories.

Since his first awaking on the beach, Benjabar had not thought of himself as black until the moment he was taken by Arturis. Indeed, he had not thought of himself as fundamentally different from any other man until that moment. Now he could think of nothing else.

Slavery was a concept that came crashing into his consciousness only after he had so abruptly lost his freedom. Slavery's reality was now sadly apparent in the demeanor of the humanity chained around him.

He knew in his heart that he had never been a slave before today. But this fact brought small consolation given his current situation. He also knew without doubt that he would find a way to win his freedom.

Benjabar suddenly became aware of a figure standing over him. He looked up and met the eyes of Captain Arturis. "I introduced myself, but you are yet to return the favor," Arturis said. "What is your name my boy?"

"Benjabar" he replied.

"Last name or first?" the Captain asked.

"Just Benjabar, no other names," Benjabar said.

"Very well," Captain Arturis replied. "Benjabar, you somehow seem to be of Jamaica, but at the same time your voice does not seem to hold a pure Jamaican accent. Tell me about yourself."

Benjabar's thoughts were racing. Somehow, keeping the Captain ignorant of his lack of memories seemed to Benjabar a strategic advantage. Although a man of extreme integrity, Benjabar determined that this was a time for deception. "I was a house slave attending the son of the Bedford plantation's owner," he began. As an afterthought he added, "The Bedford plantation is located in the Jamaican interior." Then continuing he said, "My master's son wanted me to be educated and arranged for me to attend University with him. I suppose that is where I lost much of my accent." The curious thing about this story was that, apart from the claim of being a slave, it seemed somewhat true.

Arturis' eyes seemed to pierce Benjabar's being. They seemed to say, *"I know what you have said is not true…I am only deciding how important it will be to find the truth…will it be worth damaging an excellent slave to extract the information?"* But Arturis said nothing, and after several moments nodded and turned to leave.

To his back Benjabar said without emotion, "My old master's son will pay far more than you will ever receive through my sale at market."

Without turning Arturis said, "Go on, my boy."

Again, Benjabar's mind raced and replied, "After leaving home, my old master's son became captain of a merchantman and changed his name. I do not know his new name."

Arturis turned slowly to face Benjabar. Once again, his eyes had become sharp knives cutting into Benjabar's very existence. "Why would he change his name?" he asked with a voice of ice. "And how can I sell you to him if you do not even know his name?"

"He wanted no reminders of his old life," Benjabar replied.

"Why no reminders?" asked Arturis, with doubt clearly entering his voice.

“It is a long story.”

“I love stories.”

~~~~~~~~~
~~~~~~~~~

Chapter 2 - The Boys

At first Adam Boy had not recalled his age, but ultimately, he said to himself, "I am twelve years old," and with that he became certain that he was indeed twelve. How he knew this was as mysterious to him as how the geese knew they were to fly north in the summer.

Indeed, it was a seemingly magical process that allowed him to slowly comprehend this frightening world into which he had found himself thrust.

He had awakened lying in a marsh next to a large expanse of water. Rain had beaten his face, adding to confusion and fear. He rose to his feet and fell immediately into the wet grass and mud. He stood again only when he was certain that the world had stopped turning around him.

Upon standing he noticed a duffle lying near where he had awakened. On one side of the duffle was printed *Sea Queen*. This had meaning to him, but only in the way that one sees an image in the distance through a swirling fog. He could sense an outline of recognition, but his mind could not quite form the complete and clear image. Nevertheless, he assumed the duffle was his and, not wanting the rain to wet the contents, slung it over his back without opening it.

He knew that it was late in the afternoon by a dimness not fully explained by the rain and clouds. He was desperate to find shelter from the cold, wet, and approaching darkness.

So it was that he soon found himself near naked in the shelter of an old boathouse. His wet clothes hung drying from pegs positioned along one wall while he curled under a warm, dry blanket next to a burning candle. He had found both items in the duffle. Thankfully, he had cut his hunger by chewing on a large chunk of dried meat that had also come from the duffle.

Who had packed the duffle with these items that had proven so useful and timely? Was it his mother or father, or had he packed it himself? Regardless, he was very thankful to the unknown provider.

Yes, there were many mysteries, not the least of which was the gold band around his wrist that he had noticed when removing his wet clothes. He had removed the band and read the inscription *Ad-Am-Boy*. He had known instantly that his name was Adam Boy which brought an unexpected level of calm into his situation. But think as he might, this insight had provided no clues to his past. He placed the gold band inside a pouch in his left shoe, that he somehow knew would be there.

Despite the void in his memory that should inform him who he was, Adam Boy nevertheless was able to judge his own character. He knew he was honest, loved music, excelled in mathematics, and could play games expertly and without effort. He loved life, he laughed often, and he lived each day like it was a gift given by God. Furthermore, there was a mirror in the boathouse in which Adam Boy could survey his features. He was rather tall for his age. His hair was dark and his eyes a blue that tended to sparkle in the candlelight.

Adam Boy drew upon his natural cheerfulness despite the uncertainty of his circumstances. However, as the darkness grew outside the little boathouse it seemed his mood darkened in proportion. To regain his spirits, Adam Boy decided he should find something to occupy his mind and concluded that building a fire in the boathouse fireplace would do the trick. Not only would he be able to heat the beans he had noticed in the duffel, but the fire would also give the inherent comfort provided by a fire on a damp evening.

It was when he returned to the duffle for the beans and the cooking pot that he first saw the yellow envelope sealed by wax. The wax was embedded only with three letters…*Eli*. He opened the envelope and found a note written in ink using block letters. Its message immediately gave him a purpose which improved his mental state markedly. With this note he began an adventure both marvelous and daunting.

The boy looked into the eyes of the old woman and was comforted by the kindness he saw within them. But her eyes hid sadness and an aching concern for this child. A child placed in her care by circumstances as puzzling and mysterious as life itself.

His demeanor and general appearance would indicate him to be eight or nine years of age, although he would be very tall for this age. She could tell his hair color was in transition from the gold of childhood to the darker color he would have as an adult. He was obviously an intelligent child with blue eyes that seemed to amplify that intelligence.

Four days ago, she had found him dazed and frightened wandering along the shore that was visible from her front door. His clothing was clean and neat except for the grass stain that must have resulted from the boy's laying or sitting in the grass.

Other than the mystery of his arrival, the only unusual thing about the boy was the plain gold band he wore around his wrist.

When questioned about his identity his confusion was obvious, but the boy had remained calm except when, hoping to find identifying markings, she had asked him to remove the gold band. This request agitated the boy so completely that she abandoned the effort. But knowing it would not be wise to tempt unexpected passersby with such a valuable item, she made certain that when outside the boy was always wearing his tunic. By cinching the sleeves with strings around his wrists she hoped to keep the gold band hidden.

When left to her own thoughts the woman's mind consistently returned to the same theme. That is, she was a poor widowed woman with hardly a farthing to her name. *How could she care for this child?* Her distrust and dislike of the local authorities made her doubt that they would do the right thing if she sought their help. Rather than seeking to reunite the child with his parents, they would likely send him to the local spike. It being an even more oppressive and offensive workhouse than most.

An even worse fate would be the dark and miserable orphanage. The orphanage would eventually send him to work in the horrid coal mines where he would probably die. No, she certainly would not go to the authorities.

She had no close neighbors and visitors were infrequent. Perhaps, she thought, when the Abbot came around for his monthly visit, she could ask him to care for the boy. But that was a fortnight from now, and the thought did little to relieve her concern for how she might feed and provide proper care for the boy until that time.

She had located a small duffle near where she found the boy wandering and had removed a yellow envelope, but she could not read and absently lay it on the fireplace mantle where it remained unopened. She was thankful to God for the beans and dried meat found within the duffle, but these would be gone in a week. *What would she do then?*

~~~~~~~

Adam Boy re-read the note, having lost count of how many times he had previously done so. And it was a message that presented both a puzzle and a challenge. He had read it so often that he could almost recite the note from memory. Even so, he read the note yet again…

"Adam Boy, it is extremely important that you follow the instructions in this note very carefully. I know you are confused and wondering why this could not be presented in simple and straight forward instructions. The reasons for this approach will become clear in the future. For now, please believe that for us to reunite you must solve this riddle."

The note was written in a deliberate and legible hand and signed "The Captain".
At the bottom of the sheet was the riddle:

"You must find the red horse at the Lodestar and talk to the Count. Halve the minutes and ride the steed until you see the skull. Wait for a season at the narrows until the Danelaw and Patrick flags hail."
~~~~~~~

At first, he was in even greater despair than before as he contemplated the nonsensical and unfathomable riddle. But as Adam Boy considered the puzzle, he took comfort in the fact that he was enjoying the challenge. "It seems I am good at this," he said out loud to himself as he began to consider the note's meaning in earnest.

Adam Boy waited until the next morning when his clothes were dry, and the rain had stopped, before he took his first real steps in solving the riddle. He stepped out of the boathouse and reasoned that the "red horse" must be nearby.

After a quick study of the area, he concluded that only a single road ran north and south through the farms and forest lands that bordered the sea. It would be reasonable that the red horse could be found along this road somewhere, but *which way should he walk? Should he go north or south? Was "Lodestar" a town, an estate, or something else entirely?*

He decided that for now he would go neither north nor south, but instead wander the hills and woodlands in increasingly large circles around the point where he had first awakened. Adam Boy hoped that this would result in locating the red horse or at least surface a clue to the riddle.

At the end of that first unfruitful day, he had built a fire in an open field and cooked more of the dried beans. His discouragement had returned, and he sat eating the beans in a dark mood.

I must locate this "Lodestar" he told himself earnestly. He had met three different people during his day of walking and enquired about Lodestar, red horses, and the Count. In the first instance the person was an elder man, and his only response was a quizzical look and a shake of the head. In the other two encounters, a woman and then a young girl slightly older than himself, he had at least received voiced responses. But the result was the same; neither could tell him anything useful.

His wandering had brought him the realization that he was on an island bounded on the west by an ocean and on the east by marsh and tidal waters. At the point where he had awakened the island was only about six kilometers wide, but it appeared to be several kilometers long. None of this information left him any nearer to an understanding of which way he should walk.

Adam Boy looked up at the clear star-filled sky and for a moment, and only a moment, forgot the strange circumstance in which he found himself. He forgot the riddle and forgot his loneliness. He found peace in the stars somehow. Then he realized this peace came from familiarity. He was at peace because he knew the stars. He knew their names. He knew their locations. He knew…he knew which way to walk tomorrow! Now he could go to sleep in peace with a mind cleared by the certainty of action. He would walk north tomorrow. In a flash he had remembered that "Lodestar" was another name for Polaris, the North Star. Yes, he would walk north.

~~~~~~~~

The old woman and young boy were walking along the beach. She was questioning the boy in hopes of finding some clues to his origin. She learned nothing, but the activity did seem to help them both relax.

Her attention was focused on the beach and the history it may reveal about the boy. This preoccupation made her unaware of both the dory approaching the beach and anchored offshore, the ship from which it came.
She gave a frightened start in response to the sudden hail from one of the two men in the dory. "Be ye the Widow McSparten?" he cried.

"Yes," she responded in an uncertain voice, but then more forcefully, "And who might you be?"

"Me name's Jeffrey Flyer from the merchantman *Volunteer*," he replied. "I have provisions to be delivered to ye."
~~~~~~~~

With that he and his companion stepped from each side of the dory and proceeded to pull it to shore through the knee-deep water. At the same time, the Widow's mind reeled as she tried to comprehend what was being said to her. "Provisions, did you say? Are they from the Abbot?"

"No mum," he said with a smile. "Not the Abbot." Then he proceeded with a tale that answered some questions, but at the same time deepened the mystery surrounding the boy.

Flyer told of sailing through the Straits of Gibraltar with their cargo of olive oil from Greece. He talked in hushed tones as he told of being hailed by a large merchantman and excitedly described the ship. The ship was flying a British flag, but such was its lines that he knew it had not been built in any port of the empire. He described the unusual look of the sails, the gleaming guns lining the ship from stem to stern on both sides, and the relatively small crew.

The man was absorbed with his description of the ship but became suddenly aware that his telling had diverted from the main storyline. The tall, clean-shaven captain was the real story. He had a calm demeanor that seemed somehow overshadowed by a deep and prevailing sadness.

This captain (Mr. Flyer could not recall his name) had asked to parley with Captain Harris of the *Volunteer*. Captain Harris had asked Mr. Flyer, as first mate, to sit in on the meeting. The mysterious captain had related that he had been specifically waiting for the *Volunteer* because he had heard that her captain was a man of integrity and reliability. Yet despite this high praise it took a full hour of talk before the captain was ready to make his proposal.

In exchange for a generous amount of gold the *Volunteer* would make a diversion of one day's sail from her set course to deliver the goods now found in the beached dory. They were to be delivered to a "Widow McSparten". She was to be found along an isolated section of the Scottish coast at the coordinates provided.

With that Mr. Flyer had concluded his tale, but the Widow was not satisfied. "But why did he send all this to me?" she asked.

"He would not give reasons when asked," Mr. Flyer replied. "He would say only that it was for you and the lad."

"The lad…" the Widow repeated softly.

"Yes mum," he said as he opened a sheet of paper from which he read a strange name…

"Aarondophilous".

~~~~~~~~~

Adam Boy had walked for half a day along the northbound road and was beginning to think he had misinterpreted the clue. A light rain was falling, so he decided to look for shelter. Just as the rain became heavier, he spied a building two hundred meters ahead sitting near the road. Hoisting his duffel tight to his chest he sprinted toward the building.

While still fifty meters from the building the torrent started in earnest. Adam Boy lowered his head to shield his face from the driving rain and ran to the covered doorway. The entryway afforded some protection, but the wind was whipping the rain and he continued to get soaked. As he started to look for better shelter, he noticed a sign on the door:

Welcome All Weary Travelers

Adam Boy *was* weary and felt that if the welcome was meant for anyone, it was meant for him. He slowly opened the door to a dark room lit by a single candle on a table. As his eyes adjusted to the darkness, he noticed a woman standing behind a long counter. It appeared that she had been wiping down the countertop but stopped as Adam Boy entered the room.
~~~~~~~~~

"Who or what do you seek boy?" she asked. "I seek only protection from the rain, ma'am," he replied. "Well then, take off your coat and sit at the table until the storm passes," she said with a kindly smile on her face.

Adam Boy thanked the woman as he accepted her offer. The woman proceeded to introduce herself as "Revan" as she poured Adam Boy a warm cider. Adam Boy and Revan spent the next hour exchanging information. He was hard pressed to know what warmed him more, the cider, the fire burning low in the fireplace, or the pleasant conversation.

Adam Boy felt saddened by the fact that most of the information he gave Revan was fabrication. But he knew instinctively that it was best that he should not disclose the strange facts surrounding his current situation. Therefore, to Revan he was merely a lad that was visiting his grandparents on their farm several miles away. He did not know their names (after all he called them only "Grandfather" and "Grandmother"). They lived about a mile off the road and kept to themselves most of the time.

For the most part, Adam Boy asked questions of Revan. Partly to keep her from asking him too many questions, and partly in the hope that he might learn something that would help him find the answers he needed. He learned that he had wandered into a roadside inn found midway along the length of Amelia Island on the northern coast of Florida.
Adam Boy asked her if she knew where he could find high quality horses and quickly proceeded to explain that he really liked red-colored horses. With just the trace of a smile, Revan told him she knew that almost all the farms had one or two horses, but none with any particularly good breeding, and none with the coloring he preferred.

Finally, Adam Boy noticed that the rain had stopped, so he rose from the table. He walked to the door, thanked Revan for the cider, said goodbye and opened the front door. He walked ten steps from the front door, turned to look back at the inn and noticed for the first time the name on the sign hanging over the doorway. It read "El Caballo Rojo". In the way he had learned things about himself over the past few days, Adam Boy learned that he at least read and probably spoke Spanish.

When translated to English the name of the inn was "The Red Horse".

~~~~~~~~~~

He had known his name even before he was found by the Widow. Soon after awaking disoriented on the beach, he had removed the gold band from his wrist and read *Aa-Ron-Doph-Ilous* engraved on the inside and recognized it immediately. He had chosen to guard this information until he remembered more of his past. When first asked his name by the Widow he merely shook his head and looked away.

Aarondophilous did not like the silent man that had come with Mr. Flyer to deliver the supplies. While it was apparent that Mr. Flyer was a good man with a true heart, the silent man looked as if he hid dark secrets within a greed-filled countenance. He did not know how he knew the silent man could not be trusted, but he knew this with certainty. It was the seeming inherent knowledge of the existence of such men that led him to guard his identity.

The man's silence during the entire encounter only served to heighten Aarondophilous' sense of concern. This concern turned to absolute dread when he caught a cold look in the man's eye and realized his tunic had shifted unexpectedly and the man had seen the gold band around his wrist. He knew he would not rest until the following day's ebb tide when *Volunteer* would hoist anchor and leave their coast.
~~~~~~~~~~

So it was that after the Widow was asleep that night, Aarondophilous crept silently into the room of the Widow's cottage that served as parlor, kitchen, and main living area. He prepared the room for their uninvited visitor and lit a single candle positioned so the light reflected warmly from the gold band that he placed on the table. He walked to the front door and removed the loop of rope that secured its latch. Finally, he used a length of rope to effectively latch the door to the Widow's bedroom from the outside.

He then forced himself to lay awake in bed and eventually heard the front door's latch being tried and lifted. This was followed immediately by a slight squeak of the hinge as the door opened. He heard the footsteps as they approached the table where the gold band lay.
Aarondophilous smiled when he heard his trap capture the silent man.

<p style="text-align:center">~~~~~~~~~~</p>

Revan did not appear to be surprised when Adam Boy walked through the front door of the inn for the second time. He fixed her squarely with his gaze and asked, "Do you know where I can find the Count?"

She smiled slowly and answered with a slight nod of her head. "Follow me," she said and picked up a candle, lighting it from the one on the table. She then turned to walk up the stairs located at the end of the long counter. Over her shoulder she said, "I thought you might be the one I was to expect, but your captain never told me your name and he said I would know you when you eventually asked about the Count."

As Adam Boy began to follow Revan up the stairs, he noticed for the first time two men huddled at one of the tables. The shadows in the inn were deep, but he was certain that he saw the two men exchange knowing glances as he began to climb the stairs. And glancing downward he realized that the sleeve of his tunic had caught up on the gold band at his wrist, which glinted in the candlelight. He was certain that this was the source of the two men's sudden interest in him.

One of the two men was tall, lean, and with features that reminded him of a scarecrow. The other man was short, heavy of build, and his face seemed to hold a perpetual scowl. Together the two reminded Adam Boy of a giraffe talking to a hippopotamus. The two interacted in a way that seemed sinister and gave the impression that whenever you saw one of these men you also would see the other. He smiled to himself as he named them "The Giraffopotamus".

Revan stopped at a door at the top of the stairs and with a slight wave of her hand indicated that Adam Boy should enter the room. He nodded his head and slowly opened the latch to the room.

The room was in shadows, but Revan entered the room behind him and used the candle she was holding to light a lamp sitting on the table. As illumination filled the room she nodded to the far side of the room and said, "My boy, allow me to introduce you to the Count."

Since there was no one in the room except for Adam Boy and Revan, he looked at her in confusion. But as he glanced once more in the direction in which she pointed he noticed a portrait on the wall to his left.

The portrait was of a distinguished looking man sitting at a table. A name plate on the frame identified the man as "Count Karlsky". The portrait view was from a slightly elevated perspective such that the top of the table could be seen. The man was pointing at what appeared to be a map on the top of the table. Adam Boy noticed, with some disappointment, that the details of the map were unclear and unlikely to be of any use in determining the destination of his journey.

But as Adam Boy looked closer at the painted map, he could make out what appeared to be a set of coordinates next to an "X" on the map. The coordinates read *N32⁰ 37′, W80⁰ 59′*.

Adam Boy nodded his head slightly.

He now knew exactly where he needed to go.

~~~~~~~~~

Aarondophilous' trap had been simple, and effective. A trap door was positioned in the center of the room to allow access to the small cellar. He had simply opened the trap door, and using light twigs to give it support, relocated a small carpet over the opening. He had then repositioned the few furnishings contained within the room such that the only clear access to the gold band, so temptingly placed on the table, required stepping on the carpet over the opening. Having confirmed that the open trap door was hidden within the dark shadows of the room, the only other precaution needed was to bar the Widow's bedroom door so that she would not fall victim to his surprise should she try to leave her room.
~~~~~~~~~

Upon hearing the silent man fall through the opening, Aarondophilous leapt from his bed and immediately closed and latched the trap door. He then unlatched the Widow's bedroom door as she attempted to investigate the commotion caused by the springing of the trap. Before answering the excited questions that flowed from the Widow he had yelled, "Please, help with the chest…hurry, hurry!" With that they moved a heavy chest from the corner of the room to a position directly over the trap door. This would make it difficult for the would-be thief to break the latch to the trap door and escape.

After hurriedly explaining to the Widow what had occurred and why the trap was necessary, Aarondophilous lit the Widow's oil lamp and ran to the beach to signal the ship at anchor.

The next morning with the silent man secured in the ship's brig, Captain Harris and Mr. Flyer stood with the Widow and Aarondophilous on the beach. "Madam, I am saddened and embarrassed that one of my crew would do such as this," the Captain said with a look in his eyes that matched his words. "I apologize to both you and the boy for bringing this scum to your home." And before they could respond he continued. "I feel I must do more than say I am sorry; I must show you." With that the Captain signaled to Mr. Flyer, who then placed a black bag at the feet of the Widow.

"This bag…," the Captain began, "…contains half of the gold coins that we were paid to bring the provisions to you. They are now yours."

The Widow slowly opened the bag and gasped, "Why sir, this is a fortune!"

"Not nearly enough when considering the insult to you and this lad," The Captain replied as he continued. "I am familiar with the nearby village, and with your permission I would like to take the coins there and deposit them in the local bank. I will negotiate a favorable interest rate for you and ask the Abbot to be your representative. I will also ask the Abbot to withdraw, monthly, the funds necessary to procure such provisions as you request, and to provide for the delivery of these provisions. If you like, I will also authorize the Abbot to take a monthly donation, as determined by you, to be used in support of the Abbey."

Tears began to flow from the Widow's eyes and only sobs would come when she tried to respond to this wondrous news. Finally, she could only look at Aarondophilous in wonder and quietly say, "I had no idea the miracles you would bring when you entered my life. I know grown men who do not show the character and strength that is present in you."

Aarondophilous' only response was to look at Captain Harris and ask, "Please Captain, can you tell me the name of the captain that sent you to us?"

"Why yes, I can my lad, he said his name was Eli, Captain Eli."

<p style="text-align:center">~~~~~~~~</p>

As Adam Boy and Revan came down the stairs, he noticed the Giraffopotamus trying not to be obvious in their interest of him and his quest. He then made the decision to tell them what they wanted to hear. If not, he feared they would force him to do so or possibly harm Revan in the mistaken assumption that she knew the details of his quest. For this reason, he pretended not to notice the two men and talked to Revan in hushed tones that were nonetheless loud enough for the two men to hear. "My Uncle Daylon sailed as a pirate in the Caribbean several years ago," he whispered. "A few years ago, my Uncle died of a sword wound, but not before he could tell my grandparents about the location of his buried loot. He was dying with a fever when he told them of the treasure and the location coordinates. Due to the fever, he could not think or talk clearly, and my grandparents assumed he was talking about a real red horse and a real Count, but I see now that he was talking about this inn and the painting of the Count in the room upstairs."

Revan became agitated as she glanced at the two men and gave Adam Boy a quizzical look. But Adam Boy continued as he gave Revan a conspiratorial wink, "Don't you see? My Uncle painted the coordinates of the treasure on the map. That is where the treasure is buried!"

Then after a quick glance that confirmed the two men were still closely watching him, he affected a look of sadness and disappointment as he said, "But it will take my grandparents a long time to reach the treasure. I fear it will be found and stolen long before they can complete the journey."

With that he said goodbye to Revan and left the inn.

~~~~~~~~

It was well after dark before Adam Boy returned to the inn and entered silently through the rear door that Revan had left unlatched for him. He found her sitting at a table in a back room.

"Thank you for going along with my deception," he told her as he sat at the table.
~~~~~~~~

"My pleasure, Adam Boy," she replied. "After you left your two friends found an excuse to visit the Count," she continued with a smile. "I will wager that by midday tomorrow they will be on their way to the coordinates shown on the map. But I have a feeling they will be disappointed when they reach the location."

Adam Boy did not reply to this. He was still concerned that it could be a problem for Revan if it were found she knew too much about the truth of his quest. Instead, he asked her, "Please, can you tell me all you know of who I am and what my purpose might be?"

Nodding her head Revan told of how about six months ago a ship had arrived at the nearby port, and how its Captain, Eli was his name, had visited her at the inn. He had related to her that he had made many inquiries and knew her to be a woman who lived her Christian faith as it was meant to be lived. After talking with her for over an hour he had finally outlined his purpose to her. He had returned to the wagon in which he had arrived and brought out the portrait of the Count. She was to mount the portrait in an out-of-the-way location in the inn.
Captain Eli had then described Adam Boy in detail but had instructed her to show him the portrait only after he asked about the Count. The Captain had then given Revan three papers and asked her to hide them and bring them out only when she and Adam Boy were alone. And she said, "He also recounted how your two friends might show up around the same time as you, and to be wary of them. Which is why I was alarmed when you started to talk of treasure…which I wager does not exist."

"And that is really all I know," she said in conclusion of her account.

"Captain Eli…" Adam Boy said more to himself than to Revan. There was a familiarity to the name, but the memory of who this Captain might be would not come to him.

"Are those the papers he gave you?" he said pointing at the documents lying on the table.

She simply nodded her head.

But before viewing the papers he had to ask another question. "Why did you help me?"

"I could see the kindness and the sadness in the Captain's eyes when he talked of you. My heart told me to help him. Of course, he sent me money in payment, but I gave it to the poor. I do not need to be paid for doing what is right."

Adam Boy said, "I cannot thank you for the Captain, but I do thank you for myself. You are a remarkable lady."
They smiled at one another as Adam Boy lifted the three documents. Two were maps and the other a nautical chart. "I recognize this one as a map of Fernandina, Florida. The inn is just south of town," Revan said pointing at a spot on the map. You can see that an address is marked on the map with an "X". The Captain said that you are to go there for help in getting to your destination. The other map appears to be for a section of southern South Carolina. There is not enough information on the chart for me to identify the exact area," she concluded.

Adam Boy looked at the second map and his heart sank as he noted a very prominent "X" at the coordinates *N32⁰ 37′, W80⁰ 59′*. He wondered frantically if he had mistaken the clues. If so, he had given two suspicious men the information they would need to beat him to the location. But picking up the chart he looked for the coordinates *N32⁰ 18.5′, W80⁰ 29.5′* as suggested by the clue...*halve the minutes*... and was relieved to see the name *Skull Inlet* at that location. He was further comforted when he noted that *"The Narrows"* was written on the chart with an arrow pointing to a narrow neck of land between marsh and ocean on the adjoining island.

...ride the steed until you see the skull...Wait for a season at The Narrows....

Chapter 3 - The Women

Renee Fini was furious! Her "honored position" had made her a prisoner. If she had foreseen this outcome, she may have run and left the Hos women to their fate when the opportunity presented itself. This thinking somehow calmed her, probably because it reminded her how impossible it would have been to leave those women undefended.

Fini could have no more left those women to their fate than she could abandon a child in the wilderness. For in examining her own character over these past days, she knew that there was something within that drove her to defend and help those in need. This trait went beyond that determined by her personality. She knew, somehow, that it was embedded within her very identity. She still knew little about herself, but she was certain that something in her background drove her to defend those women. In fact, this drive extended to all the innocents of the world which included children, men, *and* women.

Renee Fini smiled to herself as she realized how this self-analysis would seem self-important to anyone with whom she might share these thoughts. Oh no, although the details of who she was were still vague, she felt certain she was very much subject to human frailties.

This led her thoughts to that morning some days back, how many days ago she could not recall, when she awoke on a beach with the wide-eyed, brown-skinned man looking at her with terror, clearly startled by what she would later surmise to be her sudden appearance. He held a spear in one hand and a short sword in the other. His clothing was limited to a robe gathered at his waist with the hem stopping just below his knees.

She had risen awkwardly to her feet confused and disoriented. The man had run stumbling to a group of similarly clad and armed men. He was gesturing wildly as he rapidly spoke in a language she could not understand.

It seemed that one of the men in the group, who she immediately came to think of as the leader, was admonishing the one delivering the excited message. The leader quickly turned in her direction with a deliberate and determined stride as the others followed. She counted seven men including the leader. Their demeanor left no doubt that the men were hostile. Renee Fini became calm and, in her mind, saw very clearly how the events of the next several seconds would transpire.

By this time Fini had recovered her balance and orientation and as the leader came near, she dropped to a crouch. Using her left arm as a pivot point, she swung her body and outstretched legs in a sweeping arc that hit the leader in the back of his knees. The impact caused him to fall roughly to his back as he dropped both his spear and sword. By the way he lay she knew the leader was stunned and would no longer be a factor in this short fight.

Fini quickly picked up the leader's sword and spear from where they had fallen. In a single fluid motion, she grabbed the shaft of the spear in her right hand near its end. Swinging the spear overhead she slammed the flat surface of the spear point against the head of one of the remaining six men. As the man collapsed unconscious to the ground she spun in the direction of another attacker.

She easily blocked the man's sword thrust with the sword held in her left hand. Then she spun and jammed her elbow into the man's temple. As he collapsed Fini dropped her spear and replaced it with a second sword as she pulled it from the man's hand. She then turned to face two additional aggressors.

She parried sword thrusts from the two attackers in quick succession. As one of these men raised his spear in preparation for a follow-up attack, she swung the sword in her right hand and cut the spearhead from its shaft. Simultaneously, Renee Fini hit the cross guard of his sword with the flat of the sword she held in her left hand. This knocked the sword from his hand, leaving him open to the follow-up blow from the grip of her right- hand sword. He collapsed unconscious to the sand.

Fini spun once again to face her remaining three attackers, but these men had turned and were making a hasty retreat. She noted with a smile that one of the retreating men was he whom she had apparently startled with her awakening on the beach. He had had quite enough of her as did the fallen warriors, for as they recovered, they also retreated.

Nonetheless, she determined to put distance between herself and the beach before the men could return with reinforcements. However, it was then she saw the thing that initiated the events which established the course of her life over these past days.

Across the beach Fini saw eight terrified women huddling together as they were being guarded by two armed men. These men were clearly allied with those whom she had just fought. Rapidly crossing the thirty meters to where the women were being guarded, she rushed the two men. However, rather than fight this mad woman, they joined the others in retreat.

With their guards routed, the eight women rose and ran without hesitation into the jungle bordering the beach. Renee Fini stood alone on the sand, but before she could beat her own retreat, thirty to forty armed men stepped from the jungle. They effectively blocked her way, and their number seemed far too great to defeat.

Before an exhausted Renee Fini could drop her weapons in surrender one of the men stepped forward, dropped his weapons, and knelt before her. He then spoke in what she somehow knew to be Polynesian accented English. It took several seconds before she fully understood the implications of what he said.

The man simply said, "I surrender to you your people, oh *Great Queen.*"

Thus, began her imprisonment.

~~~~~~~~~
~~~~~~~~~

Another woman on another island awoke to complete isolation. The woman stood on unsteady legs as wave after wave of nausea assaulted her. The assault was so severe and so constant that after a few minutes of walking along the beach she finally succumbed to the temptation to fall to her knees, and then dropped prone to the sand. After what seemed an eternity, but was likely about two hours later, the nausea subsided to the point that she could stand. She then walked to a raised knoll near the point where the jungle met the beach. She sat gingerly on the knoll.

The woman had no idea who she was, from where she had come, where she was, or why she was there. She appeared to be dressed in a uniform of some kind, although all identifying markings appeared to have been removed. She wore no jewelry or ornamentation of any kind.

After an extended time of fruitless contemplation, the woman felt recovered enough to walk and thereby explore the beach. She held a hope that she would find someone who might give her answers. However, when after about twenty minutes she had yet to encounter any sign of another human, she began to fear that she was alone and without resources.

Almost instantly her growing fear turned to a fierce and unthinking anger. *Who had done this terrible thing to her?* She would find out and do whatever she must to make them pay!

Her discomfort and anger were accentuated by the fact that the sun was going down and it would soon be nightfall on what promised to be a moonless evening. It was then she recognized a sudden sense of being watched. This led her to stop walking in mid-stride and turn slowly seaward. There she saw, not twenty meters from shore, a dozen outrigger canoes making their way silently toward her position. Despite the increasing gloom, she could see that each canoe carried two men and that every man was observing her in earnest.

As the woman let out a startled cry the men began to yell and increase the tempo of their paddling. In reaction to this aggressive action, she turned and began fleeing toward the jungle that bordered the beach.

Several men jumped from their canoes and began wading rapidly ashore. As she glanced back over her shoulder at the men, the woman could see that each carried a short sword and a spear. The presence of the weapons raised the woman's level of alarm as she ran blindly into the jungle. She came to a rock outcropping and climbed upward until the ground leveled out again.

She soon came to a small stream which she jumped easily. Noticing a path which followed the stream, the woman turned inland and followed the path while desperately hoping to find some place to hide from her pursuers. The woman could hear the men running in chase behind her, but she could also begin to hear flowing water. Perhaps this stream flowed to a larger one. If so, she could jump in the stream and somehow swim to safety. These were desperate thoughts of a frightened woman. Her fear was now strong and overrode the underlying anger that remained.
As the path made a right turn around a large rock the woman's heart sank. She was confronted by a sheer cliff wall which left no escape but straight up. The sound she had heard was that of another small stream as it fell from the top of the cliff high overhead into a pool. The stream she had been following also fell into this pool; however, the joined waters exited into a maze of downed trees which presented a dangerous and possibly impassable escape.

In near panic the woman began to climb the cliff face, but soon felt a hand grab her roughly by the foot. Her hand at that moment closed around a small stone. The woman twisted her body and hurled the stone into the face of the man who was trying to stop her advance.

The man released her and yelled in pain as the stone hit his head in a glancing blow just over his right eye. But the woman's freedom was short-lived as three more men climbed the cliff below her and to each side. Each brandished a sword and used threatening gestures as they forced her to surrender.

Two of the men grabbed her. Each held an arm and forced the woman to retrace her steps down the side of the cliff. The two men led her in the direction of one whom she took to be the leader. As they neared the leader, she once again found her fear inexplicably replaced with rage. She began to struggle and screamed loudly, "Someone will pay dearly for this outrage!"

At these words, the leader looked at her wide-eyed and shouted at the two men holding her. The men immediately released the woman. With another shouted word from the leader every one of her pursuers dropped their weapons and fell on their faces before her.

In accented English, the man said, "Oh forgive us, mighty She-Warrior."

~~~~~~~~

Renee Fini had pieced together the events leading to her sudden elevation as "Queen". This was accomplished over the course of several days through conversations with the *Rangatira,* Tonee Vee. Rangatira seemed to roughly translate as "War Chief" and Fini quickly understood that it would be important to understand how this man thought.

Through strange circumstances, Fini found herself the Queen and leader of a tribe of Polynesian people calling themselves the Hos. The Hos had long been friendly with the Pitale tribe located on a nearby island. But with the coming of the large ships carrying their pale and angry masters, things had changed. The Pitale and Hos men traded the pearls they found at the bottom of their clear lagoons for the swords, spears, and other items carried within the great ships. They came to call these traders the *Outsiders*. It was through the act of trading that the Pitale and Hos learned to speak the Outsider language.
~~~~~~~~

The Hos tended to isolate their women and children from contact with the Outsiders, but the Pitale readily allowed the Outsiders into their villages. It was not long before the Outsiders began to take Pitale women for their wives. Their resulting shortage of women eventually drove the Pitale to raid the Hos and forcefully take their women as wives. It was one of these Pitale raiding parties that Renee Fini confronted and routed on that first day.

The Hos and Pitale were traditionally ruled by a council of War Chiefs. However, they learned the concept of King and Queen through their trading with the Outsiders. It was this imperfect understanding of what it meant to be a Queen that led Tonee Vee to hail this *"warrior woman"* as Queen of the Hos on that first day.

Fini had spent the first day trying to convince Tonee Vee that she was not a Queen, but her skills in battle, and her liberation of their women left him with an unmovable conviction that she was indeed a leader that deserved their unquestioning obedience.

Tonee Vee explained, "The group of females you rescued included the daughters of two of our War Chiefs. If not for you delaying them, the Pitale men would have escaped with the women and, I am certain, ransomed them. I fear payment of that ransom would have required the complete surrender of the Hos. Our tribe would exist no longer. Oh yes, without a doubt, you are our Queen."

Although her new title made Renee Fini uncomfortable, she could have accepted it as an inconvenient case of mistaken identity had it not resulted in her virtual imprisonment. There was no cell, no chains, and no shackles. Hers was a prison of devotion. She could not leave the confines of her hut without an escort of five armed men. To take a bath required the assistance of two or three "ladies-in-waiting". There were no casual strolls along the beach, no intimate dinners with a few chosen friends, or no private moments of any kind. The women of the village even took turns sleeping on the floor of the hut blocking the path to where Fini slept.

Of course, there was no hostility in the tribe's actions, and Fini understood that the Hos merely wished to protect and revere their new Queen. But the effect on Fini was a stifling oppression.

Thanks to the gold band around her wrist Fini knew her name, but little more. She felt that if she could just get away in quiet solitude for a while her memories would begin to return.

Fini stood before a mirror that had been received in trade from the Outsiders. She saw a woman of medium build with dark hair and green eyes. She caught several of the Hos men looking at her and this led her to believe that they considered her attractive. However, she had to admit that there was nothing in her appearance that would lead anyone to suspect she was capable of the combat she engaged that first day. Indeed, it was easy to see why the Pitale men were so surprised by her aggressive defense. She was sure this surprise was a major factor in her success in the fight.
As Fini pondered these things she became aware of a young woman standing patiently, but nervously before her. The young woman was carrying a duffle bag which appeared to be the source of her nervousness.

"How can I help you?" Renee Fini asked the woman.
"Please, Queen Fini, forgive my father" began the woman. "He picked this bag up near where you say you awakened on the beach. He now realizes that he was foolish to take it for himself and wishes to return it to you."

Renee Fini took the duffle from the woman and began to examine it. She realized this bag could be a key to understanding who she was.

On the side of the duffle was printed *Sea Queen*.

~~~~~~~~~~

The woman soon realized that *Rangatira* Long Dee had clearly mistaken her for another woman having similar hair color and general appearance.
~~~~~~~~~~

This was a fortunate mistake for the woman. She seized every opportunity to exploit her good fortune over the several days since being declared "Queen of the Pitale". The woman was able to learn from Long Dee about the raid on the Hos in which a woman somehow managed to single-handedly defeat the raiders. Long Dee was convinced that she was that woman and had come to claim her victory-won rights as Queen.

The stories of this unknown woman's sudden and mysterious appearance on the Hos beach led to further enhance her mystique. As did the mystery of how she was able to quickly appear on the Pitale beach after so soundly defeating their warriors on the Hos shore.

Although the woman had no memories prior to awakening on the beach, she was certain that she *was not* that woman. The woman, who defended the Hos, as described by Long Dee, was a well-trained warrior and although the woman was likely a competent fighter, she was certain she could not defeat such a grouping of well-armed men. In addition, as determined from Long Dee's description, she was certain that she was recovering from severe nausea on the Pitale's island as the battle took place on the isle of the Hos.

No, she was not the warrior that had so frightened the Pitale, but that would not keep her from using their misidentification to her advantage. The woman strategically planned how to use her position to advance her fortunes. There was never a day that she failed to renew her vow that someone would pay for what they had done to her.

Indeed, she now knew who would pay.

~~~~~~~

Within the duffle Renee Fini found dried beans and other items that were obviously intended to help her survive her first days or weeks in an unknown environment. Whoever packed her duffle may have had a premonition that her first experience on this adventure would be of confrontation and a fight for her life because the contents included a pistol, percussion caps, powder, and lead shot.
~~~~~~~

As she carefully went through the contents of the bag, Fini came upon a sealed yellow envelope with the word *Eli* embedded in the sealing wax. She quickly opened the envelope and was surprised as a small timepiece fell from the envelope. She picked up the chronometer and noted it appeared to be keeping time consistent with the actual time of day on the island, as best that she could estimate. She then read the short note also included within the envelope:

Beware of your reflection as you await a new moon. At the second bell of the first dog, stand on the head, and observe the message in the flashes of the sun.

And then:

Sorry for the mystery, will explain later…David.

At one level the message was meaningless, but in a way that would be difficult to explain she felt the key to understanding the puzzle was almost hers. She knew for example, that her "reflection" had nothing to do with mirrors or other reflective surfaces. But in the same way the mind sometimes strains to recall the reason one had just entered a room, she could not quite grasp what form this reflection would take. Similarly, the term "first dog" had an odd familiarity to it that her mind could not quite embrace.

As she continued to consider the note, she began to feel that if she could remember the "David" who signed the note, the clues would begin to fall into place.

She looked again at the exterior of the envelope and specifically the letters "*Eli*" embedded in the sealing wax. She decided that this was a name; yes, definitely it was a name. It also seemed logical to Fini that "David" was the name that should be paired with this…so *David Eli* was the author of the note…or possibly *Eli David*.

No, *David Eli* was correct.

~~~~~~~~~
~~~~~~~~~

The new "Queen of the Pitale" lost little time in preparing her army for battle. She had quickly decided that since her adversary was the superior fighter and tactician, she would need to overwhelm her in numbers. Thus, for the first time in the memory of the Pitale, the warrior caste forced new recruits into their ranks. No longer were its soldiers limited to those who wished to distinguish themselves in defense of their island, or who sought honor and glory. Now soldiers forced their way into the family huts in the early morning hours requiring every male over the age of fifteen to join their ranks. Whereas ranking in the Pitale warrior caste was traditionally by family name and status, the Queen implemented a double bracket system of hand-to-hand combat to establish leadership. The strongest fifty winners became "lieutenants". These winners then fought and the best ten of these became "captains". The Queen would keep the role of "general" for herself.

The Queen then required her captains to identify the fifty best spear makers among her subjects and force them to produce enough spears to supply her new army. Despite warnings of pearl depletion by the elders of the island, she ordered the divers to conduct repeated dives for the beautiful spheres to use in purchasing needed swords from the Outsiders. And in the face of warnings from these same elders, she proceeded to have the island canoe builders cut the largest and finest trees in the jungle for use in building a fleet of outriggers capable of transporting the large Pitale invasion force. Finally, food production was diverted from the purpose of feeding her subjects to that of feeding her army.

At the end of this process the Queen had an army of intimidating size, but little was left of the once bountiful resources of the Pitale.

~~~~~~~~~~

By her reckoning, it was about one month after awakening on the Hos beach that Renee Fini was greeted with disturbing news from Tonee Vee.
~~~~~~~~~~

One of the Hos warriors had visited Pitale under the cover of darkness in the hopes of locating his sister and rescuing her from her captors. He was unsuccessful, but as he waited in hiding throughout the following day, he witnessed the training of a Pitale army easily three times that of the Hos in size.

"What does this mean?" Renee Fini asked Tonee Vee.

"I am afraid, My Queen, that there is only one possible meaning. The Pitale intend to take the land and wealth of the Hos people. There are no other islands near the Pitale other than the Hos, and we are no threat to them. Conquest of the Hos is the only explanation."

Fini nodded and said, "Bring the man to me that saw this thing. I need to ask him a few questions." "He is waiting outside My Queen," Tonee Vee replied.

The man was tall and carried himself in a manner that suggested bravery and competency in battle. It was lucky for the Pitale that they had not discovered him during his visit to their island. He would likely have taken several of them before being subdued or killed.

"What is your name?" Fini asked. "Ry-An," the man replied.

"I understand you have seen a large army on the Pitale island. Tell me what you saw."
"The army is indeed large, but not yet well-trained. They are training from early morning until the sun drops from the sky."

"Why are they building such an army at this time?" Fini queried.
"I did not see her, but they apparently have a new Queen. I believe she has ordered the army to grow," replied Ry-An.
"But for what purpose?"

Ry-An stood several moments without saying anything, as he looked Renee Fini solidly in the eyes. He seemed to be assessing her…trying to determine how honest he could be. Apparently satisfied he began, "I heard a group of soldiers talking about the new Queen. They said she is a great warrior who is driven by hatred and revenge."

"Against whom is this revenge directed?" she asked.

"It is against you, oh Queen."

Renee Fini slowly nodded her head and said in a low voice. "Beware my reflection…"

~~~~~~~~~~

The Queen of the Pitale paced as her six remaining captains awaited her latest outburst. Some secretly hoped for the demotions experienced by their four comrades. For them, demotion was preferred to the verbal abuse and general ranting of their Queen.

One of the Queen's spies returned with unacceptable news. The Hos had learned of the growth in the Pitale army. As a result, the Pitale Queen ordered acceleration in training. Unfortunately for her captains, the day's training had not gone according to the Queen's expectations.

The new recruits were slow to respond to orders and unenthusiastic in their execution. The Queen clearly blamed her captains for this failing.
~~~~~~~~~~

"I will not tolerate this weakness I see in you and your soldiers!" the Queen growled at her captains. "I *will* have my army move on Hos within the next three days, and if you want to avoid losing half your men, I suggest you find a way to get the attention of your recruits. For as the way things now stand, although I am confident, we will win the day, the cost will be the slaughter of your soldiers by the Hos." And finally, she said through gritted teeth, "Now remove yourselves from my sight and put some backbone into those ridiculous sheep you insist on calling warriors."

The captains hurried from the "headquarters" hut that the Queen had ordered built. She then turned her focus to Long Dee. "Tell me," she began as she stared fiercely into his eyes, "Why do I feel that neither you nor my captains support me in my plans?"
"Oh Queen," he said with head bowed and eyes averted, "We truly are your loyal subjects and will do whatever you command." Then slowing raising his eyes to look her in the face he continued, "But we may hesitate because until recently we have had a peaceful existence with the Hos. In fact, some believe that at one time we were one people. It is only since we began to need wives from the Hos that either of our two peoples ever violated the other. Even now a Pitale has never actually harmed a Hos in combat. Frankly, My Queen, none of us has the hate for the Hos that would drive us to attack them with the vigor that would please you."
The Queen's gaze remained intense and steady as she coldly muttered "Call the captains back and assemble the Army. I will speak to them in one hour."

~~~~~~~~~

The Pitale Queen stood on the knoll that overlooked the main valley of the Pitale. Before her, the entire army stood in neat rows. This made her smile as she recalled how disorganized and chaotic the army had been just eighteen days before. Now she was ready to give them the fire they needed in their souls.

"Warriors of Pitale," she began, "It is with a great sadness that I must bring you news of your betrayers."
~~~~~~~~~

Pausing briefly, she continued, "Many of you know that we have received word that the Hos have a new Queen. This Queen hates the Pitale." Once again, she paused and surveyed her army.

"She has ordered her army to attack us and to take no prisoners. No Pitale are to survive including your wives and children."

The Queen saw that her words were having the intended effect. The rows of soldiers remained intact, but she could see individuals within the ranks begin to move in an agitated fashion.

"She has promised her people that they will have your forests, your rivers, your canoes, and your pearl beds. She has promised them that all memory of the Pitale will be removed from the Earth."

Now the order of the ranks began to dissolve. Individual shouts of anger and revenge could be heard throughout the valley. The woman knew that most of these shouts came from those promised special privileges by their captains, but she expected the shouts to be infectious and grow in number and intensity. All that was needed was the proper catalyst. She intended to be that catalyst.

She continued in a rising voice, "But do not despair my people! I pledge to you that I will not let this happen! I will lead you to victory over the demon Hos!"

The army cheered her continuously and enthusiastically until she finally turned and left the knoll.

~~~~~~~~
~~~~~~~~

Chapter 4 - The Girls

Kelligeen walked along Water Street near St. John's harbor and considered the 300 years of history represented by what she saw, smelled, and experienced. *How many other twelve-year-old girls had walked these smooth cobblestones brought across the ocean as ballast?* Ballast for ships not unlike those she glimpsed as she looked down the street called Ayres Cove, which intersected Water Street and led to the harbor.

She was somewhat short in stature with long dark hair that fell down her back. Her eyes were bright and reflected an intelligence undergirded by more than a little mischief. Kelligeen loved life, and she loved imagining what life would bring.

Kelligeen also loved music and cherished the violin lessons she received from Mr. Castle, the owner of the music shop that was now her destination. She was particularly excited about today's lesson because he had dropped by her home earlier in the afternoon and promised something special for today. Her imagination ran in great leaps with each thought seeming to be outdone by the next.

Kelligeen had detected a change in her parents these last few days which served to accentuate her curiosity about the surprise. She would catch them looking at her in a reflective manner and would quickly look away when noticed. Mainly, they were quiet in her presence. Uncharacteristically quiet.

What is the surprise? Was she to learn a new and complex piece? Has Mr. Castle written a new piece just for her? Was he going to give her the violin he had created and placed on sale in his store at a price greater than the salary her father made in a year?

No, Mr. Castle did like her and told her she was a gifted musician, but there is no possibility that he would give her the new violin. Its sale would represent a major portion of his shop's income and he was not a rich man.

With this last thought, Kelligeen abruptly drew in the reins on her imaginings and gave herself a mental scolding. Although Kelligeen was short in stature, she had an imagination that was very tall indeed. Her father and mother had taught her to be proud of her creativity, but occasionally she thought she had to bring herself back to reality by "giving herself a good talking to".

No, Kelligeen repeated to herself. *Mr. Castle's surprise would not be the gift of the violin.*

She was correct…his surprise was much, much more important to her life.

~~~~~~~~~~

Natalini thought herself the only seven-year-old in the world that would so love the hot and dusty streets of Madras. She loved its market, the ornate Hindu temples, and the beach that lay near Fort St. George, in which her father worked as assistant to the Governor of the Madras Province of southern India.

Her father chose to house his family in a small stone home located about three kilometers down the shoreline from the fort, which allowed for what Natalini's father considered a healthy separation from military life for his daughter. His one compromise to this separation was the three soldiers garrisoned within the walls of their home to provide security for his family.

It was Sunday morning and Natalini was on her way to St. Mary's Church located within the walls of the fort. She and her mother were closely followed by the three soldiers.
~~~~~~~~~~

Natalini's mother had moved from Varese, Italy to London with her parents when a young woman. Her mother's father had served on the staff of the Italian ambassador in London. Natalini's father was a young British officer working as a liaison to the Italian embassy. He was at the embassy attending a ball when he met and fell in love with her mother. Her mother had told her many of the specifics of their courtship, including walks along the banks of the Thames, long talks as they fed the pigeons in Trafalgar Square, and visits to the Tower of London.

After eight months of courtship, her father was assigned as an administrator in Madras. The young couple married the day before they left on the voyage to India. Nine-and-one-half-months later Natalini was born. Throughout the following years, her father had worked honestly with a reputation for excellence and had risen to his present position of power and responsibility.

Natalini loved the stories of the courtship, she loved her parents, and she loved living in Madras.

Her father had intended to accompany Natalini and her mother to church this morning but had been called to the fort unexpectedly an hour before they were to leave their home. Her mother had indulged her by riding in a carriage behind Natalini as she walked through the busy street leading from her home to the fort. The great pleasure she found in walking was due in part to the feeling of connection with the city and its people that it gave her. But an equally important reason was that she found she missed too many details when riding in the carriage. Natalini hated to miss *anything*.

It seemed the closer they got to the fort the larger the crowds became. It was becoming difficult to move the carriage through the streets. While Natalini suspected her mother was getting worried about the growing distance between her and the carriage, she was having too much fun to slow her own progress.

After they had traveled to within a kilometer of the fort, Natalini saw an Indian girl near her own age standing on a street corner selling flowers. She was much shorter than Natalini, which was true for most girls her age. Natalini did not recognize the girl, but she looked friendly and Natalini loved meeting people. Besides, she thought it would be nice to go to church with a red rose in her long black hair.

Natalini was to experience much more from this encounter than the purchase of a flower for her hair.

~~~~~~~~~

Kelligeen imagined life as a highway that contained many forks. These were not just a branching of people's lives that coincided with big events, such as deciding whom to marry. The highway also contained many small forks that one encounters many times in a single day. *What do I eat for breakfast?* (She often had French toast.) *Do I wear the purple dress or the black one?* (It was almost always purple.) *What book do I read next?* (Lately it was usually something from a new author, Sheridan Le Fanu.)

The fork in the road presented by Mr. Castle's proposal was daunting in its implications.

Kelligeen entered the shop and went directly to the small room in the back where she typically received her instruction. Mr. Castle was sitting at the table where he always sat during her lessons. However, on this day a man that she did not recognize sat across the table from Mr. Castle.

The man sat with squared shoulders and an attitude that communicated genuine dignity, not the aloofness that sometimes masqueraded as dignity. He turned to look at her as she crossed the room, his face carrying an expression that was difficult to interpret.

Mr. Castle was the first to speak. "Kelligeen, I would like for you to meet Mr. Andrewski." With that Mr. Andrewski and Kelligeen nodded greetings to each other. Continuing, Mr. Castle called to the adjoining room, "Please join us!"
~~~~~~~~~

The curtain separating the rooms parted and Kelligeen's parents stepped quickly through the doorway. Her parents had always been engaging and open with their three children. But today her parents could not bring themselves to look in her direction, instead they seemed to be fighting emotions as they stared silently at Mr. Andrewski.

Mr. Andrewski apparently took her parent's entry as his cue to speak and looking into her eyes he said, "Frankly, when Mr. Castle first told me of your talent with the violin his praise was so great that I was skeptical." Glancing briefly at Mr. Castle and then her parents he continued in a softer voice. "So, forgive me my intrusion on your privacy, but two weeks ago I asked Mr. Castle for permission to listen in the next room as you practiced. I am no longer skeptical."

Before Kelligeen could give voice to the questions begging to be asked he continued. "I have been in contact with a Mr. Hill in New York City. He is attempting to organize a philharmonic society there. This is a project that I am actively supporting financially, administratively, and emotionally. I do have considerable artistic credentials and based on my recommendations Mr. Hill and the future members of the society have voted to extend you an invitation to join."

With that Mr. Andrewski paused, but before Kelligeen could speak her father interrupted. "Forgive us my darling girl," he began. "Two days ago, Mr. Castle and Mr. Andrewski came to your mother and me and advised us that Mr. Andrewski was sponsoring you for membership in the New York society. But it was only this afternoon that Mr. Castle let us know that your membership had been approved. We hesitated to talk to you before we received word of your acceptance. Although we knew how wonderfully you play, it seemed so unlikely to us that a group of educated men in New York would accept sight-unseen a twelve-year-old girl from St. John's, Newfoundland. We could not bear to see you disappointed. Obviously, Mr. Andrewski is very persuasive." He concluded with a smile and nods of appreciation to Mr. Andrewski and Mr. Castle.

Kelligeen continued to look at her father as her questions at last found voice. "But what does this all mean?" she began tentatively. "How can I live in St. John's with you and mother while becoming a member of the society in New York City? May I continue my lessons with Mr. Castle? How do I travel to New York for the concerts?" With each subsequent question Kelligeen's voice took on greater levels of emotion, buoyed by an increasing anxiety.

"Sweetheart," began her mother as tears fell from her eyes, "You will be leaving your father and me for this wonderful opportunity. New York will become your new home."

~~~~~~~~~

Natalini approached the girl selling the flowers and spoke in the friendliest voice she could muster. "Hello, my name is Natalini," she began hoping the girl spoke English. "What is your name?"

The girl turned in her direction and smiled. "I am called Melodi," she responded.

"You looked very friendly when I saw you at your cart," said Natalini. "I was hoping we could become friends."

Melodi then turned to her flower cart and pulled from it a perfect pink lotus flower with a bright yellow center. "To celebrate our friendship to come" Melodi began, "I give you this symbol of long life, good fortune, and purity of mind."

"It is beautiful" whispered Natalini, "I will treasure this gift and I will treasure my new friend. I will think of you whenever I look upon it." She then untied the gold ribbon that gathered her long black hair at the back of her head and gave it to Melodi as she shook her hair free. "I hope you also remember me whenever you look at this ribbon."

The joy in Melodi's eyes was true and full, but "Thank you" was the only response she could muster.
~~~~~~~~~

"Will you be here at this time tomorrow?" Natalini asked. In response to the nod of Melodi's head she continued. "I will see you then when we can visit longer."

Both girls smiled as Natalini turned to continue her stroll to church, but she had gone only forty meters when she heard Melodi scream. Turning she saw a man holding Melodi around the waist. Kicking at the man, Melodi struggled desperately and continued to scream.

Natalini began to run in the direction of Melodi and yelled, "Stop! Leave her alone!" Then turning to the three soldiers guarding her and her mother Natalini screamed, "Help her! Don't let him hurt her!"

Two of the soldiers rode quickly to the aid of Melodi while the third stayed with Natalini's mother. As the two soldiers neared Melodi, her attacker released her and ran quickly into the crowd of the marketplace.

With this Natalini sighed deeply as she stopped running and stood in relief in the middle of the road. But this relief was short-lived as she found herself grabbed roughly and lifted into the air. She had the sensation of flying and realized that she was being carried away on horseback at a dead run.

Natalini heard her mother screaming from behind as she caught a glimpse of other riders blocking the paths of her guards as they attempted to pursue the man holding her. She managed to look at her captor's clothing as she struggled for freedom and recognized the style from drawings her father had shown her.

The man was dressed as an Afghan military leader known as a sirdar. She recalled from her discussions with her father that several Afghan tribes were fighting the British soldiers supporting the East India Company. She also knew the sirdars to be ruthless in fighting those they consider to be foreign invaders. The other children at the small school within the fort told terrible stories of what the sirdars and their soldiers did to the British when they were captured, even women and children.

For the first time Natalini was afraid.

~~~~~~~~~

As she stood on the stern of the steamship *Lafayette,* Kelligeen peered into the fog as St. John's harbor dissolved from view. But her mind was preoccupied, and her surroundings did not register in her consciousness.

Kelligeen's life had quickly become a blur of actions that left her somehow both numb and energized. Only two days had elapsed since the day in Mr. Castle's shop when she learned of this unbelievable turn in her life. She reflected on how much had transpired in that short time, and in some ways, it seemed she had forever been on this journey. In truth she knew her journey was only beginning.
As the last of St. John's harbor was lost to her view, Kelligeen turned to find a girl facing her from less than a meter. The girl was perhaps a year or two older than Kelligeen, and slightly taller. Otherwise, the girl was close enough in appearance to pass as her sister.

Kelligeen had been visibly startled by the proximity of the girl, which caused the girl to blush in embarrassment. To set the girl at ease Kelligeen smiled and said, "Hello...my name is Kelligeen Smythe. What is yours?"

The girl relaxed, returned the smile, and replied, "My name is Janus Andrewski." In reply to Kelligeen's unasked question Janus continued. "It is my father that you met in St. John's and is arranging for you to play with the philharmonic society in New York." Then continuing in a hopeful tone, she said, "I play the cello and wished to ask if you would like to practice together?"

"That would be wonderful," Kelligeen said with enthusiasm. "Will you too play with the society in New York?"
~~~~~~~~~

"Oh no," replied Janus matter-of-factly. "I am particularly good, but my father says your talent is rare and precious. You must understand the great honor you are being given. There will be no one else in the society remotely as young as you."

"I actually feel incredibly nervous. What will happen if I do not play well enough to satisfy the society members? Will the society pay the return passage of such a failure? Will my parents come for me?" With each question Kelligeen's voice became higher and more anxious until she noticed the smile on Janus's face, which had a wonderful calming affect.

"I know," said Kelligeen, "I am worrying about what might be instead of enjoying what is. This is not typical of me. My father says he is proud of the way I can look at things calmly and develop just the right approach to every situation. But I do have an active imagination, and I guess this has happened so suddenly, and the changes are so drastic that I have let my imagination take control."

"You will play perfectly for the society and they will love you," said Janus. "I know because my father has faith in you, and he is a very smart man. I have no concern about your ability to play perfectly." Dropping her voice, she continued, "The thing that concerns me is what I overheard two of the ship's crew discussing."

From the look on Janus' face, Kelligeen immediately knew that whatever concerned Janus should also concern her.

~~~~~~~~~

Natalini was careful to not let her fear overwhelm her. She instead began to concentrate on a means of freeing herself. Her concentration was soon rewarded as she noticed the dagger and sheath strapped to the lower right leg of the man holding her. She also noted the Afghan style saddle upon which the man sat. It was constructed using a single cloth cinch that attached to the saddle by means of a leather strap. Stretching her arm Natalini reached for the knife but found it several inches beyond her grasp.
~~~~~~~~~

She then remembered the broach that her mother had insisted she wear to church that morning. The clasp was the type that used a needle-like pin to hold the broach in place as it was passed through the material of the dress. Unfastening the clasp Natalini removed the broach from the front of her dress. She then grasped the broach in the palm of her right hand and made a fist such that the pin of the clasp protruded between her fingers extending beyond them almost an inch.

The man held Natalini firmly in his right arm and held the reins in his left. She was positioned such that her weight was partially supported by the lower neck of the man's horse. This allowed her to reach around the horse's neck and grasp the lower portion of the bridle in her left hand.

Natalini turned her head sufficiently to look in the direction from which they had come and saw approximately ten riders following at one hundred meters, with the apparent purpose of discouraging any pursuers. Waiting until she and her captor rounded a curve in the road which blocked them from the other riders, she executed her plan so quickly that it would look to an observer as a single fluid movement.

She jammed the pin of the broach into the man's upper calve and released her grip on the broach. He roared in pain and loosened his grasp on Natalini as he instinctively raised his leg to remove the pin from his calf. Natalini grabbed the knife which was now within her reach and used the sharp blade to slice through the strap holding the saddle's cinch in place.

The saddle slipped to the side and fell taking the man with it. Natalini dropped the knife and straddling the horse's neck grasped each side of the bridle with her hands.

Almost losing her grip, Natalini struggled to remain on the bare back of the horse as it continued at a full gallop. She had always loved riding horses and, in those first few moments, had a heightened appreciation for the fact that her father had insisted, over the protests of her mother, that she learn to ride bare back.

But her thoughts quickly turned to the urgent matters at hand, as a quick glance over her shoulder revealed that the other riders had rounded the curve in the road and were now in full pursuit.

~~~~~~~~

"I walked into the galley earlier looking for milk to drink with my dinner," began Janus. "There is a transom above the doorway that can be opened to provide extra ventilation for the cooking. Two crew members were standing outside the doorway talking softly, but not so softly that they could not be easily heard through the open transom. I did not intend to listen to their conversation, but I heard a word very clearly that alarmed me and demanded my attention…That word was *explosion*."
Janus then told Kelligeen the story that she had pieced together based on the portions of the conversation she could hear through the transom.

The two men that Janus heard talking were machinists on break from their duties working in the boiler room of the ship. They were clearly very worried for the safety of the ship, crew, and passengers. The origin of their worry was the fact that the captain was promised a significant bonus by its owner if the ship reached New York harbor by a set deadline. This deadline was quickly approaching, and the captain was pushing the limits of the boiler to win his bonus. One of the men had barely survived the explosion of the boiler on a steam riverboat a few years ago when that vessel had been similarly pushed to its limits. He saw the captain using dangerous techniques, such as employing a wire to defeat the boiler's safety valve. Indeed, the man swore, this was the very action that led to the steamboat disaster.

The machinist had warned the engineer in charge of the engine room of the potential for catastrophe, who in turn had passed the warning on to the captain. The captain dismissed the warning as overreaction and assured the engineer that he well knew the limits of the boiler.
~~~~~~~~

The frightening thing about this story for Janus was the fact that the concerned machinist was so sure of impending tragedy that he had decided to leave the ship when it made its scheduled stop in Halifax, Nova Scotia. He was sure he was seeing signs of strain in the riveting and general structure of the boiler and was earnestly encouraging the other machinist to leave with him.

"I am really scared," concluded Janus, "and do not know what to do. I feel that if I tell father he will dismiss it as my nervous misunderstanding of the facts. If I do manage to talk him into discussing it with the captain, I am afraid the captain will not do anything, and my story will only serve to get those two men into trouble. Yet if I do nothing, I am afraid that I will be responsible for the lives of those men in the engine room and possibly my own. Please, do you have any ideas Kelligeen?"

Kelligeen looked Janus calmly in the eyes and said, "Yes Janus, I certainly do have an idea."

~~~~~~~~~

Natalini managed to gain control of the speeding horse, but another glance over her shoulder revealed that two of the pursing horsemen had reduced the distance between her and them to less than fifty meters. She knew that if this continued as a simple horse race it would be a race she would lose. She did not intend to be recaptured, and her mind bounded from one thought to another in search of a solution. In only a few moments the solution came to her in a flash of insight that gave her a clear and clean path for escape.
The seed of this insight was brought about by the appearance of a bridge over a stream that intersected the road several hundred meters ahead. Rather than continue to the bridge, Natalini turned her mount westward from the road taking a cross-country route that paralleled the stream. She kneed the horse to increase its speed. She was determined to stay ahead of her pursuers for only a few kilometers and had no need to conserve the horse's energy for a longer ride.
~~~~~~~~~

She focused on the terrain as she rode across the landscape. The greatest danger to her plan lay in the potential for her mount to step in a hole at this speed. The horse would break its leg at the worst, and at best a stumble would result in her fall and recapture.

Five minutes after leaving the road, Natalini saw the ridgeline that intersected the flow of the stream as it traveled to the sea. Her father had brought her here two months before to fish in the waters as they tumbled through these hills, and she was beginning to recognize features along the banks of the stream. Two minutes later she saw the pyramid-shaped rock that marked the location where she and father had spent the day.

She turned her horse toward the gap in the riverbank that she knew existed just to the right of the rock. Glancing backward she saw that her nearest pursuer had closed within twenty-five meters. As Natalini descended into the stream bed she knew she would have only a few seconds in which to accomplish her plan once she dropped from sight.

Moments later as her pursuer reached the top of the stream bank, he immediately saw Natalini's horse pawing the ground and snorting in an agitated fashion. But he did not see Natalini. He quickly dismounted and ran across the large boulders that filled the bed of the stream. There was an exceptionally large boulder in the middle of the stream, and he felt certain he would find Natalini hiding behind it as he hopped to a rock that gave him a view of the boulder's backside. Natalini was not there.

The remaining riders arrived at the river and their leader gave orders to rapidly search the banks of the stream in both directions. After twenty minutes of searching, one man returned carrying the dress Natalini had been wearing. The dress had been torn on the rocks of the river and a spot of blood appeared on one sleeve.

The man began to worry about the Emir's reaction to the news that the girl had drowned.

~~~~~~~~~~
~~~~~~~~~~

Kelligeen quietly opened the door to the maintenance closet. She was not sure exactly what things she would need but hoped she would recognize them when she saw them. She had always been handy at repairing things and assumed she would be equally adept at defeating whatever methods the captain had employed to circumvent the safety features of the ship's boiler.

Kelligeen grabbed a hammer, a knife, a large screwdriver, a set of pliers, and a wire cutting tool. Considering further, she found a length of small diameter rope, a candle, and a box of wooden matches.

Satisfied that she had found what was needed, Kelligeen placed the items in a canvas bag and went back into the gangway where Janus was standing lookout for her. Nodding to Janus, they proceeded to make their way below decks. Eventually they made their way to a small compartment just outside the engine room and reviewed their plans one last time. Once Kelligeen and Janus convinced themselves they were ready, Janus picked up the canvas bag and followed Kelligeen into the engine room.

Crouching in a darkened corner, as she quickly scanned the area, Kelligeen spotted a large cylindrical vessel that she recognized as the boiler. Next to the boiler were two men manning gauges, and apparently making valve adjustments based on the readings from the gauges. The fire box was located opposite their location on the far end of the boiler. Through the gloom of the engine room, Kelligeen could just make out the form of someone whose job it was to ensure the firebox was adequately fed with coal. The girls were able to move to a position from which they could read the gauges and were alarmed to see several of them confirming the danger they faced. The needles for these gauges were pointing to the red regions of the dial faces. Kelligeen knew these regions corresponded to pressures and temperatures that were far above the safe operating values for the boiler system.

The girls looked solemnly at one another and Kelligeen nodded slowly to Janus as she took the canvas bag from her and moved further into the darkness of the engine room. Janus stood up and walked into the light cast by one of the engine room's oil lamps. "Why are you allowing the pressures to be so high?" Janus yelled at the two men manning the gauges. The startled men looked at each other and said nothing for several seconds.

Finally, one of the men said, "You should not be in here young lady." He then proceeded to approach her with the clear intention of escorting her from the engine room.

Janus began to move back toward the entrance to the engine room as she continued to address the men. "I must tell my father that you are doing things that put us all in danger." With that she began to quickly move from the engine room.

The man who had spoken turned to the other and said, "Stay here and keep an eye on things. We cannot afford to let these readings get any higher." With that he began to run in the direction Janus had gone.

The remaining man watching the gauges turned his full attention to the dials and began adjusting the valves based on what he saw. This provided Kelligeen the opportunity to work her way to the back side of the boiler as she continued to look for the safety valve. Fortunately, the valve was easy to locate, and she immediately noted a wire threaded through the mechanism. The valve was of the spring-loaded type and the wire was tied in such a way as to eliminate any tension on the spring. Kelligeen was certain that without the wire in place the high internal pressure of the boiler would have caused the safety valve to open before now.

Kelligeen feared that if she simply cut the wire restricting the valve mechanism the sudden release of superheated steam would kill her or at least cause a severe burn. To address this concern, she used the length of rope to secure the valve mechanism and thereby make the wire redundant. Once she was satisfied the rope was secure, Kelligeen used the wire cutting tool to cut the wire holding the valve closed. To her relief the just-installed rope held, and the steam was not released.

Kelligeen tied the rope in such a way as to have a taunt portion of the rope running horizontally near the floor of the room. Directly beneath this horizontal section of rope she placed the unlit candle in its holder. Finally, she used one of the matches to light the candle and then retreated a safe distance away. There she waited for the rope to burn through and consequently the steam to be released.

Just then she heard a loud conversation in the gangway outside the engine room. She recognized one voice to be that of the captain as he said, "Mr. Andrewski, I must protest your daughter's implication that we are operating this ship in an unsafe manner."

In response she heard Mr. Andrewski say, "There is no 'implication'. In fact, Janus is stating very directly and clearly that she has seen evidence of these safety violations. And furthermore, I intend to see them for myself."

"I am afraid that I cannot allow you into the engine room Mr. Andrewski, that in and of itself is a gross violation of safety procedures," she heard the captain say.

"I will not be dissuaded from this intent," exclaimed Mr. Andrewski.

"I am afraid I will have to ask my chief mate to restrain you sir," the captain replied.

"Well, I…" began Mr. Andrewski just as the candle's flame finished burning through the rope. His words were replaced by the deafening sound of large quantities of high-pressure steam being suddenly released.

The argument was immediately forgotten as everyone rushed into the engine room in response to what they all assumed was a catastrophe in the making.

~~~~~~~~

Natalini held her ear to the small opening through which came light and sounds from outside the cave. She had heard no sounds for the last hour but determined to wait until dark to leave the cave. She was concerned that someone may have been left to guard the area around the cave in which she had found refuge.

As she waited, Natalini remembered how excited her father had been when, after diving in the relatively calm pool next to the large boulder, he had resurfaced telling her about the cave. They had dived under the water together as her father held her hand and led her into the small cave formed inside the large boulder sitting in the middle of the river. There was a ledge upon which one could sit, and the small opening near the top of the chamber provided light as well as a source of fresh air.

She looked at her right arm and noticed that it was bleeding. She cupped her left hand and dipped it in the clear water. She then gently rinsed the blood from the wound.

Natalini had tripped on the hem of her dress as she hurriedly dismounted the horse and splashed into the water of the stream. As she fell her arm struck the sharp edge of a rock which must have cut her arm as it tore her dress. She frantically pulled her dress over her head and tossed it into the stream.

Holding her shoes in her hands, she dove into the water only seconds before her pursuer topped the embankment of the stream. She waited for what seemed an eternity as the Afghans searched for her. She desperately hoped that none of the men knew of the cave and was reassured that it was likely the men searching for her were foreign to this area.
~~~~~~~~

As the light grew dim in the cave, signaling that nightfall was near, Natalini slowly and quietly slipped under the water and felt her way through the opening. She fought the urge to quickly break the surface of the water and quietly raised her head into the twilight of the evening.

There was just enough light remaining for her to confirm that none of the Afghans remained in the area as she waded to the bank. She decided to wait below the embankment until full dark to ensure she would not be profiled against the horizon by the last dim rays of the sun. She gratefully noticed that the soldier who found her dress had discarded it on the bank. She deftly pulled it over her head and put on her shoes. She was very thankful for the warm night air that offset the dampness of her clothing.

When she at last climbed to the top of the embankment, she turned and followed the stream toward the east, the coast, and home.

~~~~~~~~~~

As Kelligeen prepared for bed she thought of what had happened after the boiler's safety valve released.

Mr. Andrewski, the captain, the chief mate, and Janus ran into the engine room as Kelligeen stepped from her hiding place in the shadows. It was easy to show Mr. Andrewski proof of the danger to which the captain had exposed the ship, crew, and passengers. Mr. Andrewski was a powerful and influential man. He demanded the captain turn command of the ship over to the chief mate with agreement to resign upon reaching New York. In exchange for his compliance, Mr. Andrewski agreed to not press charges.

~~~~~~~~~~

Half-a-world away, Natalini had walked all night following her escape from the Afghans, and the next morning eventually spotted a patrol from the fort.

When the patrol delivered her home, her parents cried with relief. After bathing and partaking in what she proclaimed to be the best meal she ever had, she asked that someone find her new friend, Melodi, and tell her that she was safe. Only then did Natalini fall into her bed exhausted.

Natalini awakened with the morning sun streaming through her bedroom window. She could tell that it was early morning and knew she must have been asleep for over fifteen hours.

At almost the same instant, both girls reflected on their respective experiences and said to themselves that they would never have such an adventure again.

They were very wrong.

Part II:
Reunion

Chapter 5 - Benjabar

Benjabar sat at the table with Captain Arturis. The shackles were removed from his hands and feet, but Benjabar's heart remained heavy as he thought of the men, women, and children still chained in the hold of the ship.

Captain Arturis sat upright, still, and silent as he looked into Benjabar's eyes. He seemed to lose himself in questions and doubts about Benjabar. It was as though he thought truth could be gained through a sufficient force of will. If only he looked deeply enough, and long enough, into Benjabar's eyes all the answers would come forth and present themselves for display and review.

But at last, the Captain spoke, "So, tell me my friend, who is 'Eli'?" As he asked the question, he lifted a duffle from the floor, removed a yellow envelope, and placed it upon the table. "Go ahead," he continued, "Read the note inside the envelope."

Upon hearing the name "Eli" Benjabar's memories boiled within, as if that name were the catalyst leading to the creation of all memories. Memories of Jamaica, sailing, and a bond between he and David Eli. Yet these new memories and his earlier memories remained fragmented and refused to form into a coherent identity. He needed time. Time to think. Time to concentrate. Time to remember.

Benjabar opened the yellow envelope and removed the note inside. He discovered that the mysterious envelope had been sealed, but Arturis had broken the seal, and Benjabar could not read the mark that had been stamped within the sealing wax. Written in neat block letters on the paper was the following:

Make your way to Dubignon's lair on their seaward island. Wait until the Land's birth is celebrated, and the Danelaw and Patrick flags appear.

And then...

At the bottom of the page was a carefully drawn map of a coastline. On the map was a dot next to the word "Brunswick" and an "X" near to the dot.

Benjabar assumed that the envelope was in the duffel he found on the beach, and that he had overlooked it during his initial check of the bag's contents. It could be disastrous if his assumptions were wrong. But he saw no choice but to weave this new revelation into his story.

"David Eli was my Master back in the slavery days of Jamaica," Benjabar at last whispered, "…before he left home over an argument with his father."

"About what did he and his father disagree?" asked Arturis. "Slavery, for one thing," replied Benjabar. "After slavery was abolished in Jamaica, old Master Eli continued to hold slaves on one of his plantations. The plantation was in the interior and effectively out of control of the authorities. He refused to tell those slaves that they were free. David Eli could not accept his father's conceit. But I think the thing that finally drove David Eli from his home was the matter of an arranged marriage that he in no way wanted."

All of this was pure fabrication, and Benjabar desperately hoped the deception did not show in his face or eyes. For he knew that his freedom hinged on his ability to convince Captain Arturis that he was of value to a wealthy planter whose identity had suddenly manifested in this David Eli. So, he continued with his tale...

"David Eli refused to marry the girl selected by his parents despite his father's threat to disinherit him. Eventually the disagreement became so intolerable that he decided to leave his home and set out on his own. I had been assigned as David's servant, and had become his friend. So, I asked to travel with him. David agreed to this and, unknown to his father, we both signed on as seamen on a merchantman out of Kingston." Benjabar was grateful for the way that certain facts, like "Kingston", presented themselves to his mind. He hoped these details lent credence to his story.

"David Eli quickly fell in love with the sea and sailing," continued Benjabar. "He has a way of command about him, and within a year the owner had made him captain." This last statement seemed to have a shadow of truth about it.

"What was the name of the merchantman?" asked Captain Arturis. "The Sea Queen," answered Benjabar without hesitation.

The expression on the Captain's face remained fixed as he maintained a cold stare directly into Benjabar's eyes. It took all the composure Benjabar could embrace to calmly return that stare. His answer had been another gamble. When Captain Arturis lifted the duffel to retrieve the yellow envelope Benjabar could clearly see "Clifton" stenciled to its side. Although he had been groggy and disoriented on the beach when he first found the duffel, he was certain it had been stenciled "Sea Queen" and not "Clifton". He assumed that Arturis had changed bags to confuse him, and perhaps catch him in a lie.

"I do not know this ship or her captain," Arturis at last replied. "Her keel was laid just four years ago, and David Eli assumed command only two months ago," Benjabar said in response.

"What is her flag?" Arturis demanded. "British out of Kingston," Benjabar answered without hesitation. Arturis was obviously testing the consistency of his story.

"And what led this Captain Eli to leave you on that beach?" queried the Captain.

"We had received word that old Master Eli had posted a reward for anyone returning his son home for marriage to the young woman. He was to be returned by any means necessary, short of injury to his body. Captain Eli had been identified as traveling with me, his former slave, so we agreed to separate to make him more difficult to locate. He left me on the beach where you found me, and I was to make my way to my parent's home the following morning. My parents had at last been freed and lived about five miles inland from where you found me. I planned to make my way there the following morning." Benjabar was not certain upon which beach he had found himself but based on what he had overheard one of the chained slaves say, he assumed it was Jamaica's. However, he desperately prayed that Arturis would not ask him more about where his family lived, so he quickly continued. "To further confuse those hunting him, Master David told me he planned to change his name. Therefore, I cannot tell you the name he is now using."

"Before dropping me at the beach, he wrote out the note with the map and riddle, although he had sealed it and I had not read it until you showed it to me. Captain Eli likes a good riddle which I look forward to solving, and the map tells me where to meet him."

"And I can assure you that Captain Eli will pay you far above my market price if you would deliver me there."

"But why are you so valuable to him?" demanded Arturis.

"Because I am his friend… and we each saved the other's life," said Benjabar with a smile.

~~~~~~~~~
~~~~~~~~~

Captain Eli sat at his desk, with his face aglow in the faint light, as he studied his plans. He abruptly stopped his work and adjusted the wick of the lamp that sat on the desk, and as a result the lighting level increased significantly. It was important that any crew passing his doorway see a bright lamplight shining through the crack beneath his door.

Captain Eli returned to his plans and mentally reviewed them for what seemed the hundredth time. Despite the strong temptation to first retrieve the boys, he knew that it was best to remain with the plan and rendezvous with Benjabar first. *After all this time, that name still brings up visions of a mighty warrior-king to my mind,* he said to himself.   The boys were reasonably well accommodated, and Benjabar's skills would likely be needed from the beginning to ensure success for the overall mission.

In truth, it was Renee Fini that most concerned him. The unexpected introduction of a troubling variable made her safety difficult to forecast. He would have to trust that her training and natural abilities would protect her for the time being.

He adjusted the "sextant" and again confirmed that everyone involved except Benjabar, and of course Dartous, appeared to be where they were supposed to be at this time. This was a better outcome than projected, and was due, in part, to the endless hours spent embedding critical details into everyone's memories. Captain Eli felt certain that a significant measure of luck was also involved.

But still, it bothered him...*Why was Benjabar so far off-course?* If it became necessary to vary significantly from the plan to retrieve him, everything could quickly unravel.
Perhaps, as a minimum, he should hoist sail and wait a day or so before committing to a full course change. This could result in less of a delay than continuing his determined course, since he would avoid sailing in the opposite direction from that which Benjabar appeared to be traveling.

Captain Eli sat pondering this dilemma for a long while, but in the end pushed back from his desk and said out loud, "No Benjabar, I will trust you to get back on course. I will leave my sails set, and head for where I expect to find you."

~~~~~~~~~

"Captain Eli and I were born within days of the other and grew up together. He as Master and me as slave, but neither of us were aware of what this meant until we were eleven years old."

"Old Master Eli had a leaky old sloop that he used for travel from one port to another in Jamaica. David Eli decided one day that he had watched the overseers and slaves sail the vessel so often that he could captain it, and he asked me to go along as first mate. It seemed great fun, so of course I was happy to go along with my friend in playing this game."

"We were only a mile or so offshore when a squall surprised us. We soon learned that, despite our enthusiasm, our sailing skills were severely lacking. We were blown toward shore and grounded on the rocks. The young Master was thrown by the impact and knocked unconscious. I was able to hoist him into the dinghy and row it ashore before the sloop completely broke apart."

"The old Master was furious with both of us. David's punishment was a scolding and removal of many privileges. However, he determined that I was to be sold. In the end my punishment was reduced to a light whipping, but from that time on both the young Master and I were extremely aware of the differences in our positions in the plantation's society."

Benjabar paused in the telling of his tale and Captain Arturis interjected, "and how was it that Eli saved your life?"
~~~~~~~~~

"When it came time for him to attend university, the young Master insisted that I be allowed to accompany him as his personal slave. He used his wealth and position to secure agreement that I be allowed to attend classes with him on the pretense that I was needed to carry his books, assist with his grooming, and be available to respond immediately to his various needs. This of course was ridiculous, but when money and power are joined together many are prepared to accept the ridiculous."

"Through this pretense I received an education and although I did not receive a degree, I acquired knowledge that proved to be of great value to me after I was freed. This is how David Eli saved my life."

"I do enjoy a good yarn," said Captain Arturis, "but I heard nothing that would convince me to change course for you to join with this Captain Eli. I recognized the location described in the note he wrote you and know where you are expected to rendezvous. But let us assume I believe your story and that I further believe Captain Eli would pay as much for you, his friend, as you claim. For me to sail in the waters indicated by the note would be much too dangerous. If caught with a hold filled with slaves in those waters, I could be hung. I had hoped to keep you for myself, but now, because you are such a unique black and easily recognizable as a contraband slave, I think even that carries too much risk. No, my friend, you and the rest of my cargo will have a new home in Brazil."

Benjabar was disappointed, but not surprised by Captain Arturis' response to his story. But he did not waste time or energy lamenting the outcome. Instead, he determined to initiate his backup plan at the soonest opportunity. Namely, he would attempt an escape using one of the dinghies. This was a dangerous plan, but Benjabar knew that he would die before succumbing to a life of slavery in Brazil. He was determined to attempt his escape this very night during the middle watch.

As if reading his thoughts Captain Arturis said, "If I have your word that you will not attempt escape, I will leave your shackles off." Benjabar pondered this unexpected offer for just a moment before replying with a smile that was intended to suffice as a wink, "I will promise not to escape before dinner tonight."

Even as the words came from his lips, Benjabar was planning his midnight escape. He would casually visit the shipwright, attempt to secure the tools he would need to remove the shackles in which Arturis would surely place him after dinner, somehow hide the tools near the spot to which he was previously shackled, scout out the location of the dinghy to be used, and hope to retrieve his duffel and contents.

None of this planning was needed.

~~~~~~~~

Captain Arturis was familiar with the location described in the note that he had removed from the *Sea Queen* duffel. It was Jekyll Island, a barrier island on the coast of Georgia. He had once smuggled slaves through Jekyll by bribing an overseer of the Dubignon's plantation located there.

With the overseer's help he had landed offshore at Little Cumberland Island's new lighthouse and met a pilot to take him to Jekyll. While anchored two hundred meters off Dubignon Creek, he used Dubignon's large yawl boat to transfer the slaves temporarily to a small barn in an isolated portion of the plantation. As the only white man present at the time, the crooked overseer was able to accomplish this without Dubignon's knowledge. Subsequently, they were able to reverse the process and transfer the slaves to a steamer which transported them to a plantation up the Savannah River on the South Carolina side. It was there where the slaves were sold.

This was a dangerous process with multiple opportunities for failure and arrest. He had determined that this last voyage would be one in which he minimized risks. He did not believe Benjabar's story, but even if he did, he would not change course to Jekyll.
~~~~~~~~

Arturis did like the black man though, his appreciation did not extend to trust. He had assigned his first mate to watch Benjabar closely until he was once again shackled. He determined to free the man, but only after making port in Recife, on the northeast coast of Brazil, safe from the Royal Navy.

Thinking back on these thoughts later, Arturis asked himself if his musings had somehow conjured up the near disaster. He was still in British patrolled waters when he heard the call of "Sail Ho!" He knew immediately, and without doubt, that the worst had occurred.

It was therefore in no way a surprise when the seaman pounded on his door less than a minute later and declared, "She's British sir, and armed to the teeth!"

Captain Arturis quickly considered his options. Only two came to mind. He could surrender his ship (for he was no match for a British warship), or he could dispose of the slaves.

The first option would likely leave him and his crew swinging from English nooses. The second just as surely would result in his ship being finished by the British guns, for it was midday and they were certain to see the slaves being tossed overboard.

His preference was to surrender, not because of the loss of income the other option represented, which was lost in any event. No, Arturis had come to question the life he had chosen. Indeed, he could not remember the last night that he had slept more hours than he had remained awake in shame and regret. To drown these slaves would ensure that he would never rest again.

But he knew the crew would mutiny if he determined to save the slaves. They would not agree to trading the remote possibility of outrunning the British ship for the certainty of surrender and trial. They would assume that he would try to remain out of range of the British guns at least until the slaves were weighted to the bottom of the ocean by anchor chains. If he decided otherwise it was likely Arturis would join the slaves on the bottom.

Arturis could hear the crew already preparing to remove the slaves from the hold, as they assumed that he would choose to sacrifice them. He knew he had no choice other than give the order they were expecting, but the command froze in his throat.

It was a welcome distraction when the first mate appeared at his door.

~~~~~~~~~

Benjabar had been frustrated by the constant monitoring of his every move by the first mate. He was considering how to adjust his plans when the cry proclaiming the sighted sail came about.

By the time the sail was identified as British, Benjabar had already formed his new plan. He turned to the first mate and demanded that he be taken immediately to see Captain Arturis.
The first mate had made no secret that he had been insulted when charged with "playing nursemaid to a fancy talking black that should be below in shackles and not strolling about the deck like a duke or earl." His response to Benjabar's demand was silence, framed by an ugly scowl that would have caused the rats living in the dark depths of the ship to cower.

But Benjabar was not fazed as he growled through clenched teeth. "Listen my friend, I do not care how you feel about me, but if you want to survive the British and live through this year you will take me to see the Captain! And you will take me now!"

The first mate placed his face inches from Benjabar and snarled, "This best not be some clever trick to confuse the Cap'n at a time that he's in a'need of all his wits. Otherwise, I'll be throw'n ye overboard me self! Follow me," he concluded with a wave of his hand to Benjabar.
~~~~~~~~~

With that the first mate spun on his heels and led Benjabar to the Captain's quarters. It was with a certain degree of anxiety that the first mate announced Benjabar and explained their purpose. And he was obviously much relieved when the Captain invited Benjabar to come in.

Without waiting for an invitation to speak Benjabar began. "Captain, you have but one chance to elude capture, death, or both, and I hold the key." Without awaiting a response, he continued. "I suggest that this is not a slaver, but a ship carrying free blacks from Jamaica to a new home in Brazil."

Captain Arturis' face expressed a slight hope as he began to comprehend the plan that he believed Benjabar was suggesting. "I would think you would be happy to see your British saviors," Captain Arturis responded.

"We both know that no blacks will be found on board when the English overtake your ship," Benjabar said in a low whisper. "My plan will provide a means by which we can both live to see another sunrise."

"And what else?" queried Arturis.

Benjabar gave what was becoming a familiar smile as he answered, "You will sell me and the rest of the captives to Captain Eli."

~~~~~~~~~

Captain Toddcarrol of the *HMS Minerva* was relieved to see the ship heave to in response to his signals. He was determined to do whatever it took to board the vessel, but he was happy to see that force apparently would not be necessary. Of course, he ordered all guns prepared for action should the need arise, but there was nothing in the lay of the ship that would suggest treachery.
~~~~~~~~~

Unfortunately, due to the becalmed winds it had taken over an hour to close the distance between them. But when at last his ship lay alongside the other, he signaled that its Captain, his first mate, and no more than two seamen should come unarmed to the *Minerva*. It was therefore surprising to see five figures approaching in the dinghy, not four. Two seamen were rowing the boat and the other three sat watching their approach to the ship.

As the dinghy approached and he began to make out individual features, Captain Toddcarrol became intrigued with what he saw. The man seated in the middle thwart of the dingy was a large, muscular black man. He was dressed in simple, but well-cut trousers and blouse.

The dinghy pulled alongside, and the three passengers proceeded to climb aboard the *Minerva*. One of the white men stepped forward and offered his hand. "Captain Arturis of the *Middle Passage*," said the man.

"Captain Toddcarrol of His Majesty's Navy," he replied.

"I ask your indulgence," began Captain Arturis. "In addition to my first mate, I thought it prudent to also bring my client. May I present Mr. Benjamin Bar?"

With that Benjabar stepped forward and offered his hand, affecting an air of calm and normalcy he did not feel. When the Englishman accepted his hand Benjabar began in the most refined Jamaican accent he could muster. "I am pleased to meet you Captain. When my friend Captain Arturis explained to me the likely reason you were detaining us, I agreed that it would be best if I came over to meet you."

"And why do you think we detained you?" asked Captain Toddcarrol.

"It is well understood that the Royal Navy strictly enforces the antislavery laws, and Captain Arturis was concerned that you might misinterpret the presence of my fellow colonists and me."

"What do you mean by colonists?" asked Captain Toddcarrol.

"I am the leader of a group of Jamaican free blacks who have pooled our resources and are starting a colony in Brazil," replied Benjabar. With that he handed Captain Toddcarrol a small stack of documents. "These are the letters Captain Arturis and I exchanged over the last year or so. You can see that the Captain agreed to transport us for the sum recorded within them."

Captain Toddcarrol perused the letters for several minutes before returning his gaze to Benjabar. "And how do I know you are not a slaver as well Mr. Bar?" In reply Benjabar confidently stated, "Each of my colonists will be happy to show you their papers Captain."

"May I see yours?" Captain Toddcarrol asked. "Of course," said Benjabar, as he removed an envelope from his vest pocket and handed it to the Captain.

Captain Toddcarrol opened the envelope and removed a single sheet of paper. Written in a clean hand was a declaration that one Mr. Benjamin Bar was a free man of color. It was signed by a Mr. Coxly, a magistrate of Kingston, and dated about four-and-one-half years prior. Affixed to the document was a crude stamp. The stamp would not meet the standards of a proper English court, but he supposed it was what one should expect in the colonies.

"I am certain that you will not mind if I send a detachment to your ship to confirm all is as it seems," said Captain Toddcarrol as he turned to face Arturis. "Of course not," Arturis replied.

With that, Captain Toddcarrol dismissed his visitors with a salute, turned sharply in the military way of doing so, and retired to his quarters.

~~~~~~~~
~~~~~~~~

"Commander Dayton reporting as ordered Captain," said the tall officer as he approached Captain Toddcarrol's desk.

"Take your ease Commander and tell me what you saw on the *Middle Passage*. Is she a slaver or just a simple transport as her Captain claims?"

"As the officer leading the inspection of Captain Arturis' ship, I can report that I did not see any indication of slaving. She was a bit shabby, but as clean as can be expected considering the number of passengers and crew she carries. With that many people sharing their limited accommodations it would be difficult to maintain a level of cleanliness in accordance with His Majesty's standards."

Captain Toddcarrol maintained a fixed gaze on his Commander. This gaze clearly communicated that he was not yet convinced of the innocence of the *Middle Passage*. Feeling the need to defend his position the Commander continued, "The crew included about fifteen men of color. The crew, both black and white, was armed with pistols and swords as a precaution against pirates. There was over one-hundred-fifty Negro passengers. Most were single males, but there were a few wives and children. I talked with several of the passengers and each corroborated Mr. Bar's story, and the men with whom I talked were able to show me papers. I feel certain the ship is not a slaver."
Captain Toddcarrol remained silent for several seconds before rising from his chair. "Very well," he sighed, "signal the *Middle Passage* that she is free to sail."

<center>~~~~~~~~~</center>

Benjabar stood at the railing as the *Middle Passage* sailed through the Caribbean night.   A casual glance fore and aft of the ship confirmed that the extraordinary watch was in place, a watch made up of equal numbers of blacks and whites.

He shook his head as he reflected on the unlikely plan that had brought the ship into this unusual but necessary state. He realized its success had depended on prayer and a succession of small miracles. The first miracle being the fact that Arturis had accepted a plan that called for him to arm his captives. And of equal significance was the willingness of those same captives, without exception, to agree to the charade and not renege on their promise once the Englishmen were aboard the vessel.

Perhaps everyone understood the carnage that would have ensued had either white man or black man chosen to betray the agreement that had so hastily been reached. It would have meant blacks attacking the slavers, slavers attacking blacks, slavers attacking the British, and in all probability in the confusion, the British would attack both.

Perhaps the biggest miracle of all was how slave and slaver, by working frantically side-by-side had managed to cleanse the foul-smelling ship in such a short time. Then the crew had shared clothing with the slaves, to replace the filthy rags they had been forced to wear. The new clothing also served to hide the marks of the chains visible on the wrists and ankles of the slaves. Thankfully, those chains were now at the bottom of the sea.

It was also fortunate that the crew included a former criminal who was expert in forging the official papers used by Benjabar and many of the captives. In yet another miracle, they had managed successfully to keep those slaves without forged papers away from the British sailors inspecting the *Middle Passage*.

Whether by divine intervention or luck the plan had worked. Benjabar did not place much credence in luck and said a quick prayer of thanks. He was thankful that no one was killed, that all parties had honored the unlikely truce between black and slaver, and that they were now on a heading for Little Cumberland Island where they would pick up a pilot who would take them to Jekyll. Of course, a deep distrust remained between the slavers and their former captives, but arming the blacks ensured that the agreement would be honored.

"Now if only the Danelaw and Patrick flags, and Captain Eli show when we reach Jekyll Island this might actually work," whispered Benjabar to himself.

~~~~~~~~~

It was July 3rd and the *Middle Passage* lay at anchor off Dubignon Creek. The sail up the coast, past beautiful Cumberland Island to Little Cumberland, had proven to be uneventful. It had taken three days to connect with their tall and grizzled old pilot who then maneuvered their ship through St. Andrew Sound to Jekyll Island.

So far there had been no sign of "the Danelaw and Patrick flags" as implied by Captain Eli's note, but Benjabar took some solace in the fact that the celebration of "...the Land's birth..." was still a day away.

As if reading Benjabar's mind, Captain Arturis approached the ship's rail where Benjabar was standing next to the old pilot and asked, "Do you have any idea what the Danelaw and Patrick flags would look like, or what their significance might be?"

Benjabar had pondered this very question and had a ready answer. He had also determined to share the answer with Arturis. And he believed the answer to be true, since Benjabar found that his memories were continuing to slowly return.
"The Danelaw flag is in honor of England's Danelaw region. That is where the Eli family originated. The flag is an Eli family design; a simple red pennant with the capital letter 'D' on each side. You will see the pennant atop the main mast of Captain Eli's ship."

"And Patrick's Flag?" asked Arturis.

"It is not actually a flag at all. It is a green Celtic cross woven into the ship's mainsail. It represents the Eli family holdings in Ireland and Scotland. Many associate the Celtic cross with St. Patrick."
~~~~~~~~~

Captain Arturis seemed satisfied with the explanation and started to turn away but hesitated momentarily before turning back to face Benjabar. He walked three paces forward and looked the brown man directly in the eyes. In a low voice marked with a hint of sadness Arturis said, "You know my boy, if your Captain Eli does not show, or does not honor the agreement, I will do my best to return you and your friends to chains. I would not find pleasure in this, but I am counting on the proceeds from this expedition to complete the funding of the purchase of my plantation in Virginia. I would consider leaving you free but, having observed you over these past days, I am certain you would die rather than trade your freedom for the enslavement of your fellow blacks."

Benjabar returned Arturis' gaze and replied simply, "I am confident Captain Eli will not let us down."

Captain Arturis nodded to both Benjabar and the pilot who had remained at the rail. Then Arturis quickly turned and left the deck.

The old pilot stood with a slight stoop and said in a gravelly voice, "Well me boy, I hope your trust in this Captain Eli is well placed, else this ship is in for some rough seas."
With an expression of surprise on his face Benjabar turned to face the old man. The surprise was not due to a lack of awareness of the man's presence, but rather because Benjabar had come to think of the man as perpetually silent, and because there was something familiar in the man's voice.

With a smile on his face the pilot straightened his shoulders, removed a folded paper from his breast pocket, and handed it to Benjabar. Benjabar unfolded the paper to reveal a green Celtic cross and a red pennant sketched into the respective upper and lower halves of the paper.

"It is good to see you my friend," said Captain Eli to Benjabar.

~~~~~~~
~~~~~~~

Captain Arturis sat at his desk deep in thought about his next moves. He was certain that no one would show to ransom Benjabar and the other blacks. In that event, he would be forced to return to his original plan. The arms he had been forced to provide the blacks would make this difficult and would likely result in deaths of both crew and slaves. He was trying to find a path to mitigate this possibility.

He was aroused from his musings by a knock at his door followed by the immediate entry of the hired pilot. Without waiting for an invitation to speak the pilot said in a rasp, "I'll be taking my leave of you now Captain."

"Oh?" Arturis responded. "Are you not to guide us through these waters when we depart?"

"I will return on the morrow after meeting with the representative of a merchant vessel wishing to arrange for assistance into St. Simons. When do you expect to weigh anchor?"

"The day after tomorrow," responded Arturis. To which the pilot replied, "If ye would provide me a strong crewman to help me row back to Little Cumberland, I can assure you that I will return well afore ye wish to depart."

"Very well," said Arturis. "See my mate and he will let you know who he can spare."

With that the pilot nodded, turned, and left.

It was just after dusk when the mate reported to Captain Arturis. "Captain, the pilot just left the ship along with the man you assigned."

"That I assigned?" queried Arturis.

"Yes Captain," responded the mate. "And he asked that I give you this duffel."

Opening the duffel Arturis saw a large quantity of gold coins and the following note:

Captain Arturis, Enclosed, you will find a sum well above the slave value of those you hold. The man who will return the dory will guide you to open water and accompany you as you return every captive to their home shores. Once every captive has been returned, he has the power to authorize a withdrawal in your name from the bank in Roanoke for an amount equal to the gold included here. I will advise you that it is in your best interest not to fail in completing this transaction. Similarly, I should not want to hear that you have mistreated these blacks in any way or have in any way ever again supported slavery, including the use of slaves on your own properties. Signed David Eli, Captain, the merchant ship, <u>Sea Queen</u>.

A quick search of the ship confirmed that Benjabar was no longer on board. Both he and the pilot's dory had melted into the dark of the evening.

<center>~~~~~~~~~</center>

Chapter 6 - Adam Boy

Peering through the early morning fog, Adam Boy wondered if he had made a mistake. Now that he could no longer see land the small boat seemed frail and inconsequential. He had found the boat at the location marked on the Fernandina map Captain Eli had left him. It was loaded with supplies, charts, and gear in such quantities that Adam Boy felt he could sail it around the world.

However, as he sailed through the fog with nothing but a compass and his charts for guidance, Adam Boy found himself wishing he had stayed within sight of shore. In the event of a sudden squall or other emergency it would be much easier to find a safe harbor if he had a fixed reference point toward which to sail.

So, it was with a great sense of relief that Adam Boy at last spotted the shoreline of what his charts told him was the South Carolina coast. But his relief was short-lived.

Off his port side, and between Adam Boy's location and the shore, there sailed what appeared to be a well-armed ninety-foot cutter. And even though the warship was more than two thousand meters in the distance, Adam Boy was certain that he could not avoid interception by the sleek vessel, should it choose to pursue him.

Just as he began to hope that the cutter would pass him by, it turned clearly in what appeared to be a course intended to intercept his boat. Rather than attempt to run from the cutter, Adam Boy determined to maintain his tack and hope the warship would let him be. With his full attention on the cutter, the sudden roar of cannon was so unexpected and frightening that Adam Boy became disoriented and momentarily dazed. His confusion was so complete that the nature of the thunderous noise did not register in his brain until the water exploded in front of the oncoming cutter.

After what seemed minutes, but was only seconds, Adam Boy reclaimed his composure and turned in amazement as a dark ship bore down on him as it emerged from the thick fog. It was not two hundred meters off his starboard side and the pirate's markings were clearly visible.

Grabbing the spyglass that he kept in a pouch hanging at his side, Adam Boy turned and focused it on the cutter. He could clearly see the red-striped flag that some part of his mind identified as the banner of the American Revenue Cutter Service. With a surge of adrenaline, Adam Boy realized that the pirate was using him and his boat as a shield in its battle with the cutter.

Adam Boy quickly set his sail and pulled hard on his tiller to bring the boat on a heading in the direction of the cutter. He did not like the idea of protecting the pirate ship, for if it found its range while near Adam Boy it would pound the cutter with its cannon without fear of the cutter answering in kind. The cutter would be forced to withdraw, and Adam Boy would be at the mercy of the pirate.

Adam Boy realized that the pirate would likely turn its cannon on him now that he was   closing with the cutter. For if the pirate managed to sink or damage his boat, the cutter would be obligated to provide aid, and the pirate could take the opportunity to escape. So, Adam Boy imagined the pirate's gun crew reloading after the volley fired at the cutter. He then could see in his mind's eye the crew resetting the cannon elevation and direction, as it sighted his boat's mid-section. And finally, he imagined the order being given to fire.

At that instant, Adam Boy pulled on his tiller and brought his bow hard to port. The roar of the pirate's cannon, and the explosion of the water just off his starboard side were almost simultaneous events, reflecting the fact that the pirate was now only one hundred meters off his stern.

Adam Boy's maneuver was not only successful in avoiding the fire of the pirate's guns, but also had the result of taking him out of the cutter's line of fire. The cutter responded almost immediately, releasing a volley from its forward guns that fell just short of the dark ship. This forced the pirate to redirect its attention from Adam Boy to the cutter and begin a turn that would keep it out-of-range of the cutter's guns.

This led Adam Boy to begin to hope that the pirate no longer posed a threat to him, and he almost made the fatal mistake of thinking he had taken on the role of interested observer. But he was jarred back to reality as he realized, with a start, that the pirate's turn would take it across his own course, and the pirate intended to ram him. Almost without thinking Adam Boy adjusted his sail, and once again brought his bow hard to port which afforded him the best chance of avoiding the collision.

This maneuver was almost successful, but the pirate grazed Adam Boy's stern on the port side and it seemed the small boat would surely capsize. Adam Boy lost his footing on the tilting deck and barely avoided falling into the water as he managed to cling to the bow line, dislodged by the collision.

The boat managed to right itself, and Adam Boy scrambled to his feet. He quickly surveyed the damage to his craft and was relieved to see that his hull was intact and only the upper railing had broken away.

Adam Boy returned his attention to the pirate ship as it retreated into the fog. Just before losing sight of the menacing ship, Adam Boy saw its name written across the stern...*Sea Witch*.

~~~~~~~~~
~~~~~~~~~

Captain Eli and Benjabar sat across from one another at the Captain's desk. Neither of the men seemed aware of the other. Each stared not at his companion, but seemingly at some point-in-space visible only to themselves. To an observer, it would appear they sat without movement for more than twenty minutes and showed no sign of breaking the silence between them.

But then tears began to form in Benjabar's eyes, and he at last found words to express the emotions building within his weary mind. "I did not know how much I missed my memories," he said.

Captain Eli's eyes focused on his friend and, although it was not reflected in his eyes, the slightest of smiles formed around his lips. "Yes, it is like finding old friends that you thought you would never see again," he said softly. "You likely have recovered ninety percent of your memories at this point." Lifting a large journal, he continued, "I found that by continuing this technique for just a minute or so a day has restored all but a few of the memories that I recorded prior to the event. And of course, there are several recovered memories that I had not bothered to record."

This is how the two men found themselves talking about the strange occurrences that led them to their current circumstances. Both men would occasionally mention the "event", but neither chose to dwell on its particulars. Secretly, each held a realization that it would not be a bad thing if some of the memories relating to the event remained lost.

It was almost a relief when the Chief in charge of the watch knocked heavily on the Captain's door and entered without waiting for a response. "The lookout has spotted six sails on the horizon Captain," he began. "They appear to be heavily armed, but none are showing a flag."

Whispering to Captain Eli, Benjabar said, "I thought piracy had been eliminated in these waters!" Responding hurriedly Eli said, "There was a man named Wansley who was operating along the Barbary Coast. He is a relative of a man who was hung along with Charles Gibbs back in '31. He became obsessed with the idea of coming to the Atlantic Coast of America to seek revenge and restore the family name."

Captain Eli turned back toward the Chief, pulled a chart from his desk, unrolled it, and ordered, "Show me their locations." Pointing at the chart, the Chief said, "This is our location, and the six vessels are positioned along this arc."

The single heading that would afford them escape was immediately obvious to Captain Eli. In fact, it seemed much too obvious, so he looked closely at the chart in hopes of finding a clue to what the pirates were intending. His effort was rewarded as he noted a reef on the chart that lay almost perpendicular to the heading the pirates were obviously trying to steer them. The reef would not appear on any charts available to the pirates, and they would not imagine that it appeared on the charts of Captain Eli. Indeed, Captain Eli suspected the pirates paid a high price in discovering the submerged formation and guessed that one or more of their ships had recently sunk because of hitting this reef.

After studying the chart for a few minutes Captain Eli wrote quickly on a small slate. Then turning to Benjabar he handed him the slate and said, "Take the helm and follow this heading." As he glanced at the heading instructions, Benjabar's face took on a quizzical expression as he realized the heading would take them across the reef. But after a quick check of the chart, a smile appeared on Benjabar's face, and he nodded to Captain Eli.

Returning the smile, the Captain said, "I think we have the opportunity to stop Captain Wansley's piracy career in America before it gets started. I will watch closely and let you know if we require a course correction."

~~~~~~~~~~
~~~~~~~~~~

It had been a day-and-a-half since Adam Boy witnessed the cutter chasing the *Sea Witch* into the mist. He did not see the outcome of the engagement due to the thickness of the fog. However, the lack of subsequent cannon fire led him to suspect that the pirate had escaped. This encouraged Adam Boy to sail close to shore, and thereby reduce his chances of capture should the pirate return.

So it was that Adam Boy found himself nigh caught off guard when the narrow inlet appeared between the two barrier islands. He quickly lowered anchor and double-checked his chart. Soon he convinced himself that this was indeed Skull Inlet. It was midpoint on a flood tide, and the chart confirmed the channel's location. So, Adam Boy hoisted anchor, entered the inlet, and let the tide carry him to the gentle sand beach of the island off his starboard side. He loved the sea, but as he stepped from the boat it was good to feel solid earth under his feet. He was certain that given the harrowing experience of the previous day, anyone would welcome the feel of the unmoving sand.

He crossed the narrow southern point of the island and, from a knoll, could see a tidal marsh separating two sections of the island. There was a small tidal creek running through the center of the marsh that at high tide would allow a small craft access to the interior of the island.

Adam Boy returned to his boat, nudged it into the creek, and followed the rising tide into the island's interior. Near the point labeled on his chart as "The Narrows", he tied his boat to the twisted limb of a live oak tree and prepared to explore his new temporary home. However, before he stepped from the boat, he became aware of an annoying number of mosquitoes and other insects which prompted him to recall a bottle he had noticed included in his supplies.

Rummaging through his supplies Adam Boy found the bottle bearing a label that read:

Rub on all exposed skin to repel insects.

Pouring a small portion of the clear liquid into the palm of his hand, he covered his exposed skin and was relieved to find that the insects no longer accosted him.   The words came to his mind unbidden...*Insect Repellent.* This phrase came to him in the same sudden and clear way all information came to him. However, along with the knowledge of what the mysterious solution was called came a strong understanding that he should not share this secret concoction with others.

Adam Boy knew, without a doubt, that only a few people would be familiar with the idea of "repellent", and that in some parts of the world its ability to ward off insects would be likened to wizardry. In more advanced countries the complexity of the chemical makeup would raise questions that would be difficult to answer. Either scenario could mean trouble for him. If asked about the insect repellent, he would say it was just a concoction mixed by his grandmother and that it really did not work very well. These types of deceptions were becoming an increasingly uncomfortable necessity for Adam Boy.

Adam Boy left the boat and walked toward the center of the narrow strip of island and soon found what he sought. It was a live oak tree about three meters in diameter. Adam Boy would make his home high in the gnarled branches of the tree. It would be high enough to provide commanding views of the ocean to the east and southeast, another island to the southwest of this one, and the marsh on the northwestern side of the island.

He marked his tree and walked in a direction that would take him to the central section of the beach. Adam Boy's mind roamed in imagination as he thought of the pirates, Indians, and explorers that may have wandered this island. It was, therefore, a complete surprise when Adam Boy stepped onto the beach and found himself on the edge of a fishing camp. The men in the camp were gathered about a table with heads bowed and silently praying thanksgiving. Adam Boy quickly began to back away from the scene, but one of the men heard him and looked up. "Come join us my boy," he shouted, "I can see from here you are a hungry young lad!"

Working against his instincts, Adam Boy joined the group. He was indeed hungry, but not only for food. He was hungry for companionship and conversation.

He gladly ate the offered food, and after returning to his boat to ensure it and his supplies were secure, he agreed to spend the night in camp with the fishermen. The meal was delicious, and he greatly enjoyed their company. But as he lay down on the cot that he brought from his boat, Adam Boy was saddened to learn that the fishermen would be returning to their homes in and around the nearby town of Beaufort on the morrow.

The next morning the fishermen tried to convince Adam Boy to sail with them to Beaufort, but he refused, citing the need to return home to his parents. He remembered that his charts gave "St. Helena" as the name of a large nearby island, and that is where he told the men that he lived. They seemed unconvinced.

After the fishermen loaded into their boats and left the island, Adam Boy returned to his boat and pulled a schematic from the hidden compartment, in which it was stored. He was just as amazed as the first time he saw the document. Contained within the dimensioned drawings and assembly notes was a detailed plan of how to transform the upper superstructure of the boat into a high and dry treehouse! And he was determined to complete at least the platform base before nightfall.

A memory came to Adam Boy that told him; these barrier islands were known as the hunting islands. They were so-called because the soil was too poor to support crops, and consequently, the wealthy used them as hunting preserves. Men came to hunt deer and the wild boar that were the descendants of domesticated pigs. They also came to fish and hunt waterfowl. But the islands were not without dangers.

In addition to the wild boar, the risks that confronted Adam Boy included the deadly snakes and alligators that he knew populated the island. These were the challenges that drove his desire to be off the ground before nightfall. But there was yet another predator that proved to be far more dangerous than any of these.

Captain Eli ordered that the pumps be used to remove sea water ballast from tanks located in the hold of the *Sea Queen*. As he continued to study the chart, he grew certain that the reduced ballast weight of the ship would ensure it would clear the reef, if Benjabar held to the proper heading. However, for added assurance he would confirm that the depth of the ocean's bottom was watched carefully.

The pirates were beginning to bring the *Sea Queen* within range of their cannon when Benjabar made the heading change that would take her over the submerged reef. Even with the reduced draw of the lightened ship it would clear a sharp outcropping of the reef by less than forty centimeters. Captain Eli's plan was helped by calm seas, but the current tide level made his margin-of-error less than he would have preferred.

It seemed to Captain Eli that his crew collectively breathed easier once they had cleared the reef. And as he left his quarters to join Benjabar at the helm, he sensed a curious anticipation from each one he met. But he was certain that no one, save Benjabar, anticipated his next command.

When about one thousand meters beyond the reef, and using a railing to steady himself, he yelled, "Attention all hands! Prepare for impact on my mark." Then Captain Eli pulled on two levers that were in-line with several others located next to the helm. One lever resulted in the starboard bow ballast tank quickly filling, while the other released the starboard bow anchor. Just as the anchor impacted the bottom he yelled, "Now!" Seconds later the anchor bit into the ocean's bottom, and the ship shook violently.

To the pirate captains it appeared the *Sea Queen* had hit the reef as it spun and tilted about its bow. Consequently, they all assumed that the *Sea Queen's* position marked the location of the reef and moved in quickly for the kill. As the pirates moved into their cannon range of his vessel, they unknowingly approached the reef, which was a thousand meters seaward from where they assumed it to be.

Captain Eli assessed the position of the six pirates and gave several of his cannon crews corresponding orders. It was to the great credit of the crew that they were able to efficiently prepare for firing on the tilting deck of the *Sea Queen*, and each designated gun was ready for firing within twenty seconds of receiving their orders. So it was that each of the cannons had their target sighted and ranged when the first pirate hit the reef.

As the hapless vessel ruptured its hull on the rugged reef, it pitched forward at a frightening angle. The stricken crew could be seen signaling frantically to the remaining five pirates to no benefit. Those pirates were each rapidly affecting maneuvers designed to avoid similar fates. But to the horror of their captains, two more of the pirates impacted the reef and almost immediately began to sink.

Two of the remaining three pirates had quickly dropped anchor and managed to stop their progress toward the reef. The final pirate ship was a black and menacing vessel which executed a turn that allowed it to avoid the reef and assume a heading that would carry it quickly out-of-range of the *Sea Queen's* cannon.

"Cannon group four...Fire!" commanded Captain Eli. Three cannons fired simultaneously from the port side of his ship. As he peered through his spyglass, he saw the three cannon balls tear through the mainsail of the fleeing pirate. However, no structural damage was inflicted on the black ship, and since the remaining cannons were sighted at other potential targets, he knew they would not manage another shot before it was out-of-range of his cannons.

Eli quickly turned his attention to the two pirates attempting to weigh anchor and convinced them to surrender with several well-placed shots over their respective bows. After ensuring the captured ships had dropped their cannon overboard and were busy rescuing their comrades from the sinking vessels, he began to review his encounter with the dark ship.

Just as it sailed out of the range of the *Sea Queen's* cannon, he caught sight of its name through his spyglass...the *Sea Witch*. It was Wansley's ship.

Adam Boy worked furiously all day and was satisfied with his accomplishments. His first task was to review the schematic which showed that the superstructure of the boat was made up of several sections. These sections were fitted together with a tongue-in-groove construction and were bound to the hull by large nuts and bolts. The schematic included directions on how to remove the various sections and how to use them, along with other hardware which were provided separately, for use in building his shelter. The hull would remain intact as a gig and serve as Adam Boy's means of exploring the tidal waters and marshes of the surrounding area.

Adam Boy used the tools found in the boat to disassemble three sections of the boat's deck. Each section was two-meter square that would serve as platforms upon which to build his new home. Using the block and tackle obtained from the boat's rigging, he lifted each section and secured them to three different locations high in the tree.

The platform locations were dictated by the places where two limbs forked off from the trunk of the large tree at the same height or near the same height. One area of each of the platform sections rested directly on one of the two limbs. Three points of the platforms rested on wooden spacers that Adam Boy had trimmed to the desired dimensions. These spacers were in turn secured to the limbs in locations such that the spacers served to level the platforms. Finally, he ensured the platforms were stable by nailing cast iron brackets between them and the tree.

Next, Adam Boy detached the boat's small cabin and hoisted it into the tree where he secured it to one of the platforms. With the cabin door closed, this would provide a safe place for him to spread his bedroll and sleep without fear of snakes or other real or imagined dangers.

So, it was with a sense of relief that Adam Boy opened a can of beans that night and smiled as he whispered to himself, "Good bee-uns mon."

A week later Adam Boy stood on his porch as he reviewed his new home. He mentally checked off each feature of the shelter he had come to think of as "The Tree Fort". It initially consisted only of the original three platforms to which he assigned the designations "kitchen", "bedroom", and "porch", but he also added features that transformed them into a comfortable and safe shelter.

He removed the boat's sail and spread it above the kitchen and porch platforms. This provided protection from the rain while leaving the sides open for cooking and ventilation. The sail was slanted slightly to one side and formed a "V" shape, which directed rainwater into a large bucket. The bucket hung from a rope attached to a limb next to the platform and provided Adam Boy with a source of water for drinking, bathing, and cleaning. He placed one of his two metal tubs in one corner of the platform. He built his cooking fires in this tub and kept a supply of firewood next to it. He also placed the large sea chest containing his supplies on this platform.

The bedroom platform held the former boat cabin which included a latched door. It also contained barred windows. He recalled how he had thought these bars odd when he first saw them on the boat. *After all, why would you need barred windows on a boat?* Canvas curtains were rolled above the windows but could be unrolled and tied to hooks at the bottom of the windows to provide protection from the rain. The result was a tight and safe place in which to sleep.

The porch platform held a small table and chair and, between two limbs located on opposite sides of the platform, he had hung a hammock which inhabited the space. When not hunting, exploring, or sleeping, this was the place he spent most of his time.

He joined the platforms by building rope and wood bridges between them. He then built railings around the kitchen and porch platforms. His tools, extra clothing, hunting rifle, and knives were stashed at various locations throughout the Tree Fort. Adam Boy was happy with the results of his labors, but his proudest achievement was the elevator.

For the first three days, his only means of moving materials to the porch of the Tree Fort had been to either use the block and tackle or carry the items on his back. Climbing the rope ladder, that he had secured between the ground and porch, was difficult when burdened by the weight strapped to his back. However, the block and tackle were cumbersome to use for lifting smaller items such as game or firewood. So, Adam Boy determined to build the elevator using the instructions included in the schematic for the Tree Fort.

The design utilized the boat's block and tackle as the lifting mechanism. At one end of the rope and pulley arrangement was a small platform upon which Adam Boy could place the item to be lifted. At the other end was a net in which he could place bags filled with sand, to act as counterweights to whatever was being lifted on the platform.

The upper pulley of the block and tackle was attached to a limb next to and above the porch. The lower pulley was staked to the ground directly below the upper pulley. The rope was routed through a third pulley that included a mechanical brake that, when engaged, would clamp the rope in a fixed position. The brake was set to be engaged unless the attached control lever was pulled either upward or down from its neutral position. There were holes on opposite sides of the lever, and the rope was threaded through the holes in a manner that allowed the brake to be disengaged only when the rope was being pulled. This arrangement would prevent the load from crashing to the ground in the event Adam Boy lost his grip on the rope.

When lifting or lowering items, Adam Boy would simply pull on the appropriate rope until the lifting platform was in position. When lifting heavier items, he could offset the weight of the load by adding sandbags to the net until the two opposing weights closely balanced each other. In this way, the heavy loads could be lifted with little effort.

The schematic instructions warned against using the elevator to lift people, but of course it was not long before Adam Boy had permanently balanced the system for his own weight. It was fun to ride the elevator, and a little faster than climbing the ladder. This feature of the Tree Fort nearly proved to be Adam Boy's undoing when one of the ropes frayed and he came crashing to earth from a height of three meters. He was unhurt, and while it did not stop him from riding the elevator, it did bring home the importance of periodically checking the equipment.

It was after completing the elevator that Adam Boy started his exploration of the waters, islands, and hummocks of his new home. It was on one these excursions that he found himself sparring against greed and malice.

~~~~~~~~~~

Captain Wansley was darkly morose as he peered out at the endless waters stretching before the *Sea Witch*. He had failed completely, and in a humiliating fashion, in his attempt to avenge his family name. Indeed, to his mind, he had brought even more shame to the Wansley clan. He would be forever marked as the captain who was unable to capture a single prize while losing all seven of the ships, he had persuaded to follow the *Sea Witch* from the Mediterranean to the Caribbean.

His misfortunes began when he first approached the South Carolina coast. Wansley had left the other ships anchored off Nassau, with the intention of scouting the United States coastline. He had hoped this would allow him to determine the best strategy for plundering the country's substantial trade.

He was emerging from a thick fog when he spied a cutter that he took to be one of the local merchantmen. The cutter was close to shore and had little maneuvering room, which would give the *Sea Witch* a significant advantage. In addition to this, a small boat appeared off Wansley's port side and the pirate saw, if necessary, he could use it as a screen to inhibit the cutter's return fire.
~~~~~~~~~~

So, Wansley made an impulsive decision to strike his colors and attack the cutter. It was only after he had positioned himself for the kill that the fog cleared enough for him to realize his error. His target was not a merchantman, but an American Revenue Cutter! He barely escaped disaster by maneuvering around (and probably sinking) the small boat before disappearing into the fog. While he had avoided disaster, he could see doubt in the faces of his crew. They were clearly wondering if they should be following a captain who could make such a mistake.

Then he had lost two of his best ships on the uncharted submerged reef, but his shame had been multiplied when he attempted to use this reef to his own advantage. He would never forget the name of the merchantman that had not only mysteriously avoided his trap but had managed to sink or capture all his ships except for the *Sea Witch*.

It was no surprise when the mate interrupted his thoughts in a voice that reminded him of a dog's growl. "You had best give the crew a reason to keep you as Captain," the mate began. "These cutthroats are ready to see you dance from the yardarm and then find a captain who can deliver on his promises."

"Do you have any ideas?" Wansley growled back. "Or maybe you want to be the new captain?" The mate sneered and replied, "The sooner I am off this cursed ship the happier I will be."

Wansley and the mate glared at one another for several seconds, but then the mate seemed to reconsider as he cleared his throat. "I overheard several of the men talk of the south Pacific, and how it is a paradise for blokes like us. One ugly seaman claims to have a beautiful wife on an island. Several of the men seem to regard this man highly, and I think if you offered to take him home and agreed to drop anchor there so we could lick our wounds for a while, the men might cool down a bit."

Wansley did not like the idea of giving up on his quest for vengeance, but ultimately realized he had few options at this point. "Very well," he said. "What is the name of this island?"

"The island is called 'Pitale,'" the mate answered.

~~~~~~~~~

Captain Eli and Benjabar were delayed and diverted to St. Augustine after hailing the Revenue Cutter and defeating the pirates. The legal system was a slow process, and many questions had to be answered. While some delay was expected, as they handed over Wansley's pirates and ships to the authorities, it seemed that it was taking an inordinately long time to receive their departure clearance.
The delays began when the Revenue Cutter they had sighted and signaled seemed immediately skeptical of their story, and insisted they come with them to Fort Marion. That had been almost two weeks hence, and even now it did not appear the authorities believed that they had been able to capture or sink five pirates' ships without a single shot being fired by those vessels. There had been several meetings with the Fort Commander, and they were hopeful that the meeting to which they had been summoned this morning would be the last.

There were times during the previous meetings when Benjabar and the Captain felt that they were being held captive at the old fort along with Wansley's pirates. Their frustrations with the delays were heightened by the pressing need to continue the task of retrieving Adam Boy and the others. The longer they were delayed, the greater the probability that their plans would fail.

But they were hopeful as they walked into the Commander's office that morning. The summons came shortly after breakfast and was unexpected. They imagined they could be away by noon.

"Captain Eli," began the Commander, "it is my responsibility to inform you that your ship and crew are to be detained pending your trial for piracy."

~~~~~~~~~

Adam Boy had explored every foot of the beautiful island. He started with the glorious beach and finished with the lush and vital marsh that separated his island from the adjoining islands and hummocks.

As he was exploring, he also hunted the deer and wild boar that were found in abundance. He paddled his gig around the tidal creeks and rivers where he fished, netted shrimp, and caught both blue and stone crabs. Together with the canned fruits and vegetables found in his provided supplies, Adam Boy felt he had a diet that was both tasty and nutritious. Although anxious to rendezvous with the Captain, who each day became more fixed in his memories, Adam Boy knew he was provisioned for a long wait if it was necessary. He had plenty of food and a shelter that could protect him from the elements and the island's dangerous animals. But it turned out that it was human threat to which he was most vulnerable.

It was to the immediate north of his island that Adam Boy encountered the two men. He spotted them without being seen and was inclined to keep his presence a secret. However, Adam Boy was extremely social, and it had been weeks since he had anyone with whom to talk. So, his social needs won out and Adam Boy assumed the men were hunters, forgot caution, and began to walk toward them. He also began to call out to them, since it was never a good idea to startle men holding guns. The two turned to face him and Adam Boy realized with a start that the two men were not hunters. He was instead facing the "Giraffopotamus" from not twenty meters away.

~~~~~~~~~~

As he ran through the forest toward where he had left his gig, Adam Boy remembered how funny he thought it was when he gave the two men their comical nickname, back at the "Red Horse" Inn. Even now the name made him smile, but as he remembered the men's hostile expressions the smile disappeared, and he became focused on escape.
~~~~~~~~~~

As he neared the place where his gig was secured, Adam Boy glanced back and was somewhat relieved to see that he had increased his lead over the men to fifty meters. But looking ahead once again, he realized the ebb tide had left the boat partially beached. Although the tide had turned, more than a third of the vessel's length continued to rest on dry sand and he feared the two men might reach him before he could free it. As he reached the gig, he quickly grabbed one of the oars and, using it as a lever, pushed with all his might against the boat's hull. To Adam Boy's relief the boat slid from the beach. Then after a final strong push he leapt inside the gig and began to row.

The two men reached the water's edge while he was still within ten meters of the shore, but Adam Boy guessed neither could swim because they made no attempt to stop him. As he approached the middle of the inlet that separated his island from the one just left, he saw that the men were approaching a small boat anchored to shore not one thousand meters from where he had left his gig.

Adam Boy quickly assessed his situation. He knew the two men would follow him and that it was only a matter of time before the men found his Tree Fort. He decided to use misdirection to defeat the Giraffopotamus.

~~~~~~~~

The waters were just past low tide and it had been relatively easy for Adam Boy to maintain his position in the middle of the inlet while the two men reached their boat and readied it to overtake him. As their boat came within one hundred meters of his position, he began to row. He rowed not for either the shore or the open channel. Instead, he rowed for the shallows where at low tide the waves crashed against the submerged sandbars.

Adam Boy had, in earlier explorations, studied the currents and shallows of the inlet. His purpose had been to find a safe passage that, at low tide, could take him more directly from his island to the neighboring island. He had identified a small channel that appeared to be navigable, but he had never felt confident enough in his solution to risk capsizing his boat. It now seemed the time to try.
~~~~~~~~

His plan was to lure the two men to the middle of the channel, and then take his boat back to the island from which he had just come. The two men would be forced to take the channel to the open ocean, which meant that since the tide had turned the men would be fighting the current, and Adam Boy would have at least an hour's head start. He hoped that taking his gig in this direction would lead the men to believe that he lived on the neighboring island, or one of the other islands north of his true home.

He would hide his gig in a protected cove until nightfall and use the moonless night to sneak back to his island. He knew this forced him to stay on his island and stop exploring while the men continued to search for him, but he hoped they would eventually tire of the hunt. He thought it a good plan with a reasonable chance of success, but what happened next provided a much better outcome.

Adam Boy could not believe his eyes when the two men turned their boat into the shallows while attempting to follow him! He had underestimated their greed as they pursued the imagined pirate treasure.

Adam Boy was able to successfully negotiate the shallows in his gig, but in their larger boat the two men almost immediately hit a submerged sandbar and were capsized by the pounding waves. The men were thrown from the boat but managed to wade through chest-deep water to a point on the sandbar where the water came only to their knees. They were seventy meters from shore and, since the two men could not swim, Adam Boy knew the two were effectively stranded.

As he turned his gig back toward the sandbar, Adam Boy was alarmed to see a ship's sail come into view. He imagined the ship to contain companions to the two men and was faced with a dilemma. If he turned and ran from the approaching ship, the rising tide waters would drown the two men before their companions could reach them. If he rescued the two men, he would likely be captured before he could escape.

Adam Boy knew he could not leave the men to drown, so he yelled for the "giraffe" to remove his belt and tie the hands of the "hippopotamus" behind his back. Then instructing the two to move to the far side of the sandbar, he managed to beach his gig without it being capsized by the waves crashing on the opposite side of the bar. Holding his gun on the taller of the two, he herded them into the gig and instructed the tall man to row toward the shore of the island from which they had just come. It was a risky maneuver in the heavily loaded gig, and it took them considerable time to negotiate the shallows.

By the time they reached safe water the ship, which had closed the distance between them much more quickly than Adam Boy had expected, had launched a gig of its own. Adam Boy's heart sank as he realized he would never reach shore before the men's companions overtook him. In desperation Adam Boy could come up with only one option. He decided to try a bluff. As soon as the other gig came within ear shot of him, he put the barrel of his rifle against the shorter man's head and yelled, "Back away or I will remove what few brains this fool has in his head."

In response one of the men from the other gig yelled in a laughing voice, "Easy Adam Boy, we just came to rescue those two poor souls before you hurt them!"

How did he know my name? said Adam Boy to himself. Then looking sharply back at the stranger's ship, he saw the green Celtic cross stitched into the mainsail and the red Danelaw flag towering above the main mast.

"What took you so long to get here Captain Eli?" said Adam Boy with a smile, "and don't worry about these two, my rifle is not loaded."

~~~~~~~~~~

Captain Eli sat in his cabin reviewing the events of the last several days. He silently thanked God for the blessings that most men would label "good fortune".
~~~~~~~~~~

The first blessing came when they discovered that the mate of the *Sea Queen*, Dick Bruan, was an English relative of the Commander of the old Fort in St. Augustine. The captured pirate captains were very willing to testify against them so there was a good chance that he and Benjabar would be convicted of piracy. But the word of Dick Bruan was enough to convince the Fort Commander of the veracity of Captain Eli's story, and they were quickly released.

Then it had been nothing short of a miracle that they spotted Adam Boy's gig as he attempted to rescue the two men. Despite his confidence in Adam Boy's abilities, there was a good chance that the two would have overpowered the boy once they figured out that he could never bring himself to use his rifle against them. Once they had him under their control, the two would likely have harmed the boy in their attempts to force information from him regarding the nonexistent treasure. It had become obvious that the two men were dangerous.

By questioning the pair, Captain Eli determined that at first they planned to only follow him, steal the boy's gold bracelet, and sell him as a shanghaied crewman to the shadowy captain of a Barbados-based merchantman they knew to be in port at Fernandina.

In their greed they had fallen completely for Adam Boy's contrived tale of pirate treasure ready for them to plunder. They had not believed the specifics of how the treasure came to be, but they wanted to believe that there indeed was a treasure. They had followed him up the stairs at the inn and waited in the shadows of the hallway as Adam Boy sought out the painting of the Count. Afterwards they had stolen the painting from Revan, realizing that it held one or more clues to the treasure's location... and rushed onward to beat the boy and any accomplices he may have had to the treasure. But of course, they did not have the benefit of Captain Eli's instruction to "Halve the minutes..." of the coordinates found within the painting.

These details made Captain Eli wonder at the good fortune that led Adam Boy to recognize so quickly the malice within the hearts of these two men and develop his course of action. But of course, Captain Eli also gave credit to the role that Adam's high level of intuition played in that understanding.

After searching at the coordinates indicated on the painting for several days, the two eventually assumed that they needed more information to locate the treasure, and consequently traveled to the nearby town of Beaufort to rest and consider their next steps. It was there, while drinking ale in a tavern, that they overheard two of the locals talking of the unusual young boy they had met while on a fishing trip to the barrier islands. They had described the location as "beyond St. Helena on one of the hunting islands".

The Beaufort men's description of the child matched that of Adam Boy, and they judged that he was the best hope they had in narrowing the location of the treasure. Therefore, they were determined to find him, but the exact position of the boy was unclear. However, they did receive sufficient information to reduce their search area to one of two islands. They were just finishing their search of the northern island when Adam Boy discovered them.

The two men were in the brig of the *Sea Queen*, but other than stealing a worthless painting from Revan, they had not actually committed any crime. Captain Eli ultimately convinced them that the treasure did not exist and decided to leave them at the Beaufort docks where they hopefully would find some honest employment. Unfortunately, he feared that they were not interested in honest employment, so the Captain advised the authorities to keep a watchful eye on the pair.

Captain Eli rose from his desk and walked from his quarters. As he breathed in the fresh sea air, he spotted Benjabar and Adam Boy standing together at the railing. As he approached them the Captain said, "Once we drop our two friends at Beaufort, we sail for Aarondophilous." Both man and boy nodded in agreement.

Adam Boy whispered almost to himself, "I hope we are not too late."

Both men nodded solemnly in agreement.

~~~~~~~~
~~~~~~~~

Chapter 7 - Aarondophilous

For the first time since she lost her husband more than twenty years before, Francine McSparten felt alive, hopeful, and even just a little giddy. Indeed, it had been that long since she had thought of herself as "Francine". Like everyone else, she had come to think of herself as the "Widow" McSparten. In the past when she spoke to herself, she would use terms like "Old Woman", "Old Biddy", or perhaps just "Widow". Now it was usually "Francine" or perhaps "Francy", the name her husband used when he was being especially tender.

She looked across the room at the young boy who was the source of the transformation. Aarondophilous had brought unexpected comfort into her life. Even when being mischievous and contrary (which was often) he had a way of breaking through the aggravation and making her smile. While it was true that the supplies and gold that had accompanied him into her life had significantly reduced the daily stress of survival, these were of unexpectedly secondary importance. Francine and her husband never had children, but she had begun to think of Aarondophilous as her grandson.

The boy rose from the floor next to the fireplace, which still contained the coals used to prepare their supper for the evening. "Granny Francy," he began in his strangely accented young voice, "do you think we might travel to see the lochs soon?"

Despite her discomfort with his question, Francine could not deny the smile that brightened her face. The boy had begun to refer to her as Granny Francy soon after she confessed how warm it had made her feel when her husband used her special name. "The thought of ye and me going there a frightens me deeply lad. The man who lives on the island in Loch Quoich is wicked, and I could not bear it if harm came to ye."

Francine had told Aarondophilous of Loch Quoich and Loch Garry, both of which were a few days walk from her home. She had described how romantic their stay had been when she visited there as a young bride with her new husband. The boy loved the water, and it should not have surprised her when he immediately began talking excitedly of his desire to visit the lochs.

Loch Quoich was the closer of the two, but a well-known and dangerous criminal, Ewan MacPhee, was living on an island within the loch in open defiance of the authorities. Aarondophilous had made the argument that they could travel only to Loch Garry, but the two lochs were only fifteen kilometers apart, and that was too close for her comfort.

Yet she knew the boy was both smart and stubborn, and it would be only a matter of time before he wore her down. Therefore, Francine determined to strike a bargain with him while her energy level was sufficiently high to negotiate favorable terms.

So, it was after much debate they agreed to make the journey to Loch Garry. They would travel a route that would add at least a day to their travels but would ensure they were never closer than ten kilometers to Loch Quoich, and the home of its infamous outlaw. But Aarondophilous would first walk to the village of Arisaig where he would hire Jefton McStratton to take them to Loch Garry in his carriage. Jefton was a good man and dependable; however, the attribute which commended him most was his size.

Jefton stood a head above every other man in the village, and his work as the village smith kept him stronger than any two men in the county. Francine felt these were attributes needed to discourage advances by the criminal of Loch Quoich, should he become aware of their presence in his territory. Indeed, Jefton was a man of many talents, some of which would be useful on their journey ahead.

~~~~~~~~
~~~~~~~~

The North Atlantic storm tossed the *Sea Queen* violently, as the great waves crashed over her bow. To reduce the crossing time Captain Eli had taken a more northerly route than he felt prudent, and he was beginning to question his decision to do so. But he did not really have a choice.

He knew Aarondophilous had at last left the deceptive safety of the McSparten cottage, and for this he was immensely thankful. Still, he knew without a doubt that it was important he reach the boy as quickly as possible. So, he had chosen to make the northerly crossing and, although they had not discussed the decision, he knew Benjabar, and Adam Boy were in full agreement.

Benjabar was sitting across the cabin intently monitoring the positions of the local icebergs. Even for the *Sea Queen,* a collision with one of those mountains of ice in the middle of a storm would be disastrous.

Also in the cabin was Adam Boy, who monitored the storm's intensity and looked for opportunities to find calmer water. A simple glance at the boy's face told Captain Eli that no such opportunities had presented themselves.

Captain Eli was keeping a close eye on the helm and the attitude of the ship. In this aspect he allowed himself to relax slightly. Dick Bruan had proven himself an able sailor and was keeping the ship true. Yet as the great ship began to slip down the back of a giant wave he tensed as he waited for the sign that it had reached the trough.

The Captain was rewarded by an abrupt righting of the deck, that showed the ship had survived the plunge from the top of the monstrous wall of water. However, the tremendous stresses on the ship were apparent in the groans and moans forthcoming from the ship as it hit the bottom of the wave. He found himself hoping that, for the sake of the ship and crew, this wave would be the worst.

Except for Dick Bruan at the helm, and the three in the Captain's quarters, the crew was secured below decks. As the storm approached, he had ordered the *Sea Queen* rigged for heavy seas, and then the decks cleared. Captain Eli had determined that the storm's direction would take them on a heading largely in-line with their intended course, with little correction needed. And since the ship's design was such that unless they crossed the path of an iceberg or another ship, there was no need to expose the crew to the hazards of a slippery and tilting deck in the raging storm.

The deck rose sharply underfoot, and they all braced for the climb up the face of the next wave. The deck was near vertical when, at last, the ship crested the top and began its descent down the back side of the wave.

Captain Eli could tell by the angle of the deck that this wave would be much worse than the last.

~~~~~~~~~

The carriage bounced roughly along the old drove road, but Aarondophilous hardly noticed. He was enthralled with the beauty and mystery of the Highlands as they revealed themselves with each passing mile. It seemed that he could hear each hill and stream shout to him, wanting to tell a story of clans, bravery, and honor.

In response to Aarondophilous' questions about Clan MacDonell of Glengarry, Jefton had been telling tales of the famous family. These were tales from the days before the Clearances. From the days before their families had been forced to leave the lands of their ancestors. From the days when they were strong in number and spirit and heroically fought alongside the Stuarts in their failed attempts to claim the crown.
~~~~~~~~~

Jefton told of how the clan's seat was located at Invergarry Castle after Clan Mackenzie burned Strome Castle on Loch Carron. He told of the clansmen forming a line all the way from the Rock of the Raven to the mountain called Ben Tee. How each stone had passed along that line of men until the tower had risen to six stories in height above the Rock. He told of Bonnie Prince Charlie stopping there after losing the Battle of Culloden. And described castle walls so strong that in 1746 someone he called "Butcher Cumberland" tried to blow them up and they would not fall. Indeed, Jefton proudly stated, "Those bonnie fortifications are standing to this day!"

Jefton told these tales as they traveled past the pastures and glens filled with sheep. It saddened Aarondophilous to think of the once mighty clans that had roamed the valley floors and hillsides of Glengarry. He could imagine the chiefs' laughter as they met in the Castle to plot strategy, or to assemble for a feast. Suddenly, looking up in the direction of Jefton, Aarondophilous asked, "Do you think we could see Castle Invergarry on our way to Loch Garry?"

Jefton replied, "Yes, as a matter of fact we can. This back door route to Loch Garry, that your Granny Francy insisted we use, will take us right by where it sits on Loch Oich." Aarondophilous turned to Francine and received her agreement for this unplanned stop on their journey by the nod of her head and a warm smile. Aarondophilous returned her smile and turned to face the road ahead in anticipation.

Allowing a slight smile to remain on his face, Aarondophilous said quietly to himself, *"Well Captain, I am on my way to Castle Invergarry, just as you instructed."*

The *Sea Queen* sailed up the Scottish coast showing little wear from her arduous North Atlantic crossing. The crossing had been fast but filled with tension.   Benjabar felt great relief when the sea had at last calmed, and the violent tossing of the ship ceased. There had been waves so large that it seemed a certainty the ship would capsize, but the design of the vessel was solid. There were also two icebergs that came uncomfortably close, but on each occasion the ship had maneuvered safely around them.

It was an unusually clear day, and Benjabar was straining to catch a glimpse of Francine McSparten's small cottage that the charts told him would soon come into view.   But it was not the cottage that he at last spotted in the distance. Instead, it was a trail of smoke rising into the morning sky. The sight caused his heart to sink.

"I see it too my friend," said Captain Eli, who had silently appeared at Benjabar's side. "I am concerned about Aarondophilous' well-being," continued the Captain, "but I know that he is not at the cottage, and it is highly probable that he is safe...for the time being."

~~~~~~~~~

Adam Boy looked through the ruins for clues to what had happened and why. He judged by the debris found in the remains that nothing had been removed before the structure had burned. Specifically, he found the remains of a ribbon showing the McSparten family tartan. It would have been costly and highly prized and removed before all else in the event of a sudden fire. This told him that no one was home when the fire broke out, at least no one that cared. He stooped and picked up the small metal object he saw laying in the ashes and placed it in his pocket. It was a door hinge which confirmed, beyond all doubt, that they were indeed standing among the ruins of the McSparten cottage.

"Would this be the work of MacPhee?" asked Benjabar, as they surveyed the smoldering ruins of the home.   "Possibly," replied Captain Eli, "but I don't understand why he would burn the place. Destroying a poor widow's home seems contrary to his nature."
~~~~~~~~~

At that moment Adam Boy yelled for the two of them and indicated he had found something of interest. One of the stone walls to the cottage remained standing and he was pointing at the back side of the wall. As they rounded the wall and gazed at its surface Captain Eli turned to Benjabar and murmured, "It seems I may have misjudged Mr. MacPhee's character."

There on the wall written from the smoke of a dying torch and in a semi-literate hand was:

SIRENDER

THA

BOYE

E. MACPHEE

Aarondophilous finally read the note from Captain Eli two days after the *Volunteer* lifted anchor and continued her homeward journey. Granny Francy was cleaning the mantle and found the forgotten yellow envelope. It was only then that she remembered taking it from the duffel after she found Aarondophilous and it on the beach. She was very distressed by the fact that she had forgotten the envelope and was near tears when she, at last, handed it to Aarondophilous. But he merely smiled at her and reminded her that there was a lot of excitement that day, and she could easily be forgiven for misplacing the envelope.

It had been with great eagerness and anticipation that he examined the seal that was stamped with the name "ELI". He had then carefully broken the seal, opened the envelope, and removed the note.   As he traveled through the Scotland countryside, he remembered the day he first read the note, which now seemed so long ago. As these thoughts awakened the memories, he reached inside his jacket and was comforted by the now familiar feel of the envelope.

Their travels had taken them to a small, but beautiful glen that was divided by a tumbling stream. It was mid-afternoon, but they all agreed that they were not on a timetable, and this would be the perfect spot to spend the evening. Having noticed a nearby hill, Aarondophilous had climbed to a large boulder near the top and now sat alone surveying the green landscape.

Glancing around to ensure that he indeed was alone, Aarondophilous removed the envelope from his coat pocket. Carefully extracting the note, he read it once again.

Aarondophilous, I will remind you that no one should see this note except for yourself, not even the Widow. I will explain the secrecy when we once again meet, The Captain.

Then at the bottom of the note:

Find the one who has lived long and well in a simple house by the sea. You will know the place by the ravens upon which everything hinges. Nourishment will arrive by sea, but you and your host must soon leave the nest and follow the raven to the rock upon which sits the branch of the Donald's seat. Use your bracelet to remove the raven from its perch and stay secure until Danelaw and Patrick arrive.

It was understood that Aarondophilous was meant to read the note soon after awaking on the beach, but Granny Francy's forgetfulness had delayed the actual event by several days. By the time it was read, he could easily confirm that it was intended that he stay with the Widow. Without a doubt she had "lived long and well", but the real proof was in the hinges that were used throughout the cottage.

Her husband had been skilled in working metals and had hand forged all the hinges used on the doors and shutters of the cottage. Each of the hinges was in the shape of a bird perched on a rock. Aarondophilous had taken note of the unusual and beautifully made hardware, but it was not until he read Captain Eli's note that he asked Francine about the significance of the bird design, and recognized it to be that of a raven...it was *the ravens upon which everything hinges...*

This had been the first time she had spoken of her travels to the lochs as a new bride. The days she and her husband spent on small boats touring Lochs Garry and Quoich had taken on a fairytale quality in her memories. She spoke of the morning mists that gave the bluffs and hills of the Great Glen a ghostly quality, as they rose above the clear calm waters of the lochs. This was the time when her husband first began to call her Francy, and from that time forward she associated that name with their wonderful journey.

Aarondophilous could tell by the wistful smile on Francine's face that she was reliving every detail of that long-ago journey, and it was not until she at last paused that he reminded her of the raven-on-rock hinges. Laughing at her emotional wanderings, Francine told of Clan MacDonell of Glengarry and their crest that depicted a raven sitting on a rock. They had first encountered the crest painted on the stone bluffs above Loch Garry and became enthralled with the past Highland glory the symbol represented. As a surprise for their first wedding anniversary, Francine's husband took her to her family in Arisaig and left her to visit for a week. When she returned to the cottage, her husband presented her with the gift of the hinges that he had installed in her absence. He had told her that every time she opened a door or a shutter, he wanted her to think of their grand visit to the lochs. "And ye know me lad," Francine had said in conclusion, "I do indeed remember that visit whenever a door squeaks in the old cottage."

Aarondophilous smiled and honored her memories with several minutes of silence before asking his next question. "Is there a 'Donald' Clan that also lives nearby?"

"Yes, in a way," she replied, "the MacDonells are actually a branch of the Donald Clan. As a matter of fact, at one time they were one of the most powerful branches."

Francine could not answer the questions that Aarondophilous had about the MacDonells' "seat" but, fortunately by questioning Jefton McStratton, he was able to deduce that it referred to the ruins of Invergarry Castle. At least he hoped that he had deduced correctly.

As he sat on the boulder overlooking the glen and reflecting on Francine's recollection of her long-ago visit to the lochs, Aarondophilous remembered asking her if he could ask one more question.

"May I call you 'Granny Francy'?" he had asked her, with a look on his face that he hoped was a cross between a smile and a wink.

~~~~~~~~

The next morning it began to rain one of those downpours that soak the earth, obscure the vision, and chill the spirit. The drove road quickly turned to mud, Jefton's carriage began to sink in the mire, and the horses made little headway as morning approached midday.

The carriage was covered by canvas panels, but the blowing rain managed to find its way through the gaps in the panels, so the three travelers were soaked for much of the morning. Finally, Jefton turned to face Francine and said, "This deluge is not showing signs of stopping and we are beginning to look like drowned rats. I suggest we find a dry hole and wait it out 'til morning."
~~~~~~~~

"And where will ye be a-findin' this dry hole, Jefton McStratton?" Francine asked. Jefton's only answer was a nod and a wink as he turned the carriage off the muddy road, jumped to the ground, opened a gate into the fenced pasture, led the team and carriage through the gate, closed the gate, and then proceeded to drive the carriage through the green pasture, scattering sheep as they went. Aarondophilous noted that they were following a foot path through the pasture, but the absence of ruts suggested that wagons and carriages were not often found along this route.

After following the foot path for about two kilometers they came to another gate which they quickly passed through. The foot path continued, but soon crossed a stone roadway onto which Jefton drove the carriage. The roadway shortly came to an end at a stream and Aarondophilous could see a high cast iron fence on the far side of the stream. A large structure could be seen over the top of the fence, but no details could be discerned through the heavy rain.

A small building, approximately two-and-one-half meters square in area, stood to the side of the road, and Aarondophilous could see the figure of a man within its shadows. Jefton stepped from the carriage and, despite the rain, approached the little building in what could be described as a slow and cautious manner. But despite his caution, the dark figure suddenly jumped from the building, grabbed Jefton about the neck, and appeared to be beating him about the head and shoulders. The man wore a kilt of a dark green tartan, a dark green bonnet, and a dirk held in a sheath attached to his belt.

Aarondophilous quickly grabbed the heavy walking stick that Granny Francy insisted on keeping on the floor of the carriage. He jumped to the ground and lifted the stick like a cricket bat. He was ready to hit Jefton's attacker at the back of his knees when he, at last, heard the laughter being exchanged between the two men. Stopping his swing, Aarondophilous exchanged confused glances with Granny Francy.

Finally noticing Jefton's would-be defender, the two men broke into laughter once more. In exasperation Aarondophilous said, "If you don't want me to use this club on both your heads, I suggest one of you tell me what is so hilariously funny!" At that, the two only laughed the harder, but when Aarondophilous drew back with the stick once again the stranger held out his hands with the palms outward and exclaimed between laughs, "Hold, Hold, me lad!" and turning to Jefton he continued, "Color Sergeant, I think your young friend here is ready to join the ranks of the Black Watch!" Jefton replied, "I am afraid Michael, that he might find the Black Watch too tame."

Still laughing, Jefton managed to place a hand on Aarondophilous' shoulder and say, "I will explain myself soon, but for now let's get out of the rain!" He climbed into the carriage and then nodded to the other man. Pulling on a rope next to a tall pole the man, Michael, raised a green flag. Apparently, this was a signal to someone on the other side of the fence, because almost immediately a section of the fence began to tilt downward over the stream and in-line with the roadway.

Once the section of fence had formed a bridge over the stream, and Aarondophilous was back in the carriage, Jefton began to urge the team forward. As soon as the carriage crossed the stream, the section of fence started to tilt back into an upright position.

Francine and Aarondophilous sat in silence as the carriage moved toward the large structure they had glimpsed earlier. At the front of the building there was a covered carriageway which gave access to two large ornate doors. In front of the doors stood two men dressed in the same manner as the man that Aarondophilous had threatened to beat with the walking stick, a few minutes before.

As Jefton stepped down from the carriage, the two men greeted him in only a slightly less enthusiastic manner than had Michael. After a minute or so of slapping each other on the back, and laughing over past encounters, Jefton signaled for Francine and Aarondophilous to join them.

Jefton introduced the two men as Quincy and Robin. The two shook hands with Aarondophilous and said how pleased they were to meet the young tiger that had put Michael Campbell in his place.   Both men nodded to Francine and invited her to join them inside, as they opened the massive doors to the building.

The group passed through the doorway and entered a great dining hall with a high-beamed ceiling, stone walls, and three long rows of beautiful dark walnut tables. Several men sat at the end of one table drinking from quaichs made of bone. On the side of the quaichs was a silver inlaid dirk design identical to the design engraved into the badges pinned to the bonnet fronts worn by each of the men.

As they approached the table, the tall man sitting at the end rose and assumed the rigid stance common to a man of military training. Whereas none of the other men at the table wore insignia other than the badge on their bonnets, this man wore a wide black belt around his waist.   The belt's buckle had the appearance of a silver medallion, approximately 8 centimeters in diameter. Engraved on the face of the buckle was a sunburst pattern, and overlaying the sunburst was a dirk of the same design found on the drinking vessels and bonnet badges.

Jefton stepped forward, grasped the hand of the tall man, and said, "Good to see you again, Donald."   Turning to Francine and Aarondophilous Jefton continued, "It is my honor to introduce you to the Conductor of the Keep, Donald McWilliams, and Donald, this is Francine McSparten and her charge, Aarondophilous."

Pleasantries were exchanged, and shaking each of their hands Conductor McWilliams said, "Welcome to Achnacarry Keep." Responding to their quizzical looks he continued, "Let us learn more about each other over an early dinner." Then pointing to one of the other tables he said, "Please have a seat."

"Wonderful!" exclaimed Jefton, and then giving his face a distasteful expression said emphatically, "I am famished and could eat anything but a rock or sweet potato! But if you insist on serving either, I prefer the rock!"

As they seated themselves, several men dressed in white frocks brought out bowls of a soup that Conductor McWilliams identified as "Cock-a-leekie Soup". Aarondophilous was very hungry, and the soup along with the toasted bread and warm tea was delicious. However, he suddenly recalled the taste of something he identified as "Greek Chicken Soup" that his memories told him would put this soup to shame. But try as he might, he could not remember where he had tasted the dish.

It was not until the haggis, neeps, and tatties were served that Conductor McWilliams introduced the subject of their respective histories. Aarondophilous was quick to say that he was orphaned by his American parents, who had died two years previously when their carriage had overturned, that he had been adopted by Granny Francy, and that he did not recall much of his prior life.

Francine accepted Aarondophilous' glance, that asked her to not correct his history. She therefore limited her comments to telling of her early life in the village of Arisaig, followed by her marriage and life along the coast.

As Francine finished, she and Aarondophilous looked expectantly at the Conductor. In response to their unstated question, he began to tell the story of the Keep. He told the story in a manner that was initially detached, but he became increasingly impassioned as the narrative proceeded.

The Keep was located near the local manor house known as Achnacarry Castle. It was the refuge of a group that called itself "The Guardians of the Watch". The official name of the group was "The 'Guardians of Peace' Hunting Club". This name served to remind the membership that their purpose should never be in opposition to the law, and that peace and safety among the Highland people came above all else. Of course, the group did spend much of their time hunting and was not a military organization, although the membership was made up entirely of former members of Scotland's famous "Black Watch" regiment.

The group was started by several former Black Watch soldiers, who became concerned that lawlessness was in danger of obtaining a foothold in the Highlands. The original purpose of the Black Watch was to keep order among the Highland clans, and each member felt a shared obligation to offer help when needed by the local authorities. The membership grew from that small group to a substantial number of volunteers prepared to supplement the local constabulary.

The Keep included a powder magazine along with sufficient staples to support a company of one hundred men for at least a month. Each member provided their own rifle. Requests from the authorities for support were rare, and most requests for their help came in the form of small and limited forays in pursuit of local criminals. However, the Guardians were determined to maintain the capability of sustaining a strong defensive posture, should two or more of the local clans go rogue and determine to join in a direct attack on the Keep.

The Conductor was unwilling to answer any questions about the size of the membership, or details of how many men were present at the Keep at any given time. However, at one point in the story, Jefton was called aside by one of the men for a private conversation. The Conductor took this opportunity to tell them that not only was Jefton a member of the Guardians, but that he was one of several men who served as Conductors when in-residence at the Keep. "And you should know," the Conductor had interjected, "there is not one of the Guardians held in higher esteem than Color Sergeant Jefton McStratton."

The Conductor proceeded to tell of how he and Jefton had entered the Black Watch together as young foot soldiers and saw their first action with Wellington when they met Napoleon's forces at Waterloo. The Conductor and Jefton were members of a company of more than two hundred men detached from the Black Watch Regiment and ordered to support the four light companies of Guards defending the Chateau and grounds known as Hougoumont. As they approached Hougoumont, along the sunken road known as "the Hollow Way", their company was cut off by a large force of French light infantry. Within minutes all the officers had been killed, and it began to look as if none of the company would survive the day.

But suddenly Jefton rose and yelled, "Black Watch, bayonets forward!" and without looking back to see if any of the company were following, he rushed forward and managed to lead the remaining Black Watch through the French lines and toward Hougoumont. But as they approached the wall surrounding the Chateau and its grounds, they were anguished to see that the French had used an axe to breach the North Gate of the house, and a frightful melee was taking place. It was apparent that there was an imminent danger of the French overrunning the compound. It was Jefton McStratton that urged the Black Watch into the fight, and it was the Black Watch that closed the gates. Wellington himself stated that it was the closing of the gates at Hougoumont that gave his forces the victory at Waterloo.

Less than thirty of the company survived that day, but thanks to Jefton McStratton those thirty gave Wellington the victory. Because of his heroic actions, and because of the decimation in the ranks of his company, Jefton was immediately promoted to Color Sergeant. It is generally believed that in the history of the Black Watch, he was the first to reach that rank at such an early age, and without first moving through the intermediate ranks.

It was at that point that Jefton returned to the table and the Conductor finished his story. Calling to one of the men in a white frock the Conductor yelled, "Hello laddie! I believe it is time for our special dessert!" As he turned back to those at the table, the Conductor nodded to Aarondophilous and asked, "Have ever eaten Clootie Dumpling my boy?" "No sir," replied Aarondophilous. "We usually serve it only at Christmas," explained the Conductor, "but you and Mrs. McSparten have made this a special occasion."

The dumplings were served warm and topped with a whipped cream. As Aarondophilous placed the pudding in his mouth he closed his eyes and delighted in the aroma, texture, and taste of the dessert. "I can tell that you approve of the dumpling, my young friend," said the Conductor. Aarondophilous' mouth was filled with dumpling, and his response was simply a smile and a nod of his head. Taking that as a sign to continue, the Conductor smiled and said, "The whipped cream was added because the Color Sergeant told us it was a favorite of yours." Having now swallowed the sweet concoction, Aarondophilous replied with a grin, "It is true sir, but I know for a fact that it is also Jefton's favorite. In fact, the only improvement to the entire dessert you could make from his standpoint, would be to make the dumplings from sweet potatoes!"

~~~~~~~~

Conductor McWilliams and Jefton spent the next few hours alternately telling tales of their Black Watch service, their respective childhoods, and of the clans before they were scattered by way of eviction from their ancestral lands. It was these latter tales that Aarondophilous loved the most.

Toward mid-afternoon, the Conductor and Jefton excused themselves to discuss the business of the Keep. Aarondophilous and Francine were led to their respective rooms, and Francine announced her intention to nap. Naturally Aarondophilous used this time to explore.

The rain had finally stopped, and Aarondophilous began his exploration by walking the interior perimeter of the Keep's outer wall. An interior walkway had been constructed near the top of the wall, which afforded him a good view of the surrounding terrain both inside and outside the Keep. Access to the walkway was provided by circular towers spaced about one hundred meters apart. The towers were offset to the outer portion of the wall and, thereby, provided a wide field of view along the wall's exterior.
~~~~~~~~

The Keep sat in a sweeping bend of the stream along which the entire front wall ran in a matching arc. The stream saw a drop in elevation of several meters between where it entered the bend and where the stream returned to a straighter flow. A channel had been dug on the back side of the Keep, which directly connected the upstream channel to the downstream channel. The rear wall of the Keep ran along this channel and connected to both ends of the front wall.

On the upstream side of the Keep, a dam had been constructed which insured a steady supply of water into both the natural channel and the alternate channel. This resulted in the Keep being surrounded by a rapidly flowing "moat". This, along with the surrounding outer walls, would provide a substantial defense against any lightly armed force.

Aarondophilous estimated the length of the outer wall along the rear channel to be two hundred meters and the total perimeter of the wall to be five hundred meters. Doing a quick calculation, he estimated that a compliment of one hundred men armed with Enfield Baker or Brunswick rifles could easily defend the Keep against a similarly armed force of a thousand.

At the center of the compound, enclosed within the Keep's walls, was the building in which they had dined and that Jefton had identified as the Assembly Hall. It was one of only two buildings within the Keep and served many purposes in addition to those of dining hall, housing quarters, and supply depot. The other building was a short brick structure with an arched brick roof. The single door to the building faced the rear wall of the Keep and was at the bottom of stairs that descended from ground level. This made it obvious that much of the structure was below ground level. Based on its design, Aarondophilous guessed that this was the Keep's powder magazine.

After completing a circuit of the Keep, Aarondophilous decided to return to the tower near the gate which seemed to be the only entry point to its grounds. This appeared to be the lone tower that was continuously manned, for he noted that the remaining towers were visited on a random basis, with perhaps only two of the five remaining towers occupied at any given time. In addition, he noted three men, spaced about two hundred meters apart, that continuously walked the upper wall. None of these men were armed, except with the dirks secured to their waistbands. It was clear that the Keep wished to maintain a non-military appearance, but the regimented organization, and the strong defenses made this difficult to pull off.

The gate tower was unique from the other five in that it contained the mechanism that raised and lowered the gate. It included a weighted chain, gear, and pulley arrangement that was cocked by spinning a two-meter wheel held together by eight wooden spokes. The mechanism could be tripped by pulling on a lever that would release the weights. In this manner, the gate could be quickly lowered or raised depending on the position of a lever that controlled the direction of the mechanism's gears.

The gate operation fascinated Aarondophilous, which was why he was still on the tower forty minutes later as dusk was descending. It was then that the gate was lowered to allow a supply wagon into the Keep. There was nothing unusual about the wagon, and he was effectively ignoring it until he happened to glance at the front of the wagon. His breath caught in his throat as he spotted the driver. He was almost certain that he had recognized the one that he thought of as "The Silent Man", the one that he had trapped in Granny Francy's cellar when the man attempted to steal Aarondophilous' gold band.

Aarondophilous' first thought was to raise an alarm, but immediately after he observed the man the wagon turned a corner and with the fading light, he could not, with certainty, confirm the man's identity. So, in a moment's decision, he quickly descended the stairs of the tower and ran in the direction of the departed wagon. Just as he rounded the corner to the Keep's Assembly Hall, he saw two figures jump from the wagon as it moved between the Assembly Hall and the magazine and dashed toward the side of the powder magazine, in which its door was located.

In the growing darkness, and in their apparent rush to avoid detection, it appeared that the two men had not noticed Aarondophilous, who quickly moved so that the structure of the powder magazine was between him and the mysterious visitors. As he reached the building, he attempted a casual, but silent walk next to the magazine's wall, that was opposite to the one the wagon had passed, thereby keeping the building between him and the three invaders.

As he approached the far corner of the magazine, Aarondophilous was alerted to the muted sounds of metal-on-metal. He slowly approached the corner, and cautiously peered around it. He saw the two men attempting to remove the magazine's door from its hinges by using a metal bar to dislodge the pins securing the fixed portion of the hinge to the movable piece. One of the two men chose that moment to simultaneously look up and sprint toward Aarondophilous. Without speaking, when in range of him, the man leapt at Aarondophilous, who quickly stepped to the side and narrowly avoided the man's grasp. Having missed his intended target, the man fell forward and crashed to the ground. The other man maneuvered so that Aarondophilous' intended escape route was cut off. As the large man approached Aarondophilous, he maintained his hold on the bar he had been using to remove the magazine's door. The man's menacing stance made it clear he intended to strike the boy with the bar.

Knowing that the first man would soon recover from his fall, and he would be trapped between them, Aarondophilous decided he had time to do only the unexpected. Out of the corner of his eye he saw the first man rising from the ground. Spinning on his heel with his right leg extended, Aarondophilous kicked the rising man squarely in the forehead. The man gasped in pain and collapsed once again to the ground. As he began to run, Aarondophilous wondered to himself...*how was it that I knew how to do that*?

With the larger of the two men in close pursuit, Aarondophilous ran toward the open doorway where the Silent Man was unloading supplies from the wagon and placing them in a storeroom. His decision to run in the direction of the third invader was based on three assumptions. The first assumption being that his two pursuers would be unlikely to yell a warning to their accomplice, in fear of alerting the Keep's garrison. The second assumption was that the storeroom would be connected to the kitchen where the white-frocked men would be preparing the evening meal. And the final assumption was that none of the three men would expect him to run toward where the danger was greatest.

Aarondophilous considered shouting a warning as he ran but decided instead to focus his energy on escape, since it was unlikely any of the half dozen men on the wall were close enough to hear, and if they did hear they were likely too far away to help. So instead, he found himself hoping his plan would accomplish the twofold task of escaping the intruders and warning the men of the Keep of their dangerous presence.

As he passed the parked wagon, Aarondophilous grasped the brake handle and released its wheels. Then grabbing the buggy whip next to the driver's seat, he snapped it across the lead horse's rump and the team of four horses raced away in an uncontrolled dash. *That should alert the Keep that something is amiss,* thought Aarondophilous as he sprinted for the open doorway.

Just as Aarondophilous reached the doorway, the Silent Man ran from the storeroom in response to the noise of the team and wagon being so quickly dispatched. His eyes widened in recognition and surprise as he suddenly found himself in proximity of Aarondophilous. But before he could react to these new circumstances, Aarondophilous skirted around him and struck him firmly with the buggy whip across his posterior. The man howled in pain and lashed out but failed to connect with the rapidly moving boy.

Aarondophilous spied a closed door on the far-side of the storage room and guessed it would lead to the Assembly Hall's kitchen. He ran to the door and turned the knob but found it locked. He pounded several times on the door before whirling about to face all three of the intruders. Based on the man's bearing, Aarondophilous labeled the large man as "The Leader". Continuing to clutch the heavy bar, the man pulled a knife from its sheath and began a slow approach toward the boy. At the same time, the others positioned themselves to ensure Aarondophilous could not rush past them.

The Silent Man was on his right and after feinting toward him, Aarondophilous quickly changed his direction of travel and slid feet first between the legs of The Leader. He rapidly rose to his feet and whirled to face The Leader, who attempted to follow the nimble boy by twisting his body. Using the buggy whip, Aarondophilous snapped the man's left hand which held the large bar. The Leader dropped the bar, and as it fell it struck the man on the knee. As the man cradled his throbbing leg, Aarondophilous managed to skirt past him and run for the open doorway with the two remaining men in pursuit.

Aarondophilous passed through the doorway into the courtyard where he ran as fast as he could along the rear wall of the Assembly Hall. He was heading back in the general direction of the powder magazine, hoping that the site of the original disturbance would draw rescuers to it. Aarondophilous reached the corner of the Assembly Hall, rounded it at full speed, and immediately collided with… Adam Boy.

The sight of Adam Boy lying sprawled in the courtyard triggered immediate memories for Aarondophilous. And as the surprise wore off for the two of them, their bodies began to shake with great bouts of laughter. As they rose to their feet they immediately embraced while continuing their wild and enthusiastic amusement. They were so ecstatic in their reunion, they barely noticed that Aarondophilous' two pursuers were quickly subdued by several men wearing the garb of the Guardians.

Then Aarondophilous recognized the two men standing side-by-side watching them in delighted amusement. Suddenly stopping his laughter, he released Adam Boy from his embrace and ran to the two men. Grabbing one each of the two men's legs he looked up into their faces and exclaimed, "I am so happy to see you both!" And looking down into his joyous face, Captain Eli and Benjabar could only smile as they both bent down and embraced the boy.

~~~~~~~~~

Dinner that evening was a noisy and jubilant affair. Aarondophilous thought that each morsel was the best he had ever tasted, the warm tea the most flavorful, the dessert the sweetest, and the fellowship the warmest.
He learned that the leader of the intruders, Ewan MacPhee, despite his injuries, had managed to escape by climbing the stairs to the top of the wall and dropping to the other side. However, the men of the Keep had questioned the two remaining invaders and learned the details of their plot.

The one that Aarondophilous continued to think of as the Silent Man, despite his current willingness to talk, had escaped the brig of the *Volunteer* along with two other cutthroats, as it lay at anchor in the harbor in the new village of Mallaig. The man knew Ewan MacPhee by reputation, and along with his two associates sought him out in a tavern in Fort William.
~~~~~~~~~

The Silent Man had told MacPhee of the young lad that lived with the Widow McSparten. Of course, the part of the story that got the attention of the famous bandit was that part in which the Silent Man detailed the treasure brought by his former Captain to the Widow and the boy. It would be easy to raid the home, take the money, and retreat to MacPhee's island in Loch Quoich. Apparently, it had not occurred to these bandits that the money would be in the bank and not buried in a jar somewhere near the cottage. However, this became a moot point when they discovered that the Widow and boy were not at the cottage.

Thinking the Widow and boy were somewhere in the area, they set fire to the cottage in hopes of drawing the two of them back home. After the cottage had been reduced to smoldering ruins, the Silent Man scribbled a message on the remaining wall that warned the Widow to surrender Aarondophilous and signed MacPhee's name. They had hoped to scare the Widow into paying a ransom in exchange for the boy's safety but were persuaded to retreat when the *Sea Queen* appeared off the coast, the Silent Man having recognized it from the rendezvous with the *Volunteer* several months back.

The four men had watched Captain Eli and his crew as they surveyed the ruins of the Widow's cottage. What was unknown to the scoundrels was the fact that this was the second appearance of the *Sea Queen* at the site of the cottage. The ship had previously visited the deserted cottage before sailing up the coast to the vicinity of the village. The Captain hoped to seek information on the Widow's and Aarondophilous' whereabouts, but quickly learned that the criminal MacPhee had been spotted on the road leading back to the cottage. For reasons only he, Benjabar, and Adam Boy knew, the Captain realized immediately that MacPhee posed a grave danger to the Widow and boy. So, he and the crew quickly returned to the ship and sailed down the coast, returning to the cottage.

Determining that MacPhee and company had not found the boy, Captain Eli, Benjabar and Adam Boy walked back into the village to continue the search for Aarondophilous. In the village the bandits had overheard one of the locals telling Adam Boy that they had noticed the Widow, Aarondophilous, and Jefton leaving by carriage using the road that would take them near the Keep. Knowing of Jefton's affiliation with the Keep, the informant guessed that the party would stop there. The gang was able to not only to steal one of the delivery wagons used to take supplies to the Keep, but they were also able to steal the identity papers that would give them entry to the Keep, if necessary.

One of the members of the thieving band, a man named Hilty, had been instructed to attach himself to Captain Eli and the others, with the intent of slowing their progress toward the Keep. In response to the unvoiced questions from Aarondophilous and Jefton, Captain Eli nodded, smiled, and said, "Yes, we figured out that crook very quickly and left him in the jail back in the village, but not before we obtained some very valuable information from him."

MacPhee, the Silent Man, and the other member of their group traveled directly to the Keep in hopes of finding an opportunity to kidnap Aarondophilous. They were rewarded almost immediately, for soon after they arrived at their vantage point in the hills overlooking the Keep, they spotted Aarondophilous standing on the wall of the Keep near the main gate. Judging by his interest in the gate mechanism, they correctly concluded that Aarondophilous would be at the wall long enough for them to reach it in the wagon.

They started immediately for the Keep and worked out the details of their plan in the twenty minutes or so that it took them to approach the wall. They knew that Aarondophilous would be intrigued by the sight of the Silent Man as he rode through the front gate of the Keep in the supply wagon. They correctly concluded that from his vantage point on the wall, Aarondophilous would be too distant from the Silent Man to be positive in his recognition of the criminal. They also correctly guessed that he would follow the supply wagon as it entered the Keep so that he could obtain a better view of the Silent Man, and they determined to feign an ignorance of Aarondophilous' presence as they pretended to raid the magazine of the Keep.

Using a map of the Keep found in the wagon to assist in their planning, the group determined to lure Aarondophilous into a secluded area of the Keep where they could easily capture, bind, and gag the boy. It would then be a simple matter of delivering a ransom note to the gate of the Keep once the boy had been securely hidden somewhere in the surrounding countryside.

When reaching this point in his account of their plan, the Silent Man looked at Aarondophilous with something approaching shame in his eyes and said, "The boy proved more of a challenge than any of us 'ad imagined. Even though we were expecting 'em and ready ta' snare 'em when he came 'round the corner of the powder mag-zine, he proved too slip-ry for us."

Captain Eli then looked at the Silent Man and said, "Your misjudgment of Aarondophilous' abilities will cost you dearly. Our friends here at the Keep will ensure that you are delivered to the authorities and there will be no escape for you this time."

With that the Silent Man was taken away, and Captain Eli led Benjabar, Jefton, Francine, and the boys into a separate room of the Keep and closed the door. Once the six of them were alone Captain Eli asked them to sit at the table in the room's center, but he remained standing. He slowly moved his glance from person to person until coming to rest upon Aarondophilous. Looking the boy directly in the eyes Captain Eli started to speak. "Your friend just shared with us a story that he believed to be totally accurate."

With that Captain Eli paused for several seconds before continuing. "However, the truth is that the poor, weak-minded soul had no idea what MacPhee's real plan had been."

<center>~~~~~~~~</center>

As they approached the old castle, the five men and boys along with Francine each scanned the countryside to convince themselves that MacPhee, along with any army of thieves and bandits that he may have recruited, was not in the area. They did this even though several of the Keep's Guardians tracked MacPhee back to his island and were positioned around Loch Quoich to ensure he did not leave for the next several days.

Their caution was driven by the knowledge shared with them by Captain Eli back at the Keep. Captain Eli had learned from the bandit Hilty that MacPhee was motivated by far more than the prospect of obtaining a ransom for Aarondophilous.

Captain Eli had reminded Aarondophilous of the note he had left for him in the duffel that appeared with the boy on the beach. It had given clues that Aarondophilous correctly interpreted as referring to Castle Invergarry, located on the Rock of the Raven above Loch Oich, but he had not yet been able to interpret the phrase in the note that directed him to …*Use your bracelet to remove the raven from its perch…*

Captain Eli had filled in this detail with a tale of Bonnie Prince Charlie from the time he stayed at the castle after his defeat. The nobleman had retreated to the fortress, knowing he soon would either be captured or forced to escape into exile, and there he determined to hide a vast quantity of treasure. It was this treasure that MacPhee hoped to use Aarondophilous to locate. This would be of a value far greater than any ransom that Aarondophilous might be expected to fetch and involve far less risk.

MacPhee had heard the tales of the treasure for many years, and knew it was truly a King's fortune. He also knew that it was hidden in the vicinity of Loch Oich, but he knew nothing else of the matter until he was approached by the Silent Man, Hilty, and the other man that had escaped from the *Volunteer*. MacPhee was on the verge of dismissing the Silent Man and his plans for ransom when Hilty called him to the side and told him of the real value of Aarondophilous.

Apparently Hilty had been drinking with the first mate of the *Volunteer* one evening when the first mate had a little too much to drink. The first mate had been in attendance when Captain Eli parleyed with the Captain of the *Volunteer*. Captain Eli had shared that he and his crew would be looking to pick up Bonnie Prince Charlie's treasure at Invergarry Castle when they rendezvoused with Aarondophilous. Then, he had asked that the Captain of the *Volunteer* commit to picking up Aarondophilous and the treasure, should anything happen to the *Sea Queen*. As a final piece of information, Captain Eli indicated that Aarondophilous held a key to the treasure room.

"The Captain of the *Volunteer* had assured me the first mate was an honest man," said Captain Eli, "but he apparently did not know of the mate's tendency to talk too much when intoxicated."

Once Hilty had confessed the truth about what MacPhee knew of the treasure, the Captain, Benjabar, and Adam Boy all realized MacPhee's true motivation. They knew that they had a short time frame in which to stop MacPhee from seizing Aarondophilous for the purpose of using his key. So, the three had immediately set out for the Keep.

~~~~~~~~~~

Aarondophilous approached the dark chamber of the castle ruins holding the flickering torch. He played the light along the walls looking for the "Raven" and "perch" hinted at by the note left for him back at the beach, near Granny Francy's cottage. This was his third chamber to explore, and he was on the verge of giving up the challenge by Adam Boy to find the treasure without further help from Captain Eli. But just then he saw carved into the wall of the chamber a bird, probably a raven, sitting atop a pyramid. Near the apex of the pyramid was a circle carved deep within the stone of the wall. The raven was carved into a block in the wall that had its lower edge approximately one-and-one-half meters above the floor. The block immediately below contained the carved pyramid with the circle at the top.
~~~~~~~~~~

Based on the estimated diameter and thickness of the circle, Aarondophilous made a guess regarding his next step, and removed the gold bracelet from his wrist by expanding it via cupping a finger between it and his wrist. Sliding the bracelet into the groove of the carved circle he was not surprised when he was immediately rewarded with a whirring sound and a click. Upon hearing the click, Aarondophilous pushed on the block into which the raven was etched. The block easily slid back and recessed within the wall. He had effectively "removed" the raven from his perch.

Climbing through the resulting opening, Aarondophilous found himself in another chamber. This chamber, however, was unlike the others. The others had been dark and barren of anything other than rubble, debris, and decay. This chamber was clean and contained recesses which held several unlit torches around its perimeter.

As Aarondophilous began lighting the torches he saw the room come alive with detail. Along one wall were storage containers marked with notations like "corn", "tomatoes", and "vegetable soup". But along another wall were the true wonders. He saw several gold chalices, bowls, and serving trays. He saw a jewel-encrusted gold crown, a beautiful sword with diamonds embedded in the handle, and many other marvels. This was treasure beyond all dreams.

Aarondophilous heard a chuckle come from the opening and turned to see Captain Eli smiling at him. "I found the Prince's treasure when here last year," began Captain Eli, "and decided to leave it hidden here for you, along with several months of provisions in case we were delayed in reaching you. I also installed the mechanism, which I keyed off your bracelet, to open the chamber to the storeroom.

The treasure would give you a good start in life here in Scotland, in case the *Sea Queen* was lost. However, now that we are safely together, we will hand the treasure over to Jefton for safe keeping, until it can be given to the royal museum. The fee paid for finding the treasure will be substantial, and Jefton can use it to rebuild Francine's cottage, and fund the Keep for many years to come."

At that moment Adam Boy and Benjabar came into the chamber. They were silent for several moments and then almost in unison they said, "Now we find Renee Fini!"

<div align="center">~~~~~~~~~</div>

Chapter 8 - Renee Fini

The first attack of the Pitale had been avoided entirely, and the second attack was almost entertaining, in the confusion afforded the aggressors. Its complete failure being the result of a certain legerdemain. Both achievements were the direct result of the Hos ability to sneak spies to the Pitale Island and ascertain the details of their Queen's plans of attack.

But even though a faint smile adorned Renee Fini as she recalled the surprise and frustration on the face of the Pitale Queen, as reported by her spies, she wondered if she and the Hos would survive the coming battle.

In the first case, the attack was foiled by a simple midnight visit to the island of the Pitale by the brave Ry-An and a select group of ten warriors. The brave band had paddled silently to a section of the Pitale shore that was close to the beach, upon which the Pitale army was collecting its large flotilla of canoes. The party was careful to reach the shore and complete their work on the beached canoes before the moon rose to expose their position.

And the next day before sunrise, as the Pitale army paddled toward the Hos shore in the beginning stages of their Queen's planned attack, each of the canoes began to take on water and sink. Three out of four of the attacking warriors were close enough to the Pitale shore to swim back to their furious Queen. The remainder swam to the Hos and were easily captured, having lost their weapons and because they were exhausted from the swim.

The secret to this defeat of the Pitale lay in the fact that a small hole, the size of a man's little finger, had been drilled in the underside of each canoe by Ry-An and his men. The holes had been sealed by clay so that the seal held until the clay softened upon exposure to the water. And for this reason, the seals gave way at various times depending on such variables as the thickness of the clay plug, and the quality of the clay used. So, some of the canoes began to sink soon after being launched while others made it nearer the Hos shore.

But it was the outcome of the Pitale Queen's second attempt to conquer the Hos that brought the smile to Renee Fini's face. For the second failure was due to an odd display of contradiction within the Pitale Queen herself.

Of course, the Pitale determined to ensure that the fiasco of the lost canoes would not be repeated. As the canoes and lost weapons were being replaced, a large guard was maintained on the beach during each hour of the day and night. Although the Hos were still able to secure spies on the Pitale Island, it was apparent that the Hos would not be able to repeat their sabotage of the canoes.

But it took the Pitale several weeks to resupply their army, and during this time Renee Fini studied their Queen closely through the eyes of her spies, and on two occasions through her own clandestine visits to the Pitale Island. And although the Pitale Queen, through her own network of spies, was certain that the Hos Queen knew the time and method of the upcoming attack, she was confident that her still-superior forces would win the day.
And indeed, on the day that her restored army set forth for the Hos Island it appeared that everything was going as planned. The plan was for the army to divide into two groups. One group, two thirds of the total force, would make a frontal attack onto the main beach of the Hos village while the remaining forces, having left earlier, would paddle to the back side of the Hos Island, and attack the rear of the Hos in coordination with the frontal attack.

The landing location of this group would be at the discretion of the captain assigned to lead the rear attack. This would require the Hos to spread their defenders very thin since, having no intelligence on the landing location of this group, they would in essence be required to position warriors around the periphery of the entire island. So, it was expected that the Hos resistance to the frontal attack would be weak, as they were forced to counter this attack from the rear.

Indeed, as the frontal forces drew near their beach, only a small group of Hos appeared on shore to shoot arrows and otherwise impede the advance of the Pitale. And as the Pitale Queen, from the safety of her headquarters, received the early reports of the battle from her messengers she allowed herself a small celebration of her certain victory.

But as the frontal attackers neared the Hos shore, there was a sudden surge of Hos warriors from the jungle bordering the beach. The Pitale Captain knew from their spies that the defenders of this beach now must include every warrior in the Hos army! There could be no Hos reserves to fend off the coming attack from the rear.

As hordes of Hos arrows began to fly at the frontal attackers, who were relatively exposed in their canoes, the Pitale Captain ordered their advance to stop, with his intention being to wait until the rear attack began before continuing the advance. The rear attack would distract the Hos defenders and allow his force to reach the Hos shore without the high level of casualties that the current course of action would involve.

But as the attackers waited for the rear assault to begin it eventually became apparent that something had detained, or perhaps defeated that force, and the Captain ordered his frontal attack to withdraw in the face of the deadly hail of arrows. As his forces completed their withdrawal without reaching the Hos shore, the Pitale Captain knew he would feel the wrath of his Queen because of this failure.

To understand the reason for this reversal, it is necessary to revisit that time in the attack when the forces assigned to attack the Hos' rear neared the shore opposite the Hos village. The Captain of this force had determined to land his warriors at a location that was quite a distance from the Hos village, but which offered little in the way of natural impeding obstacles or places of ambush.

Except for a handful of Hos scouts spotted along the shore, there was no sign of defenders. So, the Captain sent out his own scouts to reconnoiter the route to the Hos village and organized his men into attack formation. However, before the Captain could initiate their planned advance, one of his scouts reported that a Pitale canoe had been sighted carrying the banner of the Queen. Since the canoe appeared to be coming from the general direction of the frontal attack force, the Captain assumed that this canoe contained one of the messengers assigned specifically to communicate the will of the Queen. And he felt that it was therefore prudent to delay his advance until the messenger could deliver his new orders.

As the canoe approached the shore the Captain noted that two warriors were paddling, as a third form stood in the middle of the canoe. He assumed the standing individual was the Queen's messenger. All in the canoe wore war masks and the loose-fitting robes of Pitale war council members. Beneath the robe of the messenger the outline of a sword and breastplate could be identified. This fact puzzled the Captain because he felt it unlikely that a messenger would be so prepared for battle.

For this reason, the Captain watched the approaching canoe with a mixture of curiosity, caution, and concern. Several scenarios passed through his consciousness. These anticipated outcomes ranged from that of a message outlining a minor change in the plan of attack, to a totally new strategy that would amount to a suicide mission for his force. As it turned out, the reality was worse than every considered scenario.

The unknown canoe reached the shore and was stabilized by the two paddlers as the messenger stepped into the shallow water. The messenger, wearing the colors and markings of the Queen, walked forward toward the Captain. The apparent stare afforded the Captain never wavered as the distance between the messenger and the Captain diminished. The messenger's war mask left the Captain unsettled, as he stared back into its unchanging countenance.

The messenger removed both the war mask and the robe in one smooth motion of the hands, and as the identity of the messenger became known, all on the beach, save the Captain, fell to one knee.

Standing before the Captain, with a scowl that would freeze the blood of his mightiest warrior, was his angry and volatile Queen. The Queen maintained her cold stare for what seemed to the Captain an eternity, but when she finally spoke it was with a tone that matched her chilling demeanor.

"Thank you, Captain," began the Queen. "I have often desired to see the face of incompetence and you have at long last personified that for me."

"But my Queen..." began the Captain before the Queen silenced him with a wave of her hand, and a look of pure evil that dared the Captain to provide her the opportunity to remove his head from his shoulders.

"I made it perfectly clear that it was essential that you attack in the timeliest manner possible, and yet I find you here choosing a route greater in length than any other option available," spat out the Queen.

Of course, this was contrary to the orders given the Captain which directed him to select a random route to ensure that the Hos spies would not determine their intended approach. However, the Captain knew that a contradiction to the Queen's words would not be heard, and even more so, would not be healthy. So, the Captain merely lowered his head and muttered, "Yes, my Queen... forgive me."

The Queen next pulled a map of the Hos Island from her breastplate, and then picked up a coconut lying in the sand. Laying the map on a nearby fallen palm, she pointed to a location on the map still on the same shoreline, but near the middle of the island. She said, "I want you to immediately return your warriors to their canoes and move them to this location." And while tracing a route with her finger to the Hos village she continued, "I then want you to attack along this path which is clearly the shortest route across the island."

Despite his fear, the Captain began to protest knowing the route indicated by the Queen, while indeed shorter, would require them to traverse a small canyon which could be used to trap and destroy his command. However, before his protest could move beyond an exasperated grunt, the Queen in one swift movement drew her sword, threw the coconut into the air, and sliced it cleanly through.

"Another word Captain, and the next sphere to meet my sword will be your tiny and simple head," growled the Queen. Again, lowering his head in defeat, the Captain began the long process of returning his warriors to their canoes, and implementing the insane plan demanded by the Queen.

As he resumed the advance along the route required by the Queen, the Captain sent out multiple scouts in advance of the main body, but his fears were reinforced when none of the scouts returned. Such was his fear of the Queen and her wrath, that he would not deviate from her plan despite the near certainty of its failure. Furthermore, the Captain soon noticed that the faint sounds of battle that could be heard coming from the other side of the island had faded and were now non-existent. So, he was not surprised when soon after entering the canyon the Captain found his force boxed in by superior numbers of Hos warriors to his front and rear.

The canyon floor offered little protection from the spears and arrows that would otherwise soon descend on them, so surrendering his warriors and their weapons to the Hos Commander was the Captain's only remaining course of action. Once the Queen conquered the Hos, the Captain knew she would have his head for allowing this defeat, but there seemed no way out for the Captain, and the most honorable action available to him was to surrender his warriors rather than have them slaughtered.

Renee Fini knew that she could not continue in merely a defensive manner. The Hos had managed to capture over half of the original Pitale army. This was obviously a good thing, but on the other hand it took a substantial number of Hos warriors and resources to guard and feed these captives. And she was certain that eventually the Pitale would be successful in their attacks if they were continuously allowed to rebuild and re-arm their army. She was certain of this fact because she now knew the identity of the Pitale Queen. And she knew that this Queen would never give up in her attempts to conquer the Hos.

Her spies had provided information on the appearance and mannerisms of the Pitale leader in sufficient detail that the still-reluctant memories of Renee Fini slowly informed her of her counterpart's identity. She came to understand that the Pitale Queen was her identical twin sister, Barbara Fini.

Barbara Fini had always fallen prey to certain feelings of inferiority that, throughout their childhood, led to attempts at showing superiority over Renee Fini. And Barbara Fini had consistently demonstrated an unshakeable tenacity in everything she tried. Therefore, Renee Fini was certain that, given what she now believed to be her sister's recently altered state-of-mind, Barbara Fini would not stop in her attempts at conquest until she was successful. While the level of Barbara Fini's apparent animosity had never reached its current state, it now appeared that the recent events had drastically changed her. In fact, in her sister's current frame of mind, Renee Fini was certain she would sacrifice down to her last Pitale warrior if necessary, to win in her conquest over the Hos… and Renee Fini.

Through her network of spies on the Pitale Island, Renee Fini knew that her sister had experienced a memory loss like that endured by herself. However, it was also apparent that Barbara Fini's memories, although severely corrupted by the anger caused by the events of her arrival, were beginning to accelerate in their return. Because of these corrupted memories, she postulated that this was a conflict between her and an identical twin sister who was the source of all her problems. And it appeared that none of the love and respect she had known for her sister as an adult now shown through that anger.

Through her spies on Hos, Barbara Fini had correctly determined that the failure of the rear attack was due to Renee Fini's ability to convince the poor Pitale Captain that she was his Queen. And it was Renee Fini who had ordered the Captain into the canyon, where he had been trapped.

But by this time, it was extremely likely that Barbara Fini had recalled that the two were not only identical in appearance, but also identical in the way they thought… they did not agree in **what** they thought, but in **how** they thought. She knew it would be increasingly difficult for Barbara Fini to be fooled in future encounters, since she would now better anticipate Renee Fini's moves.

These thoughts led Renee Fini to begin planning for the Hos attack on their cousins… the Pitale. If the Hos attacked immediately, before the Pitale could recover from the last encounter, Renee Fini was certain they would be victorious. However, the cost in lives for both sides would likely be large. And this was unacceptable to Renee Fini.

She must find a way to defeat Barbara Fini without destroying either the Hos or the Pitale.

All the Hos Rangatira sat in a circle around the platform built in the central square of their village. Renee Fini stood next to the platform as she prepared to address this council of war chiefs. Each pair of eyes were fixed solidly on their reluctant Queen. All those present were aware that the future of two peoples were tied to the outcome of this council. All knew that either the Pitale or the Hos would emerge from the coming conflict in total control of both islands. This was a result that few in attendance desired, but to which all were resolved.

As Renee Fini climbed the steps to the top of the platform, it seemed the silence was complete. Only the rustling of her robes could be heard as she walked to the center of the platform. It seemed that even the crashing of the distant surf had ceased, so it could better hear what the Warrior Queen had to say.

Reaching the middle of the platform, and therefore the middle of the assembly, Renee Fini remained silent as she began a slow pivot. As she turned her body, her head and eyes remained fixed squarely between her shoulders. And as her gaze moved slowly around the circle of war chiefs, she seemed to stare darkly into each of their eyes as if she had determined to connect with each soul in attendance, so they would know her heart and her desires. After completing her full pivot, she stopped and stood looking into the night sky, as if awaiting instructions from God.

Finally, Renee Fini began speaking in a voice so low that each of the war chiefs leaned forward to better hear her, as she determined the future of their people. "War chiefs of the Hos," she began, "you have led your people well for many years." And then she paused as if the assembly needed time to absorb and accept this assessment. "However, we all know that your brethren, the Pitale, have had their hearts and minds blackened by the lies and devious maneuverings of their new Queen. And we know that because of this evil infestation of their island that they are beyond negotiations or receiving any otherwise peaceful solution to what we now face."

"I have no desire to destroy our neighbors, many of which had been your friends during the times before the big boats came with the temptations that contributed to our current unhappy circumstances. So, it is with complete candor that I admit that my mind has been tortured these last few days, as I have struggled with how we should proceed. And I must warn you that my decision will not be one that you will easily accept."

With that said, Renee Fini paused once again and completed another pivot of the assembly, but more quickly than before, and without meeting the eyes of any of the listeners. And then she continued her address, but in a voice that had slowly gained in volume until it now sounded loud and clear. "I have determined that the only way to avoid the disaster of which I have spoken, is to let the Pitale have our island without offering resistance!"

~~~~~~~~~
~~~~~~~~~

As anticipated, the war council immediately erupted into a near riot as their Queen stepped down from the platform. The thought of surrender to the evil and vengeful Pitale Queen was unthinkable, and for the first time many of the war chiefs were beginning to doubt the judgment of the Hos Queen. Renee Fini allowed the shouts and cries to continue for several minutes before stepping back onto the platform and calling for silence as she drew her sword and raised it above her head.

"My Rangatira," she began, "it is not surrender of which I speak! Our people will remain whole and at peace. It is only the island that will belong to the Pitale."   And again, silencing the excited war chiefs she continued, "Some of you have visited the island known by the name, which translates in my language as, 'Hunters Island'. But many of you have not made that journey since it is a full day's paddle from our island. You know it to have an abundant supply of sweet water, wildlife, and marvelous fruits. However, you also know it to have no beach, and to be surrounded by sheer cliffs along its entire shoreline. This feature has made it undesirable for habitation since fishing would be difficult without an accessible shoreline. And both the Hos and Pitale have been reluctant to locate so far from our islands."

"However, I have determined that it is these very features, plus one other, that offer us a solution to our current problems. Both the cliffs and the isolation will make it easy to defend against a superior force. Any approaching army could be seen several miles out to sea, which would allow sufficient time to organize a defense. And once the attacking army reached the cliffs of Hunter's Island, they would be met with stones, arrows, and spears cast down from the heights. Not a single attacker would reach the tops of the cliffs. And a nighttime attack would be disastrous, given the rocks and reefs that surround the island."

At this point one of the Rangatira stood as a signal that he wanted to speak. With a nod of her head Renee Fini granted him permission to commence. "It is true, oh Queen, that Hunter's Island could not be conquered by an army. However, it could easily be conquered by hunger. While it is true that animals, water, and fruit are there in abundance, being so high above the sea and being surrounded by treacherous breakers will make it difficult to bring the bounty of the sea to our people, and our population would soon deplete the wildlife and the fruit. I do not think we can long survive without a continuous supply of fish and other sustenance from the sea." "I agree," replied Renee Fini. "That is why it will be necessary for us to acquire a large fishing and trading fleet."

This last statement was met with stunned silence, followed by sudden and rushed whispering among the assembled war chiefs. Renee Fini allowed the whispers to continue for a minute or so before continuing. "This leads me to advise you of the other fact about Hunter's Island that is relevant to this decision. I will let Rangatira Vee tell you his story."

With that Tonee Vee stood at his place in the circle and proceeded to tell his tale. "When I was young my father took me to Hunter's Island. Only my father and I were on this excursion, and it was to be a time in which I would receive my instruction in hunting, fishing, and navigation upon the open water. However, on the way to the island our navigation was in error, and we missed our destination by several miles. My father eventually discovered his error and was able to turn us in the direction of the island. Since we were approaching the island by the opposite shore from that usually used, we happened upon a shallow shoal that my father had never seen. It covered a large area, possibly twice the size of either the Hos or Pitale islands."

"It was far out to sea from Hunter's Island shore… the tip of Hunter's highest peak was just visible over the horizon. So, my father felt that neither Hos nor Pitale had visited this shoal previously. This fact helped to explain the bounty that we found there."

At this point Tony Vee pulled a small pouch from his robe as he continued his tale. "The water is shallow, yet deep enough, such that there is little indication of its presence through an agitation of the water's surface. There was a clarity to the depth such that we could easily see the bottom. And my father had me dive to the top of the shoal to confirm close-up what he thought he could see from our canoe." Pausing, Tonee Vee then said, "What I found in the shoal was a bed of pearl oysters that covered the entire surface of the shoal." With that, Tonee Vee opened the pouch and poured out a small handful of pearls into his open palm. "These pearls were taken from that shoal," said Tonee Vee, "and I have kept them in memory of my father for these many years. But that is only a portion of the riches we found there."

Once again, Tonee Vee paused as he let the weight of his words be felt by the assembly. "During one of my dives, I swam to the edge of the shoal and thought I saw a large shape in the deeper water. I swam out to where I saw the outline of the object, and dove to where a large ship lay with its hull exterior broken by a gaping hole. Apparently, the ship had hit the shoal and quickly sank, judging by the size of the hole. I swam through this opening in the hull and by groping in the dark found these laying in piles in the hold of the ship." And with that Tonee Vee pulled his left hand from where it had been resting in a fold of his robe. In his hand were four gold coins.

Tonee Vee then completed his tale by saying, "My father made me promise to tell no one of this treasure. He had already experienced the effects of greed on our peoples as the Hos and Pitale were brought to warring through our trading with the men in the big boats." With that, Tonee Vee sat down.

Renee Fini then continued her appeal to the war council. "Rangatira Vee broke his promise to his father by bringing me his story of the shoal because he saw its riches as how we could avoid the coming destructive battle with the Pitale. He felt, and I agree, that while we do not have capability of building them ourselves, we could use the shoal's riches to purchase the large boats from the Outsiders. With this fleet, we could trade directly with other lands and also fish the waters around Hunter's Island in sufficient quantity to feed our people."

At first silence prevailed in the war council. But slowly heads began to nod, and excitement lit the faces of many of those present. Seeing the agreement around the council, Renee Fini finished the appeal by saying, "Tomorrow morning I will leave with one hundred warriors by canoe to Hunter's Island and secure it and the shoal from the Pitale. With the canoes captured from the Pitale, along with those already belonging to us, we have more than enough canoes to transport the warriors there. As soon as we can secure transport from the Outsiders, we will move all Hos to Hunter's Island."

With that, the council members rose, and the preparations began.

~~~~~~~~~~

Barbara Fini could barely contain her rage as her spy reported on the Hos war council and provided confirmation that he had watched as twenty-five canoes left Hos Island that morning, with four warriors clearly visible in each canoe, with one canoe also containing their Queen. "I will not allow them to deny my revenge!" she shouted. "They will not be allowed refuge on Hunter's Island, and the treasure of the shoal will belong to me, not that traitor of a sister!" And then in a slightly lower voice she continued, "I want one thousand warriors to leave immediately for Hunter's Island. Despite its perceived invulnerability, those one hundred Hos will not be able to defend the island from a force ten times their number."
~~~~~~~~~~

"But my Queen!" one of her captains protested. "We are already weakened in numbers of warriors and canoes from our last two attempts at conquering the Hos. We would not be able to defend a Hos attack with those warriors remaining if one thousand more are sent to Hunter's Island." Barbara Fini responded with, "Don't be a fool! Those weaklings will never attack Pitale with their Queen away leading one hundred of their warriors to Hunter's Island. Their small army cannot afford to attack with their number reduced by that amount, and without their leader. And besides, our warriors will be gone only three days. One day to travel to Hunter's Island, one day to defeat the Hos there, and one day to return after leaving three hundred warriors to secure the island. Now go...I want you to lead our warriors to Hunter's Island within the hour."

But as the Captain turned to leave, Barbara Fini cried out, "Wait!" Then staring into space, she seemed to be weighing conflicting thoughts. And then her eyes darted from side-to-side in the way that people do when they are considering alternatives. Finally, her eyes came to rest on the Captain as she said, "I have decided to accompany the expedition to Hunter's Island. I want to see the defeat of Renee Fini with my own eyes. Prepare my canoe and crew."

Once the Queen had made up her mind, the Captain realized there was nothing left to do except prepare for the advance to Hunter's Island, so he turned on his heel and left the Queen's presence.

Watching him go, Barbara Fini said in a low voice, "At last I have you, my dear sister."

Renee Fini sat on the large rock overlooking the Hos beach as she considered David Eli's cryptic note to her. It had instructed her to watch from "the head", which she had determined to be a reference to the rock upon which she now sat. Indeed, the translation of the name given the rock by the Hos was "Head" because of its shape, which somewhat resembled the shape of a woman's face and head. The message had said to watch for a sign during the new moon, and to be watching during first bell of the dog watch. Having reminded her of her sailing past, this latter instruction had been one of the clues that aided recovery of her memories.

As she puzzled through these clues, Renee Fini gradually recalled that these were nautical terms. The "first dog" was the shipboard watch that occurred between 4:00 PM and 8:00 PM, while the ships' watch bells are rung every thirty minutes.

The Captain's instructions, indicating the *Sea Queen* would approach the island at only specific times told her that somehow, he knew of the dangers posed by the hostile Pitale, and that he wanted to establish a distant contact with her as the means of planning her rescue.

And as Renee Fini glanced down at the pocket watch that her Captain had left for her, she confirmed that it was now exactly 4:30 PM, and looking into the early evening sky the faint wisp of the new moon was just visible. But, once again, there was no indication that the *Sea Queen* was within sight of the island.

She had set on this rock at every new moon since finding the Captain's note and searched for a message contained in flashes of light from the sea (*… and observe the message in the flashes of the sun.*) The signal had never come, and she now despaired that it ever would.

So even though she planned to sit here another hour this evening looking for the signal from Captain Eli, her mind began to wander back to the unexpectedly easy victory of the Hos over the Pitale.

Her orders to launch the fake expedition to Hunter's Island had been executed as planned. The twenty-five canoes had been launched from the end of a long peninsula. With five trusted warriors guarding the narrow neck of land that connected the peninsula to the main body of Hos Island, it was assured that the Pitale spies would be able to observe the launching only from a long distance. This fact made it easy to fool these hostile observers into seeing four warriors in each canoe. In fact, each canoe contained only one warrior, and three short hollowed-out palm logs adorned to resemble warriors from a distance. And of course, one canoe also contained one slightly built warrior wearing the war mask and robe of Queen Renee Fini. Since it was not known with certainty who the Pitale spies were, only Renee Fini, Tonee Vee, Ry-An, and thirty of his most trusted warriors knew of this deception.

As expected, her Hos spies on Pitale confirmed that Barbara Fini had launched a large force designed to overwhelm what appeared to be one hundred Hos warriors. However, what was not expected was that Barbara Fini would elect to accompany her force to Hunter's Island. So, with only about a hundred warriors remaining on Pitale, and without their Queen to intimidate them into action, it was much easier than expected to defeat the Pitale with the five hundred Hos that crossed the distance from Hos Island to Pitale Island using one hundred captured Pitale canoes (including the twenty-five canoes from the Hos "expedition" that had returned under cover of darkness).

This victory had occurred earlier that day, and Renee Fini would start planning in earnest on the next day for the return of Barbara Fini and her one thousand Pitale warriors to Hunter's Island. The original plan had been to capture Barbara Fini along with her remaining warriors on Pitale Island, but Barbara Fini's unexpected decision to travel with her expedition had greatly complicated matters.

Renee Fini had counted on the Pitale/Hos culture, which dictated that once a supreme leader was captured in battle, their surviving warriors would proclaim allegiance to the victorious leader. Curiously, this rule did not apply to cases in which the leader had been killed rather than captured. Since Barbara Fini was still in command of her large force, its defeat was now far from assured.

The plan to defeat this returning force was forming in Renee Fini's mind. The plan involved paddling most of the Hos warriors out to meet the returning Pitale, with large quivers of arrows allocated to each warrior. Being tired from their three-day expedition, Renee Fini felt reasonably confident that her well-armed, but slightly smaller force would be able to defeat the returning Pitale. However, this would be a costly victory, and she continued to struggle for a cleaner solution.

But for the moment, she was enjoying the relative peace and solitude that her watch here on The Head afforded her. She glanced over her shoulder and could see Ry-An and the two warriors he had designated as her bodyguards. She smiled, knowing that this was as much solitude as she could expect to receive, at least until their victory over the Pitale was completely secured.

She turned back to the sea looking for the elusive signal from her Captain. When she next looked at the pocket watch she could see that it was almost 6:00 PM, having once again overstayed her intended time… she always found it difficult to surrender her vigil, but tonight she had reason to delay even more. Indeed, from this southerly latitude at this time of year the sun had already set, and twilight was obscuring the surrounding jungle in shadows. But still, she would not allow herself to leave. So, it was some minutes later when she became aware of a disturbance behind her.

Turning and drawing her sword in one swift move, Renee Fini stood confronting some twenty Pitale Warriors that had suddenly and completely overwhelmed Ry-An and his men. With her back to the sheer drop afforded the face of the rock and waving her sword above her head, she stood prepared to defend herself against these intruders. But with knives held to the throats of her three warriors, it became apparent that they did not intend to make a frontal attack. Instead, the lives of her three bodyguards would be offered as ransom for her surrender to the Pitale.

And stepping from the shadows came a form speaking in a familiar voice. "Oh, what a joy it is to trick the trickster!" exclaimed Barbara Fini. And Renee Fini nodded her head in comprehension of what had occurred.

"I was surprised when you left for Hunter's Island, but I see that you didn't really leave," said Renee Fini calmly. "Nor did you," replied Barbara Fini, "but the important thing is that I found you rather than the other way 'round."

Continuing, Barbara Fini said, "You know, the problem with having a routine is that the routine can be used against you. I knew of your habit of coming to this rock on every new moon, even in foul weather. I do not know why you are here, some sort of religious observation perhaps, but I knew without a doubt that you would be here."

"Your spies are very observant," commented Renee Fini. "As are yours," came the response. "But the difference between you and me, dear sister, is that I am wise enough to occasionally doubt the accuracy of my spies. You, however, are naïve enough to accept whatever it is they tell you."

"Well, it is unfortunate for you that you did not believe that the treasures of Hunter's Island exist," stated Renee Fini. In reply Barbara Fini said, "Well, it remains to be seen whether the gold and pearls are at the shoal or not, which is why I did actually send nine hundred men in pursuit of your expedition. And as soon as I received the signal from my spy that he had spotted you leading your warriors against Pitale Island this morning, I left from my hiding place there and came in a circuitous route to Hos Island. With you and your men so occupied, it was easy to slip ashore and wait for you in the surrounding jungle, knowing you would be guarded only by these three. And since I have mentioned these three, I think it is time to get down to business. Unless you surrender to me, I will order these men killed one at a time."

With that Ry-An, now bound with his hands behind his back, was pushed forward and forced to kneel on the ground. And with a nod from Barbara Fini, one of the warriors behind Ry-An drew his sword and prepared to swing the blade in an arc that, without a doubt, would result in a mortal blow to Ry-An.

"Wait!" cried Renee Fini. "I will surrender, but let's first discuss the terms."

"The terms are these," said Barbara Fini, "you surrender now or your precious Ry-An will die. If you do nothing… he will die. If you are foolish enough to attack… he will die. If you keep talking… he will die."

"Please allow me to say one more thing" begged Renee Fini. And in exaggerated exasperation Barbara Fini nodded her consent.

"As I said before, it surprised me when you went with your warriors to Hunter's Island, and I wasn't totally convinced. I therefore decided on a back-up of my own. When I stood up on this rock and waved my sword above my head it was the signal for one hundred of our best warriors to silently approach through the jungle and surround you and your warriors. For this reason, I must demand that your warriors immediately release Ry-An and his men." And on cue from Renee Fini's words, an arrow struck the ground a mere fifteen centimeters in front of each of the men threatening her three warriors. "They have until I count three... one...!" And immediately, all of Barbara Fini's men dropped their weapons.

But Barbara Fini picked up the sword dropped by one of her warriors and rushed at her sister with a rage and vehemence unlike any that the hardened warriors present had ever seen. She swung her sword with the obvious intention of separating Renee Fini from this life. However, Renee Fini easily parried the attack and kicked Barbara Fini's feet out from under her. As the defeated Queen lay prone on the ground, Renee Fini placed her foot on her back and exclaimed as she looked at the Pitale warriors, "I now stand in victory over your Queen and accept her surrender of you and your army."

"I don't surrender," yelled Barbara Fini. But Renee Fini placed her foot on the back of the yelling Queen's head, forcing her face into the ground, which muffled her protests. Renee Fini then presented the Pitale warriors with a challenging look to which they responded by nodding their heads and kneeling before the Hos Queen.

~~~~~~~~~~

When the returning nine hundred Pitale warriors approached the shore of their island, they saw their comrades kneeling before the Hos Queen as a signal that their Queen had been captured. Their subsequent surrender was immediate and peaceful.
~~~~~~~~~~

It was now more than four months since that final surrender. Peace had returned to the two islands, with the Hos-Pitale united under the leadership of Queen Renee Fini. Tonee Vee and Ry-An were her trusted advisers, but they worked tirelessly to integrate the old Pitale government and military command into a single Hos-Pitale structure. And they determined to name the two islands after the inhabitants, as a move to further their unity. So, the inhabitants of both islands now referred to their unified land as Hospitale.

Together they created laws that prevented further resource depletion, by better controlling trade with the Outsiders, and by scaling the army back to a level more consistent with the proper care and defense of their population. Men that had been conscripted into the Pitale army were now back fishing, hunting, and farming. And Outsiders who married Hospitale women were required to pay large dowries, which had the effect of greatly reducing the number of abandoned wives from Hospitale/Outsider unions.

And it had been made clear to all the Hospitale, that Tonee Vee's tale of a hidden shoal and its treasures was completely fabricated. Renee Fini and her advisors understood that such an opportunity for wealth and adventure would tempt some of the Hospitale, and additional conflict would therefore result. So, it was of great importance that everyone understood that the treasure's existence had been fabricated solely to lure the Pitale from their island.

Renee Fini returned to The Head during each new moon and watched for the flashes of light on the horizon that would signal the arrival of the *Sea Queen*, her Captain, the boys, and Benjabar. But on each occasion, she returned to the village disappointed, and a little more in doubt that they would ever come.

She called on the captain of each Outsider ship that visited Hospitale, making inquiries of the *Sea Queen* and her crew. Each of the captains informed her that they had not crossed paths with the *Sea Queen*. However, many of them did indicate that they had heard tales of such a ship sailing the Mediterranean, Caribbean, and Atlantic, which seemed to be almost mystic in its capabilities and invulnerability. Invariably, Renee Fini asked the captains, that if they should meet the *Sea Queen* on the open sea, or in port, to please tell Captain Eli to hurry to Hospitale. And to ensure Captain Eli understood that it was no longer necessary to wait until the new moon.

Renee Fini told Tonee Vee and Ry-An about the *Sea Queen* and warned them that when she was reunited with the *Sea Queen's* crew, she would find it necessary to leave Hospitale. The two men understood, and although saddened were working toward the day that Renee Fini would no longer be present. They worked diligently to prepare the people and put in place a government and military structure that would eventually replace the role of Queen. But Tonee Vee and others told her constantly, although there would come a time when she was no longer among the Hospitale, there would never be a time when, in their hearts and minds, she was not their Queen.

The disposition of Barbara Fini was a difficult and painful proposition for Renee Fini. She loved her sister and could not bear to keep Barbara Fini imprisoned. Neither could she let her run free, since it was clear that the circumstances of her arrival had disturbed her mind greatly, and her defeat by Renee Fini had served only to worsen her illness. After many hours of intense deliberation, it was determined that banishment to Hunter's Island was the least severe of the options available.

Barbara Fini was taken to Hunter's Island, along with two volunteer couples who were without children. Three homes of Hospitale construction were built near the shore, and supplies were taken to the island one time per week. Renee Fini made it clear to Barbara Fini and the volunteers that this arrangement would last only until the *Sea Queen* arrived. At that time, the *Sea Queen* would pick up Barbara Fini and take her to a location where she could be cared for, and hopefully healed of her mental disturbance.

~~~~~~~~~

After three months of exile for Barbara Fini, her sister found it difficult not to travel to Hunter's Island, in hopes that she would find healing and recovery had replaced hatred and unreasonable anger. Unfortunately, Barbara Fini closed the door to her hut and refused to come out, or let Renee Fini come in. So reluctantly, Renee Fini returned to Hospitale without connecting with her sister.

A tear traced Renee Fini's cheek as the mountains of the Hospitale Islands became visible on the horizon. She knew it would not be likely that her sister's mental condition would improve while confined to her relatively isolated location on Hunter's Island, but she had at least hoped for a visual confirmation that Barbara Fini was not getting worse. She slowly became resolved to order the canoe reversed so she could return to Hunter's Island and force her sister to return to Hospitale with her. But just as she began to give the order, Renee Fini saw the outline of the ship laying off the Hospitale shores.

She knew without a doubt that this was the *Sea Queen,* even though it was not unusual for Hospitale to be visited by Outsider ships. She wasn't certain how she had come to know the ship so intimately, but she had no doubt that this indeed was the vessel she had waited for through the long and lonely months. She knew that David Eli must have met one of the captains she had asked to take him her message. He knew that her danger was past, and that there was no need to cautiously approach Hospitale. He knew there was no need to wait until the new moon!
~~~~~~~~~

The reunion with her Captain and the others was joyous. No... joyous was much too mild a word. If her arms were longer, she would have embraced her Captain and boys simultaneously. As it was, they all embraced her for what must have been almost a quarter hour. Then, she heartily embraced each of them singularly. She started with the Captain of the *Sea Queen*, then she held tightly to Adam Boy, then it was Aarondophilous, and finally there was an embrace for her friend Benjabar. After that sequence of hugs was completed, she repeated the sequence… and then once again.

They spent the next week finalizing the preparations for the Hospitale Queen to depart the islands. It was confirmed that Tonee Vee would be appointed a kind of Hospitale version of Governor for the people, with Ry-An as his Vice Governor, and the former top Pitale Captain as Commander of their army.

In the evenings, each of the reunited adventurers told their stories of how they survived the months since they were separated. They sat around a fire in the new square that was established on Hos Island, and which would serve as their seat of government for six months of the year. For the other six months the seat would transfer to Pitale Island.

Each in turn told their tale, starting with Captain Eli and finishing with Renee Fini, with the sequence being determined by the order in which they were found by the Captain. After each had told their tale, the band of adventurers all agreed that they wanted to hear each story again, for none wanted to miss a single detail. This telling seemed to make their reunion more real and had a calming effect on them all.

As part of Captain Eli's tale, he confirmed to Renee Fini the reason for the mysterious messages that he had provided to each of their party. As she suspected, one intent of the riddles that were contained within the messages was simply to stimulate their brains, and therefore aid the return of their memories. For reasons that all now recalled, Captain Eli knew that they would experience the loss of their memories, and he knew focusing on these riddles would draw out segments of their past.

After completing all the preparations for the Hospitale's pending loss of Renee Fini, and after taking on supplies provided by the islanders, the *Sea Queen* set sail for Hunter's Island. But as they approached, they were met by a canoe containing the volunteer Hospitale who were guarding Barbara Fini and providing a sort of companionship.

They told a tale of Barbara Fini covertly signaling an Outsider ship by building a fire on the back side of the island three days before. The ship having spotted the smoke from her fire, as well as flashes of sunlight reflected from her mirror, changed course, and approached the island. As the ship neared Hunter's Island, the Hospitale guardians could see that it was flying the colors of a pirate ship, with *Sea Witch* painted on the side. The guardians therefore ran to the center of the island and hid there for a full day. When they returned to their huts, they found that Barbara Fini was missing and presumably taken by the pirates.

For all these months, Renee Fini had shouldered the defense and leadership of the Hospitale with little show of emotion. But with this news, Renee Fini broke down into inconsolable sobs. The men all tried to comfort her but knew that it would take some time for her to reconcile her loss.
Turning to the boys and Benjabar, Captain Eli said, "We all need to be strong for Renee Fini for a while. And we will need to be strong for each other as well."

Then with a faint smile on his lips he said, "We need to be strong because our voyage has just begun."

~~~~~~~~~
~~~~~~~~~

Part III:
Origins

Chapter 9 – David Eli

David Eli's mind swirled in a mixture of reflections and memories as he drove through the dense smog and foul-smelling lethal air toward the Carolina Regional Coastline. For while David Eli was not the name with which he had been born, it was paramount that he thought of himself only as Captain David Eli and push memories of the past out of his consciousness. And as he crossed the last bridge to Edisto Island, he reflected that although he had indeed been a captain in the Royal American Navy, this rank of "Captain" would apply to an entirely different man, who would be on an entirely different course than that earlier version of himself.

He grimaced as he passed, once again, the ancient and derelict fish and oyster processing factories cluttering the island's shore and interior. For perhaps the thousandth time, he felt a fresh wave of sadness and loss as he considered the history of those dilapidated and barren structures. They were part of the worldwide conglomerate that had introduced a blight that ravaged the oceans and farmlands of this country. And through political manipulations, unwavering denials, and claims of social and economic benefits, this same conglomerate had repeatedly introduced this same contagion in every ocean, and in every country, on every continent.

Now, in the year 2036, the world was on the verge of economic, social, and environmental collapse. Through a series of tragic wars, government coups, and corporate takeovers, the conglomerate had at last been confronted, and the spread of the contagion slowed. But after two decades of study and analysis, it was apparent to the world's leaders that the infection could not be completely eradicated, and the coming collapse was unstoppable. The damage to the world's food supplies was beyond repair and the Earth would soon be incapable of supporting its swollen population.

This reality had led to the establishment of a complex program, one portion of which would eventually become known as "Project Sea Queen".

The project was presented to the world as an all-out effort to return abundance to the world's oceans through biological manipulation of the pitifully few examples remaining of uninfected marine species. This was a cover story that would explain the large concentration of scientists, engineers, and technical experts gathered at this one small island on the Carolina Regional Coast. But everyone with access to the facts knew that the fisheries of the world, like all sources of the world's sustenance, were beyond reclamation.

Project Sea Queen was born out of the dark reality that no known science, no known technology, or no known path could save the world from the coming chaos and destruction. Even the most secular of leaders would confide, if pressed, that only God-answered prayers could save the world.

So, many of the top minds of the planet were brought together at this one small barrier island in the old factory buildings overlooking the dying sea and told, with God's help, to invent the science and technology that could save the world. A full ten percent of the world's resources were focused on those shabby buildings, and the depleted and worn island. It was a testament to how seriously world leaders took this project that none of the resources were directed at expensive and impressive landscaping, high salaries, fancy offices, or any of the other trappings usually associated with a project of such massive scale.

At the outset, no one had any idea what the solution to this seemingly unsolvable problem would be, but the plethora of great minds began to work on the problem while the leaders of the world prayed…and six-and-a-half years after the start of the project, God heard their prayers.

Captain Eli pulled into his designated parking space, and before exposing the filtered air of the car's interior to the possibility of contamination, he pulled on the respirator and goggles which, over the past fifteen years, had become the constant companion of most people who ventured outside of controlled environments. He often considered leaving the respirator in the car and holding his breath for the twenty-five-meter walk to the air lock, which protected the building from manmade, airborne poisons. But he always discarded this notion as foolish and setting a poor example…after all, even though the blight would not harm him directly through just a short exposure, it could enter his respiratory system and be passed to the project's food supplies, rendering them useless within a few hours.

Eli had joined the project fourteen years after its start, and almost eight years after the solution to the seemingly unsolvable problem had first been proposed. According to his recent briefings, those eight years had been spent developing and perfecting the technology with the final breakthrough occurring six months prior.

It was just four months ago that he was selected as the "Lead Field Agent" (LFA). He had no idea how many candidates had been considered for his position, but guessed the number was in the hundreds since he was told it took over two years for the project's administrative team to narrow down the worldwide candidate pool. Smiling to himself, he realized that "candidates" was probably a misuse of the word. He did not apply for the job and was ordered, not asked, to take the role. So, while the word "candidate" implied that the role would be offered to another if he declined, it was obvious that, through an in-depth psychological analysis, the administrators knew he was destined to accept this role. And that he would be incapable of turning it down despite all the sacrifice, hardship, and dangers involved.

The candidate requirements for his team were so select that less than one-in-five-million people were even considered for this assignment. He had spent many long hours over the last four months selecting four of his five team members from a worldwide list of potential candidates, which had originally numbered over twenty-nine hundred. Only his second in command had been pre-selected for him. And today would be the day that he would at last "meet" his team.

<div style="text-align: center;">~~~~~~~~~</div>

Eli's task at hand was to review the list of the five selected team members and to create code names for each. While he could have opted for computerized selection of the code names, he wanted to make it a more personal and human process. After all, these are the names by which they would all be known for months and years in the future. Assigning a computer to this task seemed a cop-out to Eli, so he was given permission to assign the names himself with the only criterion being, they should be unique and easily identifiable to the project leadership. Although he could understand that the purpose of this selection criteria was to provide identifiers which were easy to search, as the administrators poured through the copious amounts of data that would be generated for the team members over the coming years, it did seem at odds with his own code name. Neither David nor Eli were exactly unique names. Perhaps this was because he spent the first four months of his assignment on the team primarily working outside the project boundaries, and the administrators wanted a name that would blend with the population.

The selection criteria for his team included extreme intelligence, superior emotional and psychological stability, high standards of integrity, and dedication as well as academic excellence in areas such as math, science, technology, and history. However, the crucial nature of the project demanded an additional specific and critical measure. So, a team of the world's leading psychologists had developed and refined the most essential measure by which the candidates would be screened…their "Intuition Quotient".

In addition to these requirements, it was determined that the ideal candidates would be without family or social ties. Hopefully, they would have no family whatsoever. And any past relationships should be such that if the candidate suddenly and inexplicably moved to unknown locations, no one would be surprised. And no one would look for them.

Up until today, from the Captain's perspective, the selection process had been completely blind. His information had not included details regarding race, religion, ethnic background, age, sex, country of origin, or even continent of origin. So, on the previous day, he had made his final selections without knowing any of the details that would give clues as to what his team members looked like. Indeed, it was likely that he would never know any actual details of the team's backgrounds, other than the selection criteria. Additionally, although each of the members had scored extremely high in all critical criteria, each one had been chosen based on one outstanding skill set.

But today he would see the faces of his team for the first time, which led him to feel the responsibility that came with the major step of giving them a name that would likely remain with them an exceptionally long time. Like Eli himself, none of the candidates could be known by their actual names. So, although Captain Eli would have preferred for each team member to select their own code name, to prevent the candidates from subconsciously assigning themselves identifiers that could lead to their true identities, it was the Captain's task to assign them for them.

So, it was with eagerness, and not a little trepidation, that he approached his desk and confirmed that a stack of 250 mm x 220 mm photographs was lying face down on his desk.
Per his agreement with his superiors, the photographs were to be in no given order. Eli closed his eyes, said a little prayer, and turned over the first photograph.

~~~~~~~~~
~~~~~~~~~

To his astonishment Eli found that he was looking at the face of a young boy. Stamped in the lower right corner read the text: "Candidate 0A1/NX19367B, Ten Years of Age, Contributing Criteria: Science, Final Selection Process: LFA Discretion".

Eli was unaware that the candidate list could include children, and he was certain that, if given the chance, he would out-of-hand have excluded anyone under twenty years of age. But, as intended, the process was designed to find the candidates that would best ensure success, regardless of age or other details of their backgrounds. He understood the only age restriction was a cap of age sixty for the potential candidates since the project was expected to take quite some years to implement, and potential debilitating issues had a greater probability of surfacing with older candidates. The future of everyone on the planet was at stake, so it was imperative that the best candidates be selected regardless of age or background. "Well," Eli whispered to the photograph, "my young friend, I am afraid that my age-prejudice cannot save you from this assignment."

So, as he looked into the intelligent eyes of the youth, David Eli continued his one-way conversation with the photograph. "You, are the first member of the team to be identified, so I think it appropriate you take the name of the first man…Adam." However, as he continued to peer at the photograph, he mused to himself that something did not quite fit with the criterion requiring the name to be unique, so after several minutes of consideration he spoke again. "You are indeed the first and I like the name Adam, but you are not yet a man. So, for the time being you will be known as Adam Boy."

~~~~~~~~~

After recording the code name and setting the first photograph aside, Eli turned over the second photograph and was struck immediately by the beauty and intensity of intelligence of the young woman in the photograph. The accompanying text read: "Candidate 0L7/SA34714Z, Contributing Criteria: Martial Arts/Second in Command, Mitigating Factor: Candidate is estranged from an identical twin sister, risk of project contamination judged to be acceptable, Final Selection Process: Administration Directive."
~~~~~~~~~

"Hello madam," he whispered. "So, you are going to be the one to hone our martial arts skills." Again, each of the candidates had scored high in self-defense, but her score had been extraordinarily high, yet he had no idea what the deciding factor had been in selecting her for the team, and why she was set as his second-in-command by the project administration. But she looked like a solid team member and her martial arts skills would be a welcome addition. "Unfortunately, I have an unshakeable feeling your skill will likely be very useful in the execution of our assignment."

"So, what will be your code name?" Eli continued. "You look like you might be French." He smiled as he said this since he had no idea what "French" would look like, and the French name Renée means "reborn" in English. "Since you are going to help give rebirth to the Earth, that fits very well. But by international agreement all names are to be anglicized to hide any hint of national identity. So, I am afraid we must drop the accent over the é." Which is exactly how the name was entered in the database.

But as the Captain continued to ponder her code name, he once again understood that additional complexity was needed. As he continued to gaze at the face of the woman in the photograph, he began to look beyond her intensity and saw an underlying sweetness in her smile and in her eyes. He saw a quiet, regal quality in that gaze, which reminded him of his visit to the Indian State of Rajasthan in northern India. Rajasthan means "Land of Royalty", and it seemed Renee would fit in well there. But this association, in turn, led him to recall the sweet dessert he grew to love there...Meethi Fini.

"So, you shall be known as Fini because you seem to have a royal look that is tempered by underlying goodness and sweetness." Eli smiled as he typed the full code name into his database: Renee Fini.

<div align="center">~~~~~~~~~</div>

The third photograph in the stack was of a middle-aged east Asian woman. Her countenance was more severe than either of the two previous candidates. But, as was his habit, Eli did not draw conclusions based on initial impressions. He instead stared intently at the photo and studied every line in the woman's face. And he read the text stamped on the photograph, hoping for additional insight: "Candidate 4P8/GV91473Y, Contributing Criteria: Environmental Specialist, Final Selection Process: LFA Discretion."

But try as he might, he couldn't quite decide what exact qualities drove this individual, or what it was that stood buried beneath her fixed stare. After over a half-hour of contemplation he finally cupped his head in his hands, and slowly shook his head as he peeked through his fingers at the image of the woman.

"You are difficult to read," he said to the photograph. "I am usually rather good at this, in fact, I believe the ability to read people is one of the traits that led to my selection as leader for this assignment. But you are a little bit of a mystery to me, and as I can imagine your eyes darting from side-to-side to remain mysterious, I will call you Dart." But as he continued to stare at the photo he said, "let's fancy it up a little bit. Let's call you 'Dartous'."

~~~~~~~~~

As he entered Dartous into the database Eli decided that he needed a break, so he stood up and decided to take a walk to the separate building that held the "Molecular Organizer". He smiled at the name for the equipment upon which the future of humanity depended.
~~~~~~~~~

The name was part of the deception and cover-up under which the project was shrouded. The story was circulated that the solution to the unsolvable problem had indeed involved biological manipulation at the molecular level. The explanation given was that through that "manipulation" process the machine would be able to restore and rebuild the damaged cell structure of the remaining marine animals. And to fuel further hope, "prominent" scientists suggested that some of the extinct species, now found only in food freezers of the rich and powerful, could be reconstituted. This of course was total fabrication and no such process existed, but circulating this story gave people hope, and provided the cover for the actual solution.

After all, although not even he knew yet what the solution was, he was told that the actual solution would be much more difficult for people to accept and would likely trigger government downfalls, and the wars they were all hoping to avoid. Hence, the reason for using only people whose identity could not be traced…if they could not be traced it was unlikely to locate them, and if they couldn't be located, they were less likely to inadvertently let clues to the true nature of the project slip out. However, Captain Eli suspected that an additional, bigger reason for untraceable identities also existed, but if so, apparently the time was not yet right to share it with any other than a very few project members.

So, as the Captain donned his respirator and goggles and stepped outside the airlock, he prepared himself to endure the seven known layers of security to which he would be subjected before he reached the Organizer. In his mind he stressed "known" layers because he felt certain that there were several layers of security beyond the usual biological and physical parameters that had been loaded in the system. He had no idea what those parameters might be, but he was virtually certain they existed.

~~~~~~~~
~~~~~~~~

As Eli entered the building housing the Organizer, he paused to observe the personnel scurrying about the facility. The technicians, engineers, and scientists were distinguishable only by the color of the coded name tags attached to the front of their white lab coats, which covered the varying military and civilian uniforms that Eli knew existed underneath. It never failed to surprise him how intensely every small detail was still being attended to by those swarming about the facility, even after so many years of frenzied activity.

Security was so intense that he, the Lead Field Agent for the project, had never seen the Organizer, and had no idea what it looked like. His security clearance would limit his access to the large room that contained the inner sanctum housing the Organizer. And as he scanned the facility, the appearance of one scientist caused him to do a shocked double take. He was sure that he caught a glimpse of the candidate that he had just designated as "Renee Fini". But he knew this should be impossible since he was assured that all the candidates were sequestered at some undisclosed location kilometers from Edisto Island. However, the similarity between the appearance of the scientist and Renee Fini was unmistakable!

Eli diverted his gaze for a few seconds as he pondered this observation. When he returned his focus to where she had been standing, the scientist was no longer to be seen. He was determined to get a better look at the surprising doppelganger, but as he searched the area with his gaze, he was unable to locate her. The need to continue with his day's tasks dictated that he return to his office, but he would keep an eye-out for the mystery scientist the next time he visited the Organizer building. For he found her mysterious appearance worrisome, as associated uncertainties nagged at the back of his mind.

~~~~~~~~~
~~~~~~~~~

As Eli settled back into his desk and the work at hand, he quickly picked up the next photograph in the stack. And the face looking back at him was of a large, well-built man with skin the color of dark mahogany.   The text read: "Candidate 8M9/RG79208Z, Contributing Criteria: Linguistics and History, Final Selection Process: LFA Discretion".

"So, you will be the one to help us understand what we are hearing, seeing, and reading," said Eli, "and ensure that we are understood by others." As he contemplated the man's strong face, he considered the appropriate code name. "You remind me of someone," Eli mused, "not in looks, but in general countenance. Although I see a basic humility in you, I also see a confident and self-assured nature." And then the revelation hit Eli. "You have the same humble-yet-cocky look that I have seen in paintings of Benjamin Franklin. So, I shall call you Benjamin." But as Eli continued to study the photograph he said, "No, Benjamin is close, but too ordinary, and it doesn't quite fit. Your look is much more exotic than a simple 'Benjamin' would suggest. But you look like one who could be the philosophical son of Benjamin Franklin, so I will borrow from the Aramaic and call you Bar-Benjamin." But Eli hesitated as he mouthed these words. "No, that doesn't sound quite right."

The Captain pondered this name for a few minutes and entering the code name into the database said, "Let's call you Benjabar".

<div style="text-align: center">~~~~~~~~</div>

One photograph remained face-down on Eli's desk and he hesitated, just a moment, before turning it over. There was something final about completing this process. It was as if completing the process would take him to the point-of-no-return in which, he was instrumental in condemning these strangers to a permanent exile. But the Captain pushed the feeling back into his subconscious and turned over the photograph.

After his experience with Adam Boy, he should have been prepared for what he saw. But he was once again startled. It was another child, another boy, but much younger than Adam Boy. And the attached text read: "Candidate 9B2/QE53823H, Six Years of Age, Contributing Criteria: Mathematics, Final Selection Process: LFA Discretion".

"So, my son, you shall be a younger brother to Adam Boy, but the mischievous look in your eyes suggest that you will present your own set of challenges. You will demand to be heard and you will speak your mind, whatever the consequence. You have a Greek look about yourself, like someone who will grow up to be a fighter…a modern-day gladiator."
Eli closed his eyes for a few minutes as he considered the things he had said to the photograph. Then opening his eyes he said, "You should be called Aaron, because in Greek the name means 'Gladiator'." But once again he paused for additional consideration before continuing. "Let's expand on your Greek look, stretch you name out a little bit, and make it sound more Greek-like. Let's call you Aarondophilous."

~~~~~~~~~

Captain Eli added Aarondophilous to the database and clicked on the "review" button. The screen responded with a summary of the five candidates and their new code names. He knew this would be the last chance to change any of the names, but Eli felt that he had thought this through, and it was unlikely he would make any changes. Yet he still hesitated momentarily before ultimately hitting the "print" button.

It wasn't a clacking paper printer that responded to the print command. Instead, Eli knew that a laser was silently printing the code names into the gold bracelets assigned to each of his team. And he reflexively felt of the gold bracelet around his own wrist, which four months before had been printed with the name "Captain David Eli".
~~~~~~~~~

After the five bracelets had ejected from the printer and were sitting in the output tray, he clicked on the "Locate" button. Immediately six distinct icons appeared on the computer screen, one for each of the five team members whose name appeared on the control screen, plus the icon representing himself. To the upper right side of the screen appeared the table that assigned the bracelet's candidate code to each icon and showed the coordinates of the bracelets' respective locations. Of course, all six icons showed the same location…Eli's office.

~~~~~~~~

The following morning the Captain, who had slept in his off-site quarters for the last time, contemplated the future. From this time forward he would be eating, sleeping, and working near his team in the dormitory nearby the training arena, to which they had all been transported the previous evening. And as he crossed the bridge to the island, his mind considered the fact that today would be the day he finally met them in the flesh. He wondered if there were issues that he or the project psychologists had missed, despite extensive reviews, that could lead one or more of the candidates to reject their assignment to the team. A portion of his mind led him to think some were likely to hesitate when the magnitude of the sacrifice they would be asked to make hit home. For this reason, he determined that his first meeting with the team members would be on an individual basis.

The previous evening, shortly after their arrival at the dormitory, each of the candidates were advised of the code names assigned to them. They were not given the process by which the names were developed or told who assigned them…only that they should expect to be addressed by these names going forward. Captain Eli determined to start each interview by introducing himself and calling the team member by their new code name, as a means of reinforcing their identification with their new identity.
~~~~~~~~

He decided to start his interview process with the boys so they could get this initial meeting quickly behind them, in case they were experiencing any anxiety associated with meeting a stranger in a strange place. A stranger who would have such a great influence over the remainder of their lives. He need not have been concerned.

He met first with Aarondophilous, who immediately crawled into his lap telling him that he was "the bomb". Eli wasn't exactly sure what that meant, but it was said in a tone that suggested being the bomb was a good thing. Of course, it would be difficult for a six-year-old to understand the complexity of the coming assignment, but the Captain helped him to understand that if he agreed to join him, he would spend a long time in an entirely different, perhaps a little scary, setting with a bunch of new friends that would help Eli take care of him. Aarondophilous smiled up at the Captain and said, "You make me feel safe, and I would really like to be with you and the others." At the end of their time together, Eli pulled out a small black bag and removed the gold bracelet designated for Aarondophilous. And placing it on the boy's small wrist touched it with his own gold bracelet, thereby activating the mechanism which would keep the bracelet snug while allowing the size to expand to accommodate the boy's growth.

Adam Boy was likewise friendly and outgoing and could understand the dangers and implications of what the team would be doing over the coming years. But his only question was, "Will I be able to listen to jazz?" This was said in a joking manner and he seemed to understand that, once they committed, none of them could return to their former lives. The "no-family" requirement probably meant that both boys were orphans, or perhaps had been removed from derelict parents. Listening to "jazz" would likely be one way to restore some degree of normalcy to his life. In any event, Adam Boy agreed to join the team and neither of the boys seemed upset about leaving their former lives.

Eli imagined that his conversations with the adults of the team would not go quite as well as with the boys. So, he decided to go first to the adult from whom he expected to receive the most objections, Dartous.

Dartous didn't disappoint him in that regard. He had not finished his summary of the Earth's descending status when she interrupted with an impatient, "Get to the point!" So, Eli decided the best route with Dartous was to present the project succinctly and without any attempt at addressing sensibilities.

"You will be part of a team that will be key to saving the planet, you will face great dangers, and you will never go home again." As Eli paused, Dartous snarled, "Is that all you are going to tell me?" "Yes, for the time being," Eli replied, as he sat across from her at a conference table. "Well, isn't that just dandy!" she said in mocking fashion. "I demand to see your superior immediately." "Request denied," Eli replied calmly.

The two sat across from each other for several long minutes. Eli remained calm, while Dartous seemed to grow angrier by the second. But finally, Dartous interrupted the stalemate by breaking into uncontrolled laughter. "You are good!" she squealed. "I would bet money that you would have gotten angry. If not at me, then at least at the errors in the psychological analysis program that would allow such an antagonistic person as I presented to slip through the screen." After another bout of hearty laughter Dartous said, "You had me when you said I would be key to saving the planet. Of course, I am in! And as far as never going home again is concerned…I am home **now**."

Now Eli understood the mysterious quality to Dartous' character that he could not cipher from her photograph…under that severe countenance, Dartous hid a weird sense of humor.

<div align="center">~~~~~~~~</div>

Eli's next interview was with Renee Fini who, unlike Dartous, calmly waited while Eli related all the background information. She only asked her first question when he came to the revelation that she would be part of a team that would be key to saving the planet. At that point she asked, "How is that possible? I know it will take the Earth at least a thousand years to recover from what we have done to it…and by that time humans will be extinct."

"I am sorry Renee Fini," replied the Captain, "I must confess to you that I do not yet know those details. However, I am assured that the solution to our problem will be extremely controversial and no one is to know the facts, including me, until their understanding is necessary to the success of the project. We will undergo some years of training together before the plan is implemented, but I promise that you will know all the facts as soon as the planning group gives them to me, along with their permission. I can only tell you that you will know everything well prior to the completion of your training."

Renee Fini nodded her head in acceptance and smiled as she said, "I know you have analyzed my psychological profile to the extent that you know I am going to agree to accept the assignment. So, I will shorten the time needed for this interview, and save any further questions for later."

Eli returned her smile as he welcomed her to the team, attached her bracelet, and advised her of their schedule for the next twenty-four hours. But at the end of her indoctrination, he added one additional request, "Tell me about your twin sister."

~~~~~~~~~

Renee Fini confirmed, as he had guessed, that she and her sister were twins, but withheld her name as dictated by the protocol, which all the project members followed. She indicated that they had lost their parents in some sort of accident shortly after they were born. They were never given the details of their parents' deaths, and they were placed in a state-run institution which clothed, fed, and educated them.
~~~~~~~~~

Captain Eli knew that all institutions of this sort followed a policy of sending only the top students to university, which led many of the children to develop a highly competitive spirit. And based on Renee Fini's body language, he guessed this was especially true of Fini's sister in terms of their sibling relationship. While Fini was making a great effort to be diplomatic, it soon became apparent to Eli that her sister was her inferior in intellect, and the sister's resulting jealously had poisoned their relationship as children. However, they had both been chosen to attend universities, although Fini supposed that her sister's school was less prestigious than her own, since her scores were below Fini's. Renee Fini concluded by saying that she never talked to or saw her sister again after they left for university.

"So, you have no idea where your sister is at this time?" asked Eli. "No idea at all," she replied, "why do you ask?" "I think I saw her here at the project yesterday working as a scientist, and from what you just told me, that may not be good news."

The shock and disbelief showed greatly on Fini's face, but Eli continued, "Try not to concern yourself, but I did want to make you aware of my suspicion. I will be talking to the project security team about this and will assign your sister a code name. In the meantime, let's keep this information to ourselves. I am not sure how the administrators will react to the fact that you have a relative working on the project." "Can you tell me what her code name will be?" asked Renee Fini.

Eli nodded agreement as he considered the code name. This was an unexpected and foreign turn of events, so remembering the Greek word "barbarous" which means "foreign" he said, "Although I will refrain from entering it into the database until we know more about her, her code name will be 'Barbara'."

~~~~~~~~~~
~~~~~~~~~~

The final interview was with the huge man code named "Benjabar", who listened intently while Eli shared the details of their mission to the extent that he could at the time. When Eli had finished, Benjabar slowly shook his head and confided to Eli that he was enough of a scientist to know that the cover story for the project was nonsense, but he also admitted that the true nature of their mission remained a mystery. And it was with a scientist's deep-seated curiosity that he agreed to join the team.

As the interview concluded, Benjabar stood across the desk from Eli and extended his hand. "I am a man of facts and data, Captain Eli," said Benjabar, "but I also have a strong sense of perception and instinct…and I know you and I will be great friends."

~~~~~~~~

The team met together for the first time the next morning. Each was escorted, one at a time, into a large room with Captain Eli standing at the apex of five chairs that were distributed around the room's periphery in a semicircle. Each remained silent, even the boys, and after all had been seated in one of the chairs, Captain Eli began to speak.
~~~~~~~~

"Good morning," he began, as he started a slow side-to-side pivot that allowed him to face each of the team members in sequence. "Each of you was asked to remain silent until I completed these welcoming comments. The reason being that we wanted to once again emphasize that none of you should communicate to the others any information that would provide details of your respective backgrounds. Do not share any information about yourself, including family history or country of origin. I can tell you that we come from more than one country. However, we are to keep our nationalities secret, which is why the administrators spent the last year training all of us, as well as the other candidates, to speak in a midcontinent North American accent. It cannot be over stressed how important it is that details of your past are not leaked to the world. At this point, to the best of my knowledge, none of those who knew you just prior to your initial selection know you are here. And, other than yourselves and a few project administrators, none of the people who know you are here now are aware of your previous identities. And this includes me. After all, the fewer people aware of your past, the less likely those details will be leaked to the outside." Eli paused for a moment and then continued.

"You have been told that your identity is being kept secret to offer as few clues as possible to the true nature of Project Sea Queen. And I am assured that should the true nature of the project become public the result would likely be protests of such a violent nature that the future of the mission would be jeopardized. I believe this to be true, but I am told there is an even greater reason to ensure the secrecy of the project. However, I have not yet been entrusted with that reason, and ask for your continued patience regarding the details of this information, which I am confident will be shared at the appropriate time." Pausing again Eli studied each of the five faces in turn, but not receiving any signals to the contrary he continued.

"I assigned each of you a code name. This code name appears on the bracelet attached to your wrist. Once I loaded your code names into the system, they replaced your legal names within all locations of the project database, and any address or other identifying information was overwritten as well." Eli expected questions at this point in the indoctrination process but receiving none he continued.

"You are requested from this time forward to answer only to your code name. Please never refer to yourself otherwise or respond to any other identifier. The bracelets are keyed to each of your voices, plus mine, and may be removed at any time by speaking your code name into the device followed by the word 'release', or by simply pulling up forcefully on the inner portion of the band. However, let me encourage you not to do so. These bracelets contain a locating circuit that will allow me to find you should you become lost, or if an emergency arises in which it is imperative that the team be located quickly. And let me stress that your training and mission will be intense and hazardous, so the likelihood of an emergency has a distinct non-zero probability of occurrence." After a short pause, the Captain continued.

"And now, it is time to introduce you to one another. But as I present each of you to the group, I challenge each of you to consider these to be your names and no longer just code names…these names now represent who we are. And do not think of the others as strangers. It is critical to our mission that from this time forward you think of them as your family and that you refer to them as family…not teammates, not colleagues, but as family…and I will start with myself…I am Captain David Eli, and my mission specialties are applied physics and leadership. I have the task of being your leader while at the same time being part of your family." And with that, Eli walked around the room and paused in front of each chair. As he looked at each team member, he recited their names and gave their mission specialties.

After completing the introductions, Eli looked around the room again and made a mental note to meet with the boys together to confirm that they had understood everything he had attempted to communicate. Fully expecting a barrage of questions from the family, he braced himself and asked, "Are there any questions?"

In response, Aarondophilous' hand shot up and he waved it frantically. "Yes Aarondophilous?" Eli asked in acknowledgment of his implied question. Standing up quickly and squirming uncomfortably Aarondophilous asked, "May I go to the bathroom?"

After all team members had taken a needed break, tables and comfortable chairs were brought into the room. And the rest of the morning was spent pairing each of the team members up one-on-one for half-hour sessions. These sessions were completely unstructured, and the members were simply encouraged to talk to one another. Eli participated in these sessions, but at the same time kept a watchful eye on the other tables. And by the break for lunch, he had total confidence in the compatibility and competency of the team. But he also knew the first real test for his new "family" would occur after lunch.

The meeting room included a single door other than the one through which everyone entered. This door opened into a corridor, which in turn led to a room containing a single large round table. In the middle of the table sat a Lazy Susan bearing a wide variety of foods. Eli smiled to himself as his new family, in response to his invitation, selected a seat at the table and continued conversations begun during the earlier exercise. To be as transparent and honest as possible, Eli was careful to point out that this eating arrangement was a further attempt to promote the idea of family, which he felt key to the expected success of their mission.

And despite the months of deep psychological, emotional, and spiritual screening that went into the selection of the team, Eli was in awe of the fact that the morning had passed without serious conflict or push-back within the team. Eli quietly considered the fact that each of the candidates expressed a common spiritual faith, which he believed would sustain them through the coming months and years of their mission, while reducing conflicts within the team. With that information in mind and knowing that none on the team would take offense, Eli led the group in a prayer of thanks for the meal which also included a plea for mission success.

Eli sat between Renee Fini and Adam Boy and was further cheered by the fact that each took one of his hands as the prayer progressed. In fact, a quick peek around the table showed that the entire team was holding the hands of the persons next to them. All this Eli took as a good sign.

So, it was with great interest and anticipation that Captain Eli led his team into the training arena for the first time that afternoon. The arena had a rectangular floor approximately two hundred meters by three hundred meters which was covered by an artificial turf. The entire arena was protected by a retractable dome which was one hundred twenty meters high at its center, and which the Captain expected would only rarely be opened, due to the harsh conditions outside of its environmentally controlled confines.

There were multiple doors of varying sizes around the periphery of the room, and the team entered the arena through a door in the middle of one wall. There was nothing on the arena floor except five large cubes, varying in size from approximately one meter on a side up to five meters on a side. The cubes were arranged such that an adult could easily reach the top of the highest cube by climbing from a shorter cube up to a higher cube.

Laying on the top of one of the smaller cubes were what appeared to be some sort of body armor, helmets, gloves, goggles, and boots. There were six sets of equipment, and it was clear by the names stenciled on the breast of the armor that there was a set sized for each of the team members. The Captain led the team to the edge of the smallest cube and began to speak: "Each of you, even the boys, have had extensive martial arts training, and even though I am your leader there will likely be times when each of you will be key to the defense of the group. Therefore, each of you will be asked to take the lead in these training exercises." And turning to face her, Eli said, "And Renee Fini, you are to lead this exercise. Please prepare your team."

With little hesitation Renee Fini picked up the body armor bearing her name and examined it closely. "This is light and serviceable armor, and I can see no reason not to assume it will be needed. Therefore, please dress yourselves in the armor, helmet, and boots assigned to you and position yourselves in a line with your backs to the largest cube."

Each of the team members quickly and quietly complied with Fini's direction and took their positions as requested. But as soon as everyone was in place, Renee Fini directed that they form a circle of about three meters in diameter and centered about twenty meters from one surface of the largest cube, and with each team member facing outward. After making a few adjustments in the relative positions of the team members, she declared that she was going to check out the cubes for offensive or defensive opportunities.

But before Fini could reach the cubes, a doorway opened abruptly in a far wall and eight hooded figures could be seen advancing toward the group. Each was dressed in black and wore body equipment like that now worn by the team. In addition to the armor, each of the figures carried a large, padded battle club. As the eight supposed antagonists fanned out in clear anticipation of an attack on the group Fini called out, "Eli and Benjabar! Each of you pick two of the attackers and take them out of action! I will take the other four and keep them busy long enough for you to finish with your attackers, so you can help me with mine. The rest of the team…please guard our rear!"

But before any of the assailants could be engaged there came a shout from Dartous, "Well, isn't this just dandy! Four more of these goons are coming out of a hidden door in the largest cube!" At this warning Fini spun and saw these aggressors were engaging Dartous and the boys.

"Retreat to a defensive position on the highest cube and try to hold them off until we can help you out!" called Renee Fini. And without waiting to confirm compliance with her directions, she charged the four attackers whom she had picked out for herself. While she was careful not to force the attack so aggressively that she would leave herself vulnerable, she quickly picked out the most isolated of the four attackers, and through a series of dodges and faints managed to wrest control of the assailant's war club. She saw the war club contained a light electroshock mechanism that she supposed would freeze the opponents battle armor, rendering them incapacitated. From that point forward Fini easily parried and fainted with the four attackers, and effortlessly kept them at bay while Benjabar and Captain Eli addressed their own sets of combatants.

Benjabar dodged the swing of an attacker's war club and used the momentum of the swing to trip and disarm his opponent. And in one continuous movement he grabbed the still-moving war club and managed to strike the second attacker at the side of the head, which sent the enemy to his knees. But before the first assailant could rise from his prone position, Benjabar continued the swing of the club to similarly immobilize his second aggressor and then, coming to the same conclusion as Renee Fini, used the shock mechanism to freeze them both. Benjabar then turned to assist Captain Eli, only to realize that Eli's attackers were similarly dazed and incapacitated.

Both Benjabar and Eli then quickly turned their attention to the four aggressors attempting to corner Renee Fini, with the result that those four soon joined their frozen comrades on the floor of the arena. All three of the team members then turned their attention to the remaining four invaders, only to see that two of them were already lying incapacitated on the ground next to the highest cube, while the remaining two were in retreat. Aarondophilous and Dartous were standing at the top of the highest cube, each holding one of the clubs dropped by two of the adult's opponents. Aarondophilous said, nodding at one of the fallen attackers, "Adam Boy tripped him, and I banged him on the head!"

Captain Eli laughed and said to himself, "this team will do…"

~~~~~~~~~
~~~~~~~~~

Chapter 10 – Renee Fini

She knew and was certain the other adults in their "family" knew as well, that given each member's prior training in martial arts, their first test had been designed so that a relatively easy victory was practically assured. But despite this knowledge, the dinner that evening was one in which they mutually toasted their success and bestowed kudos on one another. And this in turn led to the celebration and bonding of the group, which was undoubtedly the intended outcome. As she watched and participated in the celebration, Renee Fini began to feel at home for the first time in her memory. And again, although her intellect told her that this feeling of belonging was orchestrated by their oversight team, she was not resentful of this fact at all. In fact, it gave her a sense of security knowing that the unknown administrators who, among other things, coordinated their training, had thoroughly thought through their program to this degree.

"The Planners," as Captain Eli referred to the administrators, had undoubtedly understood that the intense nature of the family's assignment, and the personalities involved would dictate the need for a degree of solitude in a routine that would involve, almost exclusively, a group experience. And, indeed, Renee Fini found herself appreciating the private room to which she had been assigned. She knew that in the coming months she and the others would continue to appreciate the private retreats that their accommodations provided.

So, as she lay in her bed…bed, not bunk…she found the room to be a place of unexpected contentment. However, it was not long before her thoughts turned to the revelation about "Barbara" that Captain Eli had shared with her during their initial meeting. And contentment turned to concern.

Could it be a coincidence that Barbara turned up here working as a scientist on the mysterious piece of equipment upon which our mission depends? And although she did not know the details of the education or resulting career direction that Barbara had pursued, she knew that her intellect and interests were consistent with those needed to support this project. But still…

And as she drifted off to sleep, Renee Fini was still thinking of what Barbara's presence might mean to the mission, her "family", and to her personally. *Despite Captain Eli's assurances, could my relationship to Barbara jeopardize my position within the family? Could Barbara be a spy placed within the project by a political or corporate opponent of the mission's objectives? Or could this be an orchestrated attempt by Barbara to seek vengeance for having been forced to play second fiddle to me for her entire life? Is her presence here merely a coincidence?*

And as the folds of sleep finally began to engulf her, Renee Fini imagined that only time would answer her questions.

~~~~~~~~~~

As the days moved forward it was readily apparent to Renee Fini and the others that The Planners had established a routine of sorts, which in her mind divided the five weekdays into seven primary activities.

The day always began with breakfast at 0700, which Renee Fini and the others could take either communally or have delivered to their rooms. She noticed that at first, she and several others frequently took advantage of the "room service" option. However, as the days progressed, Renee Fini noticed that the number of meals taken in their rooms reduced significantly, which she felt reflected the increased comfort she and the other "family" members felt toward one another.
~~~~~~~~~~

Typically, the next thing on the agenda was free time from the end of their breakfast until 0830. They were encouraged to spend this time in spiritual reflection. The nature of these activities was determined by the participants and could be through some sort of self-determined communal interaction or it could be solitary.

Most of the team tended to mix up this time, preferring some days to meet with a group, and others to pass this time in solitude, but generally Renee Fini preferred to spend this time in solitary study. However, on Thursdays during this time, she met with the rest of the family who took turns leading a time of study, discussion, and prayer. She had quickly seen that all the family members had deep spiritual beliefs, which she knew would help them navigate the uncertain days ahead.

The solitary time could be spent in their rooms, or in solitude anywhere within the compound except for those areas to which they were denied access. Of course, it was rare that any of them chose to spend time in the open areas of the compound, since the toxins in the air required the use of a respirator. But Renee Fini occasionally chose to use this time to stroll within the arena, on those days when it was not undergoing modifications required for an upcoming group exercise. Of course, on those days the family was not allowed a look at the arena set-up until the scheduled start time of the exercise.

The remainder of the morning was usually devoted to either martial arts training or a group exercise of some sort. Some exercises, like that experienced on their first day together, tested their combat readiness. But sometimes the exercises were designed to test their reasoning and mental readiness, as well as their physical condition. And the mental exercises were the ones Renee Fini preferred.

The family took their lunch immediately after the training exercise, usually between 1130 and 1300, depending on how the exercises progressed, and lasted forty-five minutes. These were always communal with no option for room service. Surprisingly, lunch often turned out to be Rene Fini's favorite time of the day. She supposed that had to do with the knowledge that the arduous training and exercise activities were over for the day, and she could instead focus on the companionship of the others while anticipating a less intense afternoon.

The afternoon, after lunch, was often spent in four to six hours of academic studies for all ages. For the boys, the focus was on mathematics, the sciences, writing skills, and verbal proficiency, with two or three half-hour breaks for video games and other distractions. The adults spent much of their academic time studying history, with a focus on the period from the British and French settlement of the Americas up through the present time, with a special focus on the events and biological mismanagement that led to the disaster the world now faced. Often these studies were the most introspective part of Renee Fini's day because it reminded her how short-sighted we humans can be.

The last organized thing on the regular daily agenda was the evening meal at 1800 hours which, like breakfast, could be taken communally or in the solitude of their own rooms. Renee Fini found herself increasingly looking forward to these times, which were usually filled with laughter as the family sat around the table and decompressed after an intense day of activity. Renee Fini thought of this time as their "family time", and it was rare that anyone opted for room service.

Something that quickly became routine, to the point of being a regular ritual, was kidding Benjabar about his accent. While each had been trained to affect a midcontinent American accent, it was obvious to all that Benjabar's home was in Jamaica. This fact was first established on the evening in which a delicious dish of baked beans was served, and in dropping his guard Benjabar had said, "Good bee-uns mon", in an unmistakable Jamaican pronunciation. Adam Boy and Aarondophilous roared with laughter at Benjabar's unintended break from protocol and spent the next twenty minutes trying to "guess" from where Benjabar hailed. From that night forward, whenever beans were served...in any recipe...the other family members took turns in repeating, "Good bee-uns mon", as they poked fun at Benjabar good-naturedly.

After finishing their meal, the rest of the evening was usually spent in free time that was filled with game playing, movies, and other forms of entertainment, with the only curfew being the 2100 "lights out" rule for the boys. However, Renee Fini noticed that after a particularly intense day, the family time tended to stretch into their free time, as the family seemed to increasingly seek a sense of unity and comfort from one another.

Saturday and Sunday were off days from the usual activities, and there was no mandatory schedule. The kitchen was made available for everyone to prepare their own meals. Alternatively, everyone had the option of ordering from an extensive menu with everything on it from Avocado Pizzas to Zebra Pies. The latter being a German Chocolate pie with bands of vanilla cream pudding embedded in the chocolate, which was one of Rene Fini's favorites.

Indeed, every family member had their own favorite foods which they enjoyed eating, especially during their communal meals. There was Captain Eli's corned beef and cabbage served with cornbread, which the boys said tasted better than it smelled, and of course, Benjabar's meal of specially prepared baked beans, which always meant someone would voice a hearty, "good bee-uns mon", and there was Aarondophilous' Greek Chicken Soup with a special parmesan bread crumbled into it, which everyone claimed proved he really was Greek, and there was Adam Boys' fried elephant ear pastry, which Aarondophilous claimed were made from real elephants. But Renee Fini, in addition to the Zebra Pies, often enjoyed a large spinach and arugula salad complete with the addition of, what the boy's called, "Fini Fixin's" ... usually things like roasted chicken strips, red sweet peppers, carrots, and avocados.

Various family members often organized ball games or other types of competition, but many other forms of entertainment were also available. Renee Fini and Captain Eli often fell into the routine of riding bicycles around the arena's interior periphery. And after completing the equivalent of eighty kilometers around the arena, they would often celebrate with a slice of Zebra Pie, or some similar reward.

Captain Eli led a time of prayer, study, and sharing which he alternated between Saturday evenings and Sunday mornings, for those interested. Renee Fini looked forward to this time each week as an opportunity to understand the perspectives of the others. And as she prepared for a mission that was still largely a mystery, these sessions also reminded her of her spiritual obligations. Every family member attended these sessions almost without exception.

And as the days turned to weeks and months roughly following this schedule, Renee Fini settled into a routine of contentment in the moment, but with a constant nag of things unknown.

And chief among these unknowns...*what did Barbara Fini's presence mean?*

~~~~~~~~~
~~~~~~~~~

The training proved to be physically, mentally, and emotionally challenging. While the physical exercises typically left the family ready for an early bedtime, it was the mental portion of the exercises that sometimes kept them awake at night. And Renee Fini spent many such nights thinking about those mental exercises, and especially the first one which took place in the arena on only their third day as a family. Benjabar had been designated as the leader for this activity, which involved a large pyramidal structure with a base that covered most of the arena floor and had an apex that reached within five meters of the center of the arena's dome. As the exercise leader, Benjabar walked the perimeter of the pyramid but found only one opening in the structure. The opening was at ground level on one of the shorter sides of the pyramid. Beside the opening, inscribed on the outer wall, was a cryptic message that Benjabar identified as ancient Hebrew. Also, next to the opening were small backpacks having clasps that were keyed for the fingerprints of a specific team member. Each backpack contained a headlamp and walkie-talkie radio, each also keyed to a specific team member's fingerprint. In addition to these items, Dartous reported that a portable microscope had been included in her backpack, also keyed to her fingerprint. It was obvious that The Planners wanted them to have a specific backpack and specific contents. So, Benjabar directed each one to put on their backpack and to check the functionality of the equipment.

The equipment operated as expected except for the radios. The radios assigned to the two boys were good, but those assigned to Benjabar, the Captain, Dartous, and Renee Fini showed a "low battery" light when they transmitted. The entire family nodded knowingly to one another because they knew that The Planners did everything intentionally, and since there was not a mechanism in place to request replacement radios, they knew the low battery was an intentionally introduced variable.

Subsequently, Benjabar translated the Hebrew message as "Only a feather can open the portal beyond but open it you must." After several minutes of discussion, it was Adam Boy who suggested that the feather was a metaphor for a person of small build. He guessed that there would be pressure plates in the floor, which would trigger a mechanism that would close-off the passage if the person first walking the corridor weighed beyond the trigger value. And since they had no idea what the trigger value would be and Aarondophilous was the smallest, Benjabar determined the boy would be sent ahead to attempt to open the door that they could see at the end of the passage.

Aarondophilous reached the door without incident, found a lever next to it, and pulled it down. The door slid quietly open into a slot in the upper door frame, but a loud metallic sound was heard beneath the floor of the passage. Adam Boy suggested to the group that this was the sound of the door's trigger mechanism being disengaged, or perhaps reset for a heavier trigger weight. By Benjabar's direction, Aarondophilous immediately stepped through the open door into the passage beyond.

Benjabar doubted that the trigger mechanism had been completely disengaged, so he decided to send the team members through one at a time starting with the one having the next smallest build, Adam Boy, who was able to join Aarondophilous on the other side of the now-opened door. Subsequently, Dartous and then Renee Fini joined the boys in the passage as well. However, when Captain Eli stepped through the outer opening into the passageway, he was greeted by a loud low frequency horn that apparently signaled that the door, which had immediately begun to slide back into position, was closing. The door closed slower than it opened, but despite his best sprint, Captain Eli was not able to reach the doorway before the door had closed. As expected, the door lever would no longer move, and Benjabar and the Captain were closed off from the rest of the group, who were now trapped inside the pyramid.

From their first day together, Captain Eli had determined that the family should have a command hierarchy in case something of this nature happened, so as the highest-ranking member within the structure, Renee Fini effectively took command of the exercise. She immediately pulled her radio from the backpack and called Benjabar so he could formally agree to cede the immediate exercise command over to her. Benjabar instantly agreed to the leadership change and advised Renee Fini that he was turning his radio off to conserve the battery. But, before he did so, as the overall lead of the exercise, he directed that she check back with him in fifteen minutes.

Inside the pyramid Renee Fini turned her radio off and directed the rest of the team, except for Adam Boy, to keep their radios off to conserve their batteries. She explained that this would allow Benjabar and the Captain to communicate with them instantly in the event of an emergent issue.

As soon as the door closed their headlamps had come on automatically, but Renee Fini directed that all be turned off to conserve batteries except for hers and Dartous'. Renee Fini would take the lead, and Dartous would follow from the rear as they began to walk the upward-sloping passageway.

So, with the broad and bright beam from Renee Fini's headlamp illuminating the way, the four family members quickly moved up the passage. As best as Renee Fini could determine, the passage was leading toward the center of the pyramid at an incline of about fifteen degrees. After walking for approximately one hundred meters the passage abruptly ended in a vertical shaft and attached to one wall of the shaft there were, what appeared to be, handholds like those used during their wall-climbing training.

As Renee Fini played the beam of her light up the wall, she could see that the height of the wall extended beyond the beam's reach. But, as far as she could see up the vertical shaft, there appeared to be one-meter ledges spaced vertically about every five meters, that extended around all four sides of the shaft.

Something about this arrangement strongly suggested caution to Renee Fini, and she decided to wait until after the scheduled fifteen-minute check-in with Benjabar before proceeding up the wall. After about five minutes of waiting her caution proved to be justified as they heard a series of metallic clattering. And each time the clatter occurred it sounded closer than the last, which suggested that the sound was moving down the shaft from above. The beam of Renee Fini's headlamp could light up to the fourth ledge above their heads, and that is where she focused the beam.

As they observed this area, Renee Fini and the others could see that the source of the sounds was the action of the handholds being retracted into the wall. As a group, the handholds in each section of wall between the ledges were sequentially being retracted for about four seconds. It appeared that this sequence had started from the top of the shaft. Of course, anyone found on that section of wall when the handholds retracted would fall. If they were lucky, they would fall to the ledge below. However, especially if a fall should occur at the higher levels, it could be fatal.

Renee Fini watched as the progression of the retracting handholds moved down the shaft and confirmed that the next section in the sequence retracted at the same moment those of the previous section returned to their normal positions. When the handholds at the floor level reset, she set the timer on her chronometer and listened as the retraction sequence began at what she assumed would be the top level of the pyramid. When the full top-to-bottom sequence was complete, she punched her timer again. The entire sequence took fifty-two seconds.

Renee Fini turned to the other three and advised them that apparently their presence at the bottom of the shaft had triggered this delayed repeating sequence, and that they had only fifty seconds after the reset of the next level's handholds to reach the ledge above. She emphasized that anyone on the wall more than fifty seconds after the handholds reset would lose their grips on the wall. Aarondophilous was the best climber in the group so Renee Fini determined that he would go first, and the other three would climb side-by-side behind him with Adam Boy between Dartous and Renee Fini. She further directed that they would attempt to climb only one section of wall per sequence, to minimize the chance of being caught on the wall when the handholds retracted. It was also decided that Renee Fini's and Dartous' headlamps could adequately light the way for all, so Adam Boy's and Aarondophilous' headlamps were to remain off to conserve their batteries. After all, they had no idea how long they would be without other illumination.

Renee Fini was confident that The Planners would have built safeguards into the exercise, and it was unlikely anyone would be seriously injured. However, she was certain that if anyone were caught on the wall at the time of the retractions that the exercise would be deemed a failure. At this point the family had not failed a test, so she had no idea what the repercussions of a failure would be, however, neither she nor any of the others considered failure an option. So given the level of everyone's training, she held no major concerns for their safety, but for Renee Fini the prospect of climbing up a dark vertical shaft on movable handholds was intimidating, nevertheless.

Renee Fini contacted Benjabar at the scheduled time, quickly advised him of her plan, and agreed to report back in a half hour. And at the start of the next handhold retraction sequence, they began their climb.

The positions of the handholds varied so, the time to climb the sections of walls between the ledges varied as well. Renee Fini estimated that it took the group between twenty and thirty seconds to climb each section. This left at least twenty seconds to rest between each sequence of retractions. But everyone was in good shape, and in a little more than fifteen minutes Renee Fini estimated that they were ninety meters above the floor and could see the top ledge only fifteen meters above them.

They quickly established a routine in which immediately after the handholds had reset Aarondophilous would begin his climb. The remainder of the group would start their climbs as soon as his feet cleared the top of Adam Boy's head. This routine had quickly become automatic in its execution. So, Aarondophilous confidently began the next climb and was two meters off the ledge when the supports retracted without warning. Aarondophilous fell onto Adam Boy who had just begun his climb. Adam Boy was knocked off balance and he and Aarondophilous began to fall over the edge. With lightening reflexes Renee Fini and Dartous reached out for the boys. Renee Fini caught Aarondophilous and Dartous caught Adam Boy. Each boy was lifted to the safety of the ledge.

For just a moment, Renee Fini was in a state of near shock as the group recovered their bearings. Her shock came not from the fall, but from the fact that The Planners would place the family in such a position of danger. Although she had never met, or perhaps even seen one of The Planners, because of their meticulous attention to detail, and the obvious harm to the project that would result from death or serious injury, she had come to trust them with their lives. And this trust was in danger of evaporating like dew on the morning grass.

But this confusion lasted for only an instant as revelation and insight forced their way past the shock. Immediately Renee Fini played the beam of her headlamp down the shaft of the pyramid as a smile of understanding and relief filled her face. Rather than letting them down, The Planners once again proved themselves competent and worthy of her trust.

The light of her headlamp caught the outline of a safety net being silently retracted into the wall of the shaft. The Planners had hidden this safety mechanism from the family, and in doing so had introduced an apparent potential for mortality into the scenario of this exercise. It was apparent to Renee Fini that the out-of-sequence handhold retraction had been executed to evaluate the team's performance under significantly increased pressure.

Since The Planners wanted to evaluate the team under pressure, and since neither the boys nor Dartous seemed to be significantly upset by the incident, she decided to bite down her tendency to comfort the boys and kept this insight to herself. So, Renee Fini did not let the rest of the team know what the beam of her headlamp had revealed. Of course, this went against her nature which rebelled against the prospect of keeping secrets from the family, and she would tell the team after the exercise was complete, but if The Planners wanted the team stressed…she would let them think they were stressed.

She quickly checked her chronometer and determined that they could make it to the top before contacting Benjabar, so turning quickly to the group she told them, "New plan… Adam Boy and Aarondophilous will climb to the next ledge one at a time. Adam Boy will not start his climb until Aarondophilous is at the top. Dartous and I will stand directly below you as you each climb to ensure we catch you should this episode be repeated. Then the two of us will climb together as soon as Adam Boy has cleared the ledge. We will wait an additional fifty-two seconds, through the next set of retractions, before climbing to the next level. This of course will slow us down, but I feel the need for additional observation time, to see if a pattern emerges that will help us avoid further incidents."

But without further issues, the team made it to the top just in time to communicate with Benjabar at the appointed moment. Renee Fini reported what had occurred but left out her revelation regarding the hidden safety measure. And after agreeing to report back in five minutes, she and the team began to carefully scout their surroundings in search of a way out of the pyramid toward their goal, whatever that goal might be.

~~~~~~~~~
~~~~~~~~~

After three minutes of searching, Aarondophilous found what appeared to be a circular stud located near one wall that extended about six millimeters above the surface of the ledge's floor. The rest of the floor and walls were smooth and there were no other features apparent. There seemed no other obvious course of action than to step on the stud in the hope that an egress would be revealed, but Renee Fini decided to wait until after her call with Benjabar and Captain Eli before proceeding.

As they waited for the appointed time of the call, on a hunch, Dartous opened her backpack and pulled out the small portable microscope. It reminded her of the ones she carried into the field when examining microscopic toxins and their effects on cellular activity.

 She turned to the team and said, "It seems The Planners want us to look at something small during this exercise, and the lack of any obvious instructions on how to exit this ledge makes this a good time to look for something. And that stud would be a good place to start."
With that, kneeling, Dartous set up the microscope over the apparently smooth surface of the stud, and as she focused the lens suddenly muttered "voila" and began to read the miniscule text inscribed on the top of the stud, "Non est pluma. Uti duo Pullos. Non receptum." And then looking up at the other three asked, "How is your Latin?"

Aarondophilous replied, "We should check with Benjabar, but I think it says, 'There is no feather. Use two chickens. No Retreat.' ...but Latin isn't my best subject." The team spent the next few minutes discussing possible meanings of the three phrases and arrived at interpretations for two of the phrases. However, nothing came to their minds regarding the meaning of "Use two chickens".

At the scheduled time, Renee Fini called Benjabar who generally confirmed Aarondophilous' translation, and suggested an interpretation for two of the phrases which closely matched those offered by the team. Namely, that the reference to the lack of a feather contrasts with the instruction found at the entrance to the pyramid, which suggested that using a feather was the way to open the first door. In that instance it meant that using the lighter team members was the solution. In this case, the team agreed that it must mean that activating the stud will require a heavier force.

Benjabar also agreed that the reference to "No Retreat" meant that activation of the stud would mean that they would not be able to retrace their path by climbing down the shaft to the entrance.

But Benjabar offered a slightly different translation of the third phrase. He pointed out that the phrase could also be interpreted as "Use two chicks" and said, "I think The Planners are trying to be funny here and are referring to the slang term for women… 'chicks'…and I think they are telling us that the weight of the two women together will be required to activate the stud. And I also suggest that using a lighter weight on the stud could cause the mechanism to deactivate."

Renee Fini and Benjabar agreed to keep the radio channel open until they attempted the activation of the stud. Then, being the lighter of the two, Dartous climbed onto the back of Renee Fini who stepped on the stud, which then retracted to a position that was flush with the surface of the ledge.

At first it seemed nothing was happening, but the now familiar sound of the handholds retracting could be heard advancing down the wall of the shaft. However, this time there was no indication that the handholds were going to reset. "It certainly does look like there is no retreat," said Adam Boy.

Unexpectedly the ledge located along a wall next to their location began to slowly retract and did not stop until its outer surface was flush with the wall of the shaft. At that time, the ledge on which they stood also began to retract. Renee Fini yelled, "Quickly…move to the next ledge!" but as soon as they did so that ledge also began to retract. Without being told, the team then moved to the remaining ledge which remained motionless.

After the last of the three moving ledges retracted into the wall, the team collectively held their breath. No one offered any suggestions of what to do should the remaining ledge begin to retract. Several seconds passed with no movement of the ledge and Renee Fini began to relax a little, but then her heart leapt as the ledge began to move.

But this time the ledge did not retract. Instead, it began to tilt. One end of the ledge was fixed in place to the corner formed by two of the walls. The other end of the ledge appeared to be flexing upward as it bent into an inverted arch which progressed up the face of the shaft. The team moved to the lengthwise center of the ledge and closely watched as the moveable end of the ledge progressed upward.

At the point where the moving end of the ledge was about three meters above its fixed end, a panel slid to the side revealing a lighted passageway beyond the end of the inverted arch. Before its opening, the team had missed the outline of the panel covering the hidden passageway, because it had been shrouded by the dark shadows of the unlighted shaft. Within seconds of its opening a rope began to snake down through this new portal. The rope was clearly intended as an aid in scaling the steep curved surface.

After a quick consultation with Benjabar, Renee Fini broke their radio connection, agreeing to call back in fifteen minutes. She then directed the team to proceed up the curved surface of the ledge and then through the doorway. But after they had all entered the new passage, Adam Boy muttered, "What's with this obsession with foreign languages?" And looking in the direction of Adam Boy's gaze, Renee Fini saw the reason for his query. Attached to the wall just beyond the doorway was a sign holding the message, "Sigue a los osos y no te pierdas al a'ngel con la luz brillante."

Without waiting for a response to his murmur Adam Boy said, "It is obviously Spanish, and it says, 'Follow the bears and do not miss the angel with the shining light.' And I think I understand the reference to the bears, because we can see the outline of the bears stamped into some of the floor tiles. So, I assume that means we are to step only on the tiles with bears in them, but I have no clue about the angel thingy."

The team spent the next few minutes searching for anything looking like a winged being, or anything having to do with the popular conceptions of angels, but they could find nothing of that sort at the door opening. So, Renee Fini directed them to proceed down the hallway single file, stepping only on the large one-meter square tiles containing the bear outlines while keeping a look out for anything that might suggest an angel.

Other than the bears, there was nothing noteworthy about the hallway except the surface was inclined slightly and seemed to be following an upward spiral approaching the apex of the pyramid. However, at about ten meters up the hallway from the opening, Adam Boy noticed a coin embedded into the wall. Upon further examination, Renee Fini estimated that at intervals of about five meters additional coins were also fixed to the wall. Noting this she said, "I am guessing that one of these coins will picture an angel, so be sure to check each one as you pass."

So, the team progressed slowly...first Adam Boy, then Aarondophilous, followed by Dartous, and finally Renee Fini, each stepping carefully on the bear tiles and checking each coin as they passed. Renee Fini soon realized that Dartous was apparently somewhat of a numismatist, which made her smile because she could imagine Dartous scoffing at the use of such a big word to describe someone who is an expert in coins. So, as she passed each one, Dartous would call out... "Doubloon...Piece of Eight...Farthing...Sovereign... Liberty Dollar..." And just as Renee Fini was ready to suggest that Dartous take the lead, being the person who would most readily recognize a coin bearing an angel, Dartous yelled... "Aarondophilous! Adam Boy! Stop! You passed the angel! Be careful that you don't trigger a release before we see what this is about."

Renee Fini was in position to look past Dartous and could see the coin that had caught her attention. But she looked on in confusion, because all she could see on the embedded gold coin was the outline of a ship...not an angel. But sensing Renee Fini's questioning gaze Dartous explained, "This was a coin minted in the 15th century in England and was one of those referred to as an 'Angel' because on the other side is an image of the Archangel Michael slaying a dragon."

With that, Renee Fini signaled for the two boys to retrace their steps to a tile located before the Angel coin and she began to lead the group in a discussion of what their next move should be. They came to an agreement that the obvious move would be to push on the surface of coin in the hope of triggering the release of an egress or finding whatever it was The Planners wanted them to find. However, this seemed too obvious an answer to Renee Fini, who was reluctant to risk pushing the wrong trigger. But as she was considering what the next move should be, Renee Fini noticed a puzzled look on the face of Dartous. And in response to Renee Fini's nonverbal inquiry said, "I am a little concerned about the message which indicated the Angel would have a light...'don't miss the Angel with the shining light'...because I don't remember a 'shining light' as part of the coin's image."

"Of course!" shouted Renee Fini, "it is not that the angel has a 'shining light'…the message means for us to not miss the angel with our light…we are to shine our light on the coin." And thinking that they did not have much at risk by assuming that to be the correct answer, Renee Fini immediately turned her headlamp to the highest beam intensity and shined it directly at the coin.

Immediately, the floor tiles next to those upon which they stood began to slowly give way and revealed what appeared to be inclined chutes leading downward. It was obvious to all that this was the way out of the pyramid and all soon found themselves sliding down individual chutes. They were long curving chutes of a gentle incline that seemed to spiral down and around the interior of the pyramid. All the separate chutes joined near the bottom so that within a minute of entering the chutes, all four of the team found themselves deposited through the same opening into a common lighted chamber. The chamber had steps leading upwards, which terminated at what appeared to be an ordinary door with an ordinary doorknob. There were no instructions at the top of the steps, so Renee Fini turned the knob and tried the door which easily opened into the interior of the arena. And standing a few meters from the door were Benjabar and Captain Eli with surprised smiles on their faces.

Apparently, the team had passed the exercise.

~~~~~~~~~~

Several days later, Renee Fini decided to spend her morning free time reading in the cafeteria that served the general population of the project. She found that the rest of her family rarely used this facility, and the general population was instructed to minimize interactions with any of the family. This afforded her an opportunity to be surrounded by people, which she liked, while at the same time providing privacy, which she required. But this proved to be an unusual day.
~~~~~~~~~~

In less than a minute after sitting at the table and propping her book against the napkin dispenser sitting on the table, Renee Fini sensed a presence behind her. Turning slowly, she gasped as she recognized that she was less than two meters from her identical twin. The woman was wearing a navy-blue uniform under a lab coat that covered her name tag, and any insignia that she may have been wearing. This startling revelation momentarily stymied her thoughts and actions. But she quickly relaxed as she took in the demeanor of her sister, which was enhanced by the presence of a genuine smile.

Her sister was the first to speak, "I have been observing your habits and preferences and guessed that you would be in here today." She then paused and appeared to be gathering her thoughts. "I knew that you were aware of my presence within the project. So, it seemed to me this conversation was overdue."

Renee Fini had fully restored her calm at this point and asked, in a matter-of-fact manner, "What are you called now? After all, none of us are using our former names." Smiling once again her sister answered, "Your Captain Eli refers to me as 'Barbara', so that is the name I have assumed. But, since we are sisters, I would really like it if you thought of me as 'Barbara Fini.'" Returning the smile Renee Fini replied, "It would please me greatly to think of you that way and I will certainly address you as Fini, but you should know that I must report our relationship to The Planners. I am not sure how the fact that we are sisters will affect our positions within the project."

At that point Barbara Fini smiled broadly as she apparently suppressed a laugh. And her smile broadened even further as she said, "My job is Director of the group that you call 'The Planners'! I can assure you that our relationship is no secret." Renee Fini's immediate response was, "Well, that is certainly unexpected news."

~~~~~~~~~
~~~~~~~~~

Renee Fini sat alone at a conference room table affecting a calm exterior despite the tumultuous thoughts that beset her mind. *Did Captain Eli know that Barbara Fini was the head of The Planners? Had this all been some sort of test directed specifically at me? Why would they choose my sister, of all people, to lead The Planners? Was that a good thing? Was it a bad thing? Could it all possibly be coincidental? Could it yet result in me being removed from the family...*

She was relieved to have these thoughts interrupted by the opening of the conference room door, and the arrival of Captain Eli. Barbara Fini had suggested that they meet in this remote area of the compound to sort through the complexities of their relationships to the project. But Renee Fini had expressed a desire to have Captain Eli, as family leader, present. However, it had not been clear if this request would be granted, so while Eli's arrival was anticipated it was a great relief to know for certain that he had been permitted to meet with them.

Captain Eli and Renee Fini exchanged pleasantries as he joined her at the conference table, but she quickly determined to learn what he knew about these developments. As it turned out, he didn't know any more than she did. Like her, he had assumed she was working in the capacity of a scientist servicing the Organizer. He had learned otherwise only after Barbara Fini visited him earlier in the day to invite him to this meeting. Captain Eli expressed questions like those bouncing around her mind, but it appeared that the answers would have to await the arrival of Barbara Fini. However, there was one question that he expected Renee Fini to answer.

"In your conversation with Barbara Fini, did you detect any hint of the animosity toward you that you experienced from her when the two of you were younger?" Renee Fini delayed several seconds in answering. She was uncomfortable with this question, but ultimately decided that she had to be totally forthcoming with Captain Eli. "Yes," she replied, "she was very professional and friendly in her tone and approach, but I think I detected an underlying sharpness in her speech. I think she feels she is now in a position of superiority to me and is probably buoyed by that fact." "Well," said Captain Eli, "it does explain why I have not received a satisfactory response to my inquiries to Security about your sister. And imagine my surprise to learn that the individual presented as my supervisor was a stand-in for Barbara Fini, who is my actual superior."

Before he could elaborate further, Barbara Fini opened the door and entered the room. She was still wearing the navy-blue uniform that she had worn in her earlier encounter with Renee Fini. The uniform contained a tag that indicated her "Barbara Fini" identity along with her Director title. There was also a single insignia that indicated the title of Major. Both the tag and insignia were designed such that they could be easily removed, which Renee Fini guessed was a security precaution taken in the event of meetings and other situations in which it was best to not advertise her position in the project. Barbara Fini nodded at the two family members and gestured as if asking permission to join them at the table. They nodded their assent as she pulled a chair away from the table. She advised them that they would be talking for a while, spoke into a communicator located on her wrist, and ordered tea and coffee for them all.

She did not await the arrival of the drinks before launching into an overview of how it happened that their lives had intersected at this place and time. So, over the course of the next seventy-five minutes Barbara Fini spoke, pausing only long enough to answer an occasional question.

~~~~~~~~
~~~~~~~~

Soon after Renee Fini was accepted at her university, Barbara Fini also entered school. And while not as prestigious as Renee Fini's, it was still a respected institution (at that point in the discourse, Renee Fini thought she detected that underlying resentment in Barbara Fini's speech to which she had alluded in her conversation with Captain Eli). Barbara Fini had studied biomedical engineering with a specialty in cybernetics. After graduation, Barbara Fini had taken a position with a firm at the forefront of the development of quantum control systems for use with artificial limbs. She was assigned a position on the advanced research and development team, and even though she was still in her early twenties, had consequently made a breakthrough in the understanding of quantum fields. She shared her findings in a Thursday afternoon review meeting with the president and CEO of the firm, and on Monday she arrived at the offices of the company to find that her access card had been deactivated. Under guard she was ushered into a conference room where she found all her personal effects had been collected into plastic boxes.

As it turned out, her quantum field discovery was a means of overcoming an obstacle to furthering progress on the project. Barbara Fini was familiar with the project only from the occasional vague and guarded social media article on the subject, and she had no idea how her discovery could relate to biological manipulation. In fact, Barbara Fini thought the entire project was a boondoggle, because she could see no path for the project to successfully meet its stated objective.

It soon became clear that she was effectively a prisoner of her own government and would likely be isolated from the public for the foreseeable future. However, after several weeks of interrogation and psychological studies the true nature of the program was revealed to her which, as it turned out, was even more astonishing and unbelievable than the Molecular Organizer sham.

She was given a choice; join the project in the capacity of Director of Team Development (the people who Eli and the others referred to as The Planners) or remain under agency protection for the duration of the program. The choice was easy…remain in a nice, clean, and comfortable prison, or lead an interesting and challenging portion of a project that would have implications for all of humanity.

This was the point in the narrative when Captain Eli and Renee Fini asked the most questions…no, she never felt physically threatened while in custody…yes, she does believe her work will result in the successful implementation of the project…no, at this time she cannot share the details of her discovery or how it exactly ties into the project… no, her assignment as Director will not impact Renee Fini's role within the family.

But as she answered this last question the demeanor of Barbara Fini's face changed markedly. She appeared to be closely weighing her next words before speaking. "In fact," she muttered in a flat tone while looking Renee Fini hard in the eyes, "you were selected for this assignment only because you are my twin." Then the slightest hint of a smile appeared as she whispered, "surprise".

~~~~~~~~

Renee Fini sat alone in her room as she attempted to sort out the reality of what Barbara Fini had shared with Captain Eli and her, about the fact that she is the identical twin to the Director of Team Development, the mysterious "Planners". In fact, Barbara Fini claimed that if she had not made the quantum field breakthrough, the project would not be in the implementation phase, and none of the team would have yet been chosen. Indeed, the project would likely be in danger of being dismantled because without her breakthrough the Organizer would not be functional.
~~~~~~~~

According to Barbara Fini, Renee Fini was selected because it was assumed that it would be helpful to have one of the candidates closely related to the Director of Team Development. Having an intimate understanding of one team member's psychological and physiological profile meant the Director should quickly recognize opportunities to adjust the training plan as they presented themselves. Barbara Fini had used the recent pyramid exercise as an example of this concept. She and the members of her team had been monitoring the progress of the exercise when she recognized that Renee Fini was relying on the repeated pattern of handhold retraction to keep the team safe. So, she decided to throw Renee Fini a psychological curve ball. It would be helpful to know how Renee Fini would react if she thought, just for an instant, that she could not trust The Planners to keep her family safe in these exercises.

Barbara Fini had confirmed that there is a programmable control system that determines and controls many of the variables for each exercise. And this allowed Barbara Fini to quickly program into the controller a modification to the routine. Her intention was to make it appear that the boys were in danger of falling to their deaths as they were caught on the wall when the handholds unexpectedly retracted. She wanted to understand how Renee Fini, as exercise leader, would react during this stress situation. Renee Fini had not admitted to Barbara Fini that her "curve ball" had indeed come close to putting her into a panic situation. As it was, Renee Fini assumed she had "passed" the test associated with the introduction of this new variable, but she would likely never know for certain how her reaction had been graded by Barbara Fini and the other Planners.

Barbara Fini shared that The Planners had debated long and hard over the advisability of communicating her Director role to Renee Fini. Ultimately, The Planners determined that in such a small population as that provided by Project Sea Queen, the two of them would cross paths. Therefore, given Renee Fini's powers of deduction, it would be only a matter of time before she figured out that her twin's presence was not happenstance. In addition, it was also decided that this knowledge might add another level of complexity to their training exercises. After all, the family would never know when a new last-minute change to the training exercise might be added to test Captain Eli's second-in-command.

And as if the revelations of this day were not already challenging enough, she revealed yet another reason for Renee Fini's selection on the team. Each of the family members had a counterpart within Barbara Fini's team. These counter parts would serve as one of several back-ups, should a family member become injured or otherwise be required to drop from the project. The counterpart would not necessarily have all the skills and knowledge of the original team member, but flexibility and adaptability were deeply ingrained in the selection of each team member, as well as their counterpart. For obvious reasons, Barbara was to be Renee Fini's primary counterpart, and she held a similar skill set with the most noticeable exception being the martial arts abilities.
It was this last revelation that most intruded on the thoughts of Renee Fini as she considered all she had learned that day. She could not shake the feeling that Barbara Fini's old jealousies were still alive and held the potential to sabotage her role within the team. Renee Fini dearly hoped that she was just being overly analytical and prejudiced by a difficult childhood.

Although it turned out that Barbara Fini loved her sister and had no intention of undermining her, in the longer view of time, Renee Fini did have reason to worry.

<div align="center">~~~~~~~~~</div>

Chapter 11 – The Boys

Aarondophilous' eyes were tightly closed as he beat out the rhythm of his favorite song from his much-loved rock group, "The Hunks of Junky," on the electronic drum set. With the headphones providing the fully orchestrated, except for drums, version of the song, and with his beat merging perfectly with the score, it was easy to imagine himself preforming on a concert stage with thousands of adoring fans. Soon he was singing the lyrics of "Why was the Cat Playing Outside?" as he mimicked the famous facial expressions of the group's drummer, who went by the stage name of "Fighting Tiger".

But despite his eyes being closed, the headphones blocking out all outside sound, and his mind being lost in the lyrics of the song, Aarondophilous soon had the sense of a presence. He slowly opened his eyes and saw Captain Eli smiling as he looked down at him. Nonchalantly, Aarondophilous stopped playing and singing as he removed the headphones and addressed his visitor. "Good evening Captain," he said, "how are you this evening and what can I do for you?" "I am well, thank you. Sorry, that I came on in your room, but I had knocked several times and needed to see if you were in because it is important that we talk. May I have five minutes of your time?"

Aarondophilous nodded agreement and gestured to a chair next to the drum set. Sitting down, Captain Eli began, "Do you remember the day when we talked about how everyone in the family would occasionally be designated as the leader of our training exercises?" Aarondophilous nodded agreement and Captain Eli continued, "Well, it is your turn. You will lead tomorrow's exercise." Surprise mixed with uncertainty and just a little fear, paralyzed Aarondophilous' actions. He had understood that he would lead an exercise 'someday', but he had always assumed it would be after he was older and had more opportunity to observe how the adults handled the responsibility. It had been less than four months since he had first joined the family.

Observing the concern that was apparent within Aarondophilous' features, Captain Eli gave a reassuring smile and said, "Remember, the entire family will be there to help you, and there is neither reward nor punishment for exercise success or failure." "Yes, but we have not yet failed an exercise, and I don't want to be the first one to let the family down," replied Aarondophilous. To which Captain Eli responded, "If we fail the exercise it will not because you let us down. It will be because we, as the family, were not able to pass the test. When we fail it will not be because of a failure of whoever happens to lead the exercise that day. And notice that I said 'when' we fail, not 'if' we fail, because I am certain an exercise will come along that is simply too difficult."

"Do you know what kind of exercise it will be?" asked Aarondophilous. "No, as always, we will not receive any information about the exercise until we walk into the arena tomorrow morning," said Captain Eli as he smiled and turned toward the door of the room. Aarondophilous nodded to himself and replaced his headphones as Captain Eli closed the door after exiting the room.

<p style="text-align:center">~~~~~~~~~</p>

The next morning, despite reassurances from Captain Eli and the rest of the family, Aarondophilous nervously fidgeted as he surveyed the arena and the set-up for the morning's exercise. All that could be seen from his vantage point was a ten-meter-tall white wall that followed the contour of the arena, which was uniformly positioned about two meters from the inner arena wall. He had walked around the perimeter two times and found only one one-meter-wide opening in the wall. There were no instructions apparent, coded or otherwise, so it appeared that there was no first action dictated other than simply walking through the opening. Aarondophilous shared this conviction with the family and received nods of agreement all around.

"As the leader, I will designate Dartous to be our scout for this exercise. I don't know if size or lack thereof will present an advantage, so she is my compromise in that respect. She is heavier than Adam Boy, but lighter than Renee Fini." Turning to Dartous, he directed that she was to walk into the lighted structure and scout it for traps, clues, or hazards before he committed the entire team. She was to spend no more than five minutes before returning to the opening to report her findings. If she did not return in ten minutes, he would assume she had become incapacitated, and would send someone in to 'rescue' her.

After only two minutes Dartous returned wearing a backpack and reported that the structure appeared to be an enclosed, but well-lit maze that began with a single two-meter-wide corridor, but which split into three separate passages soon after the first turn. She also reported that the corridor's floor, at the point of the split, contained an inscription. She assumed it was a clue regarding which of the three corridors to take. Up to the point of the split, no hazards or traps were apparent. She found the backpack at the location of the split, but there did not appear to be any way to open it. "It is too heavy for a poor little woman to carry," she said with her usual smirk as she pitched the backpack to Captain Eli, who grinned as he put it on.

"Hopefully, we will figure out what we are supposed to do with the backpack, but for now, what was the clue?" asked Aarondophilous. "Don't Decide," said Dartous, with her face betraying her trade-mark grin. "What is it that you don't want me to decide?" he asked in a perplexed tone of voice. "No," she replied, "That is the clue...Don't...Decide. That is what is written on the floor of the corridor." As he looked around at the faces of the family, Aarondophilous saw the same puzzled look he himself probably wore mirrored in the faces of everyone except Dartous. She maintained her mischievous smile, which seemed to grow in delight as she observed the reactions around her.

Aarondophilous lowered his gaze as he contemplated the clue, but after half a minute or so he raised his eyes, and with a laugh said, "Well, at least it wasn't in some weird language." This brought chuckles all around, but none offered an interpretation to the clue. Finally, Aarondophilous asked, "Any suggestions?" Adam Boy was apparently waiting for an invitation to contribute, because he immediately commented, "I think it means we are to take all three corridors at the same time…that is, 'Don't Decide', take all three instead." There was a general nodding of heads as the family considered Adam Boy's interpretation.

But then Captain Eli commented, "I would like to offer a different interpretation. I wonder if the clue is telling us to go to the point of the split and wait for our next step to become apparent. That is…Don't Decide…let the maze decide for you." And continuing with a smile on his face, Captain Eli looked him directly in the eyes and said, "but, of course, it is your decision Aarondophilous." Nodding his agreement Aarondophilous murmured, "OK, let's all go to the split."

The entire family entered the maze and followed Aarondophilous along the corridor to the point where it made a ninety-degree left turn. Approximately two and a half meters beyond the corner, the corridor emptied into a small chamber about two meters on a side. Centered in each of the walls was a separate corridor and embossed in the floor of the room was the "Don't Decide" clue. Aarondophilous stepped into the chamber and motioned for the other family members to follow him. "OK," he said, "Let's check out Captain Eli's hypothesis and see if the maze tells us what to do next." A moment later when nothing happened, he looked around and noticed that all except Dartous were in the chamber. She remained in the corridor just before the chamber.

"Join us please, Dartous," he invited with his own smile and mischievous tone of voice. "It may be necessary for all of us to be in this chamber before the maze will speak to us." In response, Dartous stepped into the chamber and immediately the chamber floor appeared to sink. Reflexively Dartous jumped back into the corridor from which she had just emerged, and the downward direction of the floor immediately stopped and then reversed as it returned to its original position. Unable to resist adding a slight goading tone to his speech, Aarondophilous looked at Dartous and said, "Indeed, I think the maze is wanting you to join us." With a backward tilt of his head, Aarondophilous indicated that Dartous was to again join them in the chamber.

And when Dartous complied with Aarondophilous' direction, the chamber once again began to sink. The lowering action of the floor revealed a lighted corridor in the forward-facing wall. After the downward motion of the floor ceased Aarondophilous said, "I see no further clues, so I think the maze is telling us to move into this corridor but let me check something first." As he said this, Aarondophilous stepped into the corridor and immediately the floor began to rise once again. Aarondophilous abruptly stopped the upward motion by stepping back onto the moveable floor.

Realizing that they would not be able to return to the upper passageway once they entered the new corridor, Aarondophilous paused to survey the team regarding their choices. He pointed out that he saw only two. The first choice being that since the floor would not rise unless at least one team member stepped into the corridor, one or more of them would be forced to split from the family and explore the new passage. The only other choice was for them all to take this new route.

Benjabar was the first to voice an opinion, "It seems that if we do anything other than all take the new passage, then we are deciding something. I believe we are still under the 'Don't Decide' instruction, so I suggest we continue to let the maze instruct us and I think it is telling us to go forward." "Any other suggestions?" asked Aarondophilous.

Receiving no further comment, Aarondophilous instructed the family to position themselves so they could all quickly move into the corridor. "Everyone must move into the passage on my count of three," he instructed. The family signaled agreement, and on the three-count everyone quickly transferred to the corridor. As expected, the floor of the chamber immediately began to rise.

After the floor completed its upward movement Aarondophilous said, "Well, at first glance it appears we have only one way forward at this point. Does anyone see any new clues for how we should proceed?" A quick survey of their surroundings did not reveal any markings or patterns that would suggest what their next step would be. The corridor appeared to make a left turn only three meters ahead, so Aarondophilous decided to send Dartous ahead once again to search for traps, clues, or ploys within the corridor. This time, in less than a minute they heard a warning shout from Dartous, "I am trapped! Be careful and move slowly!"

"Captain Eli, would you go check out the situation please?" Aarondophilous asked. Captain Eli nodded agreement and moved cautiously forward, but less than a minute after turning the corner he returned with a relieved look on his face. "Dartous is okay," he said, "only a little bit embarrassed. I think it best if you all come to see for yourselves."

Following Captain Eli's example, the family moved cautiously down the passageway and all took in Dartous' predicament at the same time. The humiliated look on the face of the family's prankster made the situation almost funny, but to the credit of them all, no one laughed or even smiled.

"I became so interested in the scene that I saw painted on the wall further down the passage that I missed the obvious signs of a pressure plate. As a result, I triggered this nine-meter-wide opening in the floor behind me and at the same time a panel fell and closed off the way forward. I don't know how deep the pit is, but I cannot see the bottom, and I know it is too deep to crawl down into. There are handholds leading up this wall, but they don't seem to lead anywhere, and I was reluctant to climb on them in the possibility that they are also a part of the trap." Everyone noted the protrusions on the right-hand wall as Dartous pointed them out, "be careful that you don't trigger any other mechanisms that I may have missed," she concluded.

A careful search by the team revealed no triggers other than the pressure plate upon which Dartous stood. However, Renee Fini was quick to point out that the handholds may be the key to resetting the trap, so she said, "I suggest you take the weight off the pressure plate by using the supports." All simultaneously nodded agreement, and Dartous quickly lifted herself off the pressure plate. Immediately the opening in the floor began to close as the floor tile returned to its intended position. At the same time, the panel closing off the passageway behind Dartous slid open. The protrusions were positioned such that Dartous was able to use them to move sideways, work her way past the pressure plate, and step into the corridor beyond.

With the floor opening closed, the rest of the family used the handholds to quickly join Dartous. They then could clearly see the painting at the end of the passage that had so effectively distracted her. It was a painting of their entire family posing in front of what they took to be a large sailing ship. It was obviously a concocted painting since the family had never posed for this scene. But the thing that had most distracted Dartous, and now entranced each of them, was the name clearly visible on the side of ship: *Sea Queen*.

~~~~~~~~
~~~~~~~~

Learning from Dartous' experience, the team took several minutes to check for triggers located in the floor, walls, and ceiling that may be between themselves and the painting. At the wall upon which the painting appeared, the passageway split left and right. Other than the painting there was nothing that might offer a clue regarding which path to take, so the team began a meticulous examination of the canvas.

The family was arranged left-to-right in a line from smallest-to-largest. This, of course, placed Aarondophilous on the far left, and Benjabar on the far right. Each family member appeared to be holding a pen in one hand, and a notebook in the other. All appeared to be intensely recording something that was happening in the foreground but was not visible to the viewer. The great sailing ship behind them seemed to be docked at a wharf, but other than the lower part of a mast there was nothing shown of the ship other than the portion containing its name. Each of the family members were wearing the gray fatigues typically worn during their training exercises. The detail of the dress exactly represented every aspect of their actual appearance, down to the shape of the belt buckles supporting their pants. Even the gold bracelets on their wrists were accurately portrayed, both in appearance and in the wrist upon which the family members chose to wear them.

"Does anyone else see the one discrepancy in this painting that I see?" asked Aarondophilous. With a slight tilt of their heads, each member agreed that they indeed noted a discrepancy. Each of the family was right-handed, but in the painting, Adam Boy was holding the pen in his left hand. "It would seem to me that this painting is telling us two things," said Aarondophilous. "One thing being that Adam Boy is key to our next move, and the other being that we are to take the left-hand corridor. So, unless anyone has a better idea, I will ask Adam Boy to scout out the left-hand corridor following the same protocol as we have used previously."

No alternate interpretations were offered, and Aarondophilous indicated with a nod that Adam Boy was to reconnoiter the left-hand passage. Four minutes later Adam Boy returned with his report, which confirmed that he was the intended scout for this portion of the maze.

One of Adam Boy's accomplishments in his young life was winning the title "North American Board Game Champion" for his age group. He recognized that the floor of this passageway was painted in the pattern of cards used in a game played by few people, because of its extreme complexity. Adam Boy had avoided an irretrievable error by recognizing a rare card used in that game, one that no one else in the family would have recognized. If a player drew this card during a game, the player and all the other players not in a designated "safe zone" of the board, would immediately lose the game. Upon close inspection of the floor tile upon which the image of this card appeared, Adam Boy saw that the tile was almost certainly a pressure plate. If Dartous, or any other family member had been selected as their scout, they certainly would have stepped on that tile. Adam Boy said that while he did not know exactly what would happen, he was certain the exercise would have been counted as a loss.

"So," asked Aarondophilous, "what does this card look like? I imagine perhaps a skull and crossbones symbol, or perhaps a black snake?" "No," answered Adam Boy, "it is the picture of a baby holding a purring kitten." This brought chuckles from everyone, and all agreed that this image would not have flagged a warning to anyone but Adam Boy. Following Adam Boy, the team proceeded up the passageway, which after about fifteen meters turned left. At the point of the corridor's turn, the floor was covered with tiles that Adam Boy informed them depicted card faces from a game called "So-On". Following Adam Boy, they proceeded up the corridor until they came to the location of the tile containing the cat/baby image, of what Adam Boy called "The Card of No Return". The tile was too wide to step over and, unlike their previous challenge, there were no handholds or other means of circumventing the pressure plate.

"Any suggestions on how we get around this barrier?" asked Aarondophilous. "In fact," answered Adam Boy with a smile, "you are standing on the means of doing just that." Looking down, they all saw that they were standing on a large tile with a picture of a medieval knight in full armor carrying a bloodied broad axe. "Believe it or not," said Adam Boy, "you are standing in the 'safe zone.'" To which Aarondophilous replied, "that must be one weird game…kittens for danger and a bloody axe for safety." With a chuckle and nod of his head, Adam Boy asked Captain Eli for the heavy backpack, and then threw it onto the pressure plate of the "Card of No Return". Immediately, walls came up between them and the rest of the passageway, and a panel slid open in one of the side walls. A stairway led upward from their location toward a door.

After checking the stairway for triggers and other hazards, the team proceeded up the stairs and through the door. They found themselves emerging from the arena wall. Adam Boy slapped Aarondophilous on the shoulder and said, "Congratulations O' Fearless Leader. We have passed the exercise!"

~~~~~~~~~~

This exercise had occurred on a Friday and, per their usual Friday evening routine, after dinner Adam Boy and Aarondophilous were playing an interactive multi-player computer game of "Ubi Boys". Adam was playing the part of 'Muis' and Aarondophilous was 'Larlo'. They were closely matched in skills, with Adam Boy's greater experience giving him a slight edge. Adam Boy reached the end of the level they were playing just ahead of Aarondophilous and began the ritual celebration of victory, which included whooping and complex dance moves. Just as he was finishing the victory dance, Renee Fini walked into the game room. She smiled at the two of them and said, "I wanted to come in and congratulate the two of you on the successful completion of today's exercise."
~~~~~~~~~~

The boys nodded their thanks but looked curiously at one another. Something didn't seem quite right. She wore a navy-blue uniform rather than the gray training fatigues that they all usually wore. But in addition to that obvious difference, her demeanor did not seem quite right. She had her same beautiful smile, but there seemed a sadness in her eyes that they had never noticed before. It was a sadness that was almost palpable and permeated her entire being.

Finally, Aarondophilous turned to her and, as Adam Boy nodded agreement, said, "We had taken you for your sister, but I believe you to be Barbara Fini, am I correct?" She nodded and said, "Yes, I am, and you probably also know that I am the leader of The Planners." Not waiting for a response, she continued, "as such, I am also here to have an important conversation with the two of you." Turning to the door of the game room, she closed and locked it before continuing. "You both have intellect and abilities that are critical to the success of the project, but The Planners have spent many hours debating your participation. Your selection was through a blind process, so none of us knew how young you were. We have been observing you both closely these last weeks and have seen nothing that would suggest you are not right for the team. Nonetheless, given your age, we have decided to offer you the opportunity to withdraw from the project."

Then Barbara Fini went on to describe in greater detail the dangers and sacrifices associated with the project. She told them that in the future they would be going on a trip from which they could never return. It would be a journey to a strange and unfamiliar land. This journey and their participation in it would be important to everybody, but The Planners felt it was too much of a sacrifice to ask of two young boys without giving them the opportunity to make the decision of whether to remain or withdraw.

She further explained that although the journey would not be for another ten years, the two of them could not delay making their decision. The activities they were undergoing now were intended to train them in the combat and decision-making skills that they may need to successfully complete the mission. They would also soon start certain conditioning exercises. If one or both boys wanted out, The Planners would need to start training their replacements very soon. She assured them that if they left the team (she carefully avoided using the term "family") no one would be upset with them. She also painted a positive picture of what their life would be like if they resigned from the project. It would be a much easier life than if they remained members of the project.

As she finished, Barbara Fini said, "I know this is a big decision, and I am sorry to place the burden of making this call on yourselves. However, I trust fully in each of your abilities to make the right choice. But I will not accept an answer right now. Instead, I will meet you here one week from today at this same time. I will need your answers then. In the meantime, feel free to discuss this with your team, or let Captain Eli know if you have questions for me." With that she turned and, without allowing for questions, left the room.

~~~~~~~~~

Adam Boy could not imagine leaving his new family, but as he lay in bed at night the images of his future within the project, as painted by Barbara Fini, filled his mind. *It was an exciting but also scary future. According to what she had said, I would probably be twenty years old before we departed on the mysterious one-way journey.* He tried to imagine how his older self would feel about the decision he had to make now. He could imagine future Adam Boy being disappointed in either decision. On one hand, he might be very frustrated at the prospect of missing out on an exciting journey of such great importance. But on the other hand, would he be resentful of his younger self for denying him the opportunity of living something approaching a normal life?
~~~~~~~~~

He knew The Planners had studied closely each family member's psychological profile. He knew they had confidence in the two boy's maturity and mental capability. He knew they trusted them to make the right decision, although they were only ten and six years of age. But that didn't make the decision an easy one.

He and Aarondophilous had gone into his room that night and stayed awake well past their "lights-out" time, talking about their visit from Barbara Fini. At around midnight Captain Eli knocked on Adam Boy's door and came into the room. "Are the two of you okay?" he asked, and in response to their nods of affirmation continued, "I know of your conversation with Barbara Fini, and understand your need to talk about your decision. In fact, we intentionally delayed her visit until this evening so that, since it is Friday, you can sleep in tomorrow. However, it is getting late, and I came in to encourage you both to get some sleep." Then with a somewhat melancholy expression suddenly darkening his face, Captain Eli signaled that there was an additional reason for his visit. "I want to be absolutely certain you two clearly understand a few things. First, I want you to know that all the other members of the family fully support whatever decision you make. Second, they asked me to make certain that you know that leaving the project doesn't mean that you leave the family. We won't be able to see you every day, but we guarantee that we will visit you as often as possible, until the day we depart on our mission. We will be watching out for you and will do whatever we can to ensure you have a good life. Finally, the family asked me to emphasize that you can approach any or all of us if you need to talk through this decision."

Adam Boy had only one question for Captain Eli, "Do you think the family will have a better chance of success and meeting the mission objectives if we are replaced by people who are older?" "No," Captain Eli replied. "After watching both of you perform during our exercises to date, I can assure you that neither The Planners nor the family are concerned about the ability of either of you to support the mission. In fact, a major reason that Aarondophilous was chosen to lead the last exercise was to offer The Planners an opportunity to observe him under the added stress of leadership. And since I was part of the exhaustive selection process for screening the candidates for the family, I can say, without hesitation, that the two of you are the best fit for the family. And besides, remember that you will be older when we finally leave for our mission, so age is not an issue. Your youth at that time will likely be an important asset."

The boys had no further questions, and Captain Eli escorted Aarondophilous to his room, but it was now past 0200 hours and sleep still would not come to Adam Boy. Indeed, he would not sleep well for the next five nights, but then something happened that made the decision much easier to make.

<center>~~~~~~~~~~</center>

As he was coming into the team's cafeteria the next Monday morning, he noticed that Aarondophilous appeared to be beginning his usual breakfast of syrup-drenched pancakes, bananas, orange juice, and scrambled eggs. No other family members were present, and he was sitting alone, with his head bent, staring at his half-eaten meal. His early arrival was unusual, since Aarondophilous tended to time his breakfast so that he could maximize his time to visit with the other family members. The fact that he wasn't attacking his food with full gusto was another sign that something wasn't quite right. The two of them had agreed not to discuss their pending decision during the past weekend, although it was apparent to Adam Boy that, like him, the subject had never been far from Aarondophilous' foremost thoughts.

Adam Boy collected his own breakfast of "General Mellow" cereal with sliced peaches, French toast, and baked apples. As he sat across the table from Aarondophilous, he noticed that much of his food remained untouched. "How are you doing Squirt?" he asked, using the nickname Captain Eli often used for Aarondophilous. The only response he received was a shrug of shoulders and a shaking of head. "It's a tough decision we have to make, isn't it?" Adam Boy asked rhetorically.

Without responding, Aarondophilous looked up at last and confirmed Adam Boy's suspicion, "I am having a difficult time making my decision. I don't want to leave the family, but despite what everyone is saying, I am afraid that someone else would be better for the project than I am." "I am having similar thoughts," replied Adam Boy. "Are you concerned about the dangers and unknows about the mission?" "No," answered Aarondophilous, "I totally trust our family to be there for us, but the question I cannot answer is, will I be there for all of you when the time comes? If only I knew who would replace me, perhaps I could judge if they would be better for the mission than myself." Adam Boy was suddenly hit by an idea, "I feel the same way, but maybe there is something we can do about that."

<center>~~~~~~~~~</center>

That evening Adam Boy arrived early to the conference room, and nervously paced around the table in the center of the room. He had quickly finished his breakfast that morning and waited for Captain Eli to finish his. He then requested this meeting with the Captain and Barbara Fini. Aarondophilous would also be in the meeting but had not yet arrived. As the older of the two, he and Aarondophilous had agreed that he would lead their side of the meeting. Throughout the day, whenever the opportunity presented itself, he had rehearsed his opening and closing statements. He also had thoroughly thought through all the arguments he and Aarondophilous had developed in support of their appeal. But despite all his preparation, Adam Boy was not at all confident that their request would be granted. He could imagine several legitimate counterarguments and objections that the adults could make.

When the door to the conference room opened and all the other participants entered the room, Adam Boy found himself relieved. At least he would be getting this meeting over with, so he could find a little of the relaxation that had been eluding him all day. After the usual social greetings were completed Adam Boy began his rehearsed speech, "Aarondophilous and I requested this meeting because we are both having a difficult time deciding whether or not to withdraw from the project. We both want to stay with the family but agree that, despite assurances to the contrary, we are uncertain whether that is the best thing for the mission." Before he could continue his speech, Barbara Fini raised her hand and interjected, "I probably should have made it clear from the beginning that, unless it is a breach of security or will endanger you or others, we will give you whatever you need in order to make your decisions." This simple statement of support eliminated much of the need for Adam Boy to continue down his prepared path of arguments and justifications, and it led him to proceed directly to the part of their request that most concerned him.

"Actually, we are thinking that you may consider the implementation of our request to involve a violation of security protocol," said Adam Boy, who in response to quizzical looks from the adults continued, "because we want to meet the primary candidates selected to replace us should we decide to leave the project." If Barbara Fini and Captain Eli were surprised by this request it did not show in their demeanor. It was Barbara Fini who responded with a thoughtful look on her face, "Yes, this would violate the protocols The Planners have established for the project. However, I think it is possible to grant your request. In fact, if Captain Eli agrees, I think we can do more than just arrange a meeting. I think we can come up with something that will make it remarkably interesting and, at the same time, provide you the assurance you seek."

<center>~~~~~~~~~</center>

Three days later, Barbara Fini and the Captain obtained agreement from The Planners to use a part of the boys' academic study time to proceed with her plan. Adam Boy was standing by Aarondophilous in the middle of the training arena next to a table with four chairs, two each on the long sides of the table. He was probably one of the few people who could read the apprehension in Aarondophilous that was betrayed by subtle body movements and gestures. Shortly after their arrival, a door opened in the arena wall and two individuals entered the stadium-like space of the training floor. They wore clothing like that worn by the family, except for the color. The family's training uniform was a light gray, while that of the two strangers was a pale brown. They appeared to be in their early twenties. One was a man, and the other was a woman. Somehow, instinctively, Adam Boy knew the man was his counterpart.

After reaching the table, everyone nodded a greeting and took a seat. For reasons that were not completely explained, they had been told to avoid physical contact and to not introduce themselves, so there were no handshakes or other traditional forms of welcome. The young man sat across from Adam Boy, and the young woman was across from Aarondophilous. The young man spoke first, "I am incredibly happy to meet with the two of you. I have been very curious about the person I would replace should the need arise. I must admit that you both are much younger than I anticipated." The young woman nodded agreement with this statement. Adam Boy did not say it but thought to himself; *Funny, but I, by some means, know you are my counterpart, and you look almost exactly how I pictured you.* And he somehow knew that Aarondophilous was thinking the same thing about his counterpart.

Adam Boy smiled and responded by asking, "Were you told anything at all about why we are being allowed to meet?" This time the woman spoke, "No, we were not, can you share the reason?" Aarondophilous shook his head in answer to her question but continued to defer to Adam Boy, since this had been his idea, and they had agreed that he would lead the discussion. Adam Boy said, "We were told not to tell you our reasons, but I can confirm this meeting is at the request of the two of us." The man smiled in response and said, "Well again, whatever the reasons, we are glad to have this opportunity to meet with you. However, we were told that for security reasons we can't ask you any direct questions." Adam Boy returned the smile and said, "We were given a little more leeway. We know we can't ask about your history, but we would like to learn more about you. The first question I would like to ask is…what are your specialties?"

The woman responded that she is a historian and mathematician. The man advised that he is a martial arts specialist with a strong background in science. Adam Boy nodded as he recognized that their counterpart's skill sets overlapped their own, but something in the way they responded suggested that those overlapping talents did not reflect their primary expertise. *But* he thought to himself, *that doesn't necessarily mean they are weaker in those abilities than Aaron and me.* "How long have you been training for the mission?" Adam Boy asked. "We participated in our first training exercises thirty-eight months ago," responded the man. This was over two years before Adam Boy had been first approached by those people he now recognized were recruiting for the project. Again, this should have surprised him, but it did not. Why it did not was a puzzle to Adam Boy. Somehow, he just knew that the man and woman had been involved with the project much longer than he and Aarondophilous. *Score one point in favor of us leaving the project. Doing so would make room for these more-experienced replacements,* thought Adam Boy.

Adam Boy said, "We are limited to only five minutes for this meeting, so we may have time for only one more question." After a slight pause he continued, "why did you agree to join the project?" At this question, both the woman and the man seemed surprised and somewhat caught off guard. This time the woman answered passionately, "This is one of the greatest opportunities to help humanity in the history of the world." The man then interjected, "How could we not accept the opportunity to help save humankind by agreeing to work with the Molecular Organizer? Personally, I would look forward to working the challenging undersea environments in which the Molecular Organizer will be placed."

Both the boys maintained neutral expressions while their minds raced. Adam Boy did not expect this response. He quickly deduced that their counterparts did not know the Organizer story to be a sham, and that their assignment would involve a journey, not to the bottom of the ocean, but to a place from which they could never return. He had the distinct impression that they thought this would be an experience from which they would someday retire and perhaps write a book about. They seemed genuinely nice and intelligent people, but they were certainly working under a series of powerful misconceptions. *I score this one on the side of something that will encourage me to stay with the project,* thought Adam Boy. He suspected that if their counterparts knew the truth, they would be significantly less enthusiastic about the mission. However, before anyone could follow-up on this line of questioning, Barbara Fini stepped into the arena and said, "Okay, this is a good time to introduce the exercise we have planned for the four of you."

~~~~~~~~~

The boys stood on the opposite side of the arena from where their counterparts stood. All four were wearing body armor. In addition, each of them had been given one of the padded combat clubs, complete with the electroshock/freeze feature. Positioned near the middle of the arena floor were what appeared to be the same large cubes used in the family's first exercise. The relative orientation of the cubes was also similar.
~~~~~~~~~

Barbara Fini explained that the primary trainee group, the family, and the secondary trainee group, the family's counterparts, were undergoing training that utilized similar, but different, methods. She indicated that The Planners had decided to use this requested meeting to test the effectiveness of the two training strategies. Adam Boy was certain the activity was designed for more than just testing out differing training methods, although this reason was probably partially true. But while he couldn't say for certain, he felt the exercise had to do specifically with helping the boys make their decision.

The measurement of success was to be simple. The winners would be the team that incapacitated both of their opponents. A team could lose one of their members, provided both of their opponents were incapacitated in the end. While awaiting the sound of a horn, which would signal the beginning of the exercise, the two boys discussed their strategy. Adam Boy and Aarondophilous agreed that their counterparts would probably decide to split up and approach from opposite sides of the arena perimeter. This would be an attempt to flank them and draw them into engaging one-on-one with their counterparts. Adam Boy and Aarondophilous would take defensive stances, as if they were waiting for their opponents to reach them. Then on Adam Boy's signal they would sprint for the cubes, which they hoped would indicate an intention to set-up a protective position. Then on his second signal, they planned to execute the rest of their plan.

When their counterparts were separated from them by about twenty meters, and from each other by about twenty-five meters, Adam Boy yelled, "Now!" The two began their sprint toward the cubes, and at the appropriate time Adam Boy again yelled, "Now!", the boys made a ninety-degree turn toward Aaron's counterpart. Knowing that they would not have much time before the man, the martial arts expert, reached them, they quickly executed their attack on the woman. When only two meters away, Aarondophilous distracted her by throwing his combat club at her head. As she dodged the club, Adam Boy quickly froze her with a jab of his club to her knee. Without breaking stride, Aarondophilous retrieved his club and Adam Boy picked up the one dropped by the woman. With Adam Boy carrying both his club and the captured one, they resumed their sprint toward the large cubes. The man was trailing by only ten meters and gaining. Rather than climbing the cubes the boys split up and disappeared behind opposite sides of the cube arrangement.

The man followed Aarondophilous to the back side of the cubes and was surprised to find the boy apparently frozen in fright as he knelt in a defensive position with his back against the wall of one of the midsized cubes. The man paused for an instant, as he looked for Adam Boy and looked up just as the ten-year-old who had doubled back, jumped from the top of the cube while throwing the confiscated combat club. The man easily dodged the club, but he was distracted enough that it allowed Adam Boy to land untouched on a spot only two meters in front of him. Adam Boy used his combat club to parry an initial blow from the man, but the man easily followed up with a blow of enough force to knock the boy's club out of his hands. Just as the man prepared to freeze Adam Boy with a jab of his combat club, the "frightened" six-year-old jumped quickly to life and used his own club to freeze the man with a blow to his side. The exercise was over, and the boys had won.

<center>~~~~~~~~</center>

That evening after dinner, the boys met again with Captain Eli and Barbara Fini.   They were all drinking hot chocolate with marshmallows and the conversation was casual. The boys seemed more relaxed than they had since being given the option of withdrawing from the project. After talking for about twenty minutes, Barbara Fini congratulated the boys on their victory that afternoon and asked them how they felt about it. Adam Boy replied, "I have been surprised that the family has never lost an exercise, but I am especially surprised that Aarondophilous and I were able to pull this one off." "Both of your counterparts have combat ratings higher than either of you. Why do you think you were able to defeat them?" Captain Eli asked. "I don't know," replied Aarondophilous, "it just seems that we could guess what the other guys were going to do and could beat them to the punch."

"The fact is," said Barbara Fini, "you both are very smart young men, but we had many candidates for your positions that are equally smart. But what put you ahead of all the other candidates screened by Captain Eli was the fact that you scored off the charts when tested for intuition." "Yes," agreed Captain Eli, "when I saw your intuition scores, I knew I wanted you for the family. Your encounter with your counterparts provides examples of how strong your intuition quotient is. Just from the basis of your short conversation with them, you were able to deduce every move the others would make. In fact, I wager that each of you recognized which of those individuals had been chosen as your counterpart even before you knew their skill sets." "Yes," confirmed Adam Boy, "it seemed that I knew my counterpart by sight even before he said anything." To this Barbara Fini replied, "That was due to the amazing intuition ability each of you exhibit. So, now you know why we feel confident that, despite your youth, you can provide excellent support to the family if you should decide to stay with the project."

Aarondophilous replied to this by saying, "Adam Boy and I have decided to stay with the family." But Captain Eli replied, "You still have a few days before you have to give us an answer. So, wait until your week is up before making a final decision just in case you change your minds." They did not change their minds.

~~~~~~~~~~~
~~~~~~~~~~~

Chapter 12 - Benjabar and Dartous

Benjabar was in a contemplative mood as he considered all that had occurred in the year since he had first met Captain Eli and the rest of the family.   His thoughts included the more than two hundred combat and decision-making exercises that the family had experienced.   The objectives of which the family had always, apparently, succeeded in attaining.   He smiled to himself as he realized that the word "apparently" interjected itself because specific objectives had never been communicated to the family, although after each exercise it seemed apparent what the basic objective had been.   Of course, they never knew what less-apparent purposes Barbara Fini and The Planners had in mind for each exercise. However, Barbara Fini, their only contact within The Planners group, would occasionally share elements of the hidden agenda with the family.   The most eye-opening of these revelations was shared shortly after Aarondophilous and Adam Boy had announced their intention to stay with the program.

At that time Captain Eli received permission to share with the entire family that which he had just shared with the boys. This revelation being that intuition had been an extremely important factor in their selection. And the purpose of the exercises went far beyond combat and general mental development. Because their assignment would involve unknowable spheres of experience for which specific training could not be provided, it was critical that the exercises be designed such that they further expanded the family's already high intuition quotients.

For the next few weeks thereafter, the family discussed among themselves how each had indeed found themselves anticipating the actions of the others to a greater and greater degree. This applied even to the faceless Planners who designed the exercises, because they had found themselves more and more often anticipating the next move needed for their continued success in meeting the requirements of the day's exercise.

Sometimes the exercises included interactions with persons outside the family in which complex board games and mental exercises were involved. However, even though the faces of those persons were often covered, and they had no context in which to judge them, virtually every move made by them was anticipated by the family members. Every family member became almost unerring in their ability to anticipate the moves and needs of the others on the team.

As the months of training progressed, it became increasingly apparent to the family that these instincts and insights had led them to continued success. And Benjabar recognized the fact that they had all come to the point where they entered an exercise fully expecting to be successful. Therefore, neither he, nor any of the family, anticipated their first failure when it came.

~~~~~~~~~

Benjabar was leading the exercise which began as a simple combat drill, taking place in the empty arena using the same combat clubs and armor used in previous exercises.
The major difference, apparent from the beginning of the exercise, was the number of attackers involved. In all previous exercises the attackers had numbered between six and fifteen. Benjabar quickly counted thirty attackers mustered opposite the location of the family across the arena.

Promptly, Benjabar ordered the family into a semicircle with their backs to the arena wall. He positioned himself at the left end of the semicircle with Adam Boy on his right, between he and Renee Fini. She had Aarondophilous on her right, and to his right was Captain Eli. Anchoring the right end of the semicircle was Dartous.
~~~~~~~~~

At the sound of the starting horn, the attackers formed a V-shaped line and rushed the family. When the attackers were twenty meters from the family Benjabar yelled, "Advance!" In response, the family simultaneously moved forward with Renee Fini at the head of the advance, and the rest of the family falling back to form a tight complete circle. The unexpected nature of this maneuver allowed them to effectively split the V-formation in two. By dividing the attackers in this way, most of them were incapacitated by the family in short order. However, just as the last attacker was being frozen, a fresh set of thirty attackers entered the arena.

This was a new twist…in previous similar exercises, freezing the last attacker was usually followed by the horn signaling the end of the exercise. It was readily apparent that the second set of aggressors was more skilled than the first, because the family was rapidly engaged even though these new attackers were hampered by the disabled forms of their comrades strewn about the family's defense circle. And rather than the somewhat random nature of the first attack, the new charge appeared to be well-coordinated and specific in intent.

With a great loss of its members the aggressors executed their attack, which they initiated by forming two equal wedges. One wedge forced themselves between Benjabar and Adam Boy, and the other wedge between Renee Fini and Adam Boy. The result was that Adam Boy was quickly surrounded and cut off from the rest of the family. The family members saw what was happening and quickly adjusted their positions such that, they effectively struck the flanks of the attackers. All but eleven of the enemy were ultimately frozen, but not before they succeeded in freezing Adam Boy.

The surviving aggressors retreated to the far-side of the arena but were quickly joined by fifteen reinforcements to renew the attack, which again involved sacrificing themselves heavily. This time the assault focused on Renee Fini, who was also frozen before the sixteen surviving attackers could be forced into retreat.

Benjabar deduced that the order in which the family members were being isolated and attacked was determined in a purely random manner, as if determined by the role of a die. This randomness made it impossible for Benjabar to determine which family member the subsequent attack would target until the attacker's offensive line formed. Due to the rapid deployment of the aggressors, their actions proved too late to mount the optimum defense. So, it was apparent that The Planners had undoubtedly introduced randomness into the exercise to diminish the effectiveness of the family's high intuition quotients. This randomness, coupled with the suicide-like tactics of the attackers, made a successful defense extremely difficult, if not impossible. Indeed, during their post-exercise analysis, the family agreed that the success of any defense against even a non-random attack would have been in doubt because of the seemingly limitless number of attackers, and their willingness to sacrifice themselves.

The fourth attack wave, which included the sixteen survivors plus ten new fighters, isolated and eliminated Captain Eli. And the fifth wave contained twenty attackers who focused on Aarondophilous and then Dartous, both of whom were frozen, which left Benjabar to face the nine remaining aggressors. But, as soon as Dartous was frozen, the horn sounded signaling the end of the exercise.

Benjabar realized that his being the only family member left viable was probably the only non-random part of the exercise. The Planners obviously wanted him to make it to the end of the exercise to give him, as the leader of the exercise, the maximum opportunity to adjust his defensive strategy.

The attackers retreated from Benjabar by ten meters and assumed a parade-rest stance. A door in the wall behind Benjabar opened and Barbara Fini entered the arena. Without ceremony, apology, or comment on the outcome she looked about at the large number of debilitated individuals and said, "We thought it time to hand the family its first defeat." To this Benjabar responded, "I am sure you had your reasons."

Without responding, Barbara Fini ordered the remaining attackers to put their combat clubs on their unfreeze settings, and to release all disabled persons from their frozen state. She then turned quickly and silently and left the arena.

~~~~~~~~~

Afterwards, the family members retired to the conference room used for their debriefings and found Barbara Fini waiting for them when they arrived. She was sitting at one end of the table and with a wave of her hand invited the family to join her.

After the family was seated Barbara Fini began to speak, "Does anyone wish to hazard a guess regarding the purpose of today's exercise?" The adults nodded their heads in the affirmative, and the two boys energetically raised their hands. Through a faint smile she nodded at Aarondophilous and said, "Please tell us what you think the purpose was." To which he responded, "To show us that sometimes it is impossible to win, and we will run out of options."

Barbara Fini nodded her head and turning to Adam Boy asked, "But in the real world what other option is available to us if we are faced with impossible odds?" To which he responded, "We can surrender." Placing her hands on the top of the table she said, "You are absolutely correct Adam Boy, and that is the new variable added to your exercises starting tomorrow." Raising both arms above her head and clasping her hands together she continued, "from this day forward, if any of the team presents this signal the exercise will terminate, and it will be recorded as a surrender by the team."
Then turning to Benjabar, Renee Fini asked, "As the leader of today's exercise, please tell us the purpose of this new variable." Standing up straight and tall, Benjabar turned his eyes slowly upon each family member as he spoke with his gaze finally resting on Barbara Fini, "When our training is complete and we are on-mission, we may face situations that are impossible to overcome, and we will need to surrender to fight another day. This new variable will serve to encourage the use of our intuitive abilities to recognize when those times arrive."
~~~~~~~~~

With that Barbara Fini slowly nodded the affirmative, rose, and left the room.

~~~~~~~~~~

That evening Dartous sat at the desk in her quarters and considered this new twist in their training. She had puzzled countless times since joining the family about the nature of their assignment. *Why was their training focusing so heavily on combat scenarios? And what were they going to face that posed such a challenge that they needed to learn what unwinnable situations looked like…situations in which it would be better to surrender to a force rather than fight it?*

The entire team had been told that they would be traveling to a strange and dangerous land from which they could never return. For Dartous, this led to only one conclusion about their assignment. Although identities were well hidden, it was apparent that the family members came from widespread points across the earth. And some of them, like herself, were likely well-traveled. *So, where on Earth could they possibly go that would be as strange as they were led to understand?* For Dartous, there was only one possible answer, but she needed to confide her conclusions in someone she trusted. And at that very moment that person knocked on the door to her quarters.

~~~~~~~~~~

Dartous opened her door and invited Benjabar into the room. He was responding to her request for a private meeting. But it was unusual for one team member to request such a meeting with another, so she knew that his curiosity regarding the nature of her intended topic must have been strong. He had obviously exercised restraint and had not pressed her for information about her reasons for the meeting, so out of respect for him she wasted no time in sharing her thoughts.

"I believe we are being sent on a one-way mission to another star for the purpose of Earth colonization, and I believe the Organizer is actually some sort of quantum-drive for a spacecraft capable of traveling at or near the speed of light." Continuing she said, "I wanted to bounce my thoughts on this hypothesis off of you, and I know you have questions about how I came to this conclusion, but please let me first lay out my reasons for you."

With that, Dartous explained that the first clue was the fact that Barbara Fini had been recruited based on her work with quantum fields, and specifically quantum control systems. It seems reasonable to expect that something as sophisticated as a light-speed drive would require control complexity that would be attainable only with a quantum system.

The next clue had been Barbara Fini's use of the phrase "out of this world" to describe the project's progress several times over the course of the past year, on those rare occasions when she attended the team's post-exercise debriefings. And while at first it appeared to be only an expression of excitement over the progress the team was making toward its goal, Dartous came to believe this was a subconscious desire by Barbara Fini to communicate the nature of the project to the family.

To Dartous, this supposition also fit with the fact that this was to be a one-way trip. Even at near light-speed, it would likely take three to six years of subjective time to make the trip. However, due to the dilation of time that occurs at those speeds, Earth-based observers would likely count decades, if not centuries, before the spacecraft reached a star system with a habitable planet. Even if the technology is sufficient to make a return trip, it is unlikely civilization will survive for the long years that would be required to do so.

In Dartous' estimation, there were probably two primary objectives for their mission. The first being simply to test out the new technology with a human crew, and the second being to scout out the new planet, confirm its suitability for human habitation, and prepare it for the colonists that would follow later. This second objective would explain the diversity of skill sets within the family…all of which would be required to understand and effectively utilize an ecosystem that is likely to be completely foreign to the travelers. And the training exercises are obviously designed to enhance their problem-solving and physical capabilities, which would all be valuable assets when facing the unknown dangers and challenges of an alien world.

Dartous posited that this scenario would explain the need for the extreme secrecy associated with the project. The colony ships could carry only a small percentage of Earth's inhabitants. Chaos would rule if it became known that the Project Sea Queen plan required most of the world's population to essentially be abandoned to a dying Earth.

Dartous completed a synopsis of her thoughts, and with only a slight nod of her head and raised eyebrows made a nonverbal request of Benjabar's opinion regarding her thesis.

<center>~~~~~~~~</center>

"I have entertained thoughts of a similar concept," began Benjabar, with a nod of his head. "However, I doubt that the hopes of mankind will hinge on the successful outcome of a single scenario. My guess is that this is only one scenario among other options being pursued. Maybe there really is an Organizer under development somewhere that will be capable of restoring the biosphere of our planet, or even an approach that we cannot yet imagine." "I agree," responded Dartous, "but you do concur that that my colonization hypothesis is a likely scenario for our project?"

With a nod to the affirmative Benjabar began to ask questions, and the discussion between the two consisted of a give-and-take lasting several hours. The following reflects the gist of that conversation…

Benjabar: When did she think the family would depart?

Dartous: She assumed the timeframe given by Barbara Fini…ten years from when the family was formed…to be approximately correct. Assuming the Organizer is the ship's drive, it would probably take that long to complete testing of the drive, and to build the spacecraft that it would power.

Benjabar: When did Dartous think the colonist ship would depart?

Dartous: Given the severity of the Earth's situation, she assumed both the family's scout ship and the colony ships would undergo construction at the same time. However, assuming one gravity of acceleration, it would take the scout ship one year to approach the speed of light. Her guess was that The Planners would observe data from the scout ship for the first six months of their journey to ensure there were no problems due to hardware failures, software failures, or theoretical miscalculations. Given the great distances involved, it would take three months for the last of the six-month data from the scout ship to be received, and another three months to be fully analyzed. If these assumptions were correct, it would mean the analysis of this data stream from the scout ship would be completed approximately one year after the launch of the scout ship. If at the end of that year there were no irregularities, she theorized that The Planners would launch the colonists.

Benjabar: When did she think construction of the two ships would start?

Dartous: She guessed that both were already under construction in orbit. The colony ship, of course, would be much larger than the scout ship, and the complexity of design would be exponentially greater since the colonists' support needs would be much greater. The design would need to address issues like medical care, and accommodations for the educational needs of the children, who would likely be included among the families found within the colonist population.

Benjabar: Did Dartous have any guesses regarding the star to which they would travel?

Dartous: No, but she assumed The Planners knew exactly where they were going. Again, she suspected the quantum control breakthrough was the key to this decision. She believed that telescopes using this technology had made long-range observations of likely candidates. She also guessed that the telescopes were mounted within unmanned spacecraft powered by miniature versions of the Organizer drive, which meant the observations were likely made outside the Oort Cloud and therefore unobscured by any near-Earth objects.

Benjabar: If they were traveling to another world, why did she think The Planners had placed so much emphasis on their historical training?

Dartous: She theorized that The Planners knew surprisingly much about the destination planet due to the extremely high-resolution Quantum Telescope technology…

Benjabar: Did this mean that Dartous thought The Planners had detected a civilization on the new planet?

Dartous: Yes, she postulated that the new quantum breakthroughs had also resulted in computers with unimagined computing capabilities. Computers utilizing algorithms with the capability of projecting the current level of an observed civilization forward in time. This capability would be required, because anything observed now is likely tens or hundreds of years out of date because of the time required for light to travel to the Earth from the observed planet. This is further complicated by the fact that by the time the family reached the destination planet, its civilization would have further advanced by multiple decades, if not a century or more. Considering the focus of the family's historical studies, Dartous sensed that The Planners expected them to encounter a civilization roughly equivalent to the one found on Earth two hundred to five hundred years ago. The ability to understand the culture and to communicate with the inhabitants of the planet would obviously be critical. This also explained why The Planners wanted to include in the family a highly capable linguist, such as Benjabar, who could decipher the dominate language of the planet and teach it to the family and the colonists.

Benjabar: Much of our training seems combat-related, but do you think The Planners really think we could take on an entire planet's population should they become hostile?

Dartous: No, she was speculating that when the family arrives, the civilization will still be relatively primitive with a comparatively small population. There should be plenty of unpopulated or sparsely populated space in which the colony could settle and keep interactions and conflicts with the population at a minimum.

Benjabar: In addition to history the family's training, even the adult's, is focused considerably on geography. If we are traveling to another planet, why is this necessary?

Dartous: The answer to this question had at first eluded her, but Dartous ultimately speculated that The Planners would direct the family to assign names to geographical features that would sound familiar and reassuring to the colonists. She could imagine that they might name one of the planet's continents "New Asia", a particular mountain range, the "Himalayan Rockies", or a given portion of an ocean as the "Caribbean Gulf".

After quizzing Dartous about the details of her ideas regarding the mission objectives, Benjabar suggested some modifications. He felt that The Planners would not put all their eggs in the "Eli Family" basket. He suspected that the team that was undergoing training elsewhere were not just back-up candidates to be pulled into the family should one or more of their members become incapacitated. Benjabar felt it likely that there was a second scout ship being built that would contain the second team. This, of course, would improve the chance of project success. This alternate team may be sent to the same planet or more likely, a completely different star system. And, if so, each team would have separate colony ships following their paths.

Benjabar postulated that even if theirs was the only scout ship, The Planners would want to send two colony ships, as a means of increasing the odds that at least one group of colonists would reach their destination.

Benjabar also offered an alternate explanation regarding the family's focus on the study of geography. Yes, they would likely name certain features after their Earth counterparts, but the more immediately important reason would be to help the scouts recognize the likely geology associated with various types of terrain. In the coming years, the colonists would require access to natural resources, so Benjabar assumed it was the geology associated with each geographical feature that would become the main point of this portion of their education.

Regarding the stage of development reached by the planet's inhabitants, Benjabar speculated that to become immersed fully in this alien culture they would adopt a habit of referencing dates to the corresponding period of Earth history. For example, if they found the primary culture of the planet to correspond to Europe's early medieval period, they might adopt a convention of referring to their arrival time as 850 AD. This would amount to a psychological exercise designed to act as a constant reminder to adapt to the culture and norms of that period as a way of fitting in with the inhabitants. Of course, he admitted, if the inhabitants of the new planet happened to be giant bugs, fitting in would become moot.

At last, the two family members exhausted the subject, and agreed that Dartous' hypothesis was reasonable although unverifiable with the data at hand. And much of their speculation seemed to be somewhat of a stretch, but it still made for an interesting night's conversation.

~~~~~~~~~~

It was about six months later that Dartous heard the first rumblings of the events that would greatly accelerate their departure timeframe.

In recent weeks, each of the family members had led at least two training exercises in which it quickly became obvious that the overwhelming odds against them would make success impossible or very unlikely. And she found it interesting to note how, without much discussion among the family members, their definition of a successful exercise outcome had changed. Whereas success had previously meant that the leader of the day's exercise had managed to lead the team to discover and complete the objective for the day, their new definition of success became little or no loss of team integrity, with defeat of their opponents becoming a secondary objective. Sometimes these opponents were combatants, as in the case of Benjabar's loss, but sometimes the challenges came in the form of the exercise parameters. This had been the case with one of Dartous' own losses.
~~~~~~~~~~

Dartous and the family were faced with a baffling choice involving the need to select among thirty different doors. Benjabar had deciphered a clue provided by The Planners in a language that Dartous suspected was fabricated, to particularly challenge Benjabar's linguistic abilities. However, it was the content of the clue that led her to ultimately concede the exercise.

The full message of the clue was simple…only one of the thirty doors would lead to success. Anyone choosing any of the remaining twenty-nine doors would die of a plague… of course no one would die, but she understood that any family member passing through the "plague" door would be neutralized for the purpose of the exercise. She quickly calculated that, assuming no new information about the identity of the non-plague door was discovered, sending the team through the doors one at a time would result in less than a twenty-five percent chance of success, even if every family member were forfeited. And even allowing for the high intuitive abilities of the family members, the probability of success before all family members were neutralized was likely well below fifty percent. So, she decided to "sacrifice" herself as she randomly chose a door and passed through it. Her reasoning was that new information might be generated by the act of triggering the "kill" mechanism associated with moving through the door. But, as team leader, before entering the door she ordered Captain Eli to forfeit the exercise in the event her participation in that day's training was deactivated, and the door selection failed to reveal additional clues. Immediately upon passing through the selected door, her exercise uniform froze indicating she was "dead". Her sacrifice failed to reveal additional clues and Captain Eli capitulated.

~~~~~~~~
~~~~~~~~

It was when the frequency of the no-win exercises increased rapidly that Dartous began to suspect something had changed in The Planner's sense of urgency. Typically, changes in The Planners actions were gradual and systematic but now, over the course of less than a month's time, they had radically raised the difficulty level of the family's exercises. It seemed to her that the training intended to take place over the course of years was now being introduced at a pace designed to cram it into a timeframe measured in weeks or months. And now, exercises were being scheduled at times formally designated as rest periods. But it was when The Planners announced that educational periods would be shortened to allow for additional training exercises that Dartous was certain something drastic had occurred, forcing a significant shortening of their project initiation timeline.

The family had not discussed this sudden change in their training activities, but Dartous was certain that all suspected that the former ten-year training plan was being reduced to one substantially shorter. Although few outside the family would likely notice anything, by observing how he had reacted to the latest change in their training schedule, Dartous was certain that Captain Eli would broach the subject with the family soon.

However, patience was not a virtue that she possessed in great abundance, so Dartous decided to use her free time to reconnoiter the compound and look for clues that might explain the current urgency.

She decided the most likely building to see unusual activity was the one containing the Organizer. Although at first denied access to the perimeter building surrounding the Organizer room, the family had eventually received clearance allowing them to participate in the general project progress meetings occasionally held in the building's meeting hall. However, Dartous received her first hard clue that something had changed regarding the project character when the security system denied her access to the facility.

Dartous' next stop was the main cafeteria, which was the only eating facility available to the project's general population. She reasoned that if she observed a noticeable change in the identity or behaviors of those individuals utilizing the facility, it might give her an idea about what was driving the change in project schedule.

She arrived at the facility midafternoon, obtained a glass of milk with assorted cookies which she slowly ate while pretending to read a book. In this way, she watched the comings and goings over the next four hours. There was no one who looked unfamiliar, but it seemed to her that the traffic in the cafeteria was less than half of that expected for the time of day, and she extrapolated this information to mean that much of the project team was absent. And she further deduced that it was likely the missing project members had been evacuated from the site.

As Dartous finally stood to leave the cafeteria she received yet another clue. A technician whom Dartous recognized, but had never spoken with, approached with the clear intent to strike up a conversation with her. This was unusual since it was understood by all family members that the general population of the project had been directed to not engage any of the family unless initiated by them. This notion had been tested and verified several times by various family members, and no one ever approached them regardless of how intrusive they had made their presence. Dartous had once intentionally approached an area of the compound to which she was restricted, and it was clear the security detail was even reluctant to engage her, and when they did it was with no more conversation than was absolutely necessary…basically it had been "…please do not enter…" followed by a wave of the hand telling her to return to an authorized area.

The technician's name tag read "Rosen" which, like all project members, was certainly not the name she was known by before she joined the project. Perhaps the technician was emboldened by the fact that, like Dartous, she was Asian and female. But as Dartous turned to acknowledge her, the technician's demeanor became belligerent and openly hostile as she said, "It must be nice to have no need to worry about being pulled from bed and shipped out without notice nor opportunity to say good-bye to your friends."

Before Dartous could reply, two other technicians rushed up and each grasped an arm of the upset woman. "Come on Rosen," one of the technicians said as they pulled her toward the exit, "we need to talk to you about that defective transducer." By the panicked looks on their faces, it was obvious that these technicians were trying to keep their co-worker from saying too much, so Dartous immediately decided to follow the trio. However, as she approached the exit, one of the ever-present security personnel stepped into her path and asked to check her wrist band.

The security representative removed a device from her utility belt and passed it over Dartous' gold wrist band. She studied the screen on the device for at least a full minute, although Dartous knew the read-out on the device would be near instantaneous. She ultimately nodded to Dartous with an apology for detaining her. This had never occurred before, which led Dartous to conclude that this was simply a delaying tactic…they didn't want her talking to the agitated technician.

As expected, by the time she exited the cafeteria location Rosen was no longer in sight, and Dartous suspected that she would never see her again. At this point, any doubts about her suspicions were removed, and Dartous determined to seek out Captain Eli and ask him to get to the bottom of things.

<div align="center">~~~~~~~~~~</div>

Before she could find the Captain, an orderly found Dartous and informed her that Captain Eli had requested an immediate meeting with Dartous, along with the rest of the family. She ran to the group's debriefing room and found Captain Eli there along with the rest of the family. Clearly Captain Eli had waited for the entire family to be present before starting the meeting, because as soon as she was seated, he began. "I know you all have noticed the shifts in project operations that have transpired in recent days. Let me say first that I do not know more than any of you about what is happening. However, I have decided to ask Barbara Fini for a meeting on the issue. But before talking to her I wanted to meet with the family." Then as Captain Eli's gaze rested on Dartous he continued, "I have resisted any urges to probe the matter up until this moment, but I know that some of you have investigated these happenings on your own, and before contacting Barbara Fini I wanted to know what you have discovered. Who wants to go first?"

As it turned out, Dartous had not been the only family member to do some exploring. However, Dartous was the first to speak and told the group everything that had occurred earlier that day along with her suppositions about it all relating to a rapid evacuation of much of the project team. The others' experiences led them to come to the same general conclusion as had Dartous.

After every family member had spoken on the subject, Captain Eli concluded by saying, "I will request that Barbara Fini meet with all the family but failing that request, I will request a private meeting with her. In that event, I promise to tell you as much about what is going on as I am so authorized."

The family's remote communications with each other were via a texting device that they commonly strapped to their forearms. The only person they were linked to through this device, other than the family, was Barbara Fini. Captain Eli gazed at his device in preparation for contacting her, but as he was raising his arm holding the communicator its message alert light started blinking, a smile reached the Captain's lips, and he said, "It seems that our Director of Planners has anticipated my request and is requesting to meet with us now." With that he accepted the meeting with a single tap of the communicator's screen.

Less than a minute later Barbara Fini knocked on the door to the meeting room and entered without awaiting an acknowledgement. She began to speak and, with a shake of her head, declined the chair offered to her by the Captain. "I think it best if I stand for this meeting." Continuing she explained, "This will be more in the form of a presentation rather than a discussion. Information relative to what I will be communicating has been loaded into this room's presentation processor and will be automatically deleted at the conclusion of this presentation." Although unsaid, the message was clear...*listen closely, because this is the only time you will hear what is to follow.*

"Begin presentation," Barbara Fini commanded the artificial intelligence resident in the processor. The machine's capabilities were such that no further commands would be necessary. The audio monitoring device tied to the processor would listen for certain key words and advance the displayed information accordingly. None of the family knew the exact technology used for the electronic display screen, but suspected it utilized Barbara Fini's quantum control breakthrough to generate a three-dimensional image.

At Barbara Fini's initial command, an image of a young man appeared above the center of the conference table and rotated while slightly suspended above the table. The image had the appearance that one associates with a computer-generated representation. The man was apparently presented full-size, wearing clothing that was clearly from an earlier era. Next to the image was stationary text that could be read by all present regardless of their position at the table. The text described the man who seemed to float above the conference table:

Name: Wilder Meld
Born: 1819 near present-day Eagle Lake, New Brunswick
Died: 1904 in Paris, France
Image: Generated from a painting dated 1840
Height in 1840: 1.9 m
Weight in 1840: 85 Kg (approximate)
Occupation: Explorer, Trader, Industrialist, Philanthropist, Politician

Each of the family members nodded their heads in recognition of Wilder Meld. After all, he had figured prominently in the histories everyone had studied in school, and he had been particularly conspicuous in the history studies in which even the adults in the family were required to participate.

Meld had been born in the wilderness of what is now part of southern New Brunswick, but at the time of his birth was claimed by the United States. In 1842 the border was still in dispute between the United Kingdom and the upstart country to its south. However, the matter was settled when the United States, which was anticipating war with Mexico on its southern border, decided it had no desire to risk armed conflict on both its northern and southern boundaries. Since much more territory was at stake in the Mexican dispute, the United States withdrew all claims to the disputed Maine territory and thereby avoided the potential for war on that front. This established Meld as an undisputed British subject.

Meld's father, a successful trapper who acted as a guide to several British noblemen as well as to leaders of the powerful Hudson's Bay Company, taught his son all the tricks of the trade. In addition to his trapping skill, Wilder Meld was highly intelligent with an intense and sometimes blinding ambition. The beginning of Meld's fortune was based on a large stand of timber on property just northeast of his childhood home, given him by his father. The timber rights had been deeded to his father by the Hudson's Bay Company in payment for services rendered. Meld sold the timber to the Crown, which used it to enlarge the nearby fort, built by the Americans prior to the border dispute settlement. The Americans named it Fort Kent, but the British renamed it Fort Baring, in honor of the British diplomat that negotiated the border dispute. Meld used almost all the income from the timber sales to buy shares in the Hudson's Bay Company, and leveraged his father's friendships to obtain, at age twenty-five, a position with the firm. By his twenty-eighth birthday Meld, while on holiday in Europe, met and married Isabella Colvile. Isabella was the daughter of Andrew Colvile, a Scottish businessman who sat on the board of the Hudson's Bay Company and who was widely expected to be the company's next Governor. However, Andrew Colvile died under mysterious circumstances and, through a series of well-orchestrated political moves, Meld inherited his seat. Within three years of joining the board of the company, Meld managed to become one of the youngest persons in history to obtain the powerful position of Governor of the company when he wrested control from Sir John Henry Pelly. From that point, he used his business skills to successfully build the industrial empire that the Hudson's Bay Company was to become. By his thirty-eighth birthday he had taken over complete ownership of the company. Before he turned forty-three, Meld's fortune had grown to the point that the Hudson's Bay Company had become only one subsidiary of the massive worldwide conglomerate that became Meld Enterprises.

While heralded during his lifetime as a philanthropist known for his generosity shown to the destitute of Great Britain, including its colonies, he is now widely held responsible for development of the virus that devasted the world through its attack on the world's foodstuffs.

As sometimes occurs, the roots of the current tragedy lie buried in the deepest of good intentions. Among Meld's enterprises was a research and development laboratory located in Salisbury, which was over a century ahead of its time in terms of technological, biological, and intellectual advancements. While the objectives given those scientists working in the laboratory were many and varied, in the late 1850's Meld gave them an over-riding assignment: Develop a biological agent capable of accelerating the growth of organic materials but is benign to humans.

Meld was an intellectual who was decades ahead of his time, and he saw the burgeoning population growth of the world as the primary threat to its future. He sought to address this threat by accelerating the growth of food crops, livestock, and fisheries. His vision included limiting the application of the agent only to contained environments such as isolated fields, stockyards, and fisheries, and after twenty-three years of research and development the laboratory successfully introduced the agent into these control groups. However, an unexpected consequence of the agent's growth acceleration properties was while it left the host species with a fantastic growth rate, it inhibited their ability to mate and reproduce. As a result, the test populations soon became extinct as they quickly reached maturity and died.

Meld and his team of scientists saw this as a temporary problem and modifications to the agent continued. At some point, someone suggested that perhaps introducing the experimental subjects to large, but unmodified populations of their species would increase the potential for their reproduction. This tactic did indeed seem to work, so Meld's representatives introduced the modified species to croplands, livestock herds, and waterways throughout the world. The result was disaster of unprecedented proportions. Although Meld possessed a brilliant mind, he could not accept the fact that he made a mistake, so he fought a war of denial and deceit throughout the remainder of his life.

As the infected crops, fish, and livestock were unable to successfully reproduce within the larger populations, it became increasingly apparent that the agent was much more viral than supposed. Decades of success and notoriety were associated with Meld laboratories and its growth agent. However, it eventually became undeniable that rather than helping the world's food shortage, the shortage was being made much more severe as the world's foodstuffs became increasingly infected, and thereby depleted through their inability to reproduce. In fact, the virus spread to most of the plants, animals, and fish of the Earth, resulting in an progressively distressed ecological-economic system.

Several attempts were made throughout the late nineteenth and most of the twentieth centuries to reverse the impact of Meld Laboratories' agent. However, the company's financial and political power was so entrenched within most of the world's governments that it wasn't until late in the twentieth century, through the wars and political upheavals of those times, that the devastating abuses were held at bay.

During those times, many countries had their borders redefined and their political systems overhauled. For example, the United States joined with the British Commonwealth to establish a common military arm, the "Royal American Forces". It was this military arm that initiated the project and continued to provide overall leadership, although resources and personnel from virtually every country on Earth were poured into the project.

Barbara Fini let the family consider the image of Wilder Meld hanging in the air without comment for over a minute, which was plenty of time for each of them to dwell on his history, and the devastating effect his legacy had on the world. Finally, Barbara Fini spoke, "This is the man responsible for our involvement in this project. Without his towering intellect, Hudson's Bay Company would never have transformed into the Goliath enterprise that became Meld Enterprises. And early in the project, our leadership decided that this fact was the key to the success of the project." Pausing briefly, she added, "I will elaborate on this fully later today."

After another brief pause Barbara Fini continued, "I have led you to believe that your preparations for the family's assignment would take ten years. I did not lie to you…that is the length of time needed to complete all the technical enhancements to what we call the Molecular Organizer. This time would, of course, allow Adam Boy and Aarondophilous to mature further before being called on to serve the world in this enterprise. However, circumstances have changed." On this cue a series of images replaced that of Wilder Meld, as they floated over the conference table. The family recognized familiar places like Trafalgar Square in London, the Taj Mahal in India, the Eiffel Tower in Paris, the Washington Monument in Washington, DC, and Tiananmen Square in Beijing. In each scene was depicted uncontrolled violence as the people rioted, destroyed monuments, and set fire to the cities. "The geopolitical structure of the world is collapsing faster than anyone anticipated," continued Barbara Fini, "and we are moving our project departure date ahead substantially. We must initiate your assignment within the next year or face a worldwide revolution that will likely result in the dismantlement of our project."

~~~~~~~~
~~~~~~~~

Barbara Fini went on to explain that the world's food supply was collapsing more quickly than anticipated because of a fungus that apparently spread unchecked after the world's fish, game, and fowl populations fell below critical levels, due to Meld's agent. The world's scientists now believe the potential for this fungus has existed benignly for eons and was kept in check as it received adequate nourishment through its relationship with hosts on both land and water. However, without an adequate population of hosts for its continued survival, the fungus mutated into a much more aggressive version of itself. This mutation quickly found alternate sources of sustenance by aggressively attacking most of the world's plant species, resulting in a devastating effect on the world's food sources. Through the ages, the fungus became tolerant of countless natural defenses as it adapted to mutations in the DNA of the world's plant and animal kingdom. As a result, scientists have been unable to develop a defense against it. The one positive aspect is that, so far, human immune systems have proven generally resilient against both Meld's agent and the resulting fungus.

Riots arising from food shortages have resulted in the collapse of several third world countries, and even countries like Great Britain, France, and Russia are on the verge of disaster. The Planners estimate that within twelve to eighteen months the North American governments would fall under similar pressures. Rioting is already occurring in cities as nearby as Charleston and Savannah.

Scientists are being blamed for this worldwide disaster, due to their failure to recognize the viral agent and ensuing fungal threats early enough to halt their progress. It will only be a matter of time before science-based facilities like those surrounding Project Sea Queen will become the recipient of people's fears and anger. As a result, The Planners have made the decision to move the launch of the project ahead significantly, despite the dangers inherent in that decision.

Barbara Fini left the meeting after asking the team to meet her in one hour within the building that housed the Organizer. She promised that then she would answer the questions she knew they had, which undoubtedly included the nature of the dangers this decision introduced. Dartous translated Barbara Fini's promise to mean, that at long last they would learn the exact nature of their assignment. Regardless, Dartous was determined that she would not leave that meeting without understanding everything.

<p style="text-align:center">~~~~~~~~~</p>

Chapter 13 – Departure

Barbara Fini was the last to arrive at the door leading to the inner area housing the Organizer. She obviously wanted to delay her entry until all the family members had arrived, to avoid the possibility of being pushed for answers before all were present to hear her responses. Ordinarily, the team would be disciplined enough to hold their questions until after she had finished addressing the group. However, Barbara Fini knew, given that they were on the verge of at last learning the true purpose of the Organizer, the temptation to press her for information would be substantial. This was especially true for Dartous who, as expected, was the first to arrive for the meeting.

Barbara Fini began by directing them through a door leading directly into the control room for the Organizer. As they entered the room, all were quick to notice a mirrored window that they assumed looked out over the device. Barbara Fini was quick to inform them that the mirroring could be, and would be, removed at the appropriate time, but to minimize distractions it was decided to wait until some background information was revealed.

Although the room contained what appeared to be fifteen workstations, it was empty of personnel except for two technicians who wore headphones as they monitored complex readouts at their workstations. Nodding in the direction of the two technicians, Barbara Fini informed the family that the technicians were listening to music intended to block out any dialogue occurring between her and themselves. The implication being that the group could feel free to discuss any subject, including those which may be beyond the technicians' security clearance. Motioning at the empty workstations, Barbara Fini invited the family to sit.

She began, "As I previously alluded, it has long been believed that without the singular influence of Wilder Meld in the middle of the nineteenth century, our world would be much healthier than we find it today…probably not entirely healthy, but certainly not teetering on the brink of devastation. Meld was driven by an ego unparalleled in the history of the world, and he measured success solely on the accumulation of his personal wealth. Yes, he supported many philanthropic causes, but the object of his seeming generosity was always to garner favors from and develop alliances with powerful and influential people. The scientists of his day saw, even then, the likely price the world would pay for the unchecked expansion of his financial, industrial, and resource-consuming empire, specifically the impact of the viral agent. And there are several indications that Meld did not entirely dismiss their dire assessments, but his intensely self-absorbed personality led him to ignore anything that would diminish his accumulation of wealth and power, even if it meant future generations might suffer as a result."

"As you all know, we long ago reached the point of no-return in terms of the survivability of humanity. It became clear to the most powerful scientific minds of our time that out-of-control technologies had contributed to the destruction of the world and, ironically, only the rapid development of unknown technologies could save it. The greatest minds from around the world were recruited for the purpose of developing some technology, any technology, that would save the world."
"Many ideas were brought forward, and eventually discarded as unworkable. For example, the Molecular Organizer was one such approach, but you all know that this technology failed; although the world was made to believe it succeeded, and until recently this false knowledge had given people hope and prevented chaos."

"Another solution involved the development of large domed cities capable of protecting the inhabitants from toxins, while producing self-sustaining food supplies within sealed greenhouses. Several such cities were built around the world, but recent rioting has shown that few, if any, of these will survive. The coming food shortages, along with increasing viral concentrations which will soon be too high for a mere respirator to handle, will generate upheavals and a panic too severe for the perimeters of the domed cities to withstand. The cities can hold only a small percentage of the population, and those outside their environs will likely breach their perimeters, as they are driven to do anything to get into the perceived safe areas. Those ecosystems depend on a careful balance between population and resources and would soon become overwhelmed and collapse, even assuming the infrastructure could survive breaches by the invading populous."

"This brings me to the final two solutions our scientists considered. One involved study of the past, to determine if in history one or two key events occurred which led us down our doomed path. Historians have understood for decades that Wilder Meld is the father of our chaos, but they knew this from only a general standpoint. None could agree on the point in time in which Meld's rise became inevitable. It was hoped that a thorough understanding of the past would lead us to recognize previously unforeseen actions by Meld and others, and through this knowledge reverse the collapse. This activity was successful from the standpoint that, we now understand that the key event was Wilder Meld's ascension to the role of Governor of the Hudson's Bay Company. If that had never come about, Meld would have not obtained the power and influence that allowed him to command the resources and intellects which led to the development of Meld's virus. Unfortunately, to date, this knowledge has not led to anything that can remedy the world situation."

"This left us with one other course. The proponents of this option believed that the world could not be saved, so instead focused on preserving mankind. It was decided to build a spacecraft to carry a handpicked body of colonists on a one-way journey to another star, and in this way save humanity."

The pronouncement by Barbara Fini about the colony ship was met by nods all around because it seemed each of the family members had come to similar conclusions as Dartous.

Barbara Fini responded to the reaction by the family with a slight smile as she continued to describe the chain of events that led to what The Planners eventually called "Project Sea Queen". She detailed a series of actions remarkably like that postulated to Benjabar by Dartous. It involved the development of new technologies, which were eventually facilitated by the quantum controls developed by Barbara Fini. These developments included a new drive system, telescopes capable of viewing planetary candidates, quantum computing of algorithms designed to extrapolate planetary developments, and the decision to build a scaled-down version of the scout ship. The prototype ship utilized a small select crew to test the technology before building the actual scout and colony ships. However, at this point the narrative departed from anything the family had anticipated as Barbara Fini touched the button that removed the mirroring effect from the glass, and the family received their first look into the Organizer containment room.

Authors' note - The following narrative took place during a series of meetings over the course of the next three days, which included many hours of questioning and discussing. What follows is a summary of the key information shared during those meetings, but omits many of the technical details:

A key advancement, facilitated by Barbara Fini's work, was the ability to harness gravitons to generate a tremendous gravitational field. This field was theorized by the team charged with designing and building the scout and colony ships, and its primary purpose was to contain the enormous energies required by the ship's drive. However, the complexity of the associated physics and computations was far beyond the world's total combined computing power until Barbara Fini's advances in quantum computing and controls were realized.

The prototype scout ship was built, and successfully completed three trials using two-man crews. However, in April of 2034, on the fourth trial, a small, undetected flaw in the gravitational containment field resulted in an unmeasurable surge of gravity surrounding the ship. Radio contact and tracking locks were immediately lost and, due to the huge energy surge, it was assumed the craft had exploded with the apparent loss of both crew members.

However, the crew wore locator bracelets, like those worn by the family and other key members of the project, and the instant the ship disappeared the GPS locator within the bracelets of the two crewmembers pinged positions in Mongolia. The ship's locator GPS signal was lost, presumably damaged by the explosion. Although not in the exact same locations, the indicated positions of the crew members' bracelets were within a thirty-kilometer radius.

Barbara Fini admitted that these developments baffled her, and the others associated with that colonization project. The spacecraft was in orbit over South America at the time of the disappearance, so no one could suggest a mechanism that would allow the GPS locators to appear in Mongolia at the exact same instant contact with the orbiting ship was lost.

A team was immediately sent out to recover the bracelets and search for the remains of the ship and crew. One bracelet was found in an Erdene Zuu Buddhist monastery, while the other was eventually found in the tent of a tribal leader.

The team expected to find the bracelets charred and otherwise damaged by the explosion and fall to Earth. However, both bracelets were not only intact and fully functional, but to everyone's astonishment the crewmembers were alive and wearing the bracelets. Both crewmembers were happy and healthy, except for a severe loss of memory regarding their lives prior to the explosion. Other than the memory loss, the only other apparent changes were that, although DNA analysis confirmed the identity of both crewmembers, they both now spoke fluently in a Mongolian dialect and, most baffling of all, were estimated to be thirty to forty years older than when they launched in the scout ship.

~~~~~~~~~~

Subsequent investigations determined that one of the crewmembers was found by the monastery's monks wandering the Orkhon Valley in a confused and agitated state in 1997. At about the same time, the second crewman was taken in by a nearby nomadic tribe who found him inside the intact spacecraft. Although both crewmembers were speaking "gibberish"...probably their native languages of French and Korean...and in a similar state of confusion when found, they eventually became rational and learned the local dialect.

The tribe dismantled the ship, and several parts were found throughout the personal effects of various tribal members, who apparently considered them good luck charms. The ship's locator was never found...probably because it had been disconnected from the ship's power source. Fortunately, the fusion reactor, that would be the long-term power source for the actual scout ship, had not yet been installed for testing, so radiation poisoning was not a concern.

Both crewmembers eventually married and, although they did not recover full memories, did regain their intellectual skills, which allowed them to become leaders to the communities surrounding the monastery.

One of the crewmembers was of West European descent and the other Asian so, even though as leaders in the communities, it was inevitable that the two members would meet. However, they never made the connection to a common origin.

The crewmember discovered within the tribe had found favor with the tribal chief and was adopted by him. Upon the death of the chief, the crewmember became the tribe's leader. The other crewmember was revered throughout the area through his association with the monastery. So, it was with great difficulty that the two were persuaded to return to the project headquarters for a debriefing. Their return to the site of the launch, along with reunions with surviving family members triggered the return of some memories, but neither of the crewmembers were able to readjust to their former lives. Therefore, after a few months they returned to their Mongolian homes.
~~~~~~~~~~

These events left the project with parallel courses of action. The build and launch of the colony ships continued, but the second path involved the establishment of the area of the program now known as "Project Sea Queen".

The best of the project's theoretical physicists, Dr. Aubrent, was placed in charge of determining the cause of these extraordinary events. After six weeks of intense study, he and his team were left with only one conclusion…the surge in the ship's gravitational field resulted in a bending of time and space around the orbiting spacecraft. In essence…time bent to the point that the ship and crew were sent over thirty years into the past.

~~~~~~~~~

Dr. Aubrent and his team developed the complex mathematics necessary to explain the cause of what he called, the Temporal Event. The mathematical computations suggested that these new versions of the crewmembers did not exist in our time reality prior to the collapse of the ship's gravitational field. This explained why the GPS locator signals were not picked up until after the Temporal Event.

The mathematic extrapolations also indicated that the Temporal Travelers would be drawn into the vicinity of the closest gravitational source, but at the same time would be repelled by the mass of that same source. This explained why the crewmembers were transported to the surface of the Earth rather than being stranded in space almost forty years in the past. The fact that the Temporal Travelers appeared on dry land rather than in the middle of an ocean was found to be mere luck. Statistically, they stood a greater likelihood of landing, and probably drowning, in the ocean.

Dr. Aubrent continued to work on the calculations to determine if travel into the future is possible. He felt intuitively that forward time travel was achievable, but this possibility had neither been disproven or confirmed.
~~~~~~~~~

The mathematics had determined that interaction between the gravitational fields of the crewmembers' bodies had forced them apart, regarding their final location, although it did not affect the time to which they traveled. And since the change in their locations was related to their change in time, there were no physical barriers to their travel. This accounted for the fact that while one crewmember was found inside the spacecraft, his companion was found wandering the landscape several kilometers away.

The crewmember found in Mongolia still inside the ship had been strapped in at the time of the event, while the other was moving about the cabin inspecting the containment alarms triggered shortly before the incident. The crewmember secured to his seat had been transported in time as part of the ship, while the second crewmember and any items not tied down were sent to the same time, but a different location. Due to the large energies released at the time of the event, these displacements tended to be fifteen to thirty kilometers apart, even though the interacting gravity forces were weak.

The fact that one of the crewmembers was not buckled into the cockpit of the ship was another fortunate occurrence. It was subsequently learned that had the two crewmembers not been separated by the temporal shift, quantum interactions between the brains of the crewmembers would have led to severe psychological damage.

The first crewmember, being strapped securely to the acceleration couch, was effectively part of the ship's molecular structure. However, rather than passing through the ship's hull, the second crewmember who was not part of the ship's structure, had bypassed that barrier (and any other physical obstructions) to end up in a different location when arriving at the new timeline.

The mathematics suggested that travel into the very distant past was theoretically possible, but the practical limit was a little over two hundred years, due to currently available energy sources.

All this information led to the development of the Organizer, and subsequently to the establishment of Project Sea Queen. Captain Eli and the family's mission would be to change the damaging legacy of Wilder Meld. But to accomplish that end would require travel through both space and time.

~~~~~~~~~

Even after the inadvertent discovery that one's timeline could be changed, the colonization option continued to be pursued. However, the faster-than-expected collapse of world governments meant that time had run out on that alternative.

The Planners desired that Meld's history be impacted early in his childhood. However, due to the limitations of the Organizer's effective capabilities, they eventually compromised to the target date of 1838. Meld would be in his late teens at that time and would not yet be associated with the Hudson's Bay Company. Therefore, this timing should provide adequate opportunity for the family to prevent the association from occurring.

All family members would arrive tens of seconds apart, except Captain Eli who would arrive about six months earlier. The delays in the family arrival times would be necessary to minimize the disorientation caused by time travel. And it was felt that the Captain's six-month head start would provide him with adequate time to make the necessary preparations for the rest of the family's arrival.

Dr. Aubrent and his team identified several primary problems associated with the safe delivery of the team to 1838 (and thousands of smaller problems):
~~~~~~~~~

Problem 1: The calculations for safely positioning the time travelers were far too complex even when the world's quantum computers were processing in parallel. The Earth is turning, the solar system is spinning, and the galaxy is rotating as they move through the universe. Even though the mass of the Earth would keep the travelers in its proximity as they jump to the new time, it became increasingly clear that someone programing a time travel matrix in 2038 could not reliably deliver someone to a given location in 1838. Therefore, the delivery programing would need to be done at the time of arrival. The solution was to send twelve orbiting autonomous satellites, containing gravitational field generators, back to 1835. This would allow for some adjustment to the planned 1838 arrival date of the travelers. Calculations confirmed that due to their self-contained gravity fields, satellites locked into synchronous orbit as the jump occurred would remain in their orbits throughout the transition to the new time. This satellite cluster was referred to jointly as the Temporal Navigation System.

The System was launched to the designated time, and Dr. Aubrent's team was able to test it by sending back an oddly shaped boulder to 1838 with an embedded homing device. It was felt that this was a common enough artifact that it would likely go unnoticed throughout the intervening history but would be easy to identify by anyone searching for it. An atomic clock was embedded with the homing device and was set to activate the locator on the same date as it was sent back in time. The boulder's locator activated as planned, and the boulder was found off a beach on the island of Aruba in shallow water.

At the same time the Organizer initiates a traveler's temporal transport, it would also send a transmitter that would arrive exactly twelve hours before the transported individual's appearance. Upon arrival, the transmitter would immediately send a signal to one of the satellites, triggering it to chart the locations of all possible arrival sites and drop sets of two gravity field "grenades" from orbit to one of the locations. One grenade would be for transport of the family member, and the other would be for their supplies. As a redundancy feature, another set of grenades would be dropped to the same general area, but five to thirty kilometers apart. These grenades would contain a shielded gravitational field which would surge when the energy source maintaining the field was removed, thereby amounting to a "detonation" of the grenade. The gravity fields would detonate at the instant of the staggered arrivals. The associated surge in gravity would draw the traveler to that location. The locator bracelets of the transported family members would allow the satellites to confirm their arrival, but if the primary grenades failed to detonate it would trigger the back-up set to do so. The grenade design was such that the detonation would destroy the device, and any unused grenades were wired to self-destruct after the traveler had arrived and the satellites' infrared imagery confirmed that there was no one in the vicinity. It was required that the arrival calculations consider the effects of all gravitational fields, including the Earth and even any nearby people. Therefore, to ensure that any residual energies posed by the detonated grenades did not affect the arrival of the subsequent time travelers, Dr. Aubrent's team stipulated that the arrival sites should be widely separated on the planet. This, of course, would make retrieval of the team members somewhat difficult, but Dr. Aubrent was convinced that the possible residual effects would impact the arrival point so that the family members could find themselves kilometers offshore, or on top of an unscalable mountain.

It was determined that all arrival sites would be on isolated seaside beaches. Earth's gravity varies according to the distance from its center, which is a significant variable within the calculations for arrival determination. Therefore, placing the grenade locations at or near sea level would simplify, and therefore improve, the accuracy of delivering the travelers to locations near the grenade detonation sites. The isolation criteria were established to minimize the risk of locals being harmed by the detonations, to prevent the travelers' arrivals being witnessed, and to avoid interactions with the locals until the travelers could become oriented to their environment. Unfortunately, since the satellites were to make the calculation autonomously in 1838, the locations of the travelers would be the unknown prior to departure of the family.

*The only family member not to be sent to a beach would be Captain Eli. The gravitational fields designed to transport the others would be contained in bubbles only three meters in diameter, which would be confined within their individual Quantum Field Transport Chambers. The occupant of the chamber would lie in a hammock which allowed movement independent of their environment. In this way, only the individuals themselves would be delivered to the designated sites, and their chambers would remain in place. The Organizer and its Quantum Field Transport Chambers would be located on a ship whose exterior design was consistent with those found in 1838. There would be a transport chamber for each of the family members, other than the Captain, plus a back-up chamber in the event of a failure of one of the primary chambers. However, the Captain would be strapped into the Organizer, and the bubble surrounding him would be of sufficient size and strength to transport him, the Organizer, and the entire ship to 1838. It had been this ship that was nestled into a dry dock bay that the family saw when Barbara Fini removed the mirroring from the Organizer's control room. The name of the ship: **THE SEA QUEEN**.*

~~~~~~~~~~
~~~~~~~~~~

Problem 2: The theory that the human brain operates on a quantum level would explain why the first travelers in time suffered such disorientation and memory loss. But it was found, for reasons not yet understood, that the higher a person's intuition level and innate problem-solving skills, the less effect time transportation has on the brain. This was one important reason that the family members were chosen based on their intuition quotient, and the reason most of the daily exercises were designed to improve the family's collective intuition.

Tests were conducted in which laboratory volunteers were sent back three days in time. The volunteers underwent total isolation for one week. And then were sent back in time to another isolated location several miles away. The isolation and separation were deemed necessary to ensure that the current timeline and the new timeline did not overlap and confuse the observers assigned the responsibility of assessing the volunteers' mental state. All agreed that it would be disorienting to observe the inevitable changes that would occur because of the two timeline's merging.

These tests indicated that with proper conditioning, the time travel effects on mental states would be much reduced from that of the prototype accident. However, disorientation, nausea, and temporary memory loss upon arrival would still be a problem. Further experiments determined that recovery from the time travel effects could be expedited by reading a familiar word or phrase, which served to focus the brain's cognitive abilities. Phrases containing puzzling and uncertain content were the most effective at unraveling the figurative cobwebs in the brains of the time travelers. So, each family member would be asked to memorize key phrases which would be embedded in written notes by Captain Eli. These bewildering notes would assist in recovering memories but would likely be meaningless to anyone but the intended recipient.

The Temporal Navigation Satellites would be used by Captain Eli as a GPS structure to locate the family members through the bracelets, electronically keyed to each person. Captain Eli's early arrival would mean he would be waiting for them when they appeared. After he located their signals and assessed their condition, he would send special duffels back in time. The duffels would contain the notes designed to aid their recovery after the time jump. They would also contain several weeks' worth of protein supplements in case their recovery was delayed. The duffels would also contain a sewn-in locator chip matching that of the bracelet for the designated family member, and the bag would be made of a material treated with the respective family member's DNA. These two features would allow the Organizer to recognize the bag as belonging to that respective individual. The first of the detonation grenades would activate and facilitate the arrival of the duffel bags several minutes before the travelers' advent. This would mean their supplies would be awaiting them for a time sufficiently short to avoid interference from random occurrences, yet long enough so the residual effects of the duffels' arrival did not impact the family members' transport.

Problem 3: The Planners had always presented this as a one-way trip to the family, but, in truth, they expected to find a way to arrange a return trip. However, the accelerated destabilization of world governments meant they no longer had the luxury of time needed to develop that part of the technology. If the family were successful in their assignment, time should immediately reset upon their departure from the current timeline, so there would be no need for Project Sea Queen and the Organizer would likely not exist. There would be no one looking for them since no one still within the changed timeline would remember them, and even if there were people who somehow learned of their prior existence, the technology would likely not exist to retrieve them. After all, critical needs probably advanced this time travel technology by at least 300 years.

On the other hand, if the family failed in its mission, world government collapse would be imminent and there would be no time or resources to provide for a rescue mission, even if a means of returning the family to the current time could be developed. So, it was abundantly clear that whether the mission was successful or not, this could truly be a one-way trip.

Problem 4:   There was a distinct possibility that by sending individuals back in time, the existence of the travelers and others in this timeline could be affected. For example, should Captain Eli or Renee Fini meet one of their ancestors and interact in a way that changed key decisions in their ancestor's lives, it was possible that the ones known as David Eli or Renee Fini would never be born, or would be born under significantly different circumstances. Therefore, The Planners provided the family the following protocols: 1) They should act to prevent interactions with any of their ancestors to avoid compromising their coming history. Accordingly, The Planners traced the family members' individual ancestral histories back to the 1830's and provided sufficient details to arm them with information regarding those ancestor's movements and other factors which could aid them in avoiding unnecessary contacts. 2) The Family should avoid acting in ways that result in the death of anyone with whom they interact. This included killing anyone attempting to injure or kill them. 3) The Family should interact with as few people as possible and, therefore, they should restrict much of their movements to the ship. The inherent problem was that <u>The Sea Queen</u> was a large sailing ship and typically required a large crew. This problem was solved by incorporating hidden and disguised computer controls, armament technologies, and other means that would reduce the crewing requirements to only a handful of sailors. The controls, along with the components of the Organizer, would be hidden with a concealed entry that would be keyed to the handprints of the family members, and accessible only through Captain Eli's quarters.

Problem 5: Could the necessary work be completed within the accelerated timeline? The Organizer was already being placed in the frame of the Sea Queen and would be fully integrated with the ship's operation within three weeks. The Sea Queen would be ready for its sea trials within a month. Ideally, the technicians and scientists would have six months to work out the kinks, but theoretically the family could be launched into the past at any time after the completion of sea trials. Of course, the less time spent identifying and correcting design and procedural flaws, the greater the potential for disaster.

Problem 6: How would the individuals remain separated from each other during the time transport and thereby avoid mental stresses? The results of the initial accident, which led to the discovery of time travel, as well as subsequent testing showed that the traveling must be solo to avoid the emotional instability that apparently results from interactions among the traveler's quantum brain patterns. The Quantum Field Chambers would be energized sequentially so that no two travelers could be in transition at the same moment, and the arrival locations would be widespread and locked into the individual's DNA. Only after each of the other family members had been successfully transported would Captain Eli, along with The Organizer itself, be transported within the Sea Queen to their targeted dates.

After the three days of meetings, the family began to prepare in earnest for their departure which was scheduled to occur five-and-one-half months after these meetings concluded. As it turned out, departure came much sooner.

~~~~~~~~~~

Due to the intensity and focus of Project Sea Queen, the twins, Renee and Barbara Fini, had not felt the luxury of time needed to repair and heal what they both knew was their broken familial relationship. They had managed to maintain a detached and professional relationship throughout their shared time together on the project, but one morning, twelve days after the *Sea Queen* completed her preliminary sea trials, Renee Fini woke in a sweat to an overwhelming sense of lost opportunity. She realized that if she and Barbara Fini didn't find an opening in which to reconcile their childhood jealousies, she would likely regret it in the coming years. This feeling was intensified by the growing realization that she would soon never see her sister again.
~~~~~~~~~~

Every day, since the completion of the sea trials, the family had spent their waking moments on the *Sea Queen* improving or, in some cases, learning sailing skills and becoming familiar with the capabilities of the ship. And this training had required that each family member memorize the fabricated history of the ship and its crew, with this memorization including even small details like the significance of the small pennant attached to the top of the main mast, and of the cross emblazoned on the mainsail. So, the limited number of days remaining before departure meant that they take every opportunity to concentrate on this training, which had now been extended to seven days a week, twelve hours a day. But on this morning, rather than following the usual pre- and post-breakfast routines, Renee Fini called on Captain Eli and explained that she would be absent from that day's sea training.

As often happened with Renee Fini, she proceeded with an intense focus on the task at hand. She found herself making her way to her sister's quarters without stopping to consider the usual level of military activity she noticed throughout the compound. And it was with a combination of concern mixed with resolve she found herself knocking on the door to Barbara Fini's quarters.

Barbara Fini opened the door and, rather than expressing surprise at this early-morning unscheduled visit by her sister, merely nodded her head in a gesture that conveyed she had been expecting this call. Barbara Fini invited her sister into her quarters and asked her to wait while she called and canceled her morning's appointments.

The sisters spent the next hours in a mixture of reminiscences, frustrations, and regrets about growing up in a facility which, although it treated them well, did not provide the nurturing needed for development of a healthy sibling relationship. Renee Fini admitted that she withdrew into her studies and apologized for not making a greater effort at building a loving relationship with her sister. For her part, Barbara Fini admitted to an underlying envy of her twin's greater academic achievements. She also admitted that these emotions were not entirely absent, even though as the Director of Team Development for the project she was, in effect, Renee Fini's superior. And not even her outstanding accomplishments as inventor of the technology that may prove to be part of humanities' hope for survival was sufficient to completely quiet her envious nature.

Despite each of their tendencies to remain calm and unemotional in stress-filled situations, the two women eventually embraced and shared words of love and regret over the lost years in which they could have grown together rather than apart. Their embrace lasted for several minutes, and likely would have continued for several more if not for the alarm that signaled that the secure perimeter surrounding the project grounds was under attack, and in danger of collapsing.

~~~~~~~~~

General McDonald was a former politician with no military training. However, his inflammatory behavior commanded the attention of a large and persistent following. During a briefing held shortly after the true nature of the Organizer was revealed, the family had been given an overview of the General's activities. It was also revealed during this briefing that he was the most troubling reason for the extreme secrecy of the project, since it was known that the General was frantically attempting to place spies within the project. An in-depth psychological analysis of McDonald had revealed that he would likely use time travel technology, should he learn of its existence and gain control of it, to further his own goals, with the salvation of the world relegated as a secondary objective. It was easy to imagine a history reformed to the extent that McDonald would become dictator of a world government.
~~~~~~~~~

In a recent briefing, Barbara Fini had shared that it was this anticipated abuse by the General, as well as by others, that had led The Planners to implement excessive security measures. And she confirmed that these measures included such things as restricting the family membership to those with no close relationships. In fact, finding ways to minimize the opportunities for General McDonald and his kind to learn the true nature of the Organizer was their number one security priority.

The General made a study of authoritarian leaders and recognized that often their power came from playing into the fears and prejudices of the majority. History showed him that even intelligent and well-meaning people could be swayed when their fears were used to sow dissent. Through his studies, the General recognized common characteristics of the mechanisms by which successful tyrants gained their power. Even though each story was unique and therefore a full-treatment complicated, it seemed to him that many of these successful dictators used some version of a process which he summarized as a five-step method:

Step One: Identify the top two or three threats shared by many in the majority. It is best if these threats are, at least in part, the result of actions by members of the majority. For example, if the majority has been wasteful and self-indulgent in the consumption of a particular resource, one might focus on the hardships caused by the high prices being charged for the few reserves of that resource remaining.

Step Two: Find one or more groups to blame as the cause for the perceived threats. These could include governmental, religious, or ethnic groups. It doesn't really matter whether those blamed are in any way responsible. It is always easier to get people on board if you can show them that they themselves are in no way responsible for those things threatening them, and it is instead someone else's fault.

Step Three: Mount a campaign in public forums, such as social media, designed to "prove" that those in the target group or groups are responsible for the threats.   It is helpful if a few factual anecdotes can be included in the campaign, but this is not required, and most of the emphasis will likely be on fabricated talking points, no matter how outrageous and unsubstantiated.   The main idea is to develop a consistent message of blame and say it long enough and loud enough that the majority will begin to see it as true.

Step Four: Once a significant following has been developed, use the existing political system to obtain a position of power within the government.   This works best in democracies, by focusing on the roles of Presidents and Prime Ministers but can even be used against some authoritarian regimes by such methods as creating "a government in exile" to undermine the current leadership.

Step Five: Once in power, replace the governmental heads with your own supporters.   Then through intimidation, manipulation, and decree, change the laws of the land to consolidate your own power and legalize the persecution of the target group or groups identified in step two.   No matter the real reason behind the problems experienced by the people, from that time forward you must remain consistent in the message that the cause is due to the actions of one or more of the target groups.

The eminent collapse of the socio-economic structure provided a unique opportunity for a charismatic leader like the General to test the application of these five steps. But his rapid ascent to power surprised even him.

Step one of the process was a given…there was not a soul on the planet that did not feel threatened by the food shortages and decaying government structures. The cause of these devastating problems was, of course, the fact that governments and populations ignored the scientists' warnings regarding Meld's virus for decades, and this was obvious to any thinking person. However, the General manipulated the hearts and minds of much of the world by recasting the cause-and-effect into a dialogue in which the scientists were blamed as the originators of the plague. One conspiracy theory claimed that Meld and his company were a scapegoat for a group of scientists who had introduced the virus so that the legitimate world governments would be undermined, which would facilitate the imposition of a new world order dominated by scientists. This of course was nonsense, but steps two through five of the process rely on the expectation that many would rather blame and attack someone else rather than admit their own complicity.

As a facility containing the world's greatest concentration of scientists from diverse backgrounds, General McDonald saw the Project Sea Queen compound to be an easy target in his war against sanity. McDonald, of course, had no understanding of the project's true purpose, but he saw its destruction as a means of consolidating his power and energizing his followers. So only two weeks earlier, he sent out word through his underground network for his followers to rally at the gates providing access to the Project Sea Queen compound. To his amazement over two hundred thousand people showed up on the appointed day armed with every weapon from .22 caliber single shot rifles to automatic and semiautomatic assault weapons.

The crowd had appeared three days previously, and the military commander of the Sea Queen Project had met with McDonald and negotiated a withdrawal of his followers. The withdrawal was to take place on the morning the Fini sisters were meeting. However, this was a ruse by McDonald to lure the project's commander into a false sense of security.

The compound was well-guarded by highly trained soldiers and could have withstood a simple direct assault by even the large force assembled by McDonald and his underlings. However, the breech in defenses had occurred as McDonald's fanatics used the reduced tensions to strategically position trucks disguised as transports intended to remove the crowd. The trucks were suddenly moved to the barricades located at various points along the compound's perimeter. Each truck was filled with explosives that had been assembled at one of the compounds occupied by McDonald's followers.

At McDonald's signal, all seven of the trucks were detonated simultaneously. Without waiting for the smoke to clear, McDonald's followers immediately poured through the resultant openings. But because McDonald's people had warned the soldiers stationed at the barricades to evacuate minutes before the trucks were detonated, no one was hurt because of the explosions. As a result, the compound's officers were reluctant to order the soldiers to fire on their countrymen, so the fall of the compound, while chaotic, was amazingly bloodless.

It was this scene of chaos that greeted the Fini sisters as they stepped from Barbara Fini's quarters. The compound's defenders were being disarmed, and anyone wearing uniforms, identification badges, or anything associating them with the project were being detained.

The sisters quickly assessed the situation and immediately began to work toward implementing the protocol that was established for scenarios involving the imminent collapse of the project, such as this one. Barbara Fini realized that the identifying insignia on her uniform might make her a specific target of the invaders, and immediately removed and tossed them into a nearby trash receptacle.

Without saying a word, the sisters began to work their way toward the docks holding the launch that, with two of the project's military personnel as pilots, would already be idling in wait of Renee Fini's arrival. And through a quick check via Barbara Fini's personal communicator, it was confirmed that Captain Eli and the rest of the family were on board the *Sea Queen*. She also confirmed that the Captain had already energized The Organizer and was working through the pre-transfer checklist before initiating the final sequence that would send the family two hundred years into the past. Renee Fini knew that once she reached the docks her transfer to the *Sea Queen* would take over twenty minutes. This meant that her arrival, and positioning into her Quantum Field Chamber would be the last thing checked off that list.

<center>~~~~~~~~~~</center>

Captain Eli stared at the Organizer's status board with concern as his mind raced to absorb the implications of the day's events. Despite an awareness of heightened levels of military presence, it had begun as a normal training day, which included a test-run of the still-evolving ship and crew. As the family grew in their understanding of the ship's capabilities and unique properties, through almost constant drilling, an army of technicians adjusted the software and hardware of the Organizer daily. With its current settings, the Organizer would likely distribute the family members over distances measured in thousands of kilometers from each other. However, the technicians believed that over the coming months they could narrow that distribution such that everyone would land within a three-hundred-kilometer radius, without experiencing significant mental distress.

Until he had received the communication initiating the emergency departure protocol, nothing unusual had occurred, except for Renee Fini's request to be excused from the day's training...which was unprecedented, but the Captain had trusted she had a particularly good reason for her request. The only other thing of minor note...at the time...was that Dartous' locator bracelet had failed unexpectedly. The Captain had made a note to ensure that Dartous took the bracelet in for repair or replacement that evening but had not given the matter additional thought.

As soon as the emergency communication came in, the technicians scrambled to evacuate the *Sea Queen* using the launch secured to its side. Also, the Captain immediately began the power-up sequence of the Organizer. It is a sign of his focus on task that, it wasn't until receiving the one red light among the field of green lights, he remembered the implications of Dartous' failed bracelet...without it he would not be able to locate her after the transfer.

The Captain tapped the com-link to Dartous' private channel, but as soon as the link was established, she spoke first, "Yes, Captain...I understand the situation, but we both know that you don't have the time to worry about that now. I am attempting a repair of my bracelet, but I don't hold out much hope for it...I think the GPS circuitry is fried."

"If you want to join the technicians in the evacuation I will understand completely. None of us want to risk being left alone for the rest of our lives under unknown circumstances," said the Captain. Dartous responded, "You can't get rid of me that easily Captain...I have trained too hard and long to let a little technicality keep me from this party. Don't worry, if I can't get the bracelet to function, I will send up smoke signals. But don't spend a lot of time looking for me...you need to focus on collecting the others and finding Meld."

"Very well Dartous...I will be praying for you and will do as you say, but please know I will never stop looking for you," said the Captain as he broke the com-link.

The sisters were challenged by McDonald's followers as they wound their way to the dock, but thanks to Renee Fini's martial arts skills, and the lack of training within the invading army, they left a trail of incapacitated attackers. They were able to avoid any significant delays until they were in sight of her launch, but at that point two of McDonald's followers stepped from the shadows and started to move into a position that would block the women's path to the launch. Immediately, Renee Fini sprinted for the launch hoping to catch the soldiers off guard long enough to reach the launch and achieve her escape. But when only one-and-a-half meters from the launch, another soldier leapt from a place of concealment grabbing Renee Fini about the legs. Renee Fini tumbled onto the deck of the launch and was knocked unconscious, as she struck her head on the pilot console.

The two launch pilots immediately jumped into action and engaged McDonald's people on the dock before the intruders could raise their weapons. Barbara Fini quickly assessed the situation and determined that the two unarmed pilots would be overpowered by the three invaders. So, she hastily made her way to the launch, threw off the lines securing it, and shoved the throttle full ahead as she steered the launch from the dock.

As the launch raced on a heading toward the *Sea Queen*, automatic weapon fire was heard from the direction of the docks. The launch was rapidly out of effective range, and Barbara Fini assumed the firing had been an unsuccessful attempt to incapacitate the launch. But just then she noticed a large blip on the launch's radar screen and realized that it lacked the identifying transponder I.D. that all project vessels were required to transmit.

It then occurred to Barbara Fini that the firing from the docks was not intended to hit the launch but was instead an attempt to get the attention of this unknown vessel. And they were obviously successful in this purpose because the vessel immediately changed to a heading that was clearly intended to intercept the launch. Barbara Fini began evasive maneuvers at once while maintaining a general heading toward the *Sea Queen*. Fortunately, the speed of the launch was greater than that of the approaching vessel and she was able to avoid direct interception. However, they did come close enough to the vessel to determine it was a mid-sized Coast Guard Cutter that had apparently been commandeered by McDonald's troops.

As the launch passed in front of the oncoming cutter, McDonald's people opened fire on them from the deck gun. Several rounds managed to impact the side of the launch, including some below the waterline, and Barbara Fini soon noticed a sluggishness in the steerage of the launch, that led her to understand the launch was taking on water.

Renee Fini began to stir to wakefulness and, despite her muddled state, quickly assessed the situation. Knowing the launch was unarmed, she looked for some means of slowing the approach of the cutter and picked up four of the launch's fire extinguishers and threw each of them, in turn, into the water behind the launch. As hoped, the cutter's radar picked up the extinguishers as they were being propelled toward the ship by the launch's wake. The cutter's pilot likely interpreted them as torpedoes and took evasive action, which gave the launch the needed space to reach the *Sea Queen*. By the time the launch was moored to the side of the *Sea Queen* it was listing heavily toward the port side, and it was clear to Barbara Fini that it could not make it back to the project's dock.

The sisters were met by the Captain as they cleared the ship's railing. Barbara Fini's face seemed to shed all emotion as she stared without blinking into Captain Eli's eyes and calmly said, "I can see two options for myself in our current situation…I can either take one of your life rafts and try to make it back to shore, or I can go with you into the past. I believe our friends out there on that cutter have adopted a 'shoot-first' mentality at this point, so I judge my chances of making it alive to the coast to be slim. Therefore, I choose the second option."

Both the Captain and Renee Fini took on the postures of people preparing to protest, but Barbara Fini raised her hand in a silencing gesture. "I will use the back-up Quantum Field Chamber to make the jump…and yes, I know that it would take hours to load my DNA pattern into the system matrix, and to prepare the chamber for my proper transfer…and that this is time we do not have. Captain, please immediately copy Renee Fini's pattern into the transfer matrix of the spare chamber. I will remove my locator bracelet since the DNA sequence coded into the bracelet will not match exactly that coded into the transfer matrix. However, I believe as identical twins, our DNA patterns will be sufficiently similar that the time transfer will leave much of my sanity intact, although my memory is likely to be severely impacted. And although I will not wear a locator bracelet, if our transfers are initiated at the same instant, the positioning satellites should land me somewhere in the vicinity of Renee Fini without impacting her mental state." In response to Captain Eli's sustained objections she continued, "Let me remind you Captain, that until you make the time transfer our protocol calls for me to remain your superior…and we don't have time to argue…that cutter will be here in minutes…probably with their deck gun blazing. So, I order you to do as I say." Captain Eli reluctantly nodded his head and the women sprinted to their respective Quantum Field Chambers.

~~~~~~~~~~
~~~~~~~~~~

The protocol specified that the family make the jump, or transfer, in a specific sequence… Benjabar first…followed in order by Renee Fini, Dartous, Adam Boy, and Aarondophilus. However, given the uncertainty of Renee Fini's ability to make it safely back to the *Sea Queen*, the Captain had modified the sequence to initiate her transfer just before he initiated his own. The purpose of this modification was to make it easier to accomplish the needed programing changes, should it become necessary to eliminate Renee Fini from the transfer sequence. Understandably, this change had been a painful one for the Captain to make.

It turns out that the decision to change the transfer sequence was fortunate. Having them last in the sequence made it much easier and faster for the Captain to make the necessary programing changes.

After completing the system modifications, the Captain informed the two women via the com-link. In turn, they responded that each had initiated their individual transfer procedures within their chambers. Included within each transfer procedure was, in Renee Fini's case, a change to period clothing and a final scan of their chambers to ensure no loose materials, aside from themselves, were present. Anything not joined to the chamber would make the jump along with them. This was done to ensure that no other twenty-first century life or materials was inadvertently introduced into the nineteenth century. It would be disastrous if the Meld virus were introduced through the transfer of a contaminated fly, spider, or slice of bread. Finally, the ready lights for each of the two women turned green, except for the red light indicating that Barbara Fini's locator bracelet was missing.

Then Captain Eli began a series of master transfer sequences, starting with the sequence keyed to Benjabar.

~~~~~~~~~
~~~~~~~~~

Renee Fini lay in her station hammock within her transfer chamber looking intently at the display that informed her of the transfer status. Of particular interest was the area of the display where each of the family members' names was displayed inside a rectangular icon that provided a yellow background for the text. As each family member completed their transfer their icon color would change from yellow to green. As second-in-command, she felt a responsibility to stand vigil over those icons until each was green. And she waited expectantly to feel the tingling sensation she had been told would coincide with the peak in the quantum field associated with each transfer.

Renee Fini never took her eyes off those icons, even as the indicator light for her personal com-link channel began to blink and she activated the switch to accept the call. The display indicated the call was from Barbara Fini who said, "Sister…I am sorry we were not able to complete our earlier conversation…and I am sorry we waited so long to initiate it." "Yes," replied Renee Fini, "but I am thankful for those last few hours we had together."

At that instant Renee Fini felt a sensation that seemed to resonate within every cell inside her body, and Benjabar's icon changed from yellow to green. Neither sister commented on this, but Barbara Fini's voice seemed to take on an increased urgency as she said, "I wanted to tell you that I love you, because we both know that after the transfer, I probably will not remember you, and I will likely be in an injured mental state." The transfer sensation was again felt as Dartous' icon changed to green.

Renee Fini immediately responded to Barbara Fini, "I promise to find you and…" There was a catch in her voice as she reacted to another sensation and saw Adam Boy's status change to green, but she quickly recovered, "…I will help you to remember me…"

Another sensation and Aarondophilous' status changed to green, "…and I love you too…" then Captain Eli triggered the switch that sent the two sisters to the year 1838.

Epilogue

Those of you reading this volume know better than us how successful the mission of the Eli family proved to be. For you can look about you to discern the condition of the world. Is the air pure and clean? Are the crops bounteous? Is animal life abundant? If so, the mission was a complete success.

Is the world dying of air laden with a devastating virus? Are the fields no longer able to support the population? Do numerous animal species become extinct every month? If this is what you see, then the family failed in their mission.

Based on our incomplete knowledge of how the family fared in its mission, we believe that you are likely seeing a world that sits on a continuum, somewhere between those two extremes.

We are placing this volume, and any subsequent volumes, in a bank vault which we know will still exist for some time to come. Instructions are given to open the vault one hundred and fifty years after the completion of this draft. Funds will be available to aid in its publication as a warning to your generation. Please remember that despite the current condition of your world, there is probably a "Wilder Meld" somewhere on Earth and, without proper management, the planet can still return to the environment the family left behind before transferring to the year 1838.

Let us introduce ourselves. Although we are the narrators of this volume, we have not yet been entered into the storyline for the Eli Chronicles. However, you may meet us in future volumes. We are a sister and brother who have collaborated on the telling of this unusual narrative. When the family transferred back in time, we would not be born for another twenty years. Our names are Margarita, called Daisy, and Ikus.

Our parents are Aarondophilous and Natalini…*remember the girl who escaped her Afghan captors in India*? It was our parents, along with other members of the family, who related this story to us. And we should probably also mention that the family now includes, Kelligeen, the wife of Adam Boy. These adventures are only the beginning of those experienced by the family. We hope to someday complete the story, but will not go into those developments at this time…except for a few more details…

You undoubtedly recall that after their awakenings, the family members each experienced certain difficulty. However, what we have failed to note in this story is that there were, in fact, two separate awakenings. In the first awaking, Captain Eli reached the target year six months ahead of the rest of the family. However, he found that upon arrival, each family member had experienced complications that would place the mission in jeopardy.

For example, Adam Boy encountered scoundrels in America who attacked him for the gold bracelet he wore. And Benjabar was captured and sold into slavery in Brazil.

After unsuccessfully attempting to remedy these various ills, Captain Eli decided on a plan that would once again utilize the Organizer. He placed new supplies and revised notes in new duffel bags and sent them back to a time seconds before the arrival of the first bags. This would mean the replacement bag would trigger the locating grenade and have the effect of overriding the transfer of the original bag. Therefore, the family member would find only the second bag upon their arrival. The notes in the replacement bags provided additional warnings and instructions to the arriving family members that were designed to help them avoid their arrival crises. Then, Captain Eli sent himself back in time to 1836 to give himself more time to prepare for the arrangements designed to help the family avoid the problems associated with their arrival. For example, knowing that Adam Boy would need to be hidden away for several months from the treasure-seeking scoundrels, he prepared coded directions, and left him a special boat from the *Sea Queen's* inventory that would serve as the source of his temporary home. He hoped that by doing these several things that the family's timelines could be changed to a more favorable outcome. In each case, he coded the message so that if the notes were intercepted by their antagonists, it would be less likely that they could take steps to counter the Captain's plans.

So, it is our hope that you, the reader, can find this volume of use in better understanding how the world came to whatever state you find it. And we hope to meet you in the future-telling of this continuing narrative.

Hopefully **NOT** the End.

THE BOYS WITH CAPTAIN ELI

Adam Boy and *Aarondophilous* at 5½ years and 19 months on a voyage with Captain Eli - picture affectionately entitled *The Old Man and the Sea*

A Sea Creature created by *The Family*

THE CAPTAIN & ADAM BOY

Lovingly dedicated to *Adam Boy's* memory:
January 20, 1984-April 6, 2012

Adam Christopher Dugger (*Adam Boy*) with R. David Dugger (*Captain Eli* aka Daddy)

The origins of this book began in the 1980s when Adam said, "Daddy, tell me a story," and the creation of the book started in 2012 when David began creating chapters of this unfolding story as Christmas gifts for Aaron.

THE BOYS WITH RENEE FINI

Adam (*Adam Boy*), Aaron (*Aarondophilous*) and Renee/Mom (aka *Renee Fini* &/or *Barbara Fini*)

THE CAPTAIN & RENEE FINI

David (*The Captain*) and Renee (*Fini*) on adventures at Mount Rainier National Park and Cinque Terre, Italy. They love experiences that involve hiking, cycling, exploring, and discovering new places.

They now live in a home they built on Fripp Island, SC lovingly named *Sea Queen Cottage*.

THE BOYS

THE LOGO

Captain Eli (David) designed this logo when he and *Renee Fini* (Renee) cycled across Iowa in 2009. "E" is for *Eli* and "F" is for *Fini*, the boat is symbolic of *The Sea Queen* (in this case, our bicycles served as our trusty vessels), "Odyssey" for our continued wanderings, and the "anchor" flanked by Alpha & Omega symbolizes God as our anchor. Since then, the magnetic logo on the left has accompanied us on a multitude of adventures in our little van RV, including visiting most of the US National Parks, as well as some in Canada. We even brought it along when we visited National Parks in Hawaii…just not attached to our little RV.

www.ingramcontent.com/pod-product-compliance
Lightning Source LLC
Chambersburg PA
CBHW061504120726
48001CB00004B/1212